Set Me Free

Set Me Free

A NOVEL IN FIVE ACTS

Miranda Beverly-Whittemore

WARNER BOOKS

NEW YORK   BOSTON

The text of *The Tempest,* by William Shakespeare, is taken from *The Riverside Shakespeare.* New York: Houghton Mifflin © 1997.

The epigraph is from *National Audubon Society Field Guide to the Pacific Northwest*, Peter Alden and Dennis Paulson et al. New York: Alfred A. Knopf © 1998.

Warner Books
Hachette Book Group USA
1271 Avenue of the Americas
New York, NY 10020

Printed in the United States of America

First Edition: March 2007
10 9 8 7 6 5 4 3 2 1

Warner Books and the "W" logo are trademarks of Time Warner Inc. or an affiliated company. Used under license by Hachette Book Group USA, which is not affiliated with Time Warner Inc.

Library of Congress Cataloging-in-Publication Data

Beverly-Whittemore, Miranda.
    Set me free / Miranda Beverly-Whittemore. — 1st ed.
        p. cm.
    ISBN-13: 978-0-446-53331-7
    ISBN-10: 0-446-53331-9
    1. School principals—Oregon—Fiction.   2. Fathers and daughters—Fiction.
· 3. Domestic fiction.   I. Title.
    PS3602.E845S48   2007
    813'.6—dc22   2006020983

For David—

"I would not wish any companion

in the world but you."

And for Daddy,

who has taught me "the rarer action is

in virtue than in vengeance."

Unlike those of most conifers, the cones of Lodgepole Pines stay closed on the branches for years, until the heat from a forest fire opens them. Afterward, the fire-resistant seeds sprout en masse, producing tall, straight Lodgepoles in extensive pure stands that support many of the birds and mammals widely distributed in other coniferous forests.

—National Audubon Society Field Guide to the
  Pacific Northwest

I prithee let me bring thee where crabs grow;
And I with my long nails will dig thee pig-nuts,
Show thee a jay's nest, and instruct thee how
To snare the nimble marmazet. I'll bring thee
To clust'ring filberts, and sometimes I'll get thee
Young scamels from the rock. Wilt thou go with me?

—Caliban, *The Tempest* (II. 2. 167–72)

Set Me Free

Prologue

Spoken by
CAL

When I was a little boy, Maw-Maw would often take me on her lap and tell me about Our Way. I took Our Way to mean the Traditional Indian Way, the Neige Courante Way, because she was my toothless grandmother and her hair fell in two frayed plaits beside her face and she sometimes wore a buckskin dress that smelled of wood smoke and, on occasion, of the living thing that had once been in it. So I will never forget the moment I realized what Our Way *really* meant; the afternoon's shame is still vivid in my mind, though it shames me no more. Now I am quite fond of my boyhood embarrassment, because it is one of the few things I have from the time when Maw-Maw was the only world I knew.

I was seven years old. There were two boys who lived two houses down, with their own grandmother. This other grandmother was powerful on our reservation. This other grandmother was beautiful and well dressed. She had all her own teeth. Her hair was cut short and styled well, and her grandsons wore ironed shirts and brand-new Converse sneakers. I wanted to impress these grandsons. They were older than I. They had been to the Pendleton rodeo and showed cattle at the county fair. They could really play some basketball. I thought if I showed off for them by singing

the tribal song Maw-Maw had taught me, then perhaps they would
invite me to play with them. A game of Horse maybe, or Twenty-
one. Nothing elaborate. "That will only be the beginning," I told
myself, staring up at my ceiling in the quiet night. "Once we play
together, they'll love me. They'll invite me into their world of vac-
uums and penny candy and blue-black Levi's. Before I know it,
we'll be like brothers."

So I sang, and the whole time I thought, "I am borrowing Maw-
Maw's voice." I had to imagine I was borrowing her voice to get
the notes right, and to remember what I was supposed to say.

The quality of mercy is not strange, hey-eh, hey-eh.
It falleth as a gentle rain from hea-ven.

Those boys started laughing at me right away. "Does that sound
like an Indi'n song to you? Do those sound like Indi'n words?"
And then they laughed until they cried. When they were still
catching their breath, one said, "That's a loony old woman you live
with. Better watch out you don't catch her crazy bugs," and they
ran off and left me alone, yearning after them. I tried to take my
pride in hand. I tried to quell my anger. I went inside and found
Maw-Maw in the kitchen, humming to herself. I asked her for the
first time in my life, "Maw-Maw, is Our Way the Indi'n Way? Or
is it the Indian Way? Or is it the Traditional Way? Or is it the
Neige Courante Way?" And *she* looked at me and laughed. The
laugh she had that showed her gums and rattled her so deep, it felt
like she might die right there. The laugh that scared me because I
could not reach her when she was caught in it.

"All you need to know," she said when her breath had settled,
"is Our Way is My Way. There *is* no Indian Way, fool. 'Indi'n' is
just another way of saying you're Indian yourself. That has nothing to do with Our Way. Maybe there is a Neige Courante Way.
Maybe there is a Lakota Way. A Crow Way. A Hopi Way. But
there is also a Chinese Way. An Irish Way. A million other Ways.
Really, My Way is to learn the Human Way. Maybe that's Tradi-

tional. But that's not important. This is: you are a human living under my roof. You eat my food. You will live by My Way, which is Our Way. The Human Way. Understand?" I nodded, because I was often a little scared of how much she knew, but really, I didn't understand at all.

I have only, in these last few days, realized that you may be the only person in the world who understands what this story says about my deepest truth: I do not often understand until it is too late.

WHEN THAT SAME Maw-Maw set to dying, it was the summer I turned twelve. Two weeks into her bed rest, she had me crawl on my hands and knees and root around on the dusty floor underneath her bed. I knew her under-the-bed place was where she kept her most powerful, precious things, and so, when she asked me to do this task for her, I was afraid. It meant, for sure, she was dying.

In my search for what she wanted, I had to touch a yellowed cloth diaper, neatly folded into fourths; a bone necklace that once held powerful magic; and one silver earring tied in an embroidered handkerchief. Every time I came up for air, she prodded me with the end of her cane. "That isn't it! Keep looking!" She didn't tell me what she was looking for until I had it in my hands.

She wanted her books. The first one was quite old, at least in my mind, because it was from a decade I had never before imagined. The copyright page read 1932. The book was called *Red Mother*. It looked very boring to me, because it was the story of a Crow woman named Pretty-shield who had been a girl on the plains when there were buffalo and ancient laws and no reservations. My grandmother said this book told a tiny piece of the Crow Way, but only one woman's point of view, and that I should not forget this, that one voice alone could do only so much telling.

She leaned so close to me I could smell her peanut breath. "Did you know my husband came and got me? Took me from my mother's home. Up in Montana. Did you know that I was born a Montana Crow? Your grandfather made me an Oregon Neige

Courante. I didn't know his country. I came from big-sky country.
My people rode horses. I wanted to go with him. But I cried like
a girl every day. I was crying for the horse I had to leave behind. I
am an old woman now. I understand I was crying for my mother
and my sisters. I did not know life without them.

"My husband let me cry. He knew I would come to love this
place. He saw I was stubborn. I come from proud people. Fierce
people. People full of fighting. He knew the only way to make a
Crow love something is give her time to love it herself." Her
cataracts were like clouds passing between us, but I believe she saw
me sharply when she said, "You're a Crow. Like me, you have war
in you. A warrior. The Neige Courante? They fish. They gather.
The Crow fight. Never be ashamed. Your fighting ways come from
my blood. Be proud of that." And then she lay back and closed her
eyes.

The next day, when Maw-Maw's breathing was even shallower,
she made me go under her bed again. This time I knew what I was
looking for: I brought up the only other book I could find. There
was no date in this second book, but it was also old and heavy. I
opened it and squinted at the tiny columns of letters, all that dense
language piled up on top of itself like in the Bible. Maw-Maw did
not keep a Bible under her bed. It was not one of her most precious things. But though it was no Bible, I recognized the book
under her bed as a holy thing. I recognized it from childhood afternoons spent perched on Maw-Maw's lap. Later in my life, I
would read "The quality of mercy is not strain'd, / It droppeth as
the gentle rain from heaven" and laugh at the thought of my Maw-
Maw hearing "strain'd" as "strange," and then I would cry to think
of how merciful she was, strange herself, and strain'd too, by what
the world had asked of her. The book was a beat-up copy of *Shakespeare's Collected Works*. I have no idea who gave it to her (at the age
of twelve, I did not know to ask such things), but the inscription
reads, *November 18th, 1956. To Daisy: With undying affection for the
Brave New World you've shown me, R.*

In my twelfth summer, that summer of Maw-Maw's death, her breath grated in her chest. Women were in and out of that house, and they shooed me from her bedroom door. I was not to see her suffering. It would be too hard for me—who did not have a mother worth mentioning or a father who'd acknowledge me—to see the only person who ever loved me ravaged by sickness. But Maw-Maw and I were sneaky. I would tiptoe into her room in the moments when the house lay silent, when the sky was dark and her caretakers were sleeping. She would say to me the most beautiful things: "Tell me my story, boy. I'm in a fog, lost. Wilderness is all around me. Your voice can be my guide. Give me my life. I want to hear it."

"But I don't know your life. You've never told me. I didn't even know you were a Crow until you gave me that *Red Mother* book, Maw-Maw."

Her face made a laugh, but no sound came. "Foolish boy. I told you my life every day. It is my doings. It is my thinkings. Tell me My Way. Tell me Our Way. But tell it like I am a character in the story. Do not let me know the story is about myself. Tell me about Daisy. Her grandson Cal. Their doings. Their story will help me find my way out of this fog. Let me get the rest my bones need."

And so I would sit in the darkness and watch the Oregon moonlight shimmy across my Maw-Maw's face and tell her what I could remember of our times together. Everything we had ever done. The smell of fresh ginger cake, the taste of an alpine spring in summertime, the day I ran away from her in the grocery store, the long walks we'd taken up the meadows of Mount Jefferson. When the moon was bright enough, I sneaked in with her Shakespeare and read her that. I read her *National Geographic*. I read her *Red Mother*. I sang the songs we loved from the radio. I gave her the world. What I knew of it, at least. And when it was her time, she died.

*　*　*

So, Elliot Barrow, you're asking yourself somewhere in there, in the place where you can hear me: what does all this have to do with me? Why is he telling me all this? And now? Why, after so many years laden with secrets, full of the silence that exists between men, is Calbert Fleecing taking these moments beside my deathbed to open up? Does he take pleasure in telling me all I ever wanted to know about him, now that I cannot speak? Is he here to preach, to pontificate? To tell me I was wrong all along? Or is he turning soft? Embracing the cliché: wise Indian dispenses wisdom at just the moment when the whole world seems full of despair?

I'm not here because of me. I'm here because of you. You have a secret. I should have known. And it is only now, in knowing the secret of Shakespearean proportions that you guarded so well—my God, you should win an Academy Award for your performance—that I understand what I must do. The secret is what brings me here. It makes me understand what Maw-Maw meant when she said that My Way is Our Way, which is the Human Way. (For after all, that is your way too, isn't it? You and my grandmother, humanists united across time.) It makes me understand why the only way my Maw-Maw could leave this earth was to have me tell her the story of Daisy. Daisy's story led her out of her body, let her forgive it for the way it had betrayed her. And that is how I'm supposed to help you.

Look, Maw-Maw's Way (Our Way, if you want to get technical about it, and I know you always do) doesn't help me most of the time. She didn't give me Indian Ways, or if she did, they were all mixed up in Human Ways, and I've never known how to untangle them. When I first knew how I was supposed to help you, I was lost, man. I don't know how to make a Story Stick. No one ever taught me how to carve. If I lived a hundred years ago, I'd go to the general store and buy a ledger book and draw your story. That's what we did back then, before we'd learned your language. If you want the humiliating truth, I even tried that. Bought a notebook and a bottle of whiskey at Fred Meyer's and tried to draw you, just a few of the pieces you'd told me about. But every time I tried to get your body down on paper—your little-boy body, your teenage body, your young-man body—you were always on fire. I thought, "I must be a fucking genius. I've figured it out: Elliot Barrow was always on fire, but it was his rendezvous with actual flame that made people really see him. All this time he was dreaming of touching people, but only when he burned up and had nothing left to touch with, no body, no hands, could he actually begin to touch anyone."

Lucky for me, just then was when your secret came calling. Just then was when I understood the real reason you were holding on. That was when I understood what I had to do to help you. I saw why my drawings had failed: because I was going it alone. The truth is, I don't know you half as well as I knew Maw-Maw, because I was a little boy then and she was the woman who raised me, and you and I are straight, grown men who have loved each other in the way of which men never speak. Clearly I don't know you as well as I thought, but a little discouragement hasn't deterred me. If anything, it's emboldened my cause. I've gathered. I've imagined. And I've written it all down so I can read it to you. For perhaps the first time in your life, you're all ears.

WHEN MAW-MAW was dying and asked me to tell her her own story, she didn't want to know that it was hers. She didn't want me to say, "Maw-Maw, remember when you slipped on the front steps and I had to run and get help?" Instead, she wanted: "Daisy Lesmures slipped on her front steps the morning after the first frost. Her grandson Calbert Fleecing was so small, and his arms so weak, that instead of picking her up himself, he had to run the three miles to the nearest telephone just to get her on her feet."

At first I thought Maw-Maw wanted her story this way because she didn't want her memory to interfere with how I remembered things. This is how most twelve-year-olds think; they're the center of the universe. I thought she wanted distraction from her own point of view, and I knew I was a good storyteller, so I embellished with my usual, dramatic panache.

But now I see it's something far different. She needed me to tell her the story of Daisy Lesmures because it was Daisy Lesmures who was going to trick her body into getting its final rest. It was Daisy Lesmures, not Maw-Maw, who was going to get up from the bed where Maw-Maw lay and open the door and step out into the sunlight.

Elliot. From now on, I will not be calling you "you." From now on, I will call you "Elliot."

Set Me Free
Dramatis Personae

The Adults

Elliot Barrow — *director, founder, and headmaster, Ponderosa Academy*

Helen Bernstein — *director and founder, the First Stage Theater*

Calbert Fleecing — *assistant headmaster, Ponderosa Academy (and most certainly neither "a savage" nor "a deformed slave")*

Nat Llewelyn — *a very good liar*

The Children

Amelia Barrow — *daughter to Elliot*

Willa Llewelyn — *daughter to Nat*

Victor Littlefoot — *friend to Amelia*

Lydia Cinqchevaux — *friend to Amelia*

Sadie Hazzard — *friend to Amelia*

Wesley Hazzard — *brother to Sadie*

The Time

Autumn 1996 through Spring 1997

Act One

[OR]

We Run Ourselves Aground

Chapter One

AMELIA
Stolen, Oregon ~ Early fall, 1987

*A*melia would tell you that the story began long before it actually began. She'd say it started when she was seven and Victor Littlefoot was eight, on a day she'd almost entirely forgotten until her life made her remember.

They were playing fairies. Her father's friend Helen, back east, had sent Amelia a copy of *Shakespeare's Stories for Children*, and the tale that entranced her most was the one with Titania and Oberon and Puck and the changeling child. Victor was not very interested in the large white book with the beguiling pictures. So Amelia bribed him with the promise of a next day's game of Horse on the school's basketball court; in exchange, she got a make-believe game of Fairy Royalty. And that was what led them out of sight of the Bugle House, and her father's window, and the broad prairie of the school grounds, and down to Wiggler's Creek, where they were not supposed to go, especially not when dusk was coming on fast.

Despite Victor's valiant attempts to avoid the game, once coaxed to play, he made a very convincing king of the fairies. His upper lip, brown and earnest, was beaded with sweat that shone in the light when Amelia squinted. She could imagine him sprinkled in fairy dust, with a crown of apple blossoms, commanding an army of sprites. He seemed to be having a good time, which was why she decided to lead him farther down the creek bed, away from where the older kids might be playing or spying. She knew that any distractions would keep Victor from agreeing to something like this again. She'd felt herself losing him for some time now. So Amelia waved the wand she'd made from a juniper twig and declared that Victor was the mightiest king in all fairydom, and entreated him to walk on into the forest of Aragon and make of it what he could.

The forest of Aragon, in this case, was a stand of aspens planted on the Rudolph ranch, which lay just on the other side of Wiggler's Creek, over the fence, and in the next field. Anything on the other side of Wiggler's Creek was off limits. There was a real risk of being caught by one of Rudolph's farmhands or seen by a well-cast eye from the school. But Amelia didn't care. She knew that there was no such thing as fear of authority when one was lord of all the enchanted world. She also knew that if she commanded Victor, he might well go. She needed him to prove it to her: all the loyalty she hoped he had. So she said it again: "I entreat you, good king, walk on into the forest of Aragon and make of it what you can."

Victor ducked his head and thrust his hands into his pockets, and for a moment she thought she'd lost him for good. But then his neck straightened and his smile gleamed. "For you, my queen, I shall do this bidding," he said, and her heart skipped. Within an instant he had leaped Wiggler's Creek and was bounding up the other side of the embankment. She watched his skinny body squeezing through the wires of the fence and saw him uncurl on the other side and wave before sprinting off toward the stand of tall green trees. His blue T-shirt got smaller and smaller as he ran from her, and she beamed with pride until he stopped short ten steps from the forest.

She waited for him to move on. But he stood frozen in a tangle of sagebrush, looking down. He looked like a statue, and she knew then that only the sound of her voice could break his spell. They could both get into lots of trouble for being off campus. "Go!" she whispered, hoping him forward. She should have gone herself. Victor wasn't brave enough for discovering new places.

"Amelia!" Victor's voice rang out across the open meadow. Too loud. They would get caught for sure. She squatted so she was closer to the ground. But now she couldn't see him, and she started to wonder what was going on. Was it a rattlesnake he had discovered? He knew what to do around a rattler. But what if it was a nest? What if they were surrounding him, winding around his ankles, shaking their tails? Her heart started to pound, and then he called her name again.

Amelia launched her body across Wiggler's Creek and crept a few steps up the embankment. "What is it?" she called in as quiet a yell as she could.

"Come quick!" He wasn't moving. She looked behind her, at the school, but she didn't see anyone. She'd have to risk it.

Soon she'd pulled herself through the wire fence and was running to Victor. "What is it?" she hissed again. The bushes were as high as her face, and she had to dodge them so they didn't scratch her. When she got to Victor, she wanted to hit the back of his head for ruining their game. But then he stepped aside and pointed.

All her body went numb and buzzy at the same time. "What is it?" she asked a third time, but quietly, because it was obvious what it was. She looked at Victor and then back down at the ground.

"It's a baby," Victor said.

And it was. It was lying there on the ground, on an old gray blanket, with its eyes open, looking up at them. A real live baby. A changeling child, like the one they'd been conjuring. This was serious.

"What do we do?" she asked, but not of Victor.

He turned and looked at her, then slowly swiveled his head back toward the school. "We should get someone."

Amelia glanced back down at the baby. It was puckering its mouth. Its little hands and feet were pumping in the air. It seemed very small below them.

"I don't know," she said. "Maybe we should leave it."

Victor's jaw dropped. "We're not leaving it. I'm getting your dad."

"We'll be in trouble."

But Victor was already running. "I'm not going to let that baby die," he called. He was already nearing the fence. It seemed as if he were flying.

Death. She hadn't thought of that. Victor was right. This baby could die. Anything could die. Amelia took off her sweatshirt and laid it down over the baby, which was dressed in only a small yellow T-shirt and a diaper. When she squatted close to the baby, it smiled at her. She put her pointer finger in its warm little hand, and it tried to pull it into its mouth. The baby's breath smelled good and milky. Amelia turned to look for Victor, but he was out of sight, probably running over the creek bed, already on the grounds of the school. "He *is* brave," she thought. She was ashamed for acting like a little kid. She hoped he wouldn't tell her father what she'd said.

She'd never been alone with a baby before, this close. Part of her wanted to pick it up, but she was scared she would drop it. She couldn't really imagine how heavy it would be. Of course, she'd seen babies before. She'd even held them on her lap. There were new mothers coming by the school all the time. But she'd always felt brave with these mothers watching her, telling her where to put her hands, ready to take the baby if it started crying. This was different. She knew you weren't supposed to let the head fall back, or it could break its neck or something. She didn't want to break the baby's neck.

That was when she noticed the white cloth tied to the tree. Almost like a banner. That scared her a little, because it seemed like something a sorcerer would do. Maybe there was an invisible magic spell woven into the cloth. She began to notice how quiet the world around her was, and how alone she was in it. So she sang. First "Row, Row, Row Your Boat," then "I've Got Sunshine," then the melody to Mozart's Piano Sonata in A major, and then she ran out of songs. The baby didn't seem to care all that much. It kept puckering up its mouth and waving its hands in the air and kicking up at her. It didn't look happy, but it didn't look sad. It just looked.

Victor was taking a long time. Probably her father hadn't been in his office. Since it was after hours, there was no one else down on the main campus, not even Victor's mom, who was grading tests. Maybe her dad was making dinner. Amelia was pinched with a pang of hunger. She suddenly had to pee. It was funny she hadn't felt it before, but now she thought she might wet her pants. She would have to go to one of the bushes and pee behind it. And she would sing to the baby the whole time, so it wouldn't feel alone.

She leaned down quickly and kissed one of its toes. The baby foot was sweaty and squirmy like a thick pink worm. It smelled like it wanted to be nibbled on. "I'll be right back," Amelia said. "I just have to pee now." The baby gave a belly laugh, and she kissed its toes again. It smiled at her, and she made a funny face. "Okay," she said, "I'll be right back."

She went to the closest juniper and squatted behind it. She knew it probably didn't matter whether the baby saw her pee, but she wasn't sure if that was okay. She made sure her pants were down around her ankles and her butt was sticking far enough out that she wouldn't splatter on her clothes. The pee took a few seconds to come; she pressed her face against the juniper and breathed in deeply. Little blue berries jangled against her face. The sharp smell of the juniper was like pee, but she couldn't tell if it was her pee or the pee of the tree. She remembered she was going to sing to the baby, so she started on "Row, Row, Row Your Boat" again until she was done. Just then she heard the voices of Victor and her father. It was going to be exciting to explain about the baby to her dad. She pulled up her pants and stepped around the bush and waved.

They were running toward her, toward the spot where the baby was. Or had been. Because it wasn't until she looked at her father's face, and Victor's, that she glanced at where the baby was supposed to be, at where it had been just a moment ago, and saw that it wasn't there anymore. Not it, not the blanket, not her sweatshirt, not anything.

"Where is it?" her father asked, walking slowly forward.

"I told you, Mr. Barrow, it was right there," Victor said. He was looking at Amelia as if he didn't know who she was.

"Where'd you take it?" her father asked, taking her by the shoulders.

"It was right there." She pointed. "I swear. I just went to pee for a second."

"Did you move it?" he asked. He was starting to shake her a little bit. His grip on her shoulders was tight.

"No," she said. All she could think to say was "no."

Her father was frantic. He pushed his long fingers through his hair. "You just don't lose a baby, Amelia," he said. "Tell me where it is."

Amelia started to cry. "I don't know, Daddy. I promise, I don't know." He squatted beside her then and hugged her tight.

And that was it. They searched and searched, but nothing was found. Her father gave them a talking to for telling tall tales. He didn't want everyone to think that she and Victor were liars, so they all three agreed that this "prank" would remain a secret. Amelia knew that her father was right. If the older kids, even the ones who played pranks on one another all the time, found out, they would act like she'd done something terrible.

Even with the secret agreement, things unraveled. Victor wouldn't talk to her anymore; whenever his mom was staying late at school, he sat in her office and did his homework. It was as if they'd never been friends. And her dad gave a stern lecture at assembly about the dangers of lying.

But that wasn't what got Amelia. She knew what was true. She knew there'd been a baby. She'd smelled it. What got her was knowing she would have to hold a terrible truth inside herself for the rest of her life: something bad had happened to that baby. Death. Just like Victor said. A wolf had dragged it, or goblins. Or she and her game and her fairy wand had made the baby appear from another world, and she had done the wrong thing with it, like not saying the best magic spell, and that had made the baby disappear again, back to a horrible land where it would know no happiness. She should have taken it into her arms and held it. She should have been brave. She should not have let it die.

So Amelia vowed: no more fairy games. She didn't know her own power.

In the weeks afterward, before the memory faded and summer came and she forgot the reason that she and Victor Littlefoot would never be friends again (which seemed to matter less and less as time went on, if only because Victor and his mother moved soon thereafter to a faraway land called Chicago), Amelia could still see her father clearly, in that first moment when he'd taken her by the shoulders and asked where the baby was. He trusted her. She knew, despite what he said later, that he believed her when she swore the baby had been there only a moment before. She knew because of his eyes. She'd told him that the baby was gone like magic, and his eyes had filled with a grief she'd never known in him. He had never seemed less like a grown-up and more like a child. This was a sadness that she pondered.

WILLA
New Milford, Connecticut ~ Wednesday, May 7, 1997

Willa would tell you that the story began on the breezy morning her father sped into the parking lot where she stood at the Bellwether School, his old Volvo station wagon packed to the brim with their worldly possessions. It was the twelfth time in the past seventeen years that Willa's father had done this. Three years before, he'd promised he was never going to do it again. She'd made him promise on her life.

Willa was outside the art studio, resentfully spraying fixer on her charcoal drawing in preparation for the following week's art show. She was listening to the wind skating through the newly green maples that dotted Bellwether's main lawn. When she felt the wind splaying her ponytail, she stopped the spray and waited for the gust to pass. Though only a junior, Willa was the art star of the school. But over the last few weeks, she had come to realize that Bellwether would champion her only as long as she made the art that the school wanted her to make. This realization had replaced her initial excitement over the upcoming art show with unshakable sulkiness. Willa's terrible mood was annoying even herself. The stupid wind wasn't helping matters.

Bellwether's Catholic headmaster adored Willa's ten drawings of the Connecticut natural world, collectively named *Hill and Dale.* It had been decreed: the drawings—safe and beautiful—would be framed and hung in the main hall beside the faculty artwork and the work of the best seniors. The main hall was where the reception for the art show would take place the following Friday. Willa had been reminded more than once that it was an unprecedented honor for an eleventh-grader to be asked to participate. She pretended to be thrilled when all she could feel was a quiet kind of fury. She didn't care about the drawings. They were a technical exercise in giving people what they wanted. Willa believed they were "good" only in the eyes of people who didn't understand art.

In contrast, Willa's photography series, *Scars,* had been relegated to a drawer in the cramped darkroom, which technically was to be opened for public viewing that same Friday night. But everyone knew no parent, let alone any of the students, was going to take the long trek across campus to the art building, down the gloomy back stairway into the basement, and into the ugly, dank darkroom to open up the drawer that happened to hold Willa's series of condemned photographs. *Scars,* twelve black-and-white close-ups of the scars of twelve unidentified students, had caused a kerfuffle in the Bellwether administration, primarily because two of the photographs featured breasts, and one a pair of buttocks. Willa had argued and argued. The breasts and buttocks were there only because of the scars upon them: a removed cyst, a healed surgical incision, the remnants of a bicycle accident. The headmaster had offered his version of a compromise: remove the offending material and the photographs would be hung. No, said Willa. Nonnegotiable. And so she'd endured her first lesson in censorship. The photographs were not going to see the light of day. The students she had photographed—members of the Socialist Club, the Comic Books Club, the Democrats for Peace Club—kept their secret and smiled in solidarity at Willa across the dining hall.

Miss Finlay, the young, brightly dressed art teacher whom Willa adored, had been telling Willa since the ninth grade that she had what it took—the talent, the drive, the anger—to make it in the art world. Miss Finlay said that at her alma mater, Yale, photographic projects like Willa's were adored. She said even the drawings were to be commended for their clarity. She offered to write a glowing recommendation to Yale, and she also wanted Willa to consider RISD and Pratt. But Willa had told her New Haven was as far as she could go, and anyway, she knew her father wouldn't be able to afford it. When Willa's father had promised her they would never leave the white house with the blue shutters, Willa had made her own silent promise: she would never *want* to leave. All her life, all she'd wanted was a home. She'd made her father promise her that very thing, and he'd delivered. She wasn't going to need anything more.

Willa heard the familiar clank and thrum of the ancient Volvo before she saw it. The wind brought it to her early. Her first thought was that her father was coming to see the art. Or maybe she'd forgotten her lunch at the house. It had been so long since he'd done this that he caught her off guard. Five years before, she would have known what was to come simply from her body's reaction to the sound of his arrival: the sinking of her heart, her fallen shoulders, the mental tallying of which friends were close enough to bid goodbye. Already, she would have anticipated the resigned cold of the metal door handle under her palm.

This time she was nothing but surprised. When Nat Llewelyn

pulled around Tully Hall, he saw sadness shake down his daughter's body. He saw her limbs become taut, and he couldn't help but remember Caroline. A ball of guilt welled in his throat.

What Willa didn't know was that Nat was going to give her a choice this time. He knew what he wanted her to say, because it would make things much easier. But he had made a promise. Only a monster wouldn't give her the choice. And he knew that if she didn't come of her own volition, she would never be able to hear him. She would be too distracted by injustice. He had been a fool to keep the truth this long from Caroline's girl.

HELEN
Brooklyn, New York ~ Thursday, September 5, 1996

Helen would tell you that the story began on the Thursday just after Labor Day, when a purple bruise of a cloud was dampening the Brooklyn skyline and threatening her daily walk. Her golden retriever, Ferdinand, jangled his leash on the hook beside the door and pointed his nose toward her eagerly as she slipped on her sandals, shaking her head.

"I don't know how long this is going to hold, Fergus," she said. "You better make it quick." She could tell an umbrella would be no match for what the dark sky threatened. The maple sapling planted in front of the brownstone bent with the wind, swarmed by brittle leaves and city dust. Helen sneezed, just watching. She looked back down at the poor dog wagging his tail. "Five minutes," she said. "We'll go on a real walk tomorrow."

The phone rang, clanging open the quiet house. With a guilty glance at the dog, Helen strode to the side table and picked up. "Hello?" She cringed at her own eagerness. It was her first call of the day, and despite her better judgment, she couldn't help hoping it was Duncan. Any sign that he remembered where he lived, where his wife waited for him, was a good sign.

"Hello hello." It wasn't Duncan.

"Elliot?"

"Yes! Good to hear your voice, dearest Helen. The face that launched a thousand ships."

"Is everything all right?" Elliot Barrow never called. They had spoken on five occasions since that night in 1980 when he briefly lost his mind. And ever since then, every time they had spoken, she would worry: has he lost it again? As if he deserved her worry. She watched the dog earnestly pointing at the door and wondered at herself. Here, in the midst of terrible sorrow, only five exchanges into a conversation, and she was willing—nay, ready—to jump to Elliot's aid. How did he accomplish this so swiftly? She would have to call her therapist. She would need to pretend Elliot hadn't brought up those thousand ships. That was the line he'd used when he first took her to bed.

"Things are . . . fine," he said. A proper Protestant pause.

She asked, "It's been—what? Two years?" She tried to scroll back in her mind. Lately, time had become a tangle of sorrow. It moved strangely and left her lonely. But she was sure it had been at least two years.

"How are *you*?"

"Fine," she said, "I'm fine," even though that was a lie. "What's wrong? You sound . . ."

He sighed. One of those famous Barrow sighs that bordered on self-pity. "We're getting old, aren't we?"

She was caught off guard. Each day she felt her skin sagging, her hair thinning, her knuckles knotting up. But she was never going to admit it, least of all to Elliot Barrow. She forced a laugh. "Speak for yourself," she said as confidently as she could.

Most people would apologize. Elliot was not most people, and Helen was left to wonder at his silence.

"How's Amelia?" Helen asked finally, hoping to change the odd course of their conversation. Poor Ferdinand was loping toward Helen, pleading with his wide puppy eyes. She felt a guilty sort of relief at hearing Elliot so preoccupied. It was good to talk to someone who didn't know the details of her own particular brand of awful.

"She's great. Thanks for asking. Just started boarding school in Portland."

"She's not at Ponderosa Academy anymore?"

"Well, I can't provide her with the kind of serious musical training she's craving these days." Helen fought the urge to roll her eyes.

"And you?" he continued. "How's the First Stage? How's Duncan?"

The first drop of rain bashed against the windowpane. Helen held her breath and watched as another one hit, and another and another. The wet erected a bleary wall between her and the outside, until she heard her voice again. "The season's already begun. Duncan's tackling *Romeo and Juliet*, if you can believe it. Never thought he'd do a romance. Busy busy busy. And I'm here holding down the fort." She wanted to avoid getting into details, especially with Elliot Barrow. He'd hear weakness and pounce.

"Good, good," he said. "Listen, I'm wondering if you could do me a big favor." She'd forgotten. He sensed weakness when he wasn't too busy thinking about himself. Which was once in a blue moon.

"What's the favor?" She asked this evenly. No commitment.

"It's a little odd. But I think you'll understand." He cleared his throat. "I'm wondering if you can help me. See, I read *The Tempest* again this summer. I hadn't read it, oh, since I don't know when. I haven't the slightest idea what possessed me to pick it up off Amelia's shelf. But in reviewing it, I was struck by how much our man Will got about what people like the Neige Courante are facing. He composed the play sometime between 1609 and 1613, just a few years after Pocahontas and John Smith came face-to-face. How could he have predicted that in 1996, we'd still be dealing with these same themes: race relations, the ravages of colonialism . . ."

"You're asking me?"

"No, no, I'm saying . . . This may sound very odd, but reading it got me to thinking. It made me remember why I wanted to start this school in the first place. The project of the Academy's been sixteen years in the making. I've been so obsessed with getting things off the ground that I forgot how good it feels to have something to aspire to."

"I'm sorry, Elliot. I'm confused. What's the favor?"

"I want the school to put up a production of *The Tempest*. I want Shakespeare to sing across the prairie. There are practical reasons—this is the right time and the right place. But more than that, I realized we need some poetry in our lives. These kids need . . . I don't know. Maybe this all sounds crazy."

So Elliot still had the ability to plumb Helen's depths in a matter of seconds. "I don't think it's crazy," she said. "But you may not want to take my advice on this. You know how I feel about Shakespeare. I believe . . ." She was moved. She hadn't had a conversation like this in months.

He took her silence as a chance to press on. "I want to bring these ideas to my students, because for them, these concepts are personal. Skin color, stereotyping, discrimination will haunt them for the rest of their lives. Something like *The Tempest* will give them tools to consider these ideas critically. I'm afraid I haven't been doing enough for them in that respect. I can't take them all to a Shakespeare play in Portland or Ashland, and anyway, even if I could afford it, I'd be taking only the students. I want the whole community to be a part of this. So I've decided to bring Shakespeare here. And that's where you come in."

Helen felt an indescribable rush of flattery. Her logical mind knew that as the founder of a prestigious off-Broadway theater, she shouldn't even register a tiny gig at a school in the boondocks of Oregon. Though she would have to let him down easy, remind him with irritation that she had an actual day job that required her expertise, she couldn't help feeling a little proud. Amazing what a little approval from Elliot Barrow could still do to her after all these years. Her heart was beating faster than she would have admitted, and she found a smile resting at the corners of her mouth.

"I'm wondering," he continued, "if there's anyone you can recommend."

The sky landed on Helen's house like a great thundering beast. A burst of lightning lit the dusky room. Ferdinand curled around her feet with a whine, and she tried to soothe him as she gathered herself. She was angry with Elliot but even angrier with herself for being so stupid. Of course he would call today, of all days. Of course she would fall into this trap again. Of course she would act like a schoolgirl. And she had only herself to blame. She felt as though someone had hit her across the jaw; she was that kind of stunned, that kind of hurt.

"Helen? You there?"

"Yes," she said. "Yes, I'm here."

"Do you think you could help me? Is there anyone you can recommend?"

"I'll do my best, Elliot. I'll have to think."

"Thank you," Elliot said. "Thank you, Helen. I just want someone good. Someone who knows what they're doing."

"Yes, okay," she said, her words clipped with frustration. "I'll call you in the next few days."

"Great." He gave her his number and hung up. In the minutes that followed, Helen sat in her empty house and watched the sheets of rain come down. She would have to watch out. In under ten minutes, Elliot Barrow had opened up a longing in her that she didn't even know she had, and then he'd stolen all hope of fulfilling it.

She didn't realize how well he knew her. She didn't recognize what he'd just pulled. He knew this was the only way to get her to come. He had to make her believe it was her idea.

CAL

Amelia, Willa, Helen: each one of them would tell you the story began at the instant her world cracked open, and with that crack, her life began to change. They don't agree on the moment because they are not telling this story; they are just living their lives.

I am the one who is telling this story. So I'll begin with what my illustrious father had to say about stories in the first place. There he'd stand in front of a crowd of white senators, or Hollywood types, or—because he wasn't a total hypocrite—a flock of reservation kids, and he would say, fire in his eyes, "Only stories, true stories, can heal the crack at the heart of the world."

He was a windbag, a blowhard. But that doesn't mean he wasn't impressive. He could get you to believe that the entire field of American constitutional law and the subfield of land-use rights were an epic fashioned out of the malleable material of he said, she said. All dressed up in formal coats, sure, but what were precedents except fancy stories that illustrated the convictions of a few individuals? Who were judges except self-important, sometimes pompous literary critics, deciding how well a story held up to some standard called The Law?

My father could talk and spin stories and evoke tricksters and remind his listeners that the volcanoes on which our people once stood freely were full of fire that came from the sky. He could remind his listeners, white and Indian, that the Neige Courante, the Running Snow people, were the cold waters that had been called to soothe the fire inside the land, to make life tolerable. And in solemn gratitude, the sky and the land and the salmon and the berries had offered themselves to us. It was not simply that the Neige Courante had the "legal right" to fish the waters of the Deschutes and the Columbia, but, more basically, the Neige Courante were *of* those waters. To extricate us from that land, that life, that water, was to crack open the world, to crack open the heart of things.

My father worked well in front of audiences predisposed to liberal guilt. These people wanted to be told truths that transcended the narrow white ways of doing things. He had many, many white friends, but deep down, he hated all whites with a combination of

fierce pity and passionate respect. He hated them because, he believed, they were wrong about the world, and remarkably, they
couldn't care less so long as they got what they wanted.

When I was a little boy and had begun to ask questions about
why things were the way they were—who were those people on
television shows, anyway? where were those buildings that grew to
be so tall?—Maw-Maw gave me two little pickle jars, washed and
dried, and sent me to the creek to catch some water. "This much,"
she said, indicating with her fingers the wingspan of a blue-winged
moth.

I came back with the water. She took one jar from my hand, inspected it, and screwed on the cap. She set it on the windowsill
over the sink, next to the salt shaker, and pointed to a space right
next to the first jar, where I dutifully placed the second one, still
openmouthed. "Don't fiddle," she said. "Wait. See what happens."

I remembered the jars for a day or two, then forgot them entirely, until one day I was eating cereal and caught sight of them
out of the corner of my eye. I got up from the table and went to
the sink and grabbed the two jars. The open one was completely
empty, with a white uneven ridge circling it. The capped one still
contained water, but it was thick on the bottom, and pale brown
flecks and green blobs bobbled in the murk. When I unscrewed
the lid, things smelled. Bad.

When Maw-Maw came in, I showed her, and she sat right down
at the table and took the jars in her hands and inspected each carefully, and laughed with her eyes, and said, "He said it would work.
Just look. It worked."

"Who?" I asked.

She went on. "Do you remember why you did this with the jars?"

I nodded, but that wasn't good enough. She expected an answer
in words.

"Not exactly," I said.

"You've been asking questions about things out there. Out there
in the white world. This is an answer."

I waited, said nothing.

"Most white people act like some things about the world are true. Act like everyone should know those things. They're wrong."

"Like what?" I asked.

"How did it feel to *own* that water there?" She motioned to the jars.

"I didn't own the water," I said. "All I did was put it in jars."

"Yes," she said. "You know this. You are Neige Courante. You know no one can own water. Water is not for owning. Water is for itself. For the land and the fish and the people." She paused. "White people think you can own water. But see what happens when you catch it? It escapes or it dies." We both looked at the pitiful jar of dead water, and the empty jar too.

"But if white people are so stupid, then how come they invented TVs and those buildings and cereal in boxes?"

"Who said *stupid*?" asked Maw-Maw. "This is nothing about *stupid*. What they are is pretenders. They pretend the world is a certain way—like you can own water. While they're pretending, they pretend everyone else is pretending too. In their game, *they* buy all the water. *They* buy all the land that no one can own. When *you* go to drink this water on the land—you who are the one who didn't know you were pretending—they make you pay for it. You pay for what can never be a person's in the first place. And if they give it to you? The water? They expect you to thank them for it. Instead of thanking the water itself, for agreeing to still your thirst." Maw-Maw shook her head. "White people are pretenders, Calbert. They want us all to pretend along with them."

I thought about the way water feels in the hand—how you can't hold it, how it escapes—and I liked how smart Maw-Maw was.

She read my thoughts. "You think I came up with this myself?" She laughed. "There is a man you will meet. Someday. This is his lesson." She gathered the jars and went about the rest of the day.

That man was my father. And no matter what his public teachings entailed, his private lesson to me was simple. Stories may begin

to heal the crack at the heart of the world, but every story about a
father is, in essence, a mystery story, and who knows whether any
of us will live long enough to solve it.

When I was twenty-six, and my father had died, I had already
studied among the pretenders. I had loved some of them and hated
others. I had learned that, yes, for most of them, everything, even
people, can be bought and sold. But I had come back to the reservation with my big head swollen because of a restlessness in my
being.

Here is the crack in my life where my story begins.

It was hot and I was tired. My second cousin Eunice's car had
no air-conditioning and only two working windows. I was fresh
and agitated, steamed at everyone. Steamed at Eunice for calling up
that new school and offering my services. Steamed at myself for sitting on my ass for months and proving I was exactly what all the
wide world thought I was: a lazy Indian. Seven years on the East
Coast had changed me piece by piece. Even my fingernails seemed
sacred to me, better than all that QVC crap my cousins filled their
houses with. And yet I lived with them, eating their bread, mocking their husbands for their jobs down at the rest stop on 26. You're
smart enough to tell that my resentment was very convenient. But
that's another story.

It was like a bolt of lightning. As soon as I stepped out of the
car into the skinny gravel drive and glanced up at the empty windows of the house on Antler Hill, surveying all that ranchland, I
felt a shiver. I understood. Here I was in my homeland, but I wasn't
on the reservation anymore. Don't get confused; I was still angry.
This smart-ass white guy from New York City shows up, this *pretender*, telling everyone he's building a school for our kids, and
we're supposed to jump up and down? No, thank you. I knew all
about the Elliot Barrows of the world: at Harvard, they lined up
one by one to shake hands with me, the noble savage, mightily impressed by my ability to imitate the smatterings of pedigree.

All the same, standing there on what would become the main

drive, looking at this tangle of ranchland, wondering what the hell Elliot Barrow thought he was going to do with forty-seven arid acres, I smiled to myself. He was walking toward me with his baby in his arms. All the time I could see him talking, holding his mouth next to her ear. Her sturdy body faced out toward me, her hands flapped in the air. Then he stopped and broke into a grin, and held his baby out in front of him. He said something loud, for my benefit, but I couldn't hear him. The wind took his voice away.

But in that moment, I felt him, the weight of him, without words getting in our way. I saw the way I might come to know him. I saw that he was someone I might trust. A father holding his baby daughter, telling her something he thought she should know about the world. The wind died right then, and I heard what he was saying. "Here comes the story man!" That's what he was telling her; he was talking about me.

I paused, doubting. How convenient for him! A storytelling Indian! I was tempted, momentarily, back to the safe harbor of rage. He thought I was going to tell some cute little Indian stories for him? I reached for the keys in my pocket. But he approached, and I heard him continue, explaining to little Amelia, "Mr. Fleecing has come all the way from the East Coast to tell us stories about Beowulf and Tatiana and Becky Sharp and Sancho Panza." As he pronounced each of these names, he swayed his little girl back and forth. She laughed as she saw me. "He's coming to help us."

I knew from that moment that I loved him. I was ready to love someone. I loved him the way warriors love each other in times of war. The way they talk about fishermen up at Celilo. We were entering into an enterprise together. I knew that I would love him for the rest of my life, which was lucky—and not just because I loved Amelia—but because when you hate someone outright, you can leave him behind, but when you love someone first and then hate him later, you have to stick around. His very presence complicates you. And so it was with us.

Chapter Two

*P*laying the violin was, for Amelia, the best thing and the worst thing. It was breathing and it was drowning. It was useful and it was stupid. It was private and it was showing off. She could not remember a time when she hadn't spent her evenings with the warm wooden chin rest scalloping her chin, when she hadn't felt the high, vibrant notes pulsing through her fingers as they perched on taut strings, when she hadn't known that the resulting sounds were both as definite and as fleeting as color or taste.

Amelia's first memory of music centered on her father, her serious, wise father, blasting Mozart piano concertos from his record player—practically their only possession at the time—out onto the open land surrounding them. She realized this memory must have come from her early childhood, at two or three, for there were just a few of Ponderosa Academy's outbuildings to be seen. All she could remember was the movement of the violins over the grass, the piano notes shimmering the creek, chords in the clouds, tinkling arpeggios resonating off the piercing blue sky, and her father's voice, pointing: "The meetinghouse will be there. And the science building over there. And over there, maybe we'll have a swimming pool or a gym of some sort. We'll want to clear land for a basketball court. These kids love to play basketball."

Music had always been with her. But it had not always been natural. It had not simply flowed from her fingers, as she'd sometimes heard her father brag. No, it had been built into her, like a sturdy bit of shelving. It served a purpose. She had started playing a sixteenth-size violin at the age of three, because Elliot believed it was necessary to her development. She kept playing. When she got good, Elliot drove her to Bend for a weekly lesson with Mrs. Mercer, the former first chair of the Oregon Symphony. Amelia liked Mrs. Mercer, sure, but what she really liked was the escape from Stolen. Last year her best friend, Lydia, had been the one to drive her. The drives had been the most fun of all.

But the truth of it was—and Amelia kept this close—that the moment she stepped onto the campus of Benson Country Day Conservatory for the Arts, she knew she didn't belong there. She was not talented, she was accomplished, and those were two very different things.

Still, Amelia had assumed that she would spend her Benson year growing increasingly proficient. It would be worth it. She would study with Jackson Rice, the violin teacher for whom she'd auditioned. He was famous, only twenty-five, a former prodigy who believed that only a former prodigy could teach gifted children. Amelia would get better little by little; that would be enough.

She never believed that in the space of five short weeks, she would soar as the music raced and lilted through her body with speed and light and urgency, and then, horribly, the entire shimmering world would come crashing down around her. She couldn't have dreamed that on this evening she would be standing by the window in her dorm room, the receiver hot in her hand, persuading her father to let her come home. Back to Stolen. Now. She couldn't have dreamed that lies would flow out of her so easily. Though Amelia was not, by practice, a liar, lying was worth it if it meant she could get out of Portland fast.

Amelia had waited until any hint of crying had left her voice. She'd made sure that her roommate, Sadie, had left the room. But confronted with Elliot's endless, loving support, she was afraid she'd cry again. She was tired of pretending she was both fine and mature.

Elliot's voice was soothing. "Honey, no one wants to *make* you do anything." He paused. "I'm just so disappointed for you. Mr. Rice seemed—"

"Jackson," interrupted Amelia. "He wanted everyone to call him Jackson."

"Well, I know how much you were looking forward to studying with"—Elliot paused again, then said the name carefully—"Jackson." Amelia could hear him trying to match his tone to hers. He didn't want her to believe he was disappointed. "It's just highly unusual that he would accept another offer at the start of a school year."

"I know, Dad, but not every school inspires the same loyalty as Ponderosa." She tried to laugh, sound lighthearted.

Elliot said, "Are you sure you're all right, 'Melia? Are you sure that's the only problem? Losing your teacher?"

This was the perfect response, because it gave Amelia the chance to regain her composure, to retreat into familiar, eye-rolling sulkiness. "God, Dad, do I have to cry on the phone for you to believe I'm homesick?"

"Of course you don't, honey."

"It's just that everything is weird here. And if I have to work with that other teacher until they hire a replacement, I don't think I'll be . . ." Amelia cast about for a phrase that her father would get. "I don't think I'll be using my time to the best advantage. You know what I mean?"

No response.

"Dad?" Amelia went on. "Are you really worried about the money? Losing the semester's tuition?"

Elliot laughed. "No, honey. You're talking to an educator. That's what the money's for." She could hear his distraction.

"If it's not the money, why do you seem so hesitant?"

"Oh, sweetheart, I was just thinking about how good it will be to see you. And how great it will be to have you back here in case my Big Plan works out."

This sounded like her dad. "Big Plan?"

"Well, it's a little premature to call it that, and if I confide in you, you must promise not to tell anyone yet. Especially Lydia."

"Dad, what is it?" She remembered how contagious her father's enthusiasm was.

"If things come through, I think we might be dabbling in the theater here at Ponderosa before too long." He paused for effect, then announced: "Shakespeare!"

"Oh," Amelia said, realizing again why she'd been so ready to leave Stolen in the first place. Ponderosa was exactly the kind of place where "dabbling in the theater" would be earth-shattering news. "Oh," she repeated, trying to drive the boredom from her voice.

"Be sure not to sound too excited."

Amelia was swept with a wave of remorse. "Dad, honest, I am excited." She tried to bring the conversation up a level, to tease her father. "I was just wondering what Cal thinks. I'm sure all he hears is more work for him. You know. He's Cal."

"He's not in the loop on this yet. I'd appreciate your discretion." Elliot's voice was tinged with a familiar reprimand.

"I was kidding," she said.

"Yes, of course you were." He could sound so stern.

"I won't tell anyone, I promise," she said. "Besides, who would I tell? I'm not even back yet."

"Yes, that's right. How are we going to fix that?" Elliot's voice carried so much love that Amelia started to cry, this time with relief. She didn't care if he heard. He agreed to pick her up on Saturday. It was the earliest he could get away.

By the time Amelia hung up, she already felt halfway home, halfway back to the world that no one at Benson could even begin to understand. A sense of safety surrounded her; she often felt this way when she was reaching the end of a particularly challenging

movement, where the fast shifts and high positions, the rapid bow-
ings and measures of thirty-second notes all felt like physical ob-
stacles that she was somehow miraculously surmounting.

She allowed herself to luxuriate in this sense, but before Sadie
came back to their room, before the warmth faded, Amelia required herself to unfasten her violin case, to lift open the velvet-
lined inner compartment where she stored her resin, and to hold
the money in her hand. Eleven brand-new bills. One thousand and
one hundred dollars. The money was green and thin and crisp and
light. But most of all, it was wrong. That was why she had to leave.

HELEN
Milton, Vermont ~ Saturday, September 14, 1996

It wasn't until a week after Elliot Barrow's phone call that Helen
let herself speak about him. She thought she'd dampened that rush
of emotion for good, but leave it to old Michael Reid to recognize
the burning underneath the surface and call her on it.

They were lounging on the brightly painted Adirondack chairs
lined up in a row, facing Lake Champlain. It was sunny and bright
and astoundingly green, a day that someone from New York City
could truly savor. The perfectly mowed lawn tickled Helen's bare
feet as a breeze skipped over the afternoon. A damp Ferdinand
took turns lolling in the sun, swimming in the lake, and gobbling
crackers from Michael's outstretched hand. There were cocktails—
martinis, mixed by Michael himself—and small matching bowls
filled to the brim with salted peanuts, guacamole, pita chips, and
freshly made hummus. This was life at the Reid estate.

Perhaps "estate" was too extravagant a word; surely Michael
would say so. Yes, he was one of the Vermont Reids, and yes, he
had made a pretty penny in his own right with his film work, but
he detested being called wealthy. And though he maintained an
apartment in the city and summered here on the lake, he would be
quick to point out that his apartment was a modest loft in Chelsea,

that the house on the lake was a rustic cabin he'd inherited from his grandfather, and that really, he was no film star, just a humble aging theater queen. More than once, Helen had kept herself from commenting that only the rich call three-thousand-square-foot lofts "modest" and twenty-five acres of lakefront property "rustic."

But she was starting to understand a little more about what made Michael feel so bereft. A house with just you in it did that to you. Michael's husband, Liam, had been dead five years. Although Michael had remained healthy on the cocktail for nearly a decade, it was clear that the specter of a lonely death haunted him in the darkest shadows of his many empty rooms.

None of that was in the air today. Today there was light skipping off the water, sailboats to be counted as they flocked across the bay. The light cotton of Helen's dress was cool against her, and she could feel the sun browning her shoulders.

"And how is the First Stage?"

She took a healthy swig of her martini. "Good. Duncan's hammering out the kinks at rehearsals. *Romeo and Juliet.*" She wished she hadn't used the word "hammering." It brought to mind a most unpleasant visual, one she knew Michael was fighting the urge to acknowledge. So she wasn't as surprised as she acted when he asked, "And do you happen to be sleeping in Duncan's bed?"

"Why on earth would you even ask that?"

He shrugged, scooped up a handful of peanuts, and didn't answer. Instead, he stretched his finger out at the water. "See that point? When we got old enough, my brothers and I used to swim from here to there. My mother didn't let us start until we were twelve, though we swore up and down that we were ready at eight, nine, ten. But it's a lot farther than it looks. When you're in the water, it's a lot farther."

"Ahhh," said Helen. "The wise man preacheth. What on earth are you talking about?"

"Nothing," he said. "I just thought you might like to hear a story."

Helen sighed. "And why would you think that?"

"Because you obviously don't want to talk about real life. And I get it. This is your vacation time. Away from everything. So feel free to just sit and enjoy the environs. Drink in my little piece of heaven."

"Jesus, Michael, what do you want me to say? That my marriage is deteriorating? That rumors abound? That Duncan hasn't fucked me in five months?"

Michael turned to her in mock horror. "Ms. Bernstein, watch your tongue. There are baby animals present." He leaned toward her conspiratorially. "That's a long fucking time, Helen. Leave the bastard."

"I can't."

"Yes you can. You just don't want to."

"No," she said. "I *want* to. I can't."

"You *won't*."

"Maybe I will."

"That's the spirit, Helen. Put some balls into it. All together now: *maybe*."

She leaned her head back against the chair and closed her eyes. The sun was almost too bright against the membrane of her thought. "Elliot called."

"The plot thickens."

"Except it doesn't. And I felt like such a fool. He wanted a list of directors, with the hopes of luring one out to Oregon to direct *The Tempest* at his school."

Michael groaned. "*The Tempest*? Isn't that play dead yet? I am sick to death of the comedies."

She shook her head. "You're wrong—the comedies are the bard's true treasures—but that's not the point. The point is that I thought he was going to ask me to come and do it."

He looked at her as if she were insane. "You have a *life*. You can't just drop everything and go across the country to direct a second-rate Shakespeare play with a bunch of Indian kids."

"Of course I can't, but that's not the point."

"Anyway, are we even allowed to call them Indians? If I'm okay with calling myself queer, does that give me the right to call them Indians? Did they ever really mind it in the first place?" Michael threw a handful of pretzels toward the sleeping dog. Ferdinand immediately awoke and snuffled up the snacks from the grass.

"When Fergus throws up tonight, you're the one cleaning it up."

"The dog's name is Ferdinand. Why give your dog a dignified name if you're just going to undignify it with a nickname like Fergus?"

"I like Fergus." Helen shrugged. "And I call him Ferdinand when he's in trouble."

"You have a marriage to be miserable in," Michael declared. He had this habit of switching topics midconversation. "You can't be expected to go traipsing off every time that man calls . . ." He faltered. "Unless." His hand fluttered to his chest gracefully. Even though he was teasing, the word seemed to stop the world for a moment. "Unless you're still in love with him."

Helen laughed, drowning her mouth in the remnants of her drink. "That's ridiculous." She closed her eyes again, this time to end the conversation. She could hear Michael finishing his martini and fiddling with the olive spear; then he brought it to his mouth and took in all four olives at once. He set down the glass and leaned back in his chair, chewing. She could feel him looking at her, but she kept her eyes closed. She heard her words fading in the wind and listened to the sound of the lake lapping down in the cove, the sound of the chipmunks running, of the maple branches' slow sway. She listened so hard that she couldn't hear Michael anymore, and panic seized her. She opened her eyes in alarm. He was watching her, still as can be.

"Yes, it's ridiculous," he said in a quiet voice, all joking aside. He took her hand, which was alarming in itself. Michael Reid was not a man who did much touching. Helen looked down at his lovely fingers, perfectly soft and manicured, against hers, unkempt and ignored. He spoke again. "Love is ridiculous. But it makes us human, Helen. When was the last time you felt human?"

She squeezed his hand and waited for the moment to pass. It made her uncomfortable to feel how fiercely this man—truly alone, full of a deadly disease—pitied *her.* "You sure we can't convince you to tackle *Richard III*?"

"I'm retired, remember? I wouldn't want to ruin the legend."

"That's why we ask: so that the legend can continue."

"Oh, Helen," he said in a paper-thin voice. "Keep asking. One of these days I just might say yes."

"Well." She withdrew her hand. She didn't want this kind of seeing right now. It was too much. It was too maudlin. She stood. "I'm going inside for another round. Can I bring you one?"

"Naturally," he said. Helen picked up their glasses and headed back up to the house. A few steps away, she heard his voice again. "Love lingers. Yes, it's complicated. Yes, it's ridiculous. That's why we have a long life. So that, despite all the shit, you can still make it a *good* life." Helen waited for more, but he was done. Though his words made sense, she didn't want to hear them, no matter how much he meant them for himself too. She couldn't help hearing the judgment behind them, the empty tragedy of the world: each day you made more mistakes, missed more opportunities. Weariness washed over her. With small steps, she resumed her walk up the bright lawn and into the cool of the cabin's shade. When it hit her, she shivered and realized it was already evening, and already autumn as well.

Chapter Three

CAL

When do friends decide not to talk? Elliot was my closest friend in the world. He honored me as his baby's godfather. He welcomed my second cousin Eunice and me to Thanksgiving dinner, Christmas morning, and Easter brunch. Hell, every year I found a new drill bit or a sweater from Mervyns with my name on it sitting underneath his tree, which was more than I did in return. Giftwise, that is. Only once did he share a holiday meal at *our* table on the reservation. I chose not to be insulted by this. Maybe we offended his Puritan sensibility with our dead-from-smallpox-Indian-princess jokes that particular Thanksgiving. Or maybe it was just that he had a hard time accepting goodness from others. *He* was the one who dispensed goodness, wasn't he?

The point is, I don't know why, because I never asked. Likewise, he never asked me anything specific about my life before he knew me. What he knew were the facts: I was the son of the great Neige Courante lawyer Jasper Francoeur. I graduated summa cum laude from Harvard. I pursued a graduate degree at Harvard in literature but did not finish. I found my way back to the reservation. Six months later, Elliot Barrow showed up, and we began the endeavor of building Ponderosa Academy.

That was almost seventeen years ago. Not once, in over a decade and a half, did Elliot Barrow ask me how it came to be that my first twelve years were spent on the reservation and not in my father's home in Portland. Not once did he ask me why I didn't call my father's wife my mother. Not once did he ask me what had happened at Harvard that made me limp home like an injured animal. Not once did he doubt that I was going to stand by his side.

It's not fair to chalk it all up to his being a Wasp. He didn't pry into anyone's life, but on more than one occasion he surprised me with a juicy bit of gossip that even I had overlooked. Which meant that he listened when others spoke.

I didn't ask him about his past. I spent so much time steaming about how Elliot Barrow was interested only in his own vision, his own daughter, his own life, that I didn't notice I was just like him. It never occurred to me to wonder what had led him to such a passionate pursuit as starting a school in the country, for poor brown children. It never occurred to me to ask about Amelia's mother. All I knew was her name was Astrid and she was dead, and I thought that was all I needed to know.

Boy, was I wrong. Boy, do I wish, just once, after one of those early-summer days spent roofing the gym, I'd clinked my beer bottle against Elliot's and asked, "What happened to Astrid?" I wish he'd turned to me and asked, "What happened at Harvard?" We would have realized we were talking about the same thing: the death of love. We would have shared our secrets. I would have known him not as my salvation, or a genius, or a liar, or a charmer. I would have known him as a man.

I would have told him everything.

YOU DON'T HAPPEN into falling in love. Or perhaps that's how I comfort myself: I believe that you don't *only* happen into it. It happens to you, oh boy does it ever happen—you step in it and it won't unsmear—but more often than not, you also help it along. You do something minuscule to let it breeze in.

Afterward, when you are wretched and alone (and indulging,

with little trouble, your flair for the dramatic), somehow knowing this—that you welcomed love, that you opened up the door to it—makes you feel the slightest bit better. It makes you feel better because it makes you feel worse, and in those days, weeks, months afterward, all you want to feel is worse and worse and worse. You'd stab yourself to death with a penknife if you knew it wouldn't make you seem so goddamn pathetic to her people, who used to be your people, whom you care about only because you know they'll report back to her the second they see you wounded.

So it was.

Sometimes all I can think about, all these years and miles later, is those few seconds we had on my makeshift couch in my dusty living room in Cambridge. In the summer of 1980. In the beginning.

Blue dusk huddles outside the front window. She and I are talking about something profound, I'm sure, something impressively erudite: China's domestic policy, Derek Walcott's elegant prosody. Anything but what is happening between us. I make her laugh, and she shifts her weight, and her knee, naked, peeking from beneath her maroon corduroy skirt, grazes my leg. I expect nothing. I expect her not to notice; she's never given any indication of noticing before. But then, so slowly that I barely see it happening, she moves her knee back against my thigh. Two centimeters. Warm. Hovering. She looks at me. I look at her. And my God, I realize she's *looking*. Her face is serious, alarmed. She's discovered. Then, subtly, slowly, as I hold my breath, she presses that tiny bit of flesh against me. Time slows. I can taste the air. My arms ache. I remember it's impossible, but the world swoons so wildly that all I want to do is burrow, to be *in* her where it will finally make sense. Forget about language. It just fucking leaves me. I couldn't construct a sentence if you paid me a million dollars.

But I can now. Boy, can I ever.

You want to know what happens next, don't you? You want it to go on, vividly: my hands on her shirt, her lips on my lips, the press of new arousal. How easy it would have been, or rather, how easy it seemed to be. It seemed likely. It seemed probable. But the thing about love is that it makes you lose your grip. You become a moron. My God, I thought, life opens. Hope abounds. Forget all logic; I've got her. Here, now, she's mine.

And then her husband came back from the bathroom. She lay her smooth, bare feet back on the floor. She turned her face to him in the fading light and smiled as I stood and refilled our three wineglasses. Coq au vin was bubbling hot in that oven of mine. He flipped on the overhead light, and the brightness jolted me back to friendship, to our triumvirate and all I loved about it. Yes, I thought, I have a secret. But I will carry it inside me and I will be tight-lipped. Yes, I will worship it and tend it and pledge all fealty to its truth, for her knee was here, right here, and that's all the truth I need, for who does that hurt? What can ever be wrong about love if it is kept quiet, and honorable, and private? What indeed.

AMELIA
Stolen, Oregon ~ Saturday, September 28, 1996

Amelia had been home about ten minutes when Lydia pulled up in her enormous brown Chevrolet and stood outside the house, demanding that Amelia get in the godforsaken car already or else Lydia would die of boredom right then and there. Amelia had known it would be a matter of minutes before her best friend arrived. They had been friends so long, they couldn't remember their lives without the other.

But Amelia knew that the trickiest thing about having an old friend who's a best friend is that she'll *have* to know everything— it's one of the benefits—and the only even remotely possible way to lie to her face is to race through your true story, fast, leaving out those parts of the truth that are inconvenient or weird. When your best friend squints at you and cocks her head and looks dubious, you can just blame your awkwardness or embarrassment or squeamishness on something that makes both of you laugh. Amelia had been gone for five weeks and now she would have to look Lydia in the eye and confess some true things and delete others, all the while remembering every last thing she said. Lydia had a mind like a steel trap.

They went and got Mexican.

"So apparently, you didn't get your license yet. What did you do in the big city? Take the bus everywhere or hire a chauffeur? Or was that hottie taking you around?" The girls were settled in a booth, and Lydia had the advantage. Light from the street shone into Amelia's face, and Lydia's shadowed expression was hard to see.

Amelia grinned. "Shut up. I'll get my license by Christmas, I swear. And there wasn't much 'getting around' in Portland anyway." Amelia ran an imaginary bow over the strings of an air violin.

"Yeah, right. Looks like I'm going to be chauffeuring you well into our eighties." Lydia took a sip of water from the plastic glass. "So we've done the small-talk shit. Now tell me everything about the guy. His name's Wes. Right?"

Amelia extricated the menu from its habitual place behind the napkin holder and salsa installation. "Do you want to split some nachos?"

"Don't tell me you officially got some action!" said Lydia, hitting Amelia's arm across the tabletop. "Lookin' good, lookin' good! Sooo?"

"No, seriously, do you want to split some nachos?" Amelia couldn't help but smile.

"Oh, you are such a bitch." Lydia lifted her head and announced to the crowded restaurant: "My little baby girl's all grown up! Someone touched her titties—"

"Shut up!" Amelia hissed, blushing.

Lydia put one hand on her hip. "Spill it."

That was the moment Inez came to take their order. "Good to see you again, Amelia. Your poor father's been eating here breakfast, lunch, and dinner. Missed your company, that man."

"He's the one who sent her away," said Lydia. "Exiled to Portland, poor thing. While the rest of us live like kings."

"I'll have the chicken taco," said Amelia. "Spicy. And nachos. And a lemonade."

"And for me"—Lydia scanned the menu as if she hadn't read it a billion times before—"let's see, a burrito, I guess. A vegetarian burrito. And a Coke. And Inez?"

"Yes?"

"Congratulate our little Amelia. She's becoming a woman." Lydia sighed blissfully as Inez rolled her eyes and left to take the next booth's order. Lydia smiled smugly at Amelia. "They grow up so fast."

"Vegetarian, huh?" Amelia asked. She wasn't going to take the bait. "What happened to your love of raw meat?"

"Don't get me wrong; I still love it theoretically. But my goddamn brother got a grill for his birthday, and he's been serving us 'the perfect steak' for, like, weeks on end. The thought of cow almost turns my stomach these days. But don't think I forgot about Wes. Spill it, bitch. I want to know everything."

The time to lie had arrived. All the way back in the car with her father, Amelia had feigned sleep and schemed about what she would say to Lydia. The story Lydia would want to hear was called "My Life with Wes." But the complete story made Amelia feel so nauseated—so ashamed—there was no possible way to put it into words, even if she'd wanted to. She also knew that to talk about Wes was to talk about music, the topic of which always pushed Lydia away. A rapturous exposition on the musical dimensions of duets with Wes would get Lydia off her back immediately.

Once upon a time, Amelia and Lydia tried to have music in common. When Lydia was six and wanted to play the violin just like Amelia, Elliot had made it possible. He'd gone to Portland and bought a half-size violin, and taught the girls together on Saturday afternoons. He smiled proudly as they sawed their way through basic duets. As far as he was concerned, the girls were great. But Amelia and Lydia understood reality: Amelia was good, really good, and Lydia was, well, scratchy. She could sing the notes with her voice but couldn't quite draw them out of her instrument. Her stubbornness kept her going until she was ten, but that was that. Basketball took over. It was fine that the girls had different skills, but on raw days, they both felt the dangerous pull of music's symbolism, of the things that everyone who looked at them saw but no one dared mention: the big happy, scrappy family vs. the lonely father and daughter; the deep poverty of the reservation vs. modest, tasteful living right next to the reservation; and brown skin vs. white.

Amelia took a sip of water. "You know those Bach partitas that I've been trying to memorize for, like, I don't know, maybe ten years? Well, Wes plays them so fast, so technically perfect, you can't even hear his vibrato, it's just the way he touches the strings! And his bowing! He uses the whole thing!" Sitting there in the little restaurant in Stolen, Amelia felt how flat those words sounded. She knew this wasn't what Lydia wanted. She shrugged. "You know, he's, like, two years older than Sadie and me. I told you that, right? He's Sadie's brother? He's taking a fifth year, an extra year—you can do that."

Lydia raised her eyebrows. "You mean he failed school? Was he held back?"

"No, no, no, it's nothing like that. People do that at Benson." Amelia paused. "You know, if they're really talented and they can't decide whether or not they want to apply to Juilliard or just regular college."

"Oh yeah." Lydia looked straight ahead. "I forgot. You music prodigies do things a little differently than the rest of us."

Amelia could feel herself getting mad. "C'mon, Lydia. Don't be a jerk, okay?"

"Well, what am I supposed to be? You go away for two months, and you write me twice and call me for, like, twenty minutes. Oh yeah, and you get yourself a new best friend." Amelia could hear the hurt in Lydia's voice. "Sadie." Lydia pronounced the name carefully. "That's what she is, right? Your new best friend?"

Amelia felt both amazed and relieved, but underneath pulsed a sadness she couldn't name. "You've got to be kidding." She looked across the table at her real best friend. "Lydia. This is *me*. Amelia. Remember?" What she wanted to say but couldn't was simple: There's no way Sadie could ever be my best friend, and you know why? I lied to her and she didn't even suspect a thing, but I don't even know how to *talk* to you, Lydia, because you know me so well, you can see right through me.

It *had* been easy to lie to Sadie. Amelia had simply stood in the sparse dorm room, crying, after the conversation with her father. The moment her roommate returned from dinner, Amelia looked up and blurted out, "My dad's making me go home." She hadn't planned to say this; she'd just said it. Sadie had bought it right away. She'd protested some: "He has no right! This is your life! What will I do without my cool roomie from Stolen?" Amelia had little trouble playing the stern-but-fragile-long-grieving-widower-with-only-a-daughter-in-the-world card—he needs me!—and Sadie had helped her pack.

What hurt most was that there was no good story to tell Lydia about Wes because Lydia never would have liked or even approved of Wes in the first place. Wes *or* Sadie. They were dazzling and horrible and enticing. They were from Portland, but they boarded because their parents wanted them to have "the full-immersion experience." Amelia soon discovered that this meant Sadie and Wes were big partyers and their parents didn't actually want to be parents. They wanted their children to be someone else's responsibility, and they'd pay handsomely for that service while jetting off to the south of France, Turkey, Bali, Anguilla.

Sadie was not especially talented at the cello, but she had a lot of good stories, and a car, and knew all sorts of bohemian places to hang out. Even though Amelia was kind of afraid of her at first, she was also drawn to her, because Sadie was beautiful and funny and sarcastic. And, oh yes, because of Wes. Wes wore the same pair of dirty Levi's every day, rolled his own Drum cigarettes, and had the most beautiful blue eyes that Amelia had ever seen.

When Amelia met Wes, it was the Friday of the first week of classes. She'd returned to her dorm room and opened the door to a flurry of activity and a blast of cigarette smoke.

"Close the door! Close the door!" Sadie insisted. "We disabled the smoke alarm in here, but we can't mess with the ones in the hallway."

Wes nodded in Amelia's general direction.

"I can come back," said Amelia, her hand on the doorknob.

"Oh God, no." Sadie giggled. "He's my *brother*. Ewww."

"Who're you?" asked an unfazed Wes, taking his cigarette between his pointer and middle fingers. His bare forearm moved in slow motion. A knit cap was tugged down over his ears, and the shadow of a real shaved beard darkened the lower half of his face. Amelia almost blurted, "Who're *you*?" but she already technically knew who he was and didn't want to seem like an idiot. God, he looked good.

"I'm Sadie's roommate. I'm Amelia," she said, extending her hand, then withdrawing it, not wanting to look too dorky, too eager.

"Nice," he said. "No Chink this time, Sade. Good job."

"Oh God, pay no attention to him. You are so racist, Wes! He totally doesn't mean it, Amelia, that's just how he jokes. See, for the last two years, I've gotten some tiny Asian girl named Ming-Bo or Satuko to share a room with, and they're totally compulsive, total, like, neat freaks." Sadie jumped up and ran to Amelia and put her arms around her. "No one as cool as you, my wonderful roomie. See how much we love each other?"

"Good luck," Wes said to Amelia. "My sister's a psycho."

"Shut up, Wes. Don't be a dick. Amelia's, like, really cool. She grew up on an Indian reservation."

"For real?"

"Not *on* the reservation, technically," said Amelia automatically. "I live about twelve miles away from the Neige Courante reservation. My father runs a school there."

"Where is that?" asked Wes, leaning forward in his chair, interested.

Amelia tried not to blush. "Here in Oregon. On the other side of the mountain. Near the town called Stolen?"

"Cool," said Wes, nodding. "Fucking cool. I bet you've seen some great shit."

Amelia shrugged. She wasn't exactly sure what he meant, except that it was a good thing to have seen this "great shit." "I guess so," she said. "But mostly, it's pretty boring. I mean, it's the country. There's not much to do except study. And play the violin."

"Right," said Wes. He looked her straight in the eyes.

"Where do you live?" she asked.

"Over in Borden. The dorm of losers. I call it 'Boredom.'" He nodded toward the window and leaned back, balancing his weight on two legs of the wooden desk chair. Then he smiled. "So, sis, are we going to do this or not?"

"Yeah. Lights-out is in fifteen minutes. So you have to sign out right now and then go hide in the car. Pick us up in half an hour."

Amelia knew Sadie was talking about sneaking out, and that it was completely against the rules. Despite that, Amelia desperately hoped the "us" included her.

"So what about you, Amelia? You up for it?" Sadie asked her. "We're going to this great party. It's Friday night, and I'm *not* going to spend it sitting in here waiting to die."

"But how will we get out?"

"Wes is an expert at this shit. We already cut the screen, and lucky for you, we're both skinny enough to fit through the window. And Wes stashed the groundskeeper's ladder, didn't you, my most wonderful big brother of all?"

"See you down there," Wes said, walking past them. As he brushed past Amelia, she could smell the sweat of him, the salt of him, and it made her feel a little happy and a little embarrassed. She could feel herself blushing. "Sure," she said, "I'm in," as the door clicked shut behind him.

Later that night, after the party, as the three of them sat on a picnic table in Sellwood Park and searched the night sky for shooting stars, Wes asked Amelia if she'd like to be his little sister. That meant she would play second violin to his first in a duet partnership. It was a Benson tradition. Highly skilled upper-class musicians could choose a little brother or little sister to mentor in duets; later in the fall, they would hold an informal performance and a sight-reading competition. Amelia was overwhelmed.

"But you've never heard me play!" she protested.

Sadie laughed. "Oh, yes he has! He thinks you have talent."

"But when? When could he possibly have heard me?" asked Amelia. She'd made a point of practicing in the soundproof rooms in the basement of Haines Hall. She was, and always had been, a respecter of the rules.

"Remember when I asked you to help me with that Haydn passage? That was a setup! Go on, Wes, tell her yourself," Sadie said, shoving her brother.

"I was outside the window." He smiled slowly, spoke even more slowly. "I was checking you out." He shrugged. "So is it yes or no?"

If things had turned out differently—if Wes had been the kind of guy he'd seemed at first, and not the kind of guy who shoved a roll of eleven hundred-dollar bills into a girl's hand to make her do what he wanted—Amelia could have told Lydia everything. She could have sat in this little restaurant in Stolen and told her best friend about the Bach Double, and the thrilling rush when Wes hastened the pace in the Vivace movement and Amelia, naturally, followed, feeling the music entering her not as a series of memorized notes and corresponding motions but as risky joy, and how, as a result, she'd played better than ever before. She could have told Lydia how it had felt to hold Wes's still-warm violin under her chin, to feel the vibrato in her fingers turning the notes to honey, to feel the beautiful resonance of darkened wood. She would have told Lydia about the kiss.

But she didn't want to tell Lydia any of this, and she didn't have to, because here was the truth: the world of Benson never had to collide with the world of Ponderosa. Lydia would never meet Wes or Sadie; Sadie would never get to feel superior to Lydia. Now that Amelia was home, she didn't have to think about them either. Even if she wanted to, Amelia knew she couldn't talk about any of this; it was way too soon.

Lydia sat across the table, waiting for reassurance, for a measure of their friendship. Amelia knew the one way to make Lydia feel right, come fully home again, was to tell Lydia something *big*. She had a whole range of not quite big things, but if she picked the one that felt the furthest away from her, maybe she could make it big enough, maybe Lydia would buy it, and maybe it could explain everything.

"You know why I left? Really? Why I came home?" She saw warmth creeping into Lydia's eyes; noticed her jaw softening. "It's sort of creepy. Not just because of the thing itself but because I can't tell my dad. Ever. He can't ever know."

Lydia was poised, alert. She reached her hand across the table, toward Amelia. "You can tell me. You know that. I won't ever tell."

Amelia nodded. And blurted, "It's about sex."

"Oh my God, Amelia, you didn't, did you?"

"Oh no, it's not about me. It's about my teacher. Jackson Rice. You know, he's the guy I auditioned for to go there in the first place. He was going to change my life." Amelia held her breath for a moment, then went on quietly. "He fucked one of the students and they fired him. But not the way my dad would have fired someone. They didn't even act like what he did was bad. They acted like he was just young and it was some stupid mistake. Like if he hadn't gotten caught, it would have been okay. He went someplace else to teach, and we were all supposed to cope." She was shredding her napkin as she spoke. "I felt really stupid, Lydia. Like I was the worst musician there. I just couldn't be there anymore. I mean, he was the whole reason I went, and . . ."

Lydia looked at Amelia with concern and said, "God, that's horrible. What a creepy thing." Then she cocked her head to the side. "But honest? This Jackson guy was so important that you had to come all the way home?"

"You know me." Amelia smiled. "That oversensitive-artistic-temperament thing. It's just so far away. When I think about it now, I think I hated it there. I needed to come home, you know?" She realized what she needed to say. It was the truth: "I missed you. I didn't know how to deal with that shit alone."

"Absolutely." Lydia smiled broadly at her friend. "So is the girl okay?" Amelia didn't answer. "You know, the 'victim' of harassment? She okay?"

Amelia dropped her smile. "It wasn't a she." She sighed. And nodded as Lydia caught on. "You've got to promise not to tell anyone."

That was the way Amelia and Lydia became best friends once again. Lydia believed she knew the truth, even as a single hundred-dollar bill lay curled tight in Amelia's jeans pocket. She had intended to share it somehow with Lydia but realized that the money represented a truth too complex, too confusing. So the two friends counted out coins and rumpled bills the way they'd always done, leaving a jumble of cash on the table.

Mission accomplished.

Chapter Four

*Y*ou even brought Ariel." Disappointment skated the edge of Willa's voice. She noticed the ancient cat immediately, curled into a sleeping ball on a pillow on the front seat. Nat was reminded of how much he admired Willa in the moments before their departures. She never threw fits. She never cried. She made observations.

Nat put his hand over her fingers, where they perched on the ledge of his rolled-down window. "I thought . . ." he said, then faltered. He had planned it all on the drive over, and now he couldn't locate the right phrasing. It was so strange to think of leaving her behind. "I thought it would be easier for me to take care of Ariel."

"Than who?"

He smiled. "Than you."

Willa stepped back from the car. Just a fraction of an inch, but to her, it was miles. "You're leaving me here?"

Nat patted her hand and tried to look reassuring. "You'll be fine. I'll be back soon."

Miss Finlay emerged from the art building, a stack of papers in her hand. "Good morning, Mr. Llewelyn," she chirped. As Willa watched her walking off toward Tully Hall, she remembered all those times she'd nearly run after an adult like Miss Finlay and begged her for help. Begged her to make time stop. In North Conway, New Hampshire, it had been Willa's third-grade math teacher, Mr. Wilson, who'd sauntered obliviously by the idling car. In Chapel Hill, North Carolina, it had been the kindly Mrs. Sims, who lived next door and was on her way to buy groceries. But when it came down to it, Willa always let her intercessor carry on, unknowing. There was nothing to tell that third party. What could Willa say? "My dad makes me move when I don't want to"? "My dad keeps ruining my social life"? It wasn't as if he were kidnapping her. Willa knew it was dangerous for a little girl in America to accuse her single father of anything inappropriate, because of what people would decide to believe. The very idea that someone would think her father was capable of hurting her the way other girls were hurt, well, that was preposterous. He would never *abuse* her. And whenever he came and got her, she understood it was only because he believed something had changed that was threatening their safety. As if he could see an invisible army mounting against them both, and there were only a few moments in which rescuing was possible. Really, it was just in the seconds before they left a place for good, when it felt as if they were being scattered together into the world, that Willa felt a strange, searing pain inside, as if Nat were asking her to remove pieces of herself willingly, for a reason he would not name.

"Look, kiddo," Nat said, adopting a no-nonsense dad voice. "I'm just going on a little trip—"

"This is not a little trip, Dad, okay? I'm not fucking blind. The car is packed."

"Two suitcases. A cooler. The tent. A sleeping bag or two. Ariel's medicine. A bunch of chips. Some paperbacks. You know how I travel. I need my things."

"So this is some kind of vacation?"

"Not exactly." He wasn't going to lie.

"Dad," she said, all business, "my art show's next Friday. You'll be back by then, right?"

Nat knew to play this carefully. "I hope so." He looked away. It was worth risking her wrath.

"Where are you *going*?"

"Oregon."

Willa couldn't believe her ears. They'd never been west of the Mississippi. He had instructed her of this once, but she knew exactly where they'd been. Driving away from Rochester. Willa had been ten and bold and begging Nat—if they were just moving random places, please could they move *some*where with *some*thing interesting near it, like the Grand Canyon or Mesa Verde, where they had Indian ruins? She'd been in her Manifest Destiny phase. But her usually freewheeling father had issued a sharp "No. We do not go west of the Mississippi." His clarity on that point was unforgettable.

"You're kidding me, right?"

"Nope."

"Jesus Christ, Dad. So let me get this straight. With no warning, you've packed up half our house, even the cat, you've decided you're going to Oregon, of all places, which is, may I remind you, *west of the Mississippi*, and you're, like, leaving me here for a totally unplanned period of time."

"I guess that about sums it up."

Willa crossed her arms and caught him in her sights. "Is this some kind of trap?"

"What do you mean?"

"I mean, you *do* know what teenagers do when they have a house all to themselves, don't you? Are you going to be hiding in the bushes, watching to see if I bring any boys over?"

"Of course not, Willa," Nat said gravely. "I trust you."

Playfulness left Willa when she heard how serious her father was. "So you're just going to *leave* me." She was taut again, preparing herself. For what, she didn't know. But she'd forgotten that when he made decisions like this, she had to keep herself prepared for anything.

"Look, kiddo, you're welcome to come with me."

She laughed bitterly.

"What?" As if he didn't know why.

"I knew it. We're moving."

"No," Nat said, and it was the first time in the conversation that he sounded like *her* father and not some stock version of himself he'd summoned up for the occasion. "I promised you. This is where we live now. We will always come back."

"Dad." Willa stressed the word, so it sang out of her. "Come on. School will be over in a month. We can go camping then. My art show's next week. I don't want you to miss it."

"This cannot wait."

"You always do this. When something matters to me, when something actually matters, when I care about someone, when I finally have a friend . . . You *love* this, don't you? You love doing this to me."

"I do not love anything about this," Nat said, looking down at his hands on the steering wheel. He was not going to let Willa see the tears welling in his eyes. But she saw them anyway. The tears changed the conversation, because they brought Willa back to the car. She put both hands on the lip of the window and leaned down to get a better look.

"Dad," she said, in a soothing voice. "I know sometimes you feel like, you know, things are too hard to handle. Like it's better to leave a place, to escape it? And I understand that, I really do. But we have to stop this. We *have* stopped it. We don't need to move anymore. Remember how much I love my school? And how much we love our house? And the garden? And how you like your boss now? You're getting really good work. And you're making your furniture again." She put her hand over her father's. "We're happy here," she said. "We don't need to run away."

"I'm not running away," Nat said, and when he looked at her, his chocolate eyes were calm again. "I'm going to Oregon."

Willa sighed and withdrew. "Why?" He had seemed so much

more sensible over the last three years. She had loved him even more because he was normal, reasonable, acting like a father, but still himself. Still fun. Maybe he'd been lying all along.

"Because," he said, "I made a promise to your mother."

Willa could barely breathe. Hearing that word was like being punched in the stomach. "What did you say?"

"Before she died, I told Caroline I would find a man named Elliot Barrow. She made me promise I would find him." Nat winced from the memory. "I made a pact with her. Just before she died. And this morning I heard something on NPR. Elliot Barrow is a very well-known man, and apparently, he has been in a terrible accident. He was in a fire. He will probably die very soon. I have to get to him before that. I have to keep that promise, Wills." As an afterthought, he added, "Apparently, he runs a school. In Oregon."

"But, Dad," Willa said, her mind spinning. She cast about for more information, anything, while she tried to get a grip on what Nat had said. "You heard about it on the radio?"

"Yes," replied Nat.

"But it's something"—she hesitated—"my mom said she wanted? For you to find him?"

"Yes."

"So you looked for him before, or something, and you couldn't find him, and now you found him but he's going to die?" Nat nodded once. Willa tried to get a handle on the situation. The game had changed. She wasn't thinking about herself anymore. She said, "Why didn't you say that in the first place? I mean, you never talk about Mom. And if she wanted you to, you know, I mean . . . Go. You should go."

Nat nodded again. "The thing is, sweetheart"—here he took her hand—"I know this isn't fair. I know you've worked so hard to get to this art show. And I know how important your education is. But"—and here he paused—"and this is your decision. But. I think your mom might want you to come along. Not because you have to. Because—"

Willa was already gathering up her drawing and the fixer. "I've just got to put this stuff down," she said. "I've got to get my backpack." She had started to move away from the car when Nat called her back.

"Are you sure?" he asked. "It's going to be . . ." He sighed. He couldn't tell her how it was going to be. He had no clue.

"I'm sure," Willa said, and she smiled broadly. She had been waiting her whole life for this, to be invited into the world of information. She'd always known her mother had wonderful secrets. She'd even believed her father was privy to them. But now she knew her mother was the kind of woman who made deathbed wishes about men named Elliot Barrow. Willa's father was inviting her to fulfill these wishes with him. This was the real thing.

"Okay," said Nat, holding her gaze. "But you have to promise me it's what you want. I need to hear you promise it's your decision."

He was talking so seriously. All Willa could feel was skipping possibility, where before what she had felt was inevitable disappointment. "I promise," she said, and her smile verged on laughter.

"You can stay here," Nat went on. "You really can. You'll be very safe here—"

Willa did not want one of her father's familiar talks about safety. She would not let him back out. "I'm going to get my backpack," she said. "Give me five minutes." She ran into the art building while her father roused the sleeping Ariel and moved her to the backseat.

AMELIA
Stolen, Oregon ~ Monday, September 30, 1996

The beginning of the academic year at Ponderosa Academy was marked by an epic celebration. In the crisp light of early morning, extended families—aunts, uncles, babies, grandmothers—crammed onto the gleaming floor of the gymnasium. This great cavern of a room, at the heart of the academy's campus, usually beat with the dribbling of basketballs. The students sat cross-legged on the floor, opposite their families, lined up on folding chairs. Everyone clapped as new teachers and students were introduced. Next, they all sat patiently through another of Elliot Barrow's stirring speeches, the old women observing how animated he became, like a windup toy that worked in reverse. These women always remarked later that out of everyone there, Elliot was the one who became the most stirred of all. Elliot's speech would end "I have an unfortunate announcement: there will be no powwow tonight." Groans and giggles would ripple through the room. Clapping. Slick smiles on the faces of the older children. They had heard this before. He would go on. "It's true. We didn't have the money this year. So say goodbye to your families. They wish you well. Let us now get to work. Let us embark together on this great adventure of the mind." At that moment, the two hundred some students, ranging in age from four and a half to twenty, would stand and bid farewell to their families.

In the younger classes, rumors spread. There was always one first-grade girl who would cry: "But my brother *promised* there would be a powwow." The grade school teachers would nod sympathetically, placing their hands on top of sweaty, disappointed heads.

In the middle school, the issue of the powwow was debated; these kids were old enough to remember. But they were also getting the hang of tradition, and they loved being in on the secret. On the playground, they'd bait the kindergarteners: "It's too bad they're not having one this year. Last year's was *awesome*."

The high school students would roll their eyes, acting as though they wanted nothing to do with it. "It's stupid," they'd say. "I hate this school." That's high school. Those of us teaching them tried not to take it personally.

But even for the high-schoolers, there would come a moment in the day when, distracted by the high desert heat and the leftover smell of summer, they would relish what they knew was coming.

Someone would hear shell dresses tinkling in the background. Over the whisper of syllabi being passed to the back of the classroom, the students would hear their mothers laughing, their sisters nursing, their fathers cursing, their grandmothers bossing everyone around. As the children held soft chalk to the blackboards and scribbled long division, they would anticipate the slick gym floorboards smooth under their bare feet and smell the tantalizing smoke of the salmon bake as it wafted over campus.

At three o'clock, when learning was over, the children would open their classroom doors to find their regalia folded in their cubbies. They'd race to the academy bathrooms and change. Then the whole herd of them, whooping, hopeful, giddy, would surge back toward the gym. Just outside, in the hallway, the seniors barricaded the door and instructed the children to line up in descending age order. The impatient kindergarteners were forced to hold up the back of the line. Then two distinguished seniors, handpicked that very morning by Elliot, would hold high the school's eagle staff and U.S. flag. These seniors would ask the other children if they were ready. A whoop would rise up. And then these eldest children and their classmates would thrust open the gym doors. The children would snake into the powwow arena, making their Grand Entry. Families cheered inside as the drumming began. There was fancy dancing. Eating. Gossiping. And everyone was ready for another year of school.

IN SEPTEMBER 1996, Amelia was not at Ponderosa Academy for the first day of school. It was the first time she'd missed all the hoopla. She was across the mountain, in a green city, playing her violin, and so on that day she didn't feel that she'd missed out. The academy and Amelia had grown together, her father's twin ambitions. Amelia was infinitely proud of her father, but she couldn't help feeling that after her mother had died—a mother she could not remember, a mother she had known for only twenty-two days—Amelia had not been enough for Elliot. She was all he had in the world, and he'd started the academy because he needed more.

But since this realization, Amelia had spent her childhood caught in a logical loop: didn't she actually *want* her father to be distracted from every intimate detail of her life? Wasn't that kind of the point? By middle school, she had gotten good at ignoring the familiar cloying sensation that clung to her whenever she stepped out of bed. She hadn't imagined it could end. Even though Elliot never had time for her, he never had time without her. He was everywhere.

As she got better and better at the violin, she realized there might be ways of getting out. Amelia ran across an article about the Benson Country Day Conservatory for the Arts in one of her father's education magazines. Her heart skipped a beat as she pored over the description of a boarding school with offerings for serious musicians. She didn't know if she was a serious musician, but she knew she wanted to be. Rather, she knew that she *wanted* to want to be. Which is a different thing entirely. Perhaps more relevant, she knew her musical ambition was the argument with which she could win freedom. Even Lydia agreed: music was the sole way to get Elliot to let his daughter go.

It hadn't taken much persuasion. Elliot furrowed his brow and hemmed and hawed, but he came around to Amelia's side. He even drove her to Portland for the entrance exam. And then she got in. And then she was going. And then she was there.

But now she was back. Nearly a month into the Ponderosa Academy school year. It seemed almost impossible that she'd ever been away. She wanted to slip back into this familiar life in a way that no one would notice, but her father called an assembly on the morning of her first day back. As she heard the assembly bell ringing—a pair of second-graders was always given the task of wandering through the maze of classrooms with a cowbell—Amelia cringed. This was the last thing she wanted. It would mean everyone would notice her, as they always did, remember how different she was because of her skin, because of her father, because of her stupid shy way of being. She made her way reluctantly to the gym, where the children sat cross-legged (I can't resist any further—they sat Indian-style) and stared up at her father, looking not unlike Christ himself, expounding to the heathens.

Sure enough, her father encouraged everyone to welcome "my lovely daughter, Amelia, back into our fold." Lydia was sitting next to Amelia, providing ongoing commentary. As everyone turned to look and clap, as Amelia watched some of the boys snicker and make caustic comments to one another, Lydia whispered, "Jeez, your dad is talking more like a priest each day." Amelia waved a lame little wave at the sea of fellow students. But the truth was that she was happy to be back in this comfort. She hadn't outgrown it at all. Benson was nothing to her now. She never had to think of that place again.

A tall young man entered the door behind her father and waited patiently for him to stop speaking. Amelia and her classmates noticed him immediately. He was lean, solemn. Elliot straightened at his students' sudden raptness, oblivious to the handsome interloper behind him. The young man tapped Elliot on the shoulder and garnered a hug from the headmaster himself as a wave of curiosity rippled through the assembly.

"Mr. Littlefoot, so nice to see you," Elliot said demonstratively. "Many of you will remember Victor. He attended Ponderosa through, what, third grade? And now he joins us from Chicago. Welcome back, Victor." Amelia noticed that Victor Littlefoot's smile came on fast, like a blaze overtaking the prairie. She wanted him to smile like that at her.

Lydia mouthed, "Oh. My. God," as a forest of whispers grew up through the room. Everyone remembered Victor Littlefoot. Amelia felt a blush spread over her cheeks. Something loomed in the back of her mind, but she couldn't see it. It wouldn't take form. The room was suddenly too hot, and she felt her breath quicken as if she were panicking, but it was a good feeling, which was strange.

Victor strode toward the students, looking for a place on the floor with a bunch of twelfth-grade boys. He was gangly, and as Amelia watched him, she couldn't imagine how his long limbs would fold up properly so as to sit. As he walked, she noticed him scanning the faces of her classmates. When he saw her, he locked eyes with her and did not look away until he was sitting. He high-fived the boys, he nodded hello to the girls. He did not say anything to Amelia, did not nod, did not wave. But as they looked at each other, she saw that this looking meant something. Her stomach flipped and flipped again. Lydia squeezed Amelia's hand. "He didn't look like *that* when we were seven."

Chapter Five

*T*he First Stage Theater was on the Lower East Side, nestled in the heart of what had been, not too many years before, a genuinely bohemian (read: dangerous) neighborhood of drugs and artistic revolution. You don't need my description here; all you need is a reference to Basquiat and Haring, and you know exactly what Avenue A looked like in 1984, when Helen Bernstein and Duncan Reilly made their initial investment in an unused, uninhabitable former furniture factory. Now, twelve years later, their company was doing exceptionally well for itself. With six shows a year, a new-playwrights' contest, sold-out performances, eager benefactors, and exuberant raves, Helen and Duncan had created a wildly successful regional theater in the heart of Manhattan. It didn't get much better than that.

Except.

When they'd bought the space together, they weren't a couple. What they were was a couple of people with a crazy idea. What had happened was inevitable, not to mention terribly romantic in the eyes of the press and friends and, it seemed at times, the whole world. They had fallen in love. Sometime around 1985, Helen awoke in Duncan's sun-strewn bedroom in the West Village and knew, for the second time in her life, that her safety had been disengaged. She would go anywhere this man asked, do anything this man wanted. In retrospect, she wasn't the best judge of character. But that hadn't been the point, had it? A recurring theme.

It came to pass that on the first day of October 1996, Helen entered the First Stage to drop in on Duncan's *Romeo and Juliet* rehearsal. For years she'd reminded him that as producers, they had to hire other directors; though nepotism was convenient, it wasn't the most responsible way to run an artistic company. The main reason they had founded the First Stage was so they'd both get the chance to direct what they loved, the old masters: Shakespeare, Marlowe, Aeschylus, Euripides, Chekhov. Directing was what brought Helen her greatest joy. But as the First Stage became more legitimate, got reviewed in the *Times,* consistently drew the world's best living actors, Helen began to feel that she and Duncan should step back and be the administrators they promised to be on their letterhead. There was something profoundly embarrassing about showing off your own "brilliant" ideas year in, year out. She began to realize that the more brilliant ideas you had, the less brilliant they became. So in 1992 she cut her project, *The Bacchae,* out of the season. Duncan was enraged. She'd expected him to give her a speech about sticking to her dreams, about the tragedy of letting her talent wane in the face of others' mediocrity. She would have bought it. Instead, red-faced, he declared, "I hope you know I'm not giving up my own fucking show." And that was that.

NICK, THE FIRST Stage administrative assistant just out of NYU, was sitting behind the front desk, working on the computer. He looked surprised when Helen pushed open the front door. "Hello, hello!" he exclaimed loudly.

"Hey," she said, picking up a stack of mail. "How's it going in there?"

He shrugged, opened his mouth, then stopped himself. "Fine," he said.

"Very believable. Is she awful?"

"Not awful. No, I wouldn't say awful." Nick brought his voice down to a whisper. "She doesn't have the personality for awful."

They were talking about a sometime TV starlet whom Duncan had "discovered" on his most recent trip out to L.A. She was gracing the stage for the first time as the passionate Miss Capulet. She was gorgeous, leggy, blond. Helen had decided not to examine exactly why she felt it so necessary to look in on a rehearsal unannounced. Now that she was here, she said, "Well, I guess I better see for myself."

Nick looked terribly relieved when the phone rang.

Helen let herself in at the back of the theater. The room was dim, silent. Only a few lights were pointed at the set, which was a jumble of half-painted flats and plywood platforms. This was Helen's favorite moment in a production: when it was not yet fully formed, not yet fully itself. There were still a thousand possible ways each line could be read; a thousand possible actors could still play each part; a thousand possible costumes could still be constructed for each character. The whole act of putting the play together, of making its world come alive, consisted of honing all these thousands upon thousands of possibilities until you were left with one way, one actor, one costume, one philosophy. It was this alchemy, this electric combination of people and costumes and words that had taken Helen from the political world of her youth, that of protest and demonstration, and lifted her here. In this moment was when she was most alive, because it was here, in the space of the theater, where she felt hope. There was always one way to be. That was what theater had given her. Safety. A singular perfection she could achieve, if only on the stage.

Helen walked down the center aisle of her theater and listened for voices. She heard nothing. She softened her step and heard, in the back of her mind, a voice saying, "You may discover something here. Are you ready for it?" She reached the stage and walked beside it, running her hand along its soft wood surface, gathering sawdust. She did not call out. She did not warn him. She simply ascended the steps and walked swiftly, silently, into the dark wings. When she got there, she saw what she saw. In the past, in the darkness of her own mind, imagining this moment, she'd expected to feel grief, loss and disgust. But what she felt was pity, for him, and a kind of lifting, for herself. As if she were rising up and seeing, from above, the truth about these last twelve years, in all their sweetness and cruelty, and this seeing set her free.

CAL

Because Elliot did not talk about his past, and I did not talk about mine, a strange rift grew between us. I knew I was his wingman. He named me assistant headmaster. I was given great responsibilities. Ponderosa Academy was Elliot's vision, but I was the man on the ground floor, putting his game into play. For a long time, I did not resent my position in his grand scheme of making a school. That was what saved me, and I won't deny that, even for a second. But time pressed on. Soon I was no longer stinging from the death of love. Soon we were colleagues. Soon I began to believe that when we did not talk about our pasts, we were also saying we would not speak about our futures. And that was where we found ourselves in trouble.

I sensed this trouble long before the words "Benson Country Day" left Elliot's lips and careened into the black hole of my eardrum. I felt it in the way Ponderosa Academy grew, amoeba-like, under the watch of Elliot the dreamer. His plan for the school was not neat, or cost-effective, or regimented. If asked, I would have told you that was all fine. But inside, where the trouble brewed, I began to believe Elliot was arrogant, strong-headed, and blind to the fact that he was allowing the school to grow recklessly, wildly, and without a plan. Meanwhile, the academy was becoming a more and more integral, necessary part of the Neige Courante community. And it was all in one man's hands. I tried to rein Elliot in and scale things down, but he intimated that there was a method to his madness. He kept me away from this method with phrases like "All in good time" and "We'll see what happens." All the elders seemed unconcerned. They were happy to stay in "advisory" roles while Elliot made the big decisions. "You're there," they said to me when I complained. "You're keeping an eye on things." They trusted me. I was Jasper Francoeur's son.

I grew angry. I remembered that first day, when I met Elliot, when he told Amelia I had come to be their storyteller. I saw that Elliot kept his methods, his secrets, close. So close that even I could not see them. And I thought, "That's all he thinks I am. A fucking storyteller. I keep the children occupied while he gains power."

It was easy to jump to the next conclusion. To the difference between us. To the colors of our skin. He was white and in charge. I was brown and helped him. I began to see the way he wanted me to be something he'd conjured from a storybook, the Indian who tells tall tales. I'm not saying I never put this stereotype into play for my own uses; there's something to be said about playing up the silent-Indian type. Ladies love it. I learned this early. Give them a brooding brown man with long black braids and a will to screw, and they'll line up around the block and wait their turn until the sun goes down. I gladly pried open the tops of their tight little jars and wooed them in soothing, pithy aubades, extolling the tenderness of the aureole and denouncing the brutality of the middle class. I gave up explaining that the Neige Courante didn't use bows and arrows, that my father pulled me off the rez to send me to Phillips Exeter. I was an Indian man from west of the Mississippi, and I pretended I lived in a tepee and hunted buffalo, because that's what got me laid.

But that was my own damn business. That was my own damn birthright, and it had nothing to do with Elliot Barrow. He was a fool if he thought I was going to play the cliché for him too, the adoring aboriginal who "kemosabes" and speaks in hushed parables about Coyote.

I was not going to be his storyteller anymore. I was not going to be his right-hand man, his wise adviser, his sidekick. "Fuck him," I thought. "Sixteen years of backbreaking work, and the thanks I get is more backbreaking work in his shadow? Enough. He has no idea what I've given."

I was wrong.

Elliot wanted my blood. Elliot wanted my help. He wanted my mind, and he wanted my friendship. But he did not want my soul. I was born to tell stories. When he told me that was what he wanted of me, he didn't think he was asking a little; he knew he was asking everything. But he did not want those stories for himself. He wanted them for me. Not because I was Indian. Because I was his friend.

THIS STORY BEGINS in so many places that there shouldn't be words used to tell it. But that's all we've got: letters on the page, tongues tapping the roofs of our mouths. What I need you to remember is how much that matters. For I have known electric moments—the fleeting seconds of a hard pink knee pressing against my soft brown thigh; the low red afternoon light of an Oregon evening, streaming off an unmet Elliot Barrow's head; the violet glow of the moon on the night of my father's death; the acrid sting of a barn burning in the darkness, and this, and this, and this—but I cannot simply let them be. I return to these moments. For better or worse, they call to me in their vivid unwordness and ask me to build for them what they cannot build for themselves: phrases, sentences, paragraphs. Houses of stories. It happens again and again. No matter how many times I say no. No matter that I would rather walk across fire. We are each called to our own salvation. Mine's here, in the telling.

The Tall Tale

Once upon a time, there was a tall man who lived alone. From the outside, it looked as though he had not lived that way for long at all. He was not half as old as people who have lived alone for decades. He had not lived alone for one decade, not half a decade, not half of a half of one. The time he had lived alone sounded unimpressive when spoken in years. Even in months, it was a piddly number, and the days barely made an impression.

But from the inside, it was another story. From the inside, this lonely tall man was like a two-thousand-year-old man who'd been sitting alone in a cold house for one thousand nine hundred and ninety-nine years.

Perhaps the tall man was exceptional. Perhaps he had a biological mutation whereby his heart got lonely much faster than the hearts of most other people. Perhaps he was an unfortunate superhero, and this exponential growth of loneliness in relation to linear time was his only superpower. Or perhaps it was simply this: that a few years before, back in a warm place where the sun always hung in a bright blue sky, his life had been full of promise, of possibility, of the love of a woman who fluttered like a bird in his heart. Now that promise was gone. The bird woman was gone. And the man didn't know why. Perhaps that is, most of all, why he was so lonely.

The tall man had brought the woman who was like a bird to this new place to make a life for her. They had traveled thousands of miles, from the sunny home where he had first beheld her, to where he waited now, the place with seasons and a heavy gray sky, and a house he'd found for her to nest in and make her own. He believed this new home was where she would be happy. She had been so unhappy in that sun-filled place, and he had come to believe that what she needed was seasons. He was a little older than she, *but they were so young back in the sunny place and things were so bright that he could see deep into her eyes, and when he saw into those two azure oceans, he saw she was asking something big of him, to always promise her things in this way: happiness when there was no hope of happiness, promise when promise seemed out of reach. So he promised and he bought and he built and he led. That was the way he thought he was supposed to love her.*

But she left him alone in his house with the seasons. She left him soon. She told him, with tears in her eyes, that this was a life she could not live. She was being called by the lure of the city, and he was not to look for her there, not ever, and he was never to think it was his fault, because it was her fault that she could never be satisfied. He was to find some other woman who was nothing like a bird, and this woman would love him in the way the bird woman never could.

She didn't say whether she was coming back. But he knew that some-day she would. He knew that all the kind words she'd said to him in that sun-filled place had bound them together, no matter what she believed. So he sat. And he waited. Snow gathered and melted and gathered again, and still the tall lonely man waited for the woman. He believed that if he waited long enough, his wish could come true. His wish was simple: she would come back and stay. He believed this was the one thing that would make him happy.

He got half his wish. He didn't know what she'd been up to out there in the wide world until the winter night when he awoke out of a stark sleep to a pounding on his door. It was cold in his house. So cold that he watched his breath move ahead down the icy hallway as he padded toward the white wooden door.

He had been waiting so long that he was not surprised to see her. What surprised him had nothing to do with her. What surprised him was how tall he was. He'd been alone for so long that he'd forgotten. He realized he'd underestimated the length of his limbs, the distance between his head and the ceiling. It was in seeing her, and remembering how she had once fit against him, remembering her smallness, her leanness, her bird body, that he could remember himself. That he had a body to begin with. He let her inside.

"You look terrible," she said.

He offered her tea. She kept her coat on. She said, "I'm sorry." He thought she was talking about having left him behind in a lonely house. Now that she was back, he took a good look at her. He started to wonder if she would fit against him again. Her face looked funny. He opened his mouth to speak, to tell her something small but kind, but then she started to cry. "If I ask you to help me, do you promise you'll keep it a secret?"

He shifted his weight from one long leg to the other. "Why?"

She turned to go. Her eyes had caught a wildness. "If I can't trust you, then—"

"Wait," he said. "I'll help you. What do you need?"

"I need you to keep something for me. Promise. Not to tell a soul."

"What is it?"

"Promise first."

"Why?"

She turned to go again.

He promised.

She opened her coat and showed him.

This was the instant the tall man's loneliness ended.

Act Two

[OR]

This Is a Strange Repose, to Be Asleep with Eyes Wide Open

Chapter One

HELEN

Portland, Oregon ~ Saturday, October 5, 1996

*H*ere is where I, Calbert Fleecing, begin to break my promise. I promised you the honest, albeit subjective, truth. You knew that would be hard to deliver. But you believed I would try. But the stories have begun to merge. It's hard to stay out of them, because I was in them.

I also told you I wasn't going to speak to you anymore. That was when I thought that "you" could be only "Elliot." Now I see: "you" is other people too. Every story needs a reader. And Elliot Barrow doesn't have eyes anymore with which to read. In order for this to be a story, someone else needs to read it. Someone who isn't in it. You.

HELEN'S PLANE LANDED at the Portland airport in the early afternoon, and Cal was there to meet her. I am Cal. I am trying to tell her story. But I remember so much, and that means I am bursting to tell you what waiting for Helen's plane to land was like for me. Because I am selfish. Because I was there. Because I am the one telling this story.

It was not my choice. Elliot had a way of getting people to do things for him. He'd called me the night before, and what he had to say was simple: "My wife is coming into town." Keep in mind

I didn't even know he had a wife. Keep in mind that she wasn't his wife anymore. Did he feel the need to fully disclose? Of course not.

I said, "You're not married."

He said, "Used to be."

"Are you telling me this is Amelia's mother?"

"You know that Amelia's mother is dead."

"So you've been married twice." There was silence on the other end of the line. I said, "I didn't know you were so popular with the ladies." Again nothing. "Why is your Not-Amelia's-Mother ex-wife coming to visit? After all these years."

"Helen's going to help you with that Shakespeare project."

"There is no Shakespeare project."

"There is now."

He also forgot to mention she was landing in Portland. I agreed to pick her up because one of us had to do a phone conference with a possible donor, and I will do just about anything to avoid that kind of ass kissing. Furthermore, Elliot led me to believe she was flying into the local airport. Sure, that would have killed three hours of my Saturday, but I figured I could stop in to Rudy's and see a few people. It was when I was about to hang up the phone that he let it slip: "Four-thirty P.M., American Flight 457 from O'Hare."

"American doesn't fly into Redmond."

"Go figure," he said, and hung up. Five hours round-trip.

Why, you ask, did I not call him back and tell him to screw himself? True, he'd pulled pranks like this before, so I should have been wise to him. Perhaps it was that, the shame of being tricked once again, that kept me from saying no. Then there was the fact that Helen needed to know, regardless of whatever agreement Elliot had made with her, that her coming to the school was for recreational purposes only. I didn't know who she was. There was no way I was letting her into my classroom, or into any of the classrooms, for that matter. There was a reason I was assistant headmaster. Emperor Barrow's whims (and Emperor Barrow's dick) would not dictate the changing of curricula unchecked.

But the main reason I went? For myself. I wanted to see her for myself. Before anyone else formed an opinion. I wanted to see the kind of woman who would marry Elliot Barrow.

I WILL GIVE this story back to Helen in a moment. She had never been to the Pacific Northwest; her forays to the West Coast had been the occasional trip to L.A., and twice she'd visited San Francisco. She was a victim of that kind of New York provincialism that is blind. Let's say someone out here rarely left the same ten square miles. That's a very small space in which to spend your entire life; even those of us for whom the United States government has ever so politely reserved completely useless parcels of land usually cover at least twice this distance in our day-to-day lives. But Helen was the kind of woman who had been born and schooled in Manhattan, the kind of intellectual elitist for whom the move across the East River—and the decision to actually buy a home in an "up-and-coming" outer-borough neighborhood—had been wildly significant. Which is all to say that Helen was a New Yorker, and as a New Yorker, she initially gave off the distinct impression that the rest of the world could only ever be a kind of vacation from the real life that New York lived.

Helen, I would find out later, was scared. She had found her husband humping a bimbo, turned tail, and strode forth, his pleas falling useless in their empty theater. She had called Michael Reid and told him she was being brave, and his applause, crisp, over the line, was enough to make her even braver: she dialed Elliot Barrow's number and into the whorl of his ear declared, "I'm not asking. I'm telling you. I'm the one who can help. Do I have a job?" She had crammed her poor Ferdinand into a crate and locked the door of her home behind her.

There were all sorts of complicated legal battles to be fought about the status of the theater, which entered exhausting realms of debate over the disposition of intellectual property and the future of the company. Helen had chosen to ignore these particular aspects of her life for at least a little while. She had not begun formal divorce proceedings. She was not yet ready to punish; Duncan's guilt, if he had any, would have to be enough for now.

She was asleep when the plane landed, so she missed the Columbia River, and she missed Mount Hood, and she missed the fringes of Portland. When she awoke to the tires hitting tarmac, she was filled with excitement. Her throat thrummed with the words she would say to Elliot when she stepped from the plane. He would be waiting at the gate, and surely they would touch, if only for a hug. She dug into her purse as the plane taxied to the gate, and found a mirror and brush to try to tame her split-ended mane. The teenage girl next to her smiled with young teeth and perfect bubble gum lips. Helen put on a lipstick one shade too dark and frowned at herself in the compact mirror. Then the seat-belt sign dinged off and people leaped to their feet. She was in a window seat, so she stood up halfway, her knee resting on the seat as though to hold her place in line. She wanted to get off that plane, and to Elliot, as soon as possible.

Elliot was nowhere near the airport. Guess who was? Helen stepped from the jetway, and the anxious look on her face, peering over the crowd as people spilled from the door, was somehow familiar to me. I held my sign up higher: HELEN BERNSTEIN.

She saw me. She felt as if she were sinking. She was wrong to have come, wrong to have insisted. He had sent someone else. He did not want her here. He did not want her.

I did not see these particulars on her face. I saw her rearranging the heavy bag of books on her shoulder, and she seemed much smaller than I imagined, and very tired, very worn. "Of course," I thought. "Elliot would have married a brainy girl, the kind who travels with an entire bookshelf in a monogrammed L. L. Bean canvas tote."

She came toward me.

"Cal," I said. I stuck out my hand and she took it. Her fingers were cold.

"Helen." Her smile was a slow curl of hope. She was delivered.

AMELIA

Stolen, Oregon ~ Saturday, October 5, 1996

For at least an hour, Amelia had been trying to play the violin. She had lifted the familiar amber-hued instrument out of its velvet bed and tuned the strings until they sounded perfect. She'd swept the bow over its neat block of greenish resin until a little white spray accompanied each pull across the strings. She'd produced notes, run up and down scales accurately, but there was not a drop of music left in her. It had fled her fingers, her mind, her body. She ached to have it back. It felt as if it had gone for good. She wanted to pick up the phone to call Lydia, but she knew her friend was out shooting hoops. Afternoon light flooded the room.

Sometimes these days Amelia went through the Wes story as a series of points, like a plot outline for Calbert Fleecing's English class. It went like this:

1. Wes Hazzard was Sadie's older brother.

2. Wes chose Amelia to be his second violin.

3. Wes let her borrow his own fabulous violin because he had two of them. The one she played had cost his parents thousands of dollars. He laughed lightly when Amelia confessed it made her nervous to even touch. But when he encouraged her to play, she forgot how scared she was, seduced by the sound of her own music. There was a big difference between a good violin and a great one.

4. She sounded marginally talented as music welled up from every part of her mind and body to match Wes's line of notes. While they were inside the music, she and Wes

strode together, raced side by side, intersected, parted company, and met again.

5. Then they stopped playing and Wes turned toward her, leaned in, and kissed her. Warm, luscious. Close like music. That was the good part, the wonderful part, and it made her hungry for more.

6. The next day she went to the office of her violin teacher, Jackson, to meet Wes for duet practice; she opened the door before knocking—and yes, that was rude, but not as rude as what she had to see—Wes and Jackson Rice on the floor, kissing, kissing, kissing. Clothes all around them. A flash of naked shoulder. Of leg. Of butt.

7. Even though she wanted to shut the door before they could see her, she couldn't move, so they saw her and were totally cool and matter-of-fact; they asked her to understand, to keep quiet, and on and on and . . .

8. Of course, she said yes, anything, she would do anything, she would keep quiet, but inside she was shaking and horrified and ashamed of herself for being horrified, this was just sex and sex wasn't bad, she was from the country, she knew about sex, and it didn't matter that they were both men, she didn't care, but Wes? Wes? What have you done to me, Wes?

9. Later that day she met with Jackson Rice at his request in that very same office, and he was so kind, saying that he knew it must have been a shock to see them like that, but how wonderful of Amelia, how mature of Amelia, how liberal and kind of Amelia, to realize that if she mentioned this to anyone, he, Jackson, would lose his job and Wes would probably be expelled, and she didn't really want that, did she? She was doing so well and showed such promise. He was sure he could write her some wonderful recommendations when the time came to apply to conservatories.

10. Right outside Jackson Rice's office, Wes grabbed her by the elbow and steered her into one of the empty practice rooms and said, Hey, Amelia, don't be pissed at me, I can't help it, I think I like guys and I know I love Jackson and you have no idea how mad my dad will be, he'll kill me, and Sadie must never know, she can't know, it would kill her, and I think you're wonderful, and some really lucky guy will love you too someday, just please don't tell. I thought maybe I could help you out with your day-to-day expenses, you can get yourself a nice dress or something cool, we're absolutely good friends, and I really meant that kiss, I know that's hard to believe now, but here's some money, please don't tell Sadie, please. And into Amelia's hand he pressed more money than she had ever seen in one place at one time. And now that money was supposed to be hers. In exchange for silence.

11. Amelia didn't tell—she wasn't a snitch—but someone else *did* tell, and it wasn't even about Wes, it was about another boy, but it didn't matter because Wes thought Amelia had told, and he intercepted her under the trees between class and his eyes looked shattered, like broken glass, and what he thought had happened was what mattered, not what had actually happened. How could she have betrayed him? She couldn't say, You're not really mad at *me* for betraying you, you're mad at *him*, because he said he loved you, but all that time he was doing the same thing with someone else. Isn't that right, isn't that really why you look so broken?

12. Instead Amelia said, I promise you, I didn't tell anyone. I kept it a secret. I don't want your money. Sadie doesn't know.

13. He said, Who even cares if she knows now? She'll know someday because I'm a fag. Amelia, I'm a fag.

14. Don't say that.

15. I'll say what I want to say. Don't lie to me. Keep the fucking money.

16. Please. Here, take it.

17. That's why you liked us so much in the first place, isn't it? You wanted our money, and Jackson just wanted to love me. In peace. Keep the money. It's yours. You ruined my life and you made a bundle.

18. I didn't say anything. I don't want your money. I want to go home.

19. Then go.

The twang of the basketball on the Ponderosa Academy court brought Amelia to the window. The sound of the basketball, in itself, was not what drew her. She knew this. She wanted to see the person attached to those hands that made the ball rise and fall. In past years, she'd practiced the violin in her bedroom, facing away from the school, but ever since she'd heard that Victor was the newfound hope for the Ponderosa team, she taken up practicing in the living room, which looked out over the court. A part of her wished that her music might spill out into the open air and be heard by ears that weren't her own. She wished the delicacy and grace of her violin's song would bring such a calm to her listeners that the basketball would fall from their hands, the book bags from their shoulders, the pencils from their fingertips, and they would turn, slowly, to seek out the music's source. Victor would turn. He would see her up here, on the hill, in her father's top-floor apartment, above the math rooms, and he would want to know more.

Amelia wanted this badly, and she didn't know exactly why. She and Victor hadn't talked this whole week back at Ponderosa. Except for that glance at the first morning assembly, he didn't seem to notice she existed. Something gnawed at her, something from that other time, when they had been children together. Something told her he didn't like her. So why on earth would he look at her? And why would it make her feel like this? Still, she pressed against the window, hoping to catch a glimpse of his lean body running after the ball.

AMELIA AMBLED DOWN the hill, wishing she'd brought a sweater. She could see them out there, on the flat macadam rectangle, lights on above them. They were whooping already. The real game had begun. As she got closer, she noticed Lydia jumping up and down on the sidelines, waiting to sub in. There was a group of girls sitting cross-legged on the grass, drinking in the long swoop of the boys as they made baskets. They were talking about tonight's party: who would be there, who was likely to hook up. The conversation faded when Amelia walked by. She barely noticed. She glanced past them to her father's office, lit up. He was outlined in the window, hunched over papers. He wouldn't get back to the apartment until well after the game ended.

You would think: a Caucasian child raised adjacent to an Indian reservation, going to a school with mostly Indian teachers serving mostly Indian children, and these same children provide that child's primary option for friends. You would think: such a child must know many things. Such a child must feel a part of something. Perhaps it was precisely because Elliot so vehemently insisted that Amelia was a part of something that she didn't feel a part of something. Perhaps the other children saw how Elliot kept her separate, special. Even now that they were old enough, she wasn't allowed to go to parties, or drive, or drink a little to have a good time. No one wanted to cross Mr. B. Then there was the easily misinterpretable fact of Amelia's shyness. It made her say strange, awkward, stuck-up things. She was smart. She had read everything. And she played the violin. Who plays the violin? She was sixteen. As far as her classmates knew, she had never kissed a boy. Some of her classmates already had babies.

Amelia waved to the gaggle of girls and perched herself on the ground at their edge. A few greeted her when they were resigned to her company. None of them made any real effort to talk to her, but once they realized she was staying, their conversation drifted back to tonight's party. Amelia wondered if they were trying to make her feel jealous. She pretended not to care and leaned back on her hands. She watched Lydia join the game, shouldering her way across the court. Amelia made sure to watch Lydia and not hover too long on the other sweaty bodies bounding before her. So she was surprised by the catch in her throat when she watched as the tallest one among them vaulted into the sky, his wide hands rising improbably above the rim, bringing the basketball crashing through the hoop. The air seemed to hold Victor Littlefoot up there a moment longer than was possible. When he came back down to earth, he grinned and high-fived his teammates. The girls beside Amelia were in a frenzy: clapping, calling, shaking themselves into a dazzle, hoping to be noticed. Victor turned and smiled, like a movie star, in their direction. Then he turned a fraction of an inch farther, so that not even those other girls would see his gaze shift in the fading light. For a split second, his smile grazed Amelia. She blushed, but night was descending, and nobody knew it except her, this secret of blood rushing to skin, which had no content or meaning, but seemed a secret all the same.

Chapter Two

The rolling hills of Pennsylvania shot by in every shade of new springtime green. Here Willa was with her father, back in the car, and she felt a giddiness skipping across her knees, through her fingertips, atop her head. She and her father had done something tremendous. For the first time in her life, Willa let herself feel how fun this could be. Lifting out of your life and taking off into the world. Not asking permission. Not letting anyone know. Just going.

A part of Willa knew the reason this felt so fine was that the power dynamic had shifted. Nat had been wise to require of his daughter a desire to accompany him on this journey. He had been wise to give her that choice. But as she chattered freely at him across the front seat, he allowed himself to think about how this had been accomplished. She had agreed to come, to let him leave, only after he mentioned Caroline.

All these years he'd kept Caroline out of it. He'd let Willa believe the onus was on him. She needed him to survive. As long as it kept her safe, he didn't mind having her hate him. She would never be able to get along without him, so he didn't mind risking her wrath. He was the one who made the decisions about when to move on, the one who sensed danger lurking. By the time she was five or six and all Nat had to fear was fear itself, he rationalized: Willa hated him just a little, so much less than most daughters hated most parents. He told himself that all the moving had become easy. She would never have to know how ugly the world was. Besides, she hated him only when he made her move on. Most days of the year, he didn't do that. Most days he took her interests seriously. He respected her mind and her will. He disciplined her fairly when she required it of him. So let her think he was crazy. Let her think that his life in the construction business involved shady dealings that were best solved by fleeing. Let her believe he was a thief, a liar, dishonorable, untrustworthy. Never let her know what her mother had done. Never let her know what he, in turn, had done to save little Willa from a life of something terrible.

He had broken his rule today. He had used Caroline's name. He knew that today it had been the only way. Willa wasn't five anymore. She didn't need him to clothe and feed her. She needed answers. Dangling the promise of Caroline like a carrot was the one way to make Willa want to come along. It was also practice for what would come. They were on their way to find Elliot Barrow, after all. This *had* begun. But Nat hated having to begin this. He hated having to be the one to set it into motion.

"Dad? Dad. Hello?" Willa whistled the sharp whistle she reserved for calling the cat inside.

"Hmm?"

"I hate it when you do that." She meant his drifting off, going to the place where he kept his memories and secrets, the place she could not find him. But she did not say that.

"I'm driving," he said. "I have to concentrate."

Willa slumped back in her seat and groaned. "I thought we were going to have fun."

"We are," he said, and kept driving.

"You have no idea what I was just talking about, do you?"

"Yes I do."

"Oh yeah? What, then?" Willa challenged him.

"Reach around to the backseat and get the backpack."

Willa rolled her eyes but did just that. She pulled the backpack onto her lap and unzipped it. Reaching in, she felt the familiar cold curve of her 35-millimeter camera lens. She smiled wryly and held it up. "So it really was your plan all along to get me to come with you, wasn't it?"

"You were talking about your photographs," he said.

"Dad." He could hear her smiling through his name. "You planned it, didn't you?"

"Your beautiful photographs," he continued. He turned on the blinker and began to slow down and pull right. There was no turnoff in sight.

"What are we doing?" Willa asked, frowning.

"Time to let Ariel stretch her legs a little, wouldn't you say?"

Willa laughed at the euphemism they'd always used. When they were driving, they never said they had to go to the bathroom. She had forgotten. She glanced at the field beside their car. "Hey, look at that cool barn," she said, pointing. "What's that mean?"

The wooden structure was old and crumbling. Painted on its side was a Mail Pouch tobacco advertisement, faded white against the black of the rotting slats. He'd explained this phenomenon to Willa when she encountered her first at the age of seven. "Mail Pouch signs were the original billboards," he said now, to his nearly grown child.

"It's beautiful."

"They're very rare these days. They used to be all over the place, but now they're dying."

He pulled the car to a halt in the half-gravel of the shoulder. "Hey, do you think they'd mind if I took some pictures?" Already Willa was unbuckling her seat belt and reaching for the door handle.

"I'm sure they wouldn't mind at all," Nat said, and watched his daughter striding boldly from the car. As she straddled the fence and made her way through the field, he glanced at Ariel in the rearview mirror as she stretched herself awake. "Just a minute, girl," he said. He loved that Willa trusted him. He loved that he could orchestrate such perfect moments for her and she'd be none the wiser. He loved knowing she would always believe that this first photograph had been her own idea.

He rehearsed it in his mind. "I have four things to tell her. First I will tell her about her wonderful mother. Then I will tell her how her mother died, and what she did, and I will try to explain why. Next I will tell her what this meant for us, for you and me, Willa." He would look into her eyes and tell her all these truths. He knew how he would say them. He even knew where.

It was the fourth thing he couldn't bear to think about. It had no words yet. He had only this morning opened up the place where he had kept it for the past seventeen years. He knew he would have to make words for it so he could tell her. He knew when he told her, it was likely she would never trust him again.

For now he watched his daughter starting to shoot, her hands moving quickly over the dials as her vision sharpened. He let himself admire the ways she resembled him. Yes, he would begin to tell her. But not until tomorrow. He was glad for the drive. Oregon was a long way away. Tomorrow felt long distant as well.

CAL

Stolen, Oregon ~ Saturday, October 5, 1996

My understanding of Helen Bernstein came swiftly. Down by baggage claim. She was good-looking enough, sure, but nothing about her wardrobe—black slacks, standard-issue middle-aged-academic-woman black linen jacket, silver pendant, clog-type shoes—prepared me for the two huge black suitcases I had to lift off the conveyer belt. I thought that was all, but no. Helen smiled and announced, "Great! Now we can pick up my dog."

Dog? "Elliot didn't mention a dog."

"I'll bet Elliot doesn't mention a lot of things." She said this straight, with no apparent irony, so I scuttled our first opportunity for witty repartee. I followed her.

Forty minutes later, after filling out a pile of forms, we tried to rouse the still-drugged purebred—did I mention *huge*?—golden retriever, Ferdinand. To be honest, at first his size was a comfort. In terms of what it showed about Helen. No yappy little pooch for her. After walking Ferdinand, feeding him kibble out of a Ziploc bag she carried in her tote, coercing him to pee on the sidewalk— all this took another hour, at least—we made it to my truck. And that was when size became a concern.

Clearly, Helen was not expecting a pickup to be her means of transportation. Clearly, she did not believe that dogs are dogs. Dogs always ride in the truck bed. I don't care if two huge suitcases are rolling around under the tarp; a dog can handle that. Apparently, Helen didn't think so. So that's how I ended up sitting way too close to Elliot's ex-wife for my liking, since most of her seat was taken up by the restless if endearing Ferdinand.

I COULD TELL that for Helen, the drive from Portland to the academy passed as a dramatic lesson in geographical distinction. On the Portland side of the mountains, she saw green. Luscious, moist, verdant. Clouds hanging like batting in the low sky, dangling cobwebs of fog across the highway. But then we rose, slowly, up and out of the rain. Occasionally, she caught a glimpse of Mount Hood in front of her, just in the distance, and she gasped. Before she knew it, we were driving on a mountain; the strange experience of this is that when you're *on* the mountain, it appears to get smaller and smaller. It was only when we were on the other side, barreling down into the bright eastern Oregon high desert, that she saw the great immensity of what we had accomplished, there, like a friend, in our rearview mirror. It was white-faced and rocky. My truck cut like a river through the yellow grasses as we streamed toward Helen's future.

That's what Helen saw; that's how she might have described things. What came out of her mouth were words like "wow," like "I can't believe how gorgeous this is," like "indescribable."

"So just shut up," I thought.

I could have taught her the names of things, but I took a perverse pleasure in watching a woman of words reduced to groping for simple clichés. She didn't know how to talk about all this beauty, and she didn't know how to see it for what it was.

I could have told her the scientific version: how Route 26 from Portland passed by small basalt cinder cones that will erupt no more. I could have made her understand that Mount Hood—that magnificent crown of the Cascade Range—is a big andesite volcano made up of cooled lava flows, ash deposits, and what the mud has left behind. Driving over the mountain, you are making your way past basalt outcroppings and white feldspar crystals.

I could have told Helen that her amazement over the smooth cut of rhyolitic ash rising from the earth was caused by the recognition that what we see when we *see* geology is the inside of the earth dying to get out. She couldn't assign words to all this beauty, nor did she know how to see it for what it was. She didn't understand that the lodgepole pines, the ponderosas, and, as we descended, the juniper, all grow in response to the fundamental rules set down by rocks and soils and lava and ash. I could have told Helen the names of the birds that were too fast for her to see: the sharp-shinned hawk, the pileated woodpecker, the golden eagle. But I didn't say a word.

I could feel Helen's disappointment, her descent from the heights, as we descended from the heights into the scrub steppes. The land flattened and the color dulled. The final suggestion of elevation was rimrock skirting the horizon; the solitary green in sight was pale and dusty and resided in small herds of bunchgrass huddled against the sandy soil.

Yes, I could have told Helen many things about the place she'd come to, things that would comfort her, things that would offer her safety. But I wouldn't. Perhaps that was because she was speaking a mile a minute and I couldn't get a word in edgewise:

She: So where are we in relation to the Columbia River?

He: South.

She: And we're heading south?

He: Yup.

She: Have you ever fished on the Columbia?

He: Nope.

She: I hear it's very beautiful.

He: *Shrugs. Decides not to say:* Your people killed all the salmon and built a fucking dam that destroyed Celilo Falls and, thus, the livelihood of my people, rendering it impossible for us to fish using the methods of our ancestors. I was too young to learn these methods. There's no one left to teach me.

Wonders why he's angry at her in the way that his own father was angry at every white. There's no rhyme or reason to this anger. It comes up swift, like heartburn. He watches the speedometer slide above eighty. Hopes she's done talking.

She: So you've always lived on the reservation?

He: Lived in Portland for a while. Then on the East Coast.

She: Where on the East Coast?

He: Mostly Massachusetts.

She: Massachusetts is beautiful. Where in Massachusetts?

He: Cambridge.

She: What were you doing in Cambridge?

He: College.

She: Where did you go to college?

He: Harvard.

That one kept her quiet for a while.

By the time we got past the mountain, Helen was bunched over Ferdinand, who was snoring his drug-induced snore and sleeping hard. She leaned her head toward the window. She trusted my driving, even though I zipped around trucks and soared above the speed limit. Perhaps she trusted me because I was Indian and this was my country. Perhaps when she saw the sign for the Warm Springs Reservation, she felt a safety she had not known for a long while, even though I told her "Wrong reservation." Maybe there was something comforting about the idea of an Indian on Indian land, pulled together like magnets—she could let herself rest.

She had no idea I was going to take her straight through Stolen, where the white folks lived, where the roads were impeccably, smoothly paved. I wasn't going to drive her the eleven pockmarked gravel miles up to where I called home, the Neige Courante Reservation. She revealed her line of thought right then.

She: Neige Courante is French, right? It means Running Snow? Flowing Snow?

He: Yup.

She: That's a bit of an oxymoron, isn't it?

He: *Thinks:* She's pulling out the big guns. Wants to test if I really went to Harvard. Using words like "oxymoron." *Says to her:* The water from the mountains is cold, like snow. We fished salmon in that water.

She: Did you give yourself this name?

He: We didn't have a name before.

She: I've heard about this.

He: You have?

She: Yes, the whole notion of naming being something set-tlers . . . whites . . . You know, the whole idea being that naming was a notion settlers brought with them when they . . .

He: *Lets her talk until she sputters herself into silence.*

She: *After a long, awkward pause—you have to admire her pluck:* Well, Neige Courante is a beautiful name. It really rolls off the tongue.

He: *Deadpan:* That's exactly what we were aiming for.

After that we stopped talking, but her fluttering questions seemed to linger in the truck with us, keeping me from saying anything about the school and her place in it. I decided to let her crash and burn with the kids. They'd show her what a terrible idea a Shakespeare play was; they'd be much more eloquent than I could ever be. I turned on the tribal station and listened to Joe's slow lilt as he counted down the Top 40: "Hey hey hey! What a great day to be indigenous!" We pulled through Stolen, and I felt compelled to point it out—the gas station, grocery store, and Mexican restaurant go by in an instant—but when I leaned toward her, I noticed that she was sleeping. I kept my mouth shut. The sound of her breathing was soft. I glanced at her once, curled over her dog. It was hard to imagine this nervous little woman marrying Elliot. I guess when I was younger and looked up to him, I always imagined the women he'd been with—not that he ever talked about them—as sexy and sophisticated. They were New Yorkers, after all. He was the kind of man who could pull off a woman like that, a mythical urbanite. Now, finally meeting one of his women, I felt a combination of disappointment and smugness. *This* was his ex-wife? I'd had women with ten times more . . . well, however you want to say it. I'll put it politely: I'd had women with ten times more charisma. Helen Bernstein was a hibernating mammal. Let's face it; her name was Helen. That's a grandmother name. When I realized she looked like a mouse, albeit a pretty little mouse, I smiled to myself.

The sky was beginning to change into night. Out the truck window, the setting sun outlined the mountains with brightness. Behind them, the Pacific would be glimmering. But we did not steer toward the ocean. We turned left, off the highway, and then

turned again until we met the end of the school driveway. I wondered if I would have to wake her, but at the crunch of the gravel,
she started and turned to me. Her smile was the kind babies make
after a long, good sleep, when their heads are damp with sweat and
they have been dreaming. "Thank you," she said.

I nodded. We were pulling up to the main house and I pointed.
"Elliot will be in there."

She nudged her dog into reluctant wakefulness. He stood up
drowsily, stretched, yawned, shook. She was preoccupied with this
display, then gathered her things onto her lap. It wasn't until then
that she seemed to realize we were finally at our destination. She
looked out the window and glimpsed the school for the first time.
It sprawled out before her, a combination of hand-hewn outbuildings, prefab classrooms, pathways scuffed through sagebrush, parking lots made not by macadam but by cars. Seeing it through her
eyes, I saw, for the first time in a long time, that it looked like nothing. How easy it was to buy in to Elliot's vision if you never really
saw the place, if, through some lens of optimism, you saw the place
he imagined and the place he'd actually built as one and the same.
They were, in reality, two very different things. Apparently, he'd described to Helen the place he imagined.

"Oh," she said, surveying the land. Perhaps she was simply ac-
knowledging what I had told her—that she was mere moments
away from her ex-husband. But there was something in her voice,
a catch, like a cloud across a blue sky. She suddenly seemed as
threatening as I'd believed her to be. I heard myself defending my
territory: "Elliot is very busy these days. Maybe it's none of my
business, but he said you were coming to direct a Shakespeare program here? Not gonna happen. No money. No interest. He might
tell you otherwise, but there's the board to consider, questions of
money and time, curricula. So."

Perhaps I should have been more merciful, if only so I could
begin to complete the puzzle of Elliot myself. He was a man who
came from somewhere. She could tell me what that somewhere was.

Instead, when she got out of my car, I did not linger. Just helped her with the suitcases and the dog crate. Watched the dog pulling at his collar, which Helen clutched tightly in her fingers, as if she could restrain a dog from entering paradise. I backed up the truck, leaving her in a cloud of dust. When I hit the road, I sliced the wheel quickly and revved off into the night. I continued toward the sunset and I didn't look back.

HELEN

Stolen, Oregon ~ Saturday, October 5, 1996

The Native American left Helen and Ferdinand in the middle of a gravel road. The dog sniffed at Helen's luggage and his crate, then lifted his head and realized he was free. He was too strong for her as he pulled against his collar. She let him run down into the field below the house. If she saw a car, she'd call him. He was good about coming when she called.

Helen's wheeled suitcases didn't work on the gravel. At first she'd tried to unload them from the truck herself, but the Native American had insisted she let him do it, adding, "I've got to lift the crate down anyway," with no attempt to mask the irritation in his voice. She felt foolish. He had told her in no uncertain terms that she wasn't welcome. And she couldn't quite figure out from whence his rancor came. There had been no indication it was coming, so now she cast back over the last three and a half hours in his car: she had done something to upset him, or to offend him; she had asked too many questions; he hadn't wanted to pick her up in the first place. She hated herself when she was like this: helpless, overly apologetic. Nervous.

She could take care of herself. Granted, she could not lift her luggage, but she could drag it to the side of the road and leave it there so it would not meet a terrible end. She was soon to learn that this "road" was in fact Elliot's driveway, and that weeks went by without it being touched by a vehicle, but she was still carrying with her the mind of a New Yorker. She even worried that her luggage might be stolen; given that the town she was in was named Stolen, I suppose the thought wasn't entirely unfounded. She ran her fingers through her hair, adjusted the shoulder straps of her canvas tote and her worn leather purse, and gazed at the lit house of Elliot Barrow. She tried to quell her growing frustration at the men in her life. She tried to be sensible. Resourceful. She walked toward the tallest building in sight.

Helen didn't know this, but Elliot Barrow's home was called the Bugle House, and all four stories had been built, piece by piece, starting in the 1920s, by an eager white rancher named Jim Bugle. Jim Bugle hadn't been particularly good at handling cows, but he had initially kept his money out of the stock market and invested wisely after the crash, so by 1942 he had enough dough to build two more stories on top of his small two-story abode, then to expand outward, quadrupling his square footage. The result was a sprawling hilltop building with a porch stretching three quarters of the way around, a myriad of rooms that doubled back on themselves, creaking stairways that connected individual rooms to one another and skipped whole floors, and windows and ceilings that were unusually high or absurdly low. Jim Bugle had relied on cheap Indian labor to get the job done, and it was no great secret that the Neige Courante hired to work for him had had a good chuckle at making him a house in which he would never be able to comfortably live. The cultured women he imported from Los Angeles, San Francisco, Portland, and Seattle were at first impressed by the size and stature of the great white house with red trim as they made their way across the prairie, dust shimmying up behind their chariots. But when these ladies got inside, to their great dismay, they discovered that every room was either cramped or drafty, barren or stuffed with furniture (much of the extravagant furniture purchased from mail-order catalogs was too big to get through any except the first few doorways), too full of sunlight or too dimly lit. Added to that, despite the sweet smell of peppermint that wafted up from the newly irrigated fields, there was not a damn thing in sight. No "people." No "culture." Nothing.

Jim Bugle died alone, but the general feeling in the area was that the old bastard deserved it. He gained much more admiration in death than in life, because that ostentatious house tempted hopeful rancher after hopeful rancher through the 1960s and '70s, each one undone by the sheer difficulty of maintaining a viable ranch on forty-seven acres of scrub and brush and sand. Rumor had it that the land was cursed, that no one in his right mind could get anything worthwhile off that loveless earth. The Indians who'd been forced off it sat back, cracked their beers, and had a bitter laugh from the sidelines.

Enter the young, bright-eyed Elliot Barrow. A man with a vision. He waltzed into town in the early days of 1981, and by June he'd bought the place. Cash down. Rumor had it he was a member of a cult, like the Rajneeshis, who dressed in red and were taking over the nearby town of Antelope. Then there was the theory that he was a marijuana maven come to make some illicit bucks off the land. That would explain the beat-up car and the liquid assets. But where had the baby come from? And why did he keep talking about a school for Neige Courante kids?

Almost sixteen years later, Helen was circling the house, searching for a doorbell. Her clogs, completely inappropriate for the outdoors—she'd already rolled her ankle twice on the gravel—clacked on the wide floorboards of the porch. She'd figured out that no one lived on the bottom story; a quick peer in the windows revealed desks, chairs, and chalkboards, a kitchen, and the semblance of a cafeteria. There didn't seem to be any way inside. Scratch that; there seemed to be a lot of ways inside, but all of the doorways were dark, and she didn't want to spend her evening lost in the cavern of this huge building. (Which was a good call. Jim Bugle had taken to making pocket-sized architectural maps for all his lost lady loves.)

Helen stepped back from the house and craned her neck to the top story. The house had seemed lit from within, warm, inviting. But now she saw that had been simply an impression, a desire to get out of the Native American's car. She had wanted to feel invited and had made the house inviting. There was in fact only one light on, and it cast out from the topmost windows, brightening up the vast dusk falling around the house. There seemed to be no signs of life here, and certainly nothing like a welcoming party.

Helen called Ferdinand to her side. It was nearly dark, and she remembered there were things like coyotes in this part of the world. She called out: "Hello?" Her voice was much less bold than she would have liked. Her "hello" resounded in her head six or seven times before she called out again. Nothing. She picked up two rocks from the driveway and tossed one at the house. It hit the roof of the porch. How on earth was she going to get to the fourth floor? She tried hard to keep down a mounting sense of rage, which she had a feeling would manifest itself in a round of tears. Why was it that Duncan's infidelities had left her dry, but this man, whom she hadn't seen or really spoken to in nearly two decades, had the power to flood her tear ducts?

"Can I help you?"

Helen wheeled around to find two teenage girls, one brown and round, one white and lean, arm in arm, emerging from the dusk. Ferdinand bounded toward them and jumped up on them, slathering them in kisses.

"Oh, I'm so sorry," Helen heard herself saying. She made her voice commanding. "Ferdinand. Come." As he reluctantly made his way back to her, she said, "He's just a big teddy bear. I hope he didn't frighten you."

"What's with the rocks?" the round girl asked.

Helen glanced down at her hand, still clutching a large piece of gravel. She said meekly, "I couldn't figure out how to get inside."

The girls exchanged a look. "Um," the tall one said, "were you trying to break a window?"

"No! No. I'm just trying to get Elliot's attention—"

"You need my dad?"

"Amelia? I didn't recognize you! Sweet girl! You're beautiful! The last time I saw you, you were in a Snugli on your dad's chest!" Helen launched through the three feet between them and grasped Amelia in her arms. The girl was tall and bold and too skinny. Her long hair was pulled into a ponytail. Her T-shirt was tight on her slim frame. She smelled of the outdoors. It took Helen a moment before she realized she wasn't being hugged back. "I'm Helen," she said, letting go, by way of explanation. The girls' expressions didn't change. "Helen," she said again. "That fucker didn't tell you anything, did he?"

At the word "fucker," the girls burst into giggles. The brown one said, "Jesus, lady, how did you get here?"

"Oh. Carl drove me."

"Carl?"

"I mean Cal? Oh, dear. I mean Cal. Cal picked me up in Portland."

"*Cal?*"

"He was—he was—"

"He was Indian."

"Yes."

"I know who Cal is. I just can't believe he drove all the way to Portland to pick you up."

"Assistant Headmaster Calbert Fleecing," Amelia added.

"Assistant headmaster?"

"Yup." The brown girl stuck out her hand. "Lydia. Also Indian. We're crawling all over these parts. It's practically an infestation."

Helen didn't know how to respond. She tried to smile.

"Joking!" said Lydia. "So how do you know Elliot?"

"We're old friends. We've known each other a long time."

"How come Amelia's never heard of you?" Apparently, the girls were connected by ESP, and Lydia was their spokesperson.

"I'm not sure." Helen found herself oddly willing to open up. Lydia's questioning, though inquisitionlike, had an air of informality about it that kept the conversation breezy. "Actually," Helen heard herself saying, "we used to be married. Just briefly." She saw the alarm in Amelia register on Lydia's face. "Oh, but long before you were born, Amelia." Shit. Why on earth had she volunteered that information?

"So you're not Astrid, back from the dead?"

"No! No, I'm Helen. I'm sorry. I shouldn't have mentioned the marriage part. I'm sorry. I should just—"

"Don't apologize, Helen. This is very illuminating. Did you know Amelia's mother?"

"Um . . ." Helen was in deep water here. Better to say something vague. Better to say nothing at all. She nodded her assent.

"And now you're . . . what? Reigniting passion's flame?"

Amelia, who'd been looking at the ground, interrupted: "Where did you come from?"

"New York. Brooklyn."

"And Dad knows you're coming?"

"He bought me the plane ticket."

Lydia looked at Amelia and said, as though they were in private, "She's legit. Should we help her?"

At first Helen thought the "help her" meant in general, as though she were a wounded animal caught in a trap, needing life-or-death assistance, or someone lost in a foreign country, desperate for the right combination of words. But when a wordless Amelia walked to a suitcase and hefted it, then started trudging toward the house, Helen realized what Lydia meant. She meant helping her with the luggage. She meant helping her inside. They dragged the dog crate onto the porch and took turns in twos, carrying the suitcases through the many doorways and up the oddly circuitous set of stairs, as Ferdinand waggled and squeezed past them. They didn't stop to talk, but when they reached the top-floor apartment, a smiling Lydia offered to make burritos.

The three of them sat around the table, drinking cool water. The girls asked Helen about New York, where they had never

been, and things became positively chatty. No one mentioned Elliot's name or the fact that he wasn't there, and Helen didn't ask.
Likewise, the girls didn't ask Helen about her marriage to Elliot, or
about Amelia's mother, which was a relief. Still, Helen felt more
than a little ashamed. In retrospect, she knew why she'd mentioned
her stint as Mrs. Elliot Barrow: to make the girls her first set of al-
lies. They wanted her secrets, and now they were going to do a
dance around those secrets in hopes of getting the truth. It was a
cheap trick, but it had felt to her, in that moment, in the near dark,
locked outside Elliot's house, that it was her only ticket inside.

The Shaggy-Dog Story

Once upon a time, there was a skinny woman who was skinny in all the wrong ways. She had believed this all her life, that she was skinny in all the wrong ways. But she didn't know she believed this until the day she found her husband in bed with a different woman. The husband didn't notice the skinny woman opening the door to her own bedroom. But the different woman saw the skinny woman the second she opened that door. The different woman made a sound like a cooing, like a gasp, and the skinny woman closed the door again, quickly, and wondered in a split second whether the cooing sound was a sound of surprise or a sound of lovemaking, and then the skinny woman thought, "Well, perhaps those are one and the same."

The husband didn't try to make the skinny woman stay. He didn't do much. He shrugged his gently muscled shoulders and ran his fingers through his perfect soft hair. He didn't know what it was to be too skinny, too smart, too desperate. He was always only just those things, and being only just those things made him perfect and different: slim, and brilliant, and hungry. He didn't know what it was to be on the dark side of the moon. Now the skinny woman saw how inevitable this moment was—her leaving, his not asking her to stay.

The skinny woman and the husband shared a home with many other people. They were like a village, these people, or a clan. The clan cooked together. The clan ate together. The clan made decisions together. Up until this point, the skinny woman thought the clan didn't sleep together. But apparently, she was wrong about that. Naive. In the husband's world, this description would have been changed to "innocent."

   The skinny woman came to hate everyone in the clan. She turned against the family she had made, the family who had promised her so much. This was not what she had expected. Now that she was packing her bags and telling the husband to leave her alone, please, the skinny woman realized she didn't want any of it. She saw now, as she was being shot out the end of the cannon of love, that all the time she'd been in her husband's arms, she had been in a darkness where his close voice was the solitary truth she believed. She saw that he had this power over the whole clan, that they loved him, that they listened to him, that they would do anything for him. The skinny woman saw how dangerous this was. She felt relief. She didn't have to stay in the clan anymore. Perhaps she had been wrong. Perhaps life by committee was a fate worse than loneliness.

   That night the skinny woman undressed in front of the mirror in her mother's home. She intended to give herself a good hard look. She intended to see, once and for all, just where she was too skinny, and to make a decision about what could be done to help it. What could be done to help her: her skinniness, her smartness, her desperation. But she kept being distracted by the absence of her mother. Her mother didn't live in her own home anymore, and the quiet was unsettling. The skinny woman examined herself and felt ashamed. She had been ignoring a job for months now, which she had told her mother she'd already done, and that job was packing up her mother's home and dividing her mother's possessions and passing her mother's home on to someone else if the skinny woman didn't want it herself. The skinny woman's mother was not dead yet. But she lived as if dead, in a place with other old people. That had been the mother's choice. As with most other matters, the skinny woman hadn't known how to stop her mother from making this mistake.

   When the skinny woman looked at her nakedness, all she saw was regret. Regret and dismay. She remembered the sound the different woman had made when the door opened. She remembered how the different woman's hip looked under a flash of covers—round and supple—even though she was probably no bigger than the skinny woman and weighed no more. The skinny woman wondered how that could be. The skinny woman remembered how the different woman had shimmered and glowed, *how she had seemed to have wings of some kind, so big was her smile in the midst of her lovemaking. She was like a soaring bird in a blue sky, and the skinny woman was like a small stone at the bottom of a dirty puddle. The skinny woman realized she couldn't really blame the husband for liking the bird over the pebble. And then the skinny woman decided now that she'd realized this, she was finally allowed to buy a dog.*

The skinny woman grew up in the city. Her mother never let her have a dog. It wasn't practical. Her husband, the clan, no one would let the skinny woman live with an animal. But the next morning she put on her clothes and she went to the place where they killed dogs if they weren't rescued and she chose a dog that was wild and woolly and sweet and old and she brought it home to her mother's house and she lived with it there and made herself a new life.

She tried not to think about the different woman, whom she thought of as a bird. She tried not to think about the husband. She found success. She met new people. These people adored her, and she was no longer afraid that living in her mother's home, alone, the way her mother had, would make her sad in the way her mother was. Lots of things changed that fear, but she believed especially hard that it was the dog that had turned things around.

Meanwhile, the husband's life went somewhere unexpected. Somewhere terrible. Somewhere so terrible, that in the midst of it, the skinny woman was to be the only one on whom the husband believed he could call for help. Tell me how that is fair. But there it is. By the time the husband asked the skinny woman for help, she was not so worried about being skinny. In fact, she hardly noticed it about herself anymore. Her dog had died, but she knew how to survive it. She had a new dog. She would get a new dog when that one died, and she would tend to it until its life ended too. She had a future. She was no longer afraid. She was strong enough to help the husband when he needed her most.

It would take the husband many years to repay this kindness.

Chapter Three

*A*melia waited in the dark living room for Elliot to come home. Waiting in darkness was exactly as un-exciting as it sounds, but with each second that passed, she felt the satisfying swell of self-righteousness. When the door finally opened—she checked her watch; it was 10:47—she had to bite her tongue to wait until he was standing in front of her, as she'd planned.

"Helen's here," she said.

"Jesus! You scared the hell out of me, Amelia." Elliot fumbled over to the side table and switched on the lamp. Amelia had to cover her eyes. The light made her even more irritated.

"Did you hear me, Dad? Helen? Is here? In our house? With her dog?"

"Where's Cal?"

"I don't know. He dropped her off. I found her throwing rocks at our windows. You want to explain what your ex-wife is doing here?"

"Sweetheart." He set down his briefcase. "It's my mistake. I lost track of time. I assumed Cal would call me to tell me she'd arrived. I've been working on that grant proposal—"

"It's *so* not about that, Dad."

Elliot cleared his throat.

"Dad?"

"Yes?"

"Did you hear me? It's so not about that."

"What is it about?"

"You were *married* before?"

Elliot sighed. He didn't have to say anything, but Amelia knew that sigh was for real. He nodded.

"When the hell were you married?"

"Helen and I were married for a matter of months. Back in the seventies. I didn't tell you because it wasn't relevant. There seemed no need—"

"And you invited her *here*?"

"Yes. She's the Shakespeare expert I told you about; she's from New York. She's written two seminal works in the field and directed some of the greatest productions of our time. She's going to direct *The Tempest* for the academy." There was both accusation and questioning in his voice. "Remember? I told you on the phone."

"Yeah, you told me about a *play*, Dad, not about a *wife*, a wife whose existence you've somehow neglected to mention for—what has it been?—yes, that's right, sixteen years!"

"I didn't realize it would be such a big deal, honey. If I'd known that you were going to have to meet her alone . . . If I'd known she was going to tell you . . . Where is she right now?"

"I gave her my bedroom."

He lowered his voice. "You didn't have to do that."

Amelia got louder. "Yeah. I did, Dad. Where else was she going to sleep? She's a *person*. She was *tired*. She needed a bed." Amelia stood up. This would be her moment of triumph. She'd stayed calm. She'd given him the facts. "Anyway, I'm going out."

"Excuse me?"

Amelia edged toward the door. "Lydia and I are going to a party together. A party where there is likely to be both sex and alcohol. So. Love you. Wish I could stay for the reunion. Don't wait up."

She grabbed the doorknob and launched herself onto the landing and down the stairs as she heard her father gathering behind her.

"Amelia!" Her name as he spoke it was more of a plea than a command. But she did not turn around. Her shoes echoing on the stairs were loud against his calls, and soon she was outside. She sprinted to the end of the driveway. Lydia had the car practically in drive. Amelia slammed the door shut, and they shot off into the night. Elliot had kept a massive secret from her; it served him right that she had secrets of her own. She was tired of being so good all the time, so *thoughtful*. The wind sang, rapid and cool, through the unrolled windows, lapping the girls' long hair as they drove.

HELEN

Stolen, Oregon ~ *Saturday, October 5, 1996*

An hour earlier, Amelia, Helen, and Lydia had been sitting together at the kitchen table—where there was barely enough room for all of them—when Helen stood to do the dishes.

"Oh, don't do those," Lydia said.

Amelia nodded vehemently. "Seriously. Don't."

Helen opened up the cabinet under the sink and searched for the garbage so she could empty the soggy dregs of her burrito into it.

"Nope." Lydia giggled. "We're not even going to tell you where the trash is until you put down that plate."

The counter space in the kitchen was scant to begin with, but with the ingredients of the evening's meal spread across it, not to mention what seemed to be a week's worth of encrusted plates and utensils, there was no place for Helen to put down her plate, except the exact spot where she'd picked it up. So she hovered and hemmed until Amelia took it from her and set it right back down on the table.

"Please let me help you two," Helen said.

Amelia and Lydia exchanged one of their glances. "Oh, *we're* not cleaning anything up. Dad'll have to manage on his own."

"That hardly seems fair."

"Exactly. It isn't fair," Lydia chimed in. "Fair would have been him telling us you were coming. Fair would have been him bothering to come to dinner. Or, oh yeah, telling us he even *had* a first wife. *Please.* This mess has nothing to do with the three of us."

"Anyway," said Amelia brightly, standing up and linking arms with Helen, "it's time for you to be shown to your room. You must be exhausted."

Helen protested as she was pulled and pressed out of the tiny kitchen by the two girls. She even tried to refuse the room she was offered: as soon as the light went on, she could tell from the lavender and teal bedspread, from the scarf over the lamp shade, from the general mayhem of adolescent sprawl, that this was Amelia's own bed being sacrificed. But Ferdinand immediately jumped up onto the bed and curled into a sleepy ball.

Lydia took over. "You're going to make the poor dog move? That's just mean." She sat beside Ferdinand and leaned her head against his, saying, "Where the hell else does your crazy mama think she's going to sleep? There *is* no other bed. Except for Elliot's . . ." Lydia paused for dramatic effect.

Helen was going to let that one lie. "I was planning on the couch."

Lydia righted herself. "The couch is purely for show. Trust me. There is absolutely no way you could get even a half hour's sleep on that monstrosity. It's been in here since the sixties." Meanwhile, Amelia was gathering clothes from the floor and stuffing them into a small duffel bag. Helen couldn't tell if she was upset.

"Amelia, sweetie, you don't have to—"

Amelia righted herself and fixed Helen in her gaze. It was a not unfamiliar look of determination, as though her father were suddenly in the room. The look silenced Helen at once.

"She's staying at my house tonight," said Lydia. "We do it all the time."

"Should I give Elliot a message?"

"He'll figure it out," Lydia replied, and in the wake of Amelia's silence, Helen decided to leave it at that.

SO HELEN WAS not entirely surprised when, after forty-five minutes of silence and darkness, she heard the muffled sounds of a fight between a man to whom she'd once been married and the daughter whose will was remarkably similar to his own. Crisp whispers rose into sharp voices, then the slam of the apartment door, a flush of feet running rapidly down the stairs, a holler from Elliot, followed by the distant, lonely sound of a motor revving. Helen rose from the bed, where she'd been lying fully clothed against Ferdinand's flank, and pressed her face against the cool window. The ruby glow of the car's rear lights weakened as the girls sped into the distance. It was perfectly quiet after that.

Helen was alone again, for the first time in decades, with Elliot. It was her decision to make a greeting now or wait until the morning. When she'd first turned off the bedside lamp, she'd imagined she would sleep. She was bone-tired, and in an alternate reality, she could have closed her eyes and done some delicious dreaming. But as soon as she cast back over the day, emotion surged through her: sadness, irritation, and embarrassment. Though she didn't know all the facts, she knew she'd been manipulated. Abused, even. And she knew what she would have to say: "I need access to a phone, please. I need to make a return-trip plane reservation." Full stop. Easy. Tomorrow.

Helen made her escape plan and waited for sleep. Then a strange thing happened in that hour on Amelia's bed. She still didn't know precisely what she would say to Elliot once he came home. *If* he came home. But she found comfort in knowing she did not yet have to say it. She began to listen. What she heard, before the yelling, was a glorious chorus of nothing. She didn't think she'd ever heard anything so silent in her whole life. It was dark outside. We're talking pitch-black. So dark that Helen began to believe she wasn't really anywhere. She had arrived in the twilight, when the

edges of objects were already smudged and dreamlike. Her body
was unmoving and unmovable, and she pushed her reality into that
same crepuscular light where the concrete world faded into nothingness. Elliot didn't exist, his academy was illusory, she had never
been married to an asshole named Duncan, there was no New
York City, bright and bustling even as she lay there, a country away.
Even Helen's own body was a trick she'd conjured. Only Ferdinand's breath kept her constant. She began to think: "Perhaps this
is rock bottom. But perhaps rock bottom is not so terrible after all."

By the time the taillights evaporated into the night, Helen was
ready. There was already enough enmity to go around, so she
smiled at herself, which was odd, considering her earlier anxieties.
For now she felt a paucity of panic. She opened the door to the
bright hallway and was not the slightest bit afraid. She *knew* Elliot.
She'd been married to him, for Christ's sake. There was no need to
be timid or needy. Hadn't she known the second she heard his
voice that there would be something accomplished in seeing him
with her own eyes? Hadn't she known she would gain back a part
of herself she had not known in years?

"Elliot."

"I hope we didn't wake you."

Helen's eyes adjusted as she took in Elliot's perch on the couch.
There he was. Older, yes. But his eyes were still that blue, fringed
in thick black lashes. The kind of eyes that told you this man held
mystery. Amelia had those eyes. Elliot's brown hair was still dusty—
though now with brushstrokes of gray instead of flecks of blond—
and he was as strong and long as he'd been the day she'd met him,
in a chemistry class freshman year at Columbia. He'd been the
same color then, tanned in the way of a man who is not fussy. But
damn, those eyes. She was reminded, as she stood in his hallway,
leaning against the door frame, exactly why she had first fallen in
love.

"Not at all. It's fine."

He came toward her, touched her arm, and leaned in to peck

her on the cheek. "Hello, Helen," he said. "I seem to have screwed up all around. I can't believe Cal didn't call me. And I'm afraid I didn't mention your coming to Amelia. And now she's stormed out." He sighed. He *did* look older.

"You seem not to have mentioned anything about me."

He was silent. He nodded. "Haven't known what to say. I'm sorry," he said, looking down at his hands. "I should have picked you up myself."

"Yes. You really should have." She couldn't believe her honesty. But there it was.

"Sit?"

"I'm happy," she said, staying where she was. He had moved away from her. She wanted to watch him like this, outside of the frame of the picture, before she was a part of it. He glanced toward the front door. Helen added, "I don't think she's coming back tonight."

He sighed again, full of worry.

"If I remember correctly, Elliot, you were only two years older than Amelia is now when I met you. And you were doing a hell of a lot more than drinking with your friends in the middle of the desert."

"That's what scares the shit out of me."

"She'll be fine."

Ferdinand loped into the room, and Elliot raised an eyebrow. "I don't go anywhere without old Fergus," Helen said. "Hope he won't be a problem."

"We've got plenty of land to go around," Elliot said, patting the couch beside him so the dog would come. And then Elliot smiled. A weary smile. But a smile nonetheless. "It's good to have you here."

She wasn't going to say anything about that, about what was between them. "She's a good kid." It felt right to dispense a little mercy.

Chapter Four

CAL

The first time I knew who my father was, I couldn't have been more than four years old. My mother was long gone, but aside from the occasional nightmare, I was a pretty happy boy. Maw-Maw kept me busy. She didn't give me the option of feeling sorry for myself.

The Neige Courante hosted one of the biggest powwows east of the Cascades in those days. I guess we were much more prone to celebrating ourselves then, eager to dance in honor of our heritage. That's probably because there were so many more elders alive, people who could look way back into our past and remember the fiber of what our people are made of. Young people were required to get in line. Eye rolling was not permitted. Perhaps it's just that the grown-ups have gotten lazy.

In any case, here is what I remember: Jimmy Marron, an older boy, a fancy dancer, came up to me with a piece of straw between his teeth and said, "I've got a secret." He was smug and proud and he knew that, more than anything else, secrets were the one thing I could not stand being kept from. All people had to do was tell me they had a secret and I'd do just about anything to find out what that secret was. It didn't matter if I didn't know who Sharon and Bill were, let alone what "making it" meant. All that mattered was that I got to be in on the secret too.

I begged Jimmy to tell me what his secret was. And as I was begging, a slew of other children gathered around us, salmon cakes in their hands. The girls jingled and caught the light on their shell dresses. The jingling sounded like laughter in the breeze.

"Here's what I'll do," Jimmy said. He squatted down beside me and pointed his finger. There, across the park, was a tall Indian man in a suit, leaning against a fancy black car. "See that guy?" Jimmy asked. I nodded. "Guess who he is."

"That's not a secret!" I whined.

One of Jimmy's older sisters, Alice, came up to him and pushed his shoulder. "Shut up," she said to him. To me she said, "Let's go." She reached down to pick me up.

But I didn't want to be carried. "Tell me the secret!" I said.

The boys all laughed, and the girls shook their heads. "You heard him," Jimmy said. "He wants to know the secret."

"Come on," Alice said, trying to pick me up, but I stood my ground.

"The secret," Jimmy said, "is *that's* your daddy." All the boys laughed for real. Alice picked me up and perched me on her hip.

"You're a real asshole, you know that?" she yelled over her shoulder to Jimmy as we walked away.

I didn't see what was bad or funny or secret about knowing that this man was my daddy. I had never seen him before, and dads were the kind of people who were always around. I decided I must have heard the word wrong. The man must have been something else. (Incidentally, the charming Jimmy Marron is now a "self-employed" mechanic, which means that he sits on his couch night and day, complaining. Needless to say, I've never given him the opportunity to fix my car.)

When I got old enough to understand what my own memory was telling me, I was already old enough to understand that what made that man with the fancy black car my daddy was also what made me different. I was caught between two worlds, even though the only world I'd ever lived in was that of the Neige Courante reservation. Even then I knew that something was going to lead me away from the home my people had been assigned. It was as if I could see ahead, into the future, though I didn't know what the future was. All I knew was that every day I woke up feeling as if I could never be happy where I was.

In that, I am not unlike the Neige Courante people as a whole. Hell, our name means "running snow," and everyone knows that once snow hits the ground, it's a stationary substance. It takes a special kind of people to make snow move fast. We're born movers. Before the reservation, we were people of the Deschutes River. Some say French trappers gave us our name; the water that sustained the Neige Courante is ice-cold, fed by mountain streams. It is hard to touch that water in the middle of the hottest August afternoon.

In the old days, the Neige Courante camped. We roamed the length of the Deschutes River. We stayed mostly in the high elevations, near what is now called Elk Lake on the mountain we now call Bachelor, and then, as salmon season approached, we made our way north, up past the Metolius River, up past the mountain we now call Hood, to the Columbia, where we fished and fished at Celilo Falls. We lived mostly underneath the verdant expanse of the lodgepole pine canopy. We came down from those regal trees only for the salmon.

In the late nineteenth century, our tribal leaders signed a treaty—get this, "in good faith"—relinquishing the land we had roamed for centuries to the white federal government. In exchange, we were "given" twenty-five square miles of steppe grassland. This demotion likely means little to you, so let me explain it this way: let's say you lived in Tuscany and someone decided you "got" to live in Siberia instead. What happened to our traditions next, especially after we realized we were no longer "allowed" to fish on the Columbia River—especially after they built a dam that drowned Celilo Falls—is on par with what you're imagining right this minute.

So there we were, the Neige Courante and me, locked in oddly parallel existences, bound to fates not fully our own. I did not know that at the time, however. All I knew was that the man with the fancy black car was strange and enticing and mine.

HELEN

Stolen, Oregon ~ Sunday, October 6, 1996

Elliot was striding far ahead of Helen across the brusque landscape. It was a chilly seven A.M. on her first morning at the academy, and he had insisted that since it was Sunday, they should take a brisk walk before breakfast. He had something special to show her. Helen considered herself to be in very good shape; her daily walks with Ferdinand around the Prospect Park loop were a good three miles long. But apparently, she had nothing on Elliot. Beside him, she felt like a gnome of a woman, round, huffing, unsteady, no match for his Nordic stride. They were heading north, the surprisingly warm sun making a determined appearance to their right. Helen was proud of herself for knowing the direction they were walking. She was proud of herself for remembering to pack two pairs of sensible shoes. She desperately needed caffeine, and as she trailed Elliot and the eager, bounding dog, she tried to remember if she'd seen a coffee machine in his minuscule kitchen.

Helen realized how familiar this all felt. She remembered afternoons spent scuttling down Upper Broadway as Elliot made his way south. From behind him, she was able to see what people thought. Especially women. He'd been striking in his brazen youth. Long hair, T-shirt emblazoned with political slogans, a generous stride. Old women pitied him as if he were a stray puppy, young mothers seethed against him with a kind of unnamed hunger, and single girls, free to flirt, made it clear they simply loved what they saw. In the early days, Helen found this attention flattering. She told herself that every woman who wanted Elliot was paying her a compliment. When she concentrated on this concept, she almost believed it. And when he held her in his arms, she would repeat it to herself: the most desired man at Columbia had chosen *her*. And he was not simply eye candy. He was brilliant. He was going to change the world. He had said more than once that he could not change the world without her. They were lovers *and* they were comrades. Surely there was nothing more she could ask for.

Helen shivered and pulled herself out of the past. She was not going to do this. Dredging up that life, the person she had been so brutally long ago, would simply cause her more pain. Elliot glanced back over his shoulder and motioned for her to move faster. She pushed the memory of his taste as far out of her mind as was humanly possible.

When she caught up to him at the top of the hill, she had to brace her hands on her knees. She needed air. Elliot didn't give her much breathing room. He pointed eagerly. "Look!"

"What am I looking at?" She was looking. She was looking hard. All she could see was a shed at the bottom of the hill, and Ferdinand lifting his leg against it. Literally. That was the only thing of note between where she was standing and the distant horizon. Her stomach sank as Elliot spoke in excited tones.

"You can stay here! The nearest hotel is at least ten miles away, and anyway, I don't have the money to put you up there for more than a couple of weeks. The kids have been fixing up this old building since last year. There are pictures of it from, oh, I'd say the fifties, maybe even before. And the kids! They've been having an absolute blast! It doesn't look like much, but let's see—they've installed insulation, a generator for emergencies, we've got solar panels on the roof, a hand pump from the creek. We even dug an outhouse!"

The use of the word "building" was generous at best. Helen numbly followed Elliot as he barreled down the hill, he in a euphoria of explanation, she in a state of shock. He was pointing out all the fantastic details, and all she could see was a shack a little bigger than a minivan parked in the middle of an open, dusty prairie, without another man-made structure of any kind in sight. Elliot flung open the door and continued his sell.

"We wanted to cut down the trees ourselves and plane the wood, but it seems there are laws about kids using power tools. Insurance we don't have. But the kids picked out the wood themselves, and they measured and designed and built the bunk bed, the table, the desk, that chair—it's really quite comfortable, Helen, go ahead, try it. And the countertop—that was tricky, because we had to get Formica down here, and we had to have a professional come in and install the gas stove, as well as a gas heater for the water. No shower yet, but you can use the ones in the gym for now . . ."

Elliot rattled on while Helen peeked into the dark shack with horror. She didn't know much about Oregon, but she could see that there were big mountains surrounding the fields where the school lay, and she knew that people skied in those mountains, and skiing meant snow, and snow meant winter, and winter meant cold. Freezing cold.

"It's vital for them to learn practical skills like this. How to *build* things. How to build *homes* for themselves." Elliot stopped midsentence. "What's wrong? You look like you've seen a ghost."

How perceptive. Helen sized Elliot up and remembered how hard it was to tell him anything that might be unpleasant for him to hear. For example, she had never spoken of the growing rift in their marriage until she was presented with its dissolution in its most obvious, naked form. "How am I going to live here?" she finally managed to ask.

"What do you mean?"

She picked her words carefully. "Elliot, I live in a brownstone in the middle of Brooklyn. I'm constantly surrounded by people. And I don't mean to sound unreasonable here, but I'm also used to a certain number of amenities: a toilet, a shower, running water, heat."

"There's running water here."

"There's a hand pump for a creek. Which will probably be frozen in about a week."

"No, we've taken care of that. A gas heater. And you haven't seen the woodstove."

"No. Elliot, no. I don't want to turn down your hospitality, but are you actually serious?" It was time to let him down. "Anyway, I spoke to Cal. I know he doesn't want me here, and his warm reception would have told me that even if he hadn't. It's untenable. You don't need your ex-wife directing a production of *The Tempest* with a bunch of teenagers and an audience who—don't give me that look, Elliot, we both know I'm right—won't be terribly enthusiastic or—"

"Or smart enough to understand it."

"I didn't say that!"

"You didn't need to. It's written all over you."

"What is?"

"Your privilege."

"Ex*cuse* me?"

"When was the last time you sacrificed something, Helen?"

"Oh, Jesus," she said, "here comes the martyr speech. Are you really still giving this pep talk after all these years?"

"Just answer me, Helen, when was the last time—"

"Save it," she said. She was already seething. She'd forgotten how easily she became the fuse and he the match.

"What have you done lately that isn't about yourself?"

"I came to help you, you fucker. Which ranks among the biggest mistakes I've ever made." She remembered how easy it was to confuse this rage with love. She pulled her arms tightly around herself and, safely contained, headed back up the hill, calling Ferdinand to her side. He scuffled up against her, glancing up at her expression. He always knew when she was upset.

"Wrong direction," Elliot called.

"Screw you."

"You're going back the way we came. If you want to go back faster, walk that way. I took you the scenic route. Trust me. You'll see the main building from the top of the hill."

Indeed she did. But she did not wish to give him the satisfaction of being right. She waited for him at the top of the hill, and when he got there, she tried to bait him. She got her voice under control. "I always forget what an asshole you are. It's such a disappointment."

"I tell the truth the way I see it."

"You tell a self-righteous, self-aggrandizing, self-promoting truth where you get to feel holier than every other goddamn person you meet." He didn't say anything. This was encouraging. She went on. "You win. You're the best. You've helped the most people. Is that what you want me to say?" He was looking out across the land as the morning light arrowed over it. She was losing him. And then she was losing her grasp on her fury. It had resigned itself. "Jesus, Elliot. What the hell am I doing here?"

He didn't answer. Just kept looking west. She had no more fight left. She couldn't remember what had been said or what had started the argument in the first place. So she made her way down the hill alone, in the direction he'd pointed. "Fergus," she called. The dog stayed beside Elliot. "Fergus! Come here!" But he did not come. Of course he did not come. She would walk alone.

The ground was prickly with sagebrush, and she had to fight her way around the juniper trees. That's what he'd called them. Juniper. The smell of the earth was salty and wild, a smell she'd never smelled before. Silky. Rasping in her lungs. A lozenge of pine that unwound itself inside her as it began to bake in the daylight. The sand beneath her feet was red and soft. She moved quickly. She knew he would watch her as she made her way all the way back to the school. So she kept on steadily, her back to him. She swore she would not look back. All the mercy between them was gone.

"EXACTLY HOW ARE you getting to the airport?"

She was surprised he had followed her back to the house. The

Elliot she'd married would not have done so. She pretended not to be impressed. She gathered up her toiletries in a frantic fury as his frame filled the bathroom doorway. She was looking forward to shoving him out of her way.

"I'm guessing you're not going to offer."

"I don't think you should leave."

"I'll call a cab."

"There *are* no cabs."

"I'll find someone to drive me."

"You don't know anyone."

"I know Cal. He'll be pleased to hear I'm leaving. And I know Lydia. I know she has a car. Or I'll walk down to the highway and hitchhike." Elliot's judgmental silence raised Helen's hackles. "I've hitchhiked before. And I'll do it again. If forced." She grabbed the shampoo and headed for the doorway.

Elliot stopped her, putting his arms on his shoulders. "Please listen," he said. He seemed amused.

"I don't need you laughing at me."

"I'm sorry." He made his face serious. "We got off on the wrong foot. Amelia gave me some good advice last night. In the middle of all the yelling. She was right. I should have picked you up at the airport myself. It was very rude of me to send someone else to do my job. I was swept up in my work, distracted, but the real truth is I was afraid to see you again." He dropped his arms from her shoulders. "We've spoken on the phone all these years, on and off. But I haven't seen you. I haven't seen you since . . ." His body seemed to cave.

"I know."

"So," he said.

Helen felt exhausted. She had been so determined to leave the bathroom, but now it seemed the safest place in the world. She wanted to stay in its womb. She set her toiletries down in the sink and closed the toilet cover, then sat on it. Elliot leaned in the doorway, silent.

"I'm not sure how to proceed," she said. "I really don't think it's a good idea for me to stay."

Elliot nodded. "I'm sure Duncan will be happy to have you home."

"Oh." She examined the tile grout. "Well. I wouldn't be so sure."

Elliot coughed his Wasp cough, deflecting any talk of private tensions.

Helen picked up a shampoo bottle for security and fiddled with the flip top. "Look," she said. "It's a very nice offer. The house and all. I appreciate it, I really do. I guess I'm just sensitive right now about feeling like a charity case."

"But you aren't," said Elliot.

"You didn't even want me for the job! You asked me to suggest a director for the play. And I volunteered myself! I don't think I have to tell you how unusual it is, someone in my position—and I mean this with no vanity—but it's a strange career move, to say the least, coming all the way out here."

"I'm thrilled that you're here, Helen."

"Don't I deserve an ounce of respect?"

He ran his fingers through his hair. "I had to figure out what I was going to say."

"About what?"

"I've been thinking. A lot. About that night, over sixteen years ago. After I found out that Astrid was gone. And the way you came and helped me after what I'd done to you. After leaving you. You were . . . you were amazing."

Helen couldn't help her smile. "Nah."

"You were. I was out of my head. I lost my mind. But you helped me get back to myself. So I could be there for Amelia. I'll never be able to thank you enough."

Helen shrugged. "What can I say? You needed me. I had to help."

"This is another one of those moments. I need your help."

"You mean directing *The Tempest*?"

"Yes," he said, but his voice didn't commit. "That and more."

"You haven't lost your marbles again, have you?"

"I'll let you be the judge of that."

HE MADE HER breakfast. Omelettes and toast. No coffee, but strong black tea, and that would do for now.

"I've had to reimagine my goals for Ponderosa Academy as it's grown. The problem is, as I see it, that the school and I are too closely linked. I fear that if something were to happen to me—"

"God forbid."

"God forbid, yes, but those things do happen, and if it did, I fear the school would be unable to sustain itself. Look. The first decade and a half of this school have been about surviving on a day-to-day basis. But there hasn't been much nourishment. There hasn't been any kind of long-term plan. And that's got to change, if only because of the financial side of things. We make do—on my inheritance, on federal and state grants, on private donations—but everything's held together with Scotch tape and rubber bands." He held the spatula in the air and gazed out the narrow window at the end of the kitchen. "These kids deserve more than that," he said. "They deserve more than just me lifting everyone around on my back. I'll admit, it's tiring, but that's not why we need to change the way things are run. We need to change things so these kids can go to the best colleges in the nation. So they can be doctors and senators and presidents. That's what I imagined when I started this place. And we're getting there. But I realize we can't get there alone."

"And my directing a production of *The Tempest* is going to fix all that." Helen was amused. Elliot relied so heavily on other's abilities to save. He was an optimist at heart, but she had no idea where he was going with this line of thought.

"I know what you're thinking," he said, placing her meal before her. "Go on, eat up while it's hot."

"What am I thinking?" she asked through the bite as she commanded Ferdinand away from the table: "Sit, boy. Settle."

"You're thinking I'm a worthless liberal idealist with a lot of big concepts and no practical solutions."

Helen waved her arms open. "This school is the most practical solution I've ever seen! If anyone knows how to turn idealism into reality, it's you. Most of our former comrades are renovating their prewar apartments and fretting over their second homes. Anyway, what do I know? I direct plays."

Elliot concentrated his efforts on his omelette, but Helen could tell he was pleased. She couldn't help smiling. This wasn't flirting, exactly, what they were doing. But it was what they had always done. Danced around each other's ideas. It felt good to be known again.

When he sat, he told her, "There's a school in Portland. The school where Amelia started this fall—Benson Country Day. They call themselves a conservatory for the arts, but they have the potential to be so much more. I've been talking to the headmaster and the board of directors. They're excited about the opportunity to combine forces. Making one school out of two. They're not sure yet. But they've given me a year to see what kind of proposal I could come up with. I mean, we're talking a big opportunity here. They're talking full integration; some of our kids go there and board. Get exposed to the arts in a way they won't out here. Get the kind of education I can only dream about giving them. Get some of those Portland private-school kids out here. Create a new kind of community, one that expands the students' world at both schools."

"And you'd be giving up control?"

"I don't know yet."

"But the academy wouldn't be yours anymore."

"No," he said. "No, I suppose it wouldn't be *only* mine. But it isn't that now, and that was never the point. I don't want to keep it to myself. All I did was imagine the possibility of the school and put some of that possibility into play."

"And *The Tempest*?"

"There will be a festival in the spring, with an art show, a pow-wow, classroom presentations, and *The Tempest*. We'll invite the Benson people and show them what an extraordinary amount we have to offer. We'll show them that we have the potential to be a world-class institution."

Helen leaned back in her chair and sized Elliot up. "You seem in surprisingly good spirits in the midst of all of this."

"As I said, I've been thinking a lot about that night sixteen years ago. For so long, I've shied away from it. I was sure I'd gone insane. I couldn't forgive myself for making such a terrible choice in marrying Astrid, in starting a family with her. I couldn't forgive myself for loving a woman who could leave behind her own child and commit such heinous acts. But lately . . ." He shook his head, obviously moved. Helen had rarely seen Elliot like this: open and vulnerable. She felt compelled to reach out and comfort him.

"Lately," he went on, "I've had some stunning revelations. About the way we rejuvenate ourselves. The funny way life moves and works. I can tell you this much: I believe in hope now. In a way I had forgotten."

Helen put her hands around her mug and closed her eyes. She didn't know what exactly he meant, but she liked the thought of it. Hope. "I can't believe I'm going to live in that shack."

"You don't have to stay."

"If I don't show up one morning, you've got to promise to send a search party."

"Only stay if you want to," he said.

"I think I want to."

"You can live up here."

"We'd kill each other. And anyway. That would be a little strange."

"You can stay here, with Amelia, and I can live down there."

"No," she said. "No, she needs you. And I need my space." She added, "Perhaps it's none of my business. But you've shared these ideas about the future of the school with the assistant headmaster, right?"

"You mean Cal?"

"Yeah," she said. "He seems a bit . . ." She cast about for a polite word. "He seems *concerned*. About the school. I don't want to get in the middle of anything, but—"

"Of course," said Elliot, and in those two words, Helen was reminded how deftly Elliot always moved her from feeling included to feeling like an outcast. How he shut her out the second he believed she'd judged him. "I haven't had the chance," he said, rising to clear his plate.

Perhaps I underestimated her.

Chapter Five

WILLA
Day Two
Columbus, Ohio, to Mitchell, Illinois ~
Thursday, May 8, 1997

One of Willa's absolute favorite things to do on the road was eat. There was something thrilling about ingesting immeasurable pounds of potatoes and red meat while streaming through the world. They ordered chicken-fried steaks from shiny red truck-stop booths with built-in pay phones. They parked at small-town burger joints and scarfed down fries from trays attached to their windows. Though this food was not forbidden in the Llewelyns'"real" life, the ritual of it was something they rarely engaged in once they'd settled into a place. When they lived somewhere, they ate at home. When they were on the road, it was all fast food and greasy spoons.

It was no surprise, then, that the morning Nat and Willa awoke in Columbus, Ohio, she insisted they eat their first road breakfast at Denny's. She'd exerted her influence in other ways too. She'd gotten Nat to agree on sleeping in hotels instead of that god-awful tent from the 1970s. At first he'd made a big deal about whether he had enough cash on him to pay for a week's worth of room bills, but in the end, he relented. She kept herself from saying that normal fathers used credit cards instead of worrying about a paper trail. While her father checked in at the Motel 6 front desk, Willa put her head to the cat's and thought about how there were many things about her father she was never going to understand or like. She was wise to enjoy her father in spite of these things.

Their hotel room was dark and dank, but it had two beds, and beds were better than the ground. Willa sneaked Ariel in under her jean jacket, and the cat patrolled the room for mice. It was a good sign that she found none. In the morning, when Willa repacked her suitcase—she knew now for sure that Nat had hoped she was going to come along, because he'd packed a bag for her, albeit full of her least favorite and worst-fitting clothes—she felt the giddiness again. In her normal life, she would be sitting in biology right this second. Nat had put in a call to Bellwether from the pay phone downstairs and let them know there was a family emergency. He'd try to get Willa back in time for the art show.

When at Denny's, Nat always ordered the Lumberjack Slam: three buttermilk pancakes, a slice of grilled honey ham, two bacon strips, two sausage links, two eggs, grits, and an English muffin. He nodded each time the waitress rounded the table with her carafe of coffee, so he'd have imbibed six or so cups by the time his plate was clean. Willa's strategy was more conservative, if no less ambitious, given her size: two eggs sunny-side up, bacon, hash browns, rye toast, orange juice, hot chocolate, and a piece of cherry pie. When else in your life did you get dessert after breakfast?

"You know those underpants you packed for me?" They were already done with the first round of food and waiting for the second. Willa was trying to tease Nat. She kicked him under the table to try and jolly him up. "They're, like, from sixth grade. There's absolutely no way I can fit into them."

Nat smiled gloomily. He wasn't really listening.

"It's okay," Willa continued. "We can just stop at Kmart or something. But I think it's pretty funny that you thought I'd fit into them. They're, like, the size of my *hand*."

"They're the only ones I could find," he said finally, fiddling with the sugar packets.

"Did you check my top drawer?"

"Of course I did, Wills."

"Oh. Then all my other ones must've been dirty."

The waitress wedged Willa's pie onto the table and cleared a few plates. Willa took a bite and, with her mouth full, said, "And what's with that pink polka-dotted shirt?"

"What about it?" Nat asked, slathering his pancakes in maple syrup.

"I *hate* that shirt."

"I guess I didn't know that."

"Yes, you do. Remember who gave it to me?"

Nat paused as if considering. "Can't say that I do."

"Yes, you do, Dad. Cute-as-a-button Cassie. No lesbian buys a teenager a pink shirt with polka dots on it." Cassie had lived next door before they moved to Connecticut. Despite the fact that the place was Northampton, Massachusetts—and thus, Nat had insisted, this generous, gift-giving woman was most likely lesbian—Willa hadn't bought it. She saw Cassie as one in a long line of women who tried to get their talons into Nat by buttering up his daughter. It was all well and good if they wanted to date him, but it creeped her out when they acted like they'd be dating *her* if things went according to plan.

Nat busied himself with his bacon. He could sense the lightness and ease Willa was attempting to coax out of him, but he wasn't feeling it. All he could think about were the four things he needed to say. He wanted to rein her in, get her to pay attention. He wished he had a way to still her, even for a moment. To make her listen to what he had to say. He cleared his throat.

She went on. "I appreciate you packing those clothes for me, I really do. But I think it's safe to say, once and for all, that you have absolutely no fashion sense."

"I need to talk to you, Willa," Nat said.

"Well, then, Father, let us commence to talk." Willa mimicked the seriousness in his voice and sat up straighter. She raised an eyebrow, a smile skirting the edges of her mouth.

"It's about your mother," Nat said, and all of Willa's pretense disintegrated. She hadn't brought Caroline up since he'd mentioned her name yesterday. She knew her father well. She knew that mentioning her mother would bury that information deeper. She'd become an expert in this truth. All her life, the best way to get the dirt on anything—her mother, especially—had been to wait in the wings and listen. Eventually, Nat would say something that teased at more. Getting beyond that was the trick. If you asked, you lost any chance. He'd gather the troops and surround that particular nugget steadfastly. Let him think you didn't care, and that was when you got the good stuff. It was rare, however, to get anything this direct from her father on any point, especially Caroline. Willa wasn't sure how to proceed.

"Okay," she said cautiously, and put down her fork.

"I just want you to know," Nat said, his heart beating fast, "that your mother loved you very, very much."

"I know, Dad. I know." She was graceful when she comforted him.

"I know you know. But I want to be sure you really understand. She was a riveting, strange, illuminating woman, and it breaks my heart that she'll never get the chance to see how beautiful you are."

"Da-ad." Willa blushed. Nat used words like "illuminating" on rare occasions. She didn't know whether it was a good idea to start asking questions. But she had to take the risk. "Do I look like her?"

Nat eased back into the booth. "Every day, more and more."

Willa nodded. "I thought so. From the album she made for your first anniversary. I was looking at the pictures again the other night. I mean, my hair isn't quite as long, but I think . . ." She smiled. "I'm glad. I guess I looked more like you when I was little."

"I guess," Nat said.

She'd said something wrong. She could see it beginning. The way her dad would close up. She scooped up another round of pie and took a bite, nonchalantly asking, "What else do you remember? About her? I mean, what was so strange?"

"She had the dirtiest sense of humor. Just absolutely wicked. People didn't expect it, because she was so tiny and looked so innocent. She got away with a lot because of how she looked. When I met her in high school, everyone called her 'the hummingbird.' She was so tiny and fast."

"And that was in California, right?"

"Yup," he said. "Los Angeles. We've got to get out there someday."

"Maybe we could stop on our way back from Oregon," Willa said hopefully.

"It's a long way out of the way."

"I'm just saying that maybe—"

"Someday, Wills, someday, you'll see where your mother and I met. I promise you that."

"I know your parents died a long time ago, Dad. And I know you weren't very close to them or whatever. But maybe her parents, you know—"

"Her parents . . ." Nat sighed. "Your mom had it rough, kiddo. That's one of the reasons we moved east, actually. It was something we shared. There wasn't anything for us in California. We needed a new beginning."

"And that's why you loved each other so much? Because you were like two peas in a pod, right? Just like you used to say?"

Nat nodded. "That's right," he said, more quietly than before.

Willa knew to nudge Nat off the touchy ground. She could tell if they kept talking about this part of things, he'd stop soon. She should make him laugh. "Remember that story you told me about how you guys first got together? About the junior prom and that creep who kept dancing with her, and you saved her from him by pretending to be sick? And then she had to take care of you and the guy left her alone?"

"Yes," Nat said. He had to be so careful with what he told her.

Willa's mind was a sponge. He'd told that story once, and she'd been seven at the time.

"You said she had on a green dress. And whenever I picture it, it's always satin, but I realized you never told me if it was satin or not. And I was just wondering: was it?"

Nat closed his eyes and let himself see Caroline. Long, wild hair. Hips gliding side to side to the music. Lips moving along with the words. He couldn't remember the dress at all. "Is satin the shiny stuff?" he asked.

"Yes." Willa smiled triumphantly.

"Then you're right."

"I knew it." The waitress brought more coffee. "And what else?"

"Your mother and I took a cross-country trip together. Because I got an apprenticeship, learning how to build furniture, and she was thinking about college. We started driving at the end of June. Right after we graduated from high school. From California back to Connecticut, the reverse way we're going. That's how we ended up back east."

"Will you ever show me the house you guys bought together? You keep saying you will, Dad, but you never do. And now we live in Connecticut. But you won't even tell me where it is."

"I'll take you there."

"When we're back from Oregon?"

"Yes," Nat said, and told himself wishful thinking wasn't lying, exactly. "It was a cottage with a door that was black on the outside and white on the inside. And we had very little, just a bed we'd gotten on sale, and a table and chairs the neighbors were throwing away."

"And me," said Willa, beaming. "You also had me."

Nat withdrew his fingers from the table, taking them into his lap. He watched them move as though they were not his own. "There are parts of your mother that are hard to understand," he said, fixing his daughter in his gaze.

Willa nodded. "I know you guys had problems."

"But no matter what you hear, Willa, you must never forget how much she loved you."

Willa cocked her head to the side. "What would I hear? And who would tell me?"

Nat cleared his throat again. It wasn't time for this yet. He took out his wallet and handed her a twenty. "I've got to stretch my legs. Get the check, will ya? I'll take care of Ariel and meet you at the car."

Willa watched him walk away and tried to measure her emotions. She should be happy, she told herself. She had gotten more already than she'd ever had before, and there was promise of more yet to come. Still and all, she couldn't shake the feeling that something wasn't right. She was old enough to know that when someone tells you wonderful things about someone else, there is often something bad close behind. That, and when Nat handed her the money, his hand was shaking like crazy.

AMELIA
Where-We-Have-the-Parties ~ Saturday, October 5, 1996

The party everyone had been talking about was east of the academy, away from the mountains. It was on a dusty yellow spot of land that everyone knew about but had no name. A lot of places around here don't have names. Names are given to a piece of land when something happens on it. Take some local favorites: Broken Balls Creek, Infidelity Peak, Maidenhead Point. And you think I'm kidding.

Aside from the parties held on the land where the parties happened, there was nothing much to distinguish it from any of the wide space surrounding it. There was nothing denoting its limits. This place was as wide and as long as the number of bored Friday-night teenagers who could spread across it under a wide, cloudless sky.

In retrospect, it is easy to note that this land *was* distinguishable; there was an ancient skeleton of an old homesteader barn lying a quarter mile or so away from where the bonfire was usually lit. The crisp gray wood of the barn lay against the earth like the ribs of a whale beached long ago, swept clean of flesh by a sand-filled wind. But no one would notice that barn until After.

Because nothing important had happened in a very long time at the place where Amelia and Lydia were going for the party, the name that the place had gotten for itself, which was not written on a map and did not exist at a latitude or a longitude, was simple: Where-We-Have-the-Parties. That is not the name of that place now. Now it is called Don't-Go-There-Because-of-What-Happened. But I'm getting ahead of myself.

Where-We-Have-the-Parties is not, contrary to what you may think, an Indian name. This was a place named by teenagers, most of whom were Indian, but their age is a much more relevant fact than their cultural heritage or the color of their skin. They had been given access to this place because no one else wanted it, as is often the way with teenagers. Teenagers will turn an unwanted piece of land into a kingdom, because simply being there offers a freedom of the soul. (I am contradicting my own mind when I say that people had never been over this land, when I say they had never named it. When I use the word "people" like that, I mean white people. All these places have Neige Courante names, and these names are not the ones given by Neige Courante teenagers. Except among the tribal elders, most of those names sound inconsequential, and even then they mean nothing compared to what they meant to our wandering ancestors.)

Lydia had been to parties here five or six times over the course of the summer. It was not an Always-Party place, because some of the kids—those adept at buying cheap beer and making well-placed phone calls—were afraid that word would spread and unwanted kids would show up. We all know them. The dorks. The goody-goodies. Had Lydia not been at Amelia's side, vouching for her, Amelia definitely would have been considered an unwanted. She had been to only one of these parties. I have already told you that she was not prone to participating in the other kids' activities, and it was a catch-22: the less she did with them because she felt too different, the more different she became in their eyes. She knew this. But she did not know how to change it. There were all sorts of reasons she hadn't participated. At first it had been about her father: she hated the disappointment in his eyes when he found out she'd done something disobedient. She knew this disappointment wouldn't kill him, but she also knew that Elliot Barrow was a far easier man to keep happy than to pick up from the sad, unreachable place he was willing to go. So she stayed close to him, like a calf sheltered from the storm under the limbs of a shade tree.

But there was something more, and by this point in her life, Amelia knew it. She was a coward. Leaving Benson Country Day—running away, more like it—just proved it. And though she was furious at her father for not telling her about Helen's existence or impending visit, Amelia understood how easy it was to keep unpleasant truths to yourself, praying all the time that people would never find out about them and, if they did, that they'd have the sense to forgive you. Under the same circumstances, she would have been capable of doing exactly the same thing her dad had done.

Which was why jumping into Lydia's car and gunning into the distance was such a big deal. As they got closer and closer to Where-We-Have-the-Parties, Lydia was talking a mile a minute. Amelia's doubts became second thoughts.

"Seriously, if Victor is there, you are *going* to talk to him. I mean, he's definitely going to be there, but if, like, his grandmother won't let him leave the house or something . . . But don't worry. He'll be there, and you'll talk to him and . . . Oh my *God*, I'm so excited you're coming with me!" Amelia nodded once, and Lydia caught the drift. "There is absolutely no reason to be nervous. You're with me. Everyone loves me."

Amelia sat quietly, refusing to smile, to laugh, to be swept up in Lydia's enthusiasm.

"Okay." Lydia slowed the car and pulled to the side of the gravel road. Rocks ticked up loudly against the underbelly of the car. "What the fuck is up with you?"

"Nothing."

"Yeah, right. 'Nothing.' Do not tell me you are feeling guilty."

"It's nothing."

"You *are*, aren't you? You're feeling guilty. Don't do this to me, Amelia. Seriously, please do not do this."

"I'm not doing anything, Lydia."

"Yes, you are. You are taking our one night of fun, just about *ever*, and turning it into a gloomfest."

" 'Gloomfest' isn't even a word."

"C'mon. You love your dad because, yes, he's a good guy—we all know that—which is why it's so terrible that he just lied to you. I don't know if you've noticed, but when people start lying to you, you stop trusting them. That's how things *work*."

"He wasn't lying—"

"Not telling your daughter that you have an ex-wife is lying, no matter how you try to whitewash things. Your father is the master of whitewashing. He would beat Tom Sawyer at his game." Lydia nudged Amelia in the ribs, smiling. "Oh, come on, I don't even get one smile for my completely unprompted literary reference, proving that I've already done my reading for Monday? You know: Tom Sawyer, the white paint, the fence?" When Amelia didn't respond, Lydia groaned and leaned back against the headrest. "Jesus, you really are a downer tonight."

Amelia shrugged and pressed her cheek against the side window. The night was fully dark now, and a car full of partying kids came up fast behind them out of nowhere, then slowed when they noticed the red glow of Lydia's brake lights. The other car's windows were down, and the smell of cigarettes and the sound of the Stones blasted from it.

"You coming or what?" Alex Speakseasy leaned out the car window and handed Lydia an open beer.

"Yeah, we're coming."

Alex leaned farther into the night, peering around Lydia, until he made out Amelia's face. He jerked his head quickly when he saw her, unable to hide his surprise. "I thought you were alone," he said, retreating into the car.

"Yeah, well, I'm not."

"Cool, cool," he said, nodding. "See you." And they were off.

"You see?" said Amelia when the night was again dark.

"Don't pay attention to those assholes," Lydia said. "They don't know you." She took a swig from the beer and handed it to Amelia, pressing on the accelerator. The car lurched forward, gaining speed. "And they *won't* know you unless we get to the fucking party already. I command you to be in a good mood."

VICTOR LITTLEFOOT WAS at the party, but he was surrounded by the familiar entourage of admirers. Girls leaned against his pickup, guzzling beer from bottles, giggling, telling stories on themselves. Boys stood a few yards away, spitting, recounting basketball plays just loud enough so Victor could hear the bravado in their voices.

"This is bullshit," said Lydia, after she'd gotten a beer into Amelia's hand. "We should just go talk to him. Those girls are nothing but bitches and hos."

"Do you have to talk like your brothers?"

"I don't have to do anything I don't want to. Why? You've got a fucking problem with the goddamn way I talk?"

Amelia raised her eyebrows and downed a gulp of Miller Lite. It was watery and lukewarm. The stuff that Sadie and Wes drank was high-end, microbrewed, and ice-cold.

"I'm glad to see you drinking. To be perfectly honest, I thought that was going to be the hardest part, getting you to even hold a beer in your hand."

"I drink."

Lydia smiled. "So I guess some things *did* change while you were in Portland." There was a twinge of pride in her voice. She grabbed Amelia's hand, and before Amelia could resist, they were heading in Victor's direction.

"Hey hey hey! The party has begun!" Lydia said. They were too close for Amelia to pull away.

"What's *she* doing here?"

"You got a fucking problem with my best friend, asshead?" Lydia was in Johnny Courrament's face in a split second. All the boys laughed.

"No problem, no problem," Johnny said, backing up. "Great that you could make it," he said to Amelia, bowing low. The boys laughed louder.

"I'm watching you," said Lydia, her finger still in the air. Johnny and some of the boys sauntered in the direction of the bonfire. "I'm keeping my eye on you. I beat you up when we were ten, and I can still take you, and you fucking know it!"

"I don't think threatening to beat people up is the best way to go, Lydia." Amelia spoke in a low voice.

"The only way to talk to these kids is to let them know where you stand."

"I know how to talk to them. I've known them my whole life, just like you."

"Yeah?" Lydia put a hand on her hip. "And how many friends do you have?"

"Just don't be so aggressive, okay? Settle down."

"If you want me to settle down, you better start learning how to defend yourself." Lydia launched farther in Victor's direction.

Soon they were sidled against the crush of girls flirting with Victor. He was barely visible through the thicket of teased hair, flailing arms, and suggestive laughter, and Amelia felt stupid standing there. But she made conversation—at least girls pretended they liked you when they didn't—and kept Victor in the corner of her eye. She saw an opening, but just then another car pulled up. The kids inside it beckoned Victor over. Lydia put her arm on Amelia's shoulder as he disappeared into the backseat. "We need more beer," she said, and Amelia was inclined to agree.

HOURS PASSED. THE desert air cooled. Most of the children pulled comforters and heavy jackets out of the trunks of their cars, and the bonfire grew bigger and bigger. Because there was nothing in the vicinity to burn, it was always someone's job to load a pickup with downed limbs and branches from the forest on reservation land. Because Lydia had sauntered off with her arms around her sometime boyfriend, Bobby Marron, long before the moon had set, and because there was no one else to talk to, and because Victor too had last been seen heading into the wilderness with a girl on each arm, Amelia assigned herself the task of fire duty. She was wrapped in a ratty wool blanket, her face toward the flames, next to the unloaded wood. Every ten minutes or so, she'd reach onto the waning pile of logs and disentangle a branch, then fling it into the fire. Sparks would fly up toward the stars and vanish. All around her, people were talking, laughing, kissing in the glow of the fire. She pulled the blanket tighter.

"Hey."

You knew he was going to show up, didn't you? Of course he was. Amelia was the only one who didn't know.

Amelia was surprised to hear a voice so close. She turned toward its source and blanched when she saw that it was Victor. "Hey," she said, glancing back at the fire. He was so near she could have touched him. She was glad for the blanket.

"Great fire."

"Thanks." As if it were hers.

Silence. Then Victor reached across her, brushing her leg through all those layers of cloth. She felt herself blushing and was thankful for the darkness. He lifted one of the branches off the pile and brought it back to his lap. The branch chafed against the blanket as it crossed her. He started peeling off its bark. Amelia pulled her knees to her chest and buried her chin against them. This was not happening.

"You having fun?"

She nodded. "Yeah. You?"

He shrugged and threw a piece of bark onto the flames. It popped against the heat. "You know," he said.

"Yeah." She did not know.

"Are the parties always like this?"

Here was a moment when she could have been honest. But "I don't know because I've only had the balls to go to one party before, and that was two years ago" didn't have the same ring as something effortlessly cool. She tried to untangle what that effortlessly cool thing would be, but she was tongue-tied. "You know," she echoed. She did not know.

"Ah." They listened to the fire crackling. "Is that girl Lydia your best friend?"

Amelia nodded. "She comes on a little strong."

"She kind of freaks me out," he said, and because there was humor in his voice, Amelia felt brave enough to look at him. His eyes crinkled and he started to laugh, and then she was laughing too.

"You're taller than I thought you'd be," he said when their laughter had died down.

"That's weird," she said, trying not to think about the fact that he'd been thinking about her and was willing to admit it. "Then again, you were always really tall. So you probably thought I was a short kid even though I wasn't."

"Yeah," he said, looking up at the stars. "I was always taller than you." He threw another piece of bark on the fire. "When was the last time we saw each other?"

"I don't know," she said. "Sometime when I was seven and you were eight. Before you moved to Chicago."

"Yeah," he said. "I just wondered if you knew exactly when."

"Why?" she asked.

He shrugged. "I just can't remember much about living here. Before."

"How's Chicago?"

"I like it there. I mean, it sucks sometimes; in the winter you freeze, in the summer you roast. And the city is totally split. Black people live on the South Side, white people live on the North. The South Side is dangerous and there are drugs and guns there, everywhere, really. You'll get mugged in broad daylight and no one will do anything. But the lake is beautiful. And it's where my friends live. And my mom. She likes that there are so many Indians."

"She must miss you."

"Nah," he said, breaking the branch in two. "She's the one who sent me back." Victor's voice loosened, and he kept talking. "Yeah, Grandma is having a really hard time, and Mom thought it would be good to have a grandkid living with her." He paused. "I kept getting into trouble. My mom calls it 'urban trouble.' She decided to send me to the country." He gestured to the party around them and laughed. "If she only knew."

Amelia couldn't believe it, but she felt relaxed, as if she were capable of reassuring someone else, even. Someone like Victor. She felt calm. As if she knew what to do and say. She said, "Well, we can try to get in a little trouble together," but after it was out of her mouth, she realized that could mean something much more flirtatious than she intended. She buried her face against her knees again and laughed nervously. Victor didn't respond and she wanted to die. She never should have opened her big stupid mouth.

"You remember that baby?"

"What?" Victor's words jostled the embarrassment right out of her.

"The baby," Victor persisted. "The baby we found on the other side of Wiggler's Creek."

"No," she said, but even as she spoke, she knew that she *did* remember. Pulling that baby back into her senses took a few moments. She remembered the infant cooing up at her. She remembered fear. And she remembered loneliness.

"We were playing together. And for some reason we went beyond that old fence that isn't there anymore, you remember, and we found this baby—"

"And then you went to get my father, and I went to pee, and by the time you got back—"

"The baby was gone." Victor nodded. "You *do* remember. I've been wondering since I first saw you. And we weren't allowed to play together after that, were we?"

Amelia felt as if she might burst. "We weren't. You're right, we weren't. But how long was that before you moved?"

"A while," he said. "I remember you trying to play with me a couple of times after that, but that's it. That's all I can remember: the baby and then not being allowed to play."

"There was something tied in the air over the baby. A piece of white cloth or something, remember?"

"Yeah," he said, "it's something ranchers do. It's called flagging. See, when a cow has a calf that's too young to walk, ranchers tie white tags on the shrubs around that area to keep the coyotes away."

She was surprised he knew this and she didn't. He was the one who'd been living in Chicago all this time. "Why would that keep coyotes away?"

"Because of the movement. Coyotes see the cloth fluttering and it scares them off." Victor was dead serious. He was looking at her. There were no clouds between them. "All I remember about this place is you."

It had been said. Amelia felt a shiver swoop up her, from the bottoms of her feet to the top of her head. She didn't know what to say. He hadn't looked away yet.

"I'm going to find that baby," Victor said.

"Oh."

"I'm going to find out what happened."

"It's not a baby anymore."

"I know that," he said. "We can't tell anyone. I don't want anyone else to know. You have to promise, if you're going to help me. We have to find out what happened together."

That's how Amelia Barrow and Victor Littlefoot became friends for the second time in their lives.

The Cock-and-Bull Story

Once upon a time, a boy was sent to live with his father. This father was a man the boy did not know well. I would say the boy did not know him at all, but that is hyperbolic even for this kind of story. The boy knew who his father was because another boy had told him. Since then the boy and the father had spoken to each other a few times at a few community occasions. But the father did not live where the boy lived—he lived in a city over the mountain, with children he called his own. Besides, the father was not the kind of man to take the boy on his lap and praise him. The father was not one for praising, generally, or for children, unless his wife had given birth to them.

Circumstances changed when the boy's grandmother died. Up until this point, though the boy knew who his father was, and knew what being a father meant, and though the boy knew that all around him, there were all sorts of distant relatives he could call his own, he had always somehow suspected that his grandmother was the one person in the world with whom he shared any kind of blood. He believed that meant that only she could claim him, and that when she died, he would be like a man himself: free to do as he pleased, to live where he wanted. He was wrong.

The father showed up at the grandmother's funeral and simultaneously confused and clarified the boy's world. The boy knew his mother was the one who had left him in his grandmother's care before leaving, never to return. He could not remember this mother, nor the things she had said into his ear the night she ran off into the moonlight. Still, when the father showed up at the grandmother's funeral, the boy knew something about what kind of man the father was. By which I mean: something the mother said into that infant's ear must have stayed with him, even though the boy did not know it until that moment. Something about how this man who was his father was good at making promises, expert at cajoling, skillful at temptation. The boy saw that he was going to want the father even though he did not want to want him. The boy's first thought was to flee, but by the time the father's clean black car pulled up beside the church, it was already too late, although nothing had yet begun.

The boy could not flee. There was a funeral going on, and the boy was trapped in the front row, with all eyes on him. All eyes shifted when the father's form darkened the church's doorway. All eyes popped out of all heads at the social afterward, when the father placed his hand on the boy's bony shoulder and told him it was time to gather his things. "This is what she wanted," the father said, so the boy was bound to obey. His grandmother knew best.

Twelve years had passed since the boy was born, and it seemed to him all that time that no one but his grandmother wanted him. He did not think this in a self-pitying way. He thought himself quite lucky. His grandmother was the kind of woman who made discussion of love irrelevant. But suddenly, here was a man saying, "I am your father. I have come to take you to your new home. My wife is ready to be your mother." The boy knew the father was also saying, "Don't be fooled: it's not as if we had a choice." The boy knew this meant the grandmother had somehow cajoled the father into taking the boy in. And even though the boy was scared, he thought, "This is what she wanted." He would do it just for her.

The father drove the boy up to the grandmother's falling-down house, and for the first time in his life, the boy felt embarrassed. He saw that the house might be ugly. He thought, for the first time in his life, that only poor people would live in that house. The boy realized that perhaps this was what his grandmother had wanted for him: to see a life beyond the falling-down house. This was why she had sent for the father.

The boy did not want to let the father in to help him gather his things. He did not want the father to see how his life really looked. But there was no choice. The father pushed open the front door and decided what the boy did and did not need. When it came down to it, all the boy took with him *was a suitcase with two books hidden inside. Everything else, as the father said, was useless.*

"You'll come back here in the summers," the father said. "It's important for you to maintain your ties to your heritage."

When the boy met the father's real children, the children who were all the father's own, the boy wondered why they spent no summers being tied to their heritage. Instead, the real children attended space camps and Model United Nations conferences and Johns Hopkins science programs.

But the boy hadn't met those children yet. All that was to happen had not yet happened. What happened was this.

As the father drove the boy from the land that was in the boy's blood, the boy caught a glimpse of the old bull he'd been warned about hundreds of times by old ladies like his grandmother. This bull lived in a field with a falling-down fence around him. For the most part, the bull was a quiet creature, just something wild and distant, a foreboding possibility on the fringe of childhood games. There were always threats of the bull going crazy, on a rampage, leaving bloody children in his wake, but nothing like that ever happened.

Suddenly, the boy turned to the father. "I gotta go," he said.

The father opened his mouth to respond, then understood. "Number one or number two?"

"I gotta piss."

"We'll talk about that word at home. For now . . ." The father pulled the car to the side of the gravel road, beside the field where the bull stood idly by.

The boy opened the door and smelled the sour mash of weathered straw. A breeze cut through the thin jacket a cousin had lent him for the funeral. The sun was warm on his back as he made his way to the fence. He unzipped his pants and waited for the piss to come. But this was silly, because he hadn't had to piss in the first place. He didn't know why he'd asked the father to stop the car. It wasn't as if he didn't want to go with him. He did want to go. It seemed as if he'd been waiting to go for years but hadn't known it all this time.

The bull raised his head and looked at the boy. The boy's chest started hammering. He felt himself piss a little bit. He looked right in the bull's eyes. He wondered what it would take to get the bull to gore him. He wanted to say something to get the bull riled up, wave his arms in the air, anything, but the father leaned out the passenger side and said, "Son, we gotta get."

And the boy thought, "I'm someone's son."

Act Three

[OR]

Do You Love Me?

Chapter One

*D*ay three began with crossing the Mississippi. Naturally, Willa was old enough to have studied geography and to know, rationally, that what lay on the other side of that national divide was much the same as what lay before it: people, houses, roads. But in all her seventeen years, she had never actually crossed the big river, so there was something mystical about this accomplishment. She'd never been allowed on the other side. She'd begged her father the night before to do this crossing in the daylight. Here, now, was her first glimpse of the waterway: it shimmered and shone like hammered metal. It was much wider than the Hudson, and much wilder. Full of boats the likes of which she'd never seen, and they were all heading someplace southern, someplace with swampy bayous and zydeco music. The Mississippi seemed cut from the cloth of a country far different than the one she'd always known, a landscape much messier and more unpredictable. The Wild West.

On the other side of the river, Willa made her father find a bluff from which she could take pictures. She loaded her camera in the relative darkness of the car, shadowing the film with her body. When she started to shoot, she wished she could be as nimble a

photographer as she wanted. She wanted to capture the feelings she
had while she was making the pictures and somehow project those
feelings into the photographs themselves. But she already knew,
from her limited experience, that that was much harder than it
seemed. Miss Finlay had told her the best practice was to use the
film as a tool, and without hesitation. Willa worked silently and
diligently, as Ariel wound around her legs, purring, and Nat
perched on the hood of the car, watching his daughter work.

Nat considered the possibility of making this the moment. It
was a beautiful morning, and they were alone, and there was sun in
the sky and spring on the air and a breeze that tossed their hair
gingerly. But he didn't want to take her work from her. She was
happy shooting so he let her be. Afterward, she clambered up beside him onto the warm hood of the car.

"I should have shot from the other side," she said. "I just wasted
two rolls shooting into the sun."

"We can go back," Nat said instinctively. "I don't mind."

"Aren't we in a big fat rush? To get to that Elliot guy before he
dies?"

"Yes—"

"Thought so. So no, we can't go back. Anyway, we can just stop
again on our way east." The wind carried Willa's voice away. She
leaned against her father's warm arm. "What's with that Elliot guy,
anyway? Why are you supposed to find him? Why did she make
you promise?"

So the time had come. Just like that, without his instigation. Nat
put his arm around Willa and squeezed. He began slowly. "After
Caroline and I moved to Connecticut, we started to have some
problems. I guess the honeymoon phase wore off. We should have
been a little smarter about how we did things. We were babies. We
were only eighteen, and we decided to move across the country
alone, to a place where we didn't know anyone and had never been
before, and start a new life together." He listed all these things on
his free hand and shook his head. "We weren't ready for how hard

it was going to be. I thought all I needed was a steady job, just to show her I could be a man in her life who provided for her, made her safe, all that, and then she'd be happy. You know? But it didn't work out that way."

Willa nodded against him, looking out across the water, and he continued. "One day I came home from work, and she was just . . . sobbing. She'd have these . . . episodes when I knew her in California. But I guess I had no idea how deep she got. That first day in Connecticut was just the tip of the iceberg. Over the next few months, she got really hard to talk to, really distant. Angry. She'd say all sorts of awful things, about what a terrible state the world was in, how children were dying everywhere of all sorts of horrible diseases, how we weren't doing anything to help. I didn't know what to do. When she got like that, it was like she wasn't the same person. I didn't know how to talk to her. And she said the most horrible things about me, about how all I wanted was to own her, to keep her locked up, to . . ." He swallowed and tried to keep his voice measured.

"It's okay," Willa said, putting her arm around his waist but not looking at him. "We don't have to talk about this."

"Oh, but Willa, we do," he said, and it was the wistfulness in his voice that kept them still and silent for a moment before he began again.

"I thought some change would do her good. I bought us train tickets down to New York City, and we spent a weekend in a cheap motel in Times Square. The city was really gritty then, nothing close to what it's like today, and our hotel room was disgusting. But even then that city was the fanciest place we'd ever been. I'd always promised her I was going to take her to Europe. New York was the closest I got. But oh my God"—here he smiled—"you should have seen her in the sculpture wing at the Met. She was so happy. I hadn't seen her like that in . . . well, since we'd moved. She earned her hummingbird nickname all over again just in that one day. And when we went back up to Connecticut, she didn't seem so sad anymore. So for her birthday, I saved up and bought her ten round-trips. I meant for them to be five for her and five for me. I thought we could make it a monthly thing together. A tradition. But one day I got home from work, and she was the happiest I'd seen her in months. She was making this delicious meal for us—meatballs, garlic bread, broccoli—and she told me she'd spent the day in New York. Walked to the train station, hopped on a train all by herself. Wandered around Central Park. She was just . . . glowing. She said she loved the city. And even though I felt a little . . . well, jealous, I was also glad to see her feeling well again. I told her she needed to be careful, keep her purse close to her body, not ride the subway alone, that kind of thing, and she laughed the way she had in high school when she knew I was right but she was going to do things her way anyway. I decided to drop the subject. I thought if visiting New York made her happy, then so be it."

A barge down on the Mississippi let out a low, long bellow. The cat jumped up on Nat's lap and meowed at him a few times until he scratched behind her ears. She hopped over to Willa's lap and leaned steadily against the girl. Willa bit her lip and waited. Then she asked in a soft voice, "And what happened then?"

"What happened then is that Caroline left me. She announced it to me one evening. She said she'd found a new life for herself. In New York. Apparently, she'd been busy on those trips down to the city. She said she'd found a group of people who believed what she believed. She said she was going to help them. They were going to change the world. She had already packed a bag. She left most of her things behind. She said she wasn't going to need them anymore."

"Just like that?" Willa asked, petting the cat instead of touching her father.

"Just like that."

"And you let her go?"

"Your mother wasn't the kind of woman I could keep still. She had her own mind, Willa."

"But what about me?" Her eyes were blurry, and her voice was uncontrollable. "And who were those people? What does that mean, they believed what she believed? What's that supposed to mean?"

"What it means," Nat said gently, "is that she fell in with a group of radicals. They were involved in what they called the Movement. Their idea was to repatriate the southern states and call them New Africa."

"What do you mean?"

"They wanted those states to secede from the Union, and they wanted to give those states to African-Americans whose ancestors had been brought over during slavery."

"I don't know what any of that means," Willa said. She was frustrated at how calm he sounded. She wanted him to get to the point.

"It means she became very politically involved. With this group of people she left me for." He paused. "She left *us* for."

"But she loved you," Willa said. "I know she loved you. And what about *me*?"

"Yes," he said, laying his hand on top of her head before she shook it off. "She loved me. She loved you. But she reminded me that I had always been the one who wanted kids. I was the one who would know what to do as a father." He was careful when he said this, trying to keep the anger from his voice. "*She* needed to change the world."

"But that's crazy," Willa said. "That's crazy, Dad. She really believed that stuff about New Africa? She really thought that was going to happen?"

"She said she did, yes."

"But she wasn't crazy, was she? I know she was hard to get along with, and I know you guys fought, but I didn't think she was—"

"She wasn't crazy," Nat said, resisting the urge to physically comfort her. "She developed firm beliefs. After she died, I—"

"You said she died in a fire," Willa said as she studied Nat's face. "That's true, right? You said that's what happened. You said you guys lived together, but then one night, she was with a group of friends, and the house—"

"I'm getting to that."

"She came back to you, right? You're going to tell me that after she came back to us, she died in the fire?"

Nat sighed. "Your mother died in something like a fire."

"What the hell is that supposed to mean?" The pitch of Willa's voice was rising.

"She died in an explosion."

"An explosion?" Willa pushed Ariel from her lap and leaped up from the car. Her body was one long swerve of kinetic energy. "What are you talking about?" she asked, raising her voice. She was angry, accusatory. "That's not how my mother died," she said. "She died in a fire."

"Listen to me," Nat said, though he made no move to touch her. "Hear me out. I need to finish telling you—"

Willa's hands were over her ears. "No," she said, but she looked at him with hope in her eyes.

"After she left, I looked for her," Nat said, "but the city was too big. I didn't even know where to begin. Besides, when she left, she told me there was no point in my looking. She said she had found her new family. It broke my heart, Willa, but I had to let her go. I knew her. I knew that if I kept looking, even if I found her, it wasn't going to do any good. She wasn't going to come back to me. She didn't want me. She told me, to my face, that she would die if she had to spend even one more day in the house we'd shared. So I let her go, Willa. I let her go."

Willa wasn't moving away, but she wasn't coming back either. Nat decided to keep this part succinct.

"One day she came back. She told me she'd done something terrible. Something terrible for 'the cause.' That's what she called it. She told me she wasn't staying. She had to go to a place they called a safe house. She said she'd be okay there. But she made me promise that if anything ever happened to her, I would find a man named Elliot Barrow and deliver a message for her. I begged her to stay. I begged her to tell me what she'd done. But she left. And she never came back. Three days later, she was killed in an explosion in New Jersey. I read about it in the newspaper. She was staying in a house with six other people, and they were making bombs in the basement. And that's how she died."

"I don't believe you," Willa said through her teeth.

"I know you don't," Nat said, "but I'm telling you the truth. It was time for you to know it. I'm sorry that it is the truth. And I'm sorry you have to know it."

Willa was shaking her head.

"You can ask me anything," Nat said. "You can say anything you want."

Willa seemed beyond words, but she gathered herself enough to ask, on a sharp intake of breath, "What did she do?"

"What do you mean?"

"What was the terrible thing she did? The reason she had to go to the safe house? The place they were making those bombs." Her lower lip quivered.

"She helped kidnap a man. And then the man died."

There was a beat. "You mean she murdered him."

"No one knows, Willa. No one knows what really happened, because most of the people who helped in the kidnapping died when the explosion—"

"I have to be alone," Willa said, gripping her stomach as though she was about to be sick. "I have to take a walk or something." She strode quickly away, up the edge of the bluff, skirting the edge of the Mississippi. He watched her determined walk until she was a small dot in the distance. He did nothing. In the past, he would have followed behind unobtrusively, just to make sure she was all right. But this time he knew she wouldn't fall. She had too many questions to waste them with a fall. She would be back. He was sure of that. He wished he could have told the story more kindly. He wished he could have said, "Your mother was a gentle woman. I'm sure she had nothing to do with that man's death." He wished he could have told Willa all the facts up front. But he wanted more time. Surely, all the truth would come. There were jagged connections and undefined time lines in the story he had cast. Willa was a smart girl. She would begin to unravel the past he'd given her and start to worry at the frayed truth.

AMELIA
Stolen, Oregon ~ Sunday, October 6, 1996

Lydia dropped Amelia off at the end of the driveway. "Sorry," Lydia said as she braked, "I'm not up for the Wrath of Barrow. Good luck." As Amelia blinked her way into the early afternoon, Lydia unrolled the passenger window and called out, "Remember, no matter what happens: it was worth it. Just remember Victor's luscious ass."

Amelia smiled over her shoulder and waved as Lydia pulled a U-ie and headed back toward the highway. The gravel skipped under Amelia's feet as she walked. She hadn't told Lydia everything, just that she and Victor had spoken. These delicious secrets were the kind everyone kept. The sky spilled golden light in shafts, parting the clouds. It was as though the world had decided to open today, bigger, better, brighter, than it ever had before. She shivered, but she was not cold. Her fingers felt electric, as though by touching something, she could infuse it with life. She hugged herself and smiled.

At the house, as she opened the screen door, she heard voices coming around from the side porch, where kids usually sat between classes. But today was Sunday, and the voices were earnest and clear. The voices of adults. She had a choice. She could sneak upstairs and wait for the inevitable or face it right then. And then it was not her choice anymore, because as Amelia stood with her hand on the door handle, Helen's head peeked around the side of the house. Ferdinand appeared right after Helen. He slathered Amelia's hands in giddy kisses.

"Hello! Come join us!" Helen pulled the dog back by the collar and beamed at Amelia. Such jollity had not been heard in this place just about ever. And though Amelia was feeling positively jolly in her deepest self, the sight of her father's ex-wife, the physical proof that Helen existed, triggered Amelia's defensiveness.

"Oh. Hey."

"Your dad's been telling me all about the school and how you helped him build it."

"I didn't help. I was, like, a baby."

Helen came toward her. Amelia's first instinct was to recoil. But she fought it. She simply stood there until Helen's arm was around her shoulder, and then she was being steered around the side of the house, into the shadow of the porch. As they walked, Helen leaned in to whisper, "I've loosened him up for you. I think we can get through this without any yelling." Helen's familiarity was jostling and new.

Elliot was sitting in a rocking chair, a mug of tea in his hand. The autumn air was cool and he was smiling. The word "lounging" occurred to Amelia. He looked the closest she had ever seen him to being perfectly relaxed. He even smiled, the smile of the lazy who don't plan to get up anytime soon.

"Hey," said Amelia.

"I'm going to bring down another pot of tea," said Helen. "Do you want anything else, Elliot?"

"I'm fine, thanks." Helen left. The dog settled down for a snooze. Amelia stood at the edge of the porch, trying to quell the flutter in her stomach, from Victor, from too much beer, and from having to face this strange vision of her father, the way she often dreamed of him being. The way he never was. It was very confusing.

"Listen, Dad, I'm sorry." He had this way of making her apologize when she least expected it.

"I know," he said. "I need to do a better job."

"You do a good job. I shouldn't have spoken to you like that."

He nodded. "I should have gotten on my own that you're growing up. I keep you too close sometimes. I have my reasons. But I know it can't be easy."

Why did Amelia feel as if she was going to cry, as if all the happiness she'd gained in Victor's company was dispersing? She
wanted to hold on to how mature she'd been the night before, like
a real adult. At the moment she felt about nine years old. And more
than a little self-righteous. If only Elliot could have seen his
beloved Ponderosa students getting wasted by the bonfire. "Do you
even begin to get how responsible I am? If I told you the things
people my age are *doing*, you wouldn't believe it."

Elliot's chair made a gnawing sound against the floorboards as
he rocked back and forth. "I'd have you sainted, huh? That's what
you mean?"

Amelia nodded. She didn't want to cry. Already, great hot tears
were spilling from her eyes. She hated crying. She was glad when
Elliot took it from there.

"I propose we start over. We make new rules. I try to trust you
more. I tell you when I am inviting my ex-wives to come live with
us." He smiled. "I'm kidding, Amelia."

"I know," she said reluctantly.

"And you must inform me when my rules are terribly unfair."

"Okay."

"The rules exist because I want you to be safe. I would never
forgive myself if something happened to you. You're all I have,
Amelia. Perhaps that makes me an uncool father."

"No." Though Amelia did not want Elliot to dump this responsibility upon her, it was what he did. He believed, and would
always believe, that she was all he had. She wanted him to have
so much more, and in truth, he did. He did not see any of the rest
of it; all he saw was her. She went to him. She wanted to crawl
on his lap, the way she used to in the ancient days between them,
but she was too big. Too tall. Too heavy. She sat at his feet and
put her head on his lap. She examined the heavy blue of his Sunday jeans, the snags in them, the paint on them, and rubbed the
thick denim between her fingers. It was good to be this close to
him, the way they had been when her only way around had been

in his arms. The chair rocked her back and forth. Her tears seemed to disappear the second her cheek touched his legs. She hugged her arms around his calves. She wished she could hand him her happiness. She wished it could always be like this, and that this would be enough.

He began to sing to her. The simple song she knew in her bones. The song he had always sung to her and had not sung in a long, long time. There were words, and the words mattered, but more than that was the joy she felt as his voice hummed through her body and made her feel small, cared for, at peace.

The gypsy rover came over the hill,
Down through the valley so shady,
He whistled and he sang till the green woods rang
And he won the heart of a lady.
She left her father's castle gate,
She left her own true lover,
She left her servants and her estate
To follow the gypsy rover.

Ah-di-doo ah-di-doo-dah-day
Ah-di-doo ah-di-day-dee
He whistled and he sang till the green woods rang
And he won the heart of the lady.

Her father saddled his fastest steed
And roamed the free lands all over.
He found her at last in a mansion fine
With the whistling gypsy rover.
"He's no gypsy, my father," said she.
"He's lord of the free lands all over.
And I will stay till my dying day
With the whistling gypsy rover."

Helen came back. Amelia could feel her footsteps shimmying through the floorboards. Elliot kept singing. This was the part they

could never remember the words to. Something about marriage.
Something about a feast.

> *. . . down by the River Clady*
> *And there was music and there was wine*
> *For the gypsy and his lady.*

Elliot's voice hummed the rest of the chorus, so that it reverber-
ated through his chest, down into his legs, and into Amelia. She kept
her eyes closed and remembered how this felt, just the two of them.

The song ended. There was a rest in things, and Amelia knew
someone would speak, but she wished they wouldn't. She held her
breath and was surprised when no one spoke at all. She kept this
silence, leaning against her father, feeling his warm hand on the
back of her head. The smell of peppermint wafted up from the
fields near the highway, and she breathed in deeply, savoring its
familiarity.

The sound of a car coming up the driveway was what finally
broke the moment. Amelia was nearly asleep when the purring engine and the crunch of gravel under tires pulled her back into herself. She heard the dog perk up and run to the driveway. She heard
Helen stand—she hadn't heard her sit—and follow. Amelia reluctantly opened her eyes. Elliot rubbed her back for a few moments,
and she broke from him, sitting back, stretching her arms.

"Let's never fight again," he said.

"Yeah, right."

"You're sixteen, Amelia. Last night was an important reminder.
I can vaguely, in the darkest corners of my mind, remember sixteen. I wanted more freedom. So how's this? One night every two
weekends." It wasn't much. But it was something. "Just promise me
you won't drink—you won't drink too much, anyway. And no sex.
Please, no sex."

"Oh God, Dad."

"We don't have to talk about it. Just understand that I'm not old
enough to be a grandfather."

"Please stop."

"Because if you have sex, I'll know. I'll see it on your face."

"I'm going to die." Amelia blushed. Her embarrassment was an odd comfort. As she wished it away, she also wanted it. She wanted him to speak this way to her, to forbid her things, to discipline, to lead her, when she also wanted exactly the opposite. This is what you feel if you are lucky enough to be loved, and in the world between the children and the adults.

Elliot's face lit up as he looked beyond Amelia and greeted someone. She turned to see Victor standing awkwardly beside Helen. Amelia stood—too fast, she realized, as the world spun around her then swerved to a halt. "Hi!" she said loudly, brightly, much too eagerly. She promptly wished she could find a hiding place.

"Come sit, Victor," said Elliot. "What a pleasant surprise! I see you've met Helen. She's going to be directing a production of *The Tempest* this year. Victor is one of our best and brightest. We knew him when he was very small, but then he made the move to Chicago. Come sit, Victor. Tell us about your mother!"

"Hey," said a somewhat overwhelmed-looking Victor, who didn't move an inch. "Actually, I came to see if Amelia's free."

"Oh." Surprise clipped Elliot's voice, but he recovered quickly. "Sure." He smiled broadly, genuinely.

An awkward silence fell over the group. The smell of the peppermint was beginning to make Amelia feel a little sick. She had no idea what to do or say. All the joy she'd felt earlier in the day had blossomed into pure terror. As each second ticked by, she could remember fewer and fewer words. So she could have kissed Helen for speaking next. "What do you two have planned?"

Victor caught Amelia's eye and cleared his throat. "We're on a . . . on a kind of mission, I guess you could say. Looking for something."

"Like a treasure hunt?"

"Yeah, sure. Like a treasure hunt."

"Sounds like fun," Helen said. "I'm sure Amelia will want to freshen up a bit—she just got back from Lydia's—so why don't you do that, Amelia, and in the meantime, Victor can have some tea and tell me all about living in Chicago and what it's been like to move back here." Helen pulled Victor and Elliot into a breezy kind of chitchat as Amelia fled the porch and sought out the cool of the stairwell. The privacy of it.

She remembered as she climbed what she always forgot when she was alone with her father like that: how hard it was afterward, reentering the world, being around anyone else whose company she enjoyed. If she was allied with someone else, it seemed she was Elliot's enemy. She wished she could keep Helen on retainer, for her smooth transitions, for her directorial authority.

SOON AMELIA WAS riding in Victor's Chevy pickup, which was high off the ground and moved fast through the world. It was red and beat up and being in it was like being in a dream. Victor himself was a dream—a white T-shirt, dirty jeans, and a wide smile. If Amelia could have cast this moment in a fantasy, this was exactly how she would have wished it. In that imaginary world, she never knew what Victor would say to her. For that matter, she never knew that she would have anything worthwhile to say to him. But here they were, making fluid conversation about nothing in particular. It was unreal.

"So your dad's not mad?"

"Nah. I mean, he's disappointed. Which is sometimes worse than mad. He doesn't really get mad, actually. Just disapproving."

"Was it okay I came over?"

"Of course!" Again a little too eager. "Tone it down," she told herself, then said, "I mean, it's cool." She added quietly, so that even she had a hard time hearing herself, "I guess I didn't expect to see you."

"What? You serious?"

"I mean, you have so many friends, and . . ." She shrugged.

"You didn't think we had a good talk last night?"

"Oh, sure, *I* did. I just . . . I didn't know if you meant it."

Victor shook his head, matching her seriousness. "I don't break my word. I ask you for your help, I need your help. I believe in keeping a word of honor."

They were driving the back road now, looping around to the other side of the school, and Wiggler's Creek, to the ranch next door. Amelia wanted to ask why exactly it was her help he needed. Yes, she could muster interest and passion about the subject of the disappearing baby, if it meant he wanted her alone. Most of all— even more than finding the baby for Victor—she wanted that moment back: when he told her she was all he remembered about Stolen. It was like wanting back the moment before one flipped a coin. That moment in which everything was possible.

Amelia was realizing what we all realize, that in the seconds when someone reveals that he needs us, we are made vaster, wiser, and more capable than we have ever been. We are altered by that need. Afterward, we are faced with the cruel truth of coming back here, to earth, which makes no mention of our alteration. Victor's mouth had delivered a warm wash of need to Amelia's ears, and twelve hours later, she was already discovering she could relive this conversation only so many times.

She was in trouble. She was ready for more. But she didn't know how to begin. Victor tapped against the glass of his window, pointing into the distance at the stand of alders, ashen-leaved, rattling in the soft breeze, much taller than they had been ten years before. He asked simply, "We found the baby near there, right?"

"Yes," said Amelia. "You're right."

Chapter Two

These days I like to think of the negotiations over the Benson-Ponderosa merger as a string of pitched battles in what would become my private bloodless war with Elliot Barrow. The first skirmish took place on the Monday morning after Helen arrived. I knew Elliot was up to something when he made his appearance in the teachers' lounge. All right, that's unfair. I'm making it sound as if he never came in there, and he came in all the time. Enamored of the brassy shine of academic euphemism, he always referred to it as the Faculty Lounge. It seemed I was the only one who could detect the difference between his purely social visits and the ones where he expected something. He poked his head in the door: "Hello, Doris! Looking forward to sitting in on the frog dissections tomorrow! Ray, Amelia's dreading today's quiz. Make her squirm!" Soon he was tapping my shoulder, drawing me out from behind my carefully erected wall: the *Times* arts section. "Cal, can I have a word? Are you free this period?" He knew I was free.

Assistant Headmaster Calbert Fleecing. Has a lovely ring to it. But I knew it would be a meaningless title unless I supplied the meaning. When Elliot Barrow came to our end of the earth to start a school for our Neige Courante children, everyone here suspected he was running from something. It's amazing how quickly people forget. A rich man decides to spend his inheritance educating your children, and all your questions disappear. I'll be the first to admit that I understood what it felt like to run away. That was one thing we had in common. Perhaps that's why he jumped the moment my name was dangled before him. Given my circumstances at the time, I embodied a strange blend of open hostility and pleased-as-punchness. I'm not saying Elliot didn't have to work hard to nab me. I was not an easy get. But I mean, come on. I had fled the preeminent academic institution on earth with a shroud of shame to show for my time there. I had moved back to a place where I had zero friends and a reluctant family. Something would have to end my misery.

Even before Elliot showed up—and even through my self-hatred, which we can discuss later ad nauseam, if you're really all that interested—I began to notice something. Because of who my father was, and what the people owed him, those same people seemed to want me to lead them a little too. Kind of as a way to pay my father back for what he'd given. This unspoken investment in me was something that followed me down the aisles of the grocery store and came roaring across the prairie. People didn't like me. But that hardly mattered. They liked what I stood for.

For a while I resisted. My moniker for a time was Harvard Graduate Calbert Fleecing. Okay, fine. Not my favorite but fine. And then this: "They loved him so much, they asked him to stay on for graduate school! And Lord knows we don't know how they taught him this, but they taught him poetry. They taught him literature. Law might have been more useful. Medicine. The tribe could have used a proper doctor. But poetry, that's good too, and no one can say anything bad about it, because a literature degree from Harvard must be the best literature degree in the world! You can tell he excelled. Just look at him! All he does all day is sit around and brood! Now, *there's* a writer if we've ever seen one!" What came next was the downward spiral of a young man trying to match wits with a whole nation's set of elderly women.

Me: NONONO. DON'T introduce me like that. STOP mentioning Harvard.

Them: You're ashamed of us? Think the word "Harvard" can't sit easy in our mouths? Too good for us? That what you think?

Me: You keep missing the point. I never got my degree.

Them: He's saying we're stupid!

Me: No. I'm saying I never even got my master's. I'd rather you didn't tell people—

Them: We tell people the truth. You went to college at Harvard.

Me: So tell them that. Don't tell them about the literature. Don't tell them anything beyond college.

Them: If you're so ashamed of literature, we don't know why you studied it in the first place.

Me: I'm not ashamed. I just don't want everyone talking about it.

Them: You're a cocky one! They teach you that at Harvard? Bet so. Thinking everyone's sitting around on their front porches talking about you.

Me: Anyway, it's none of your business.

Them: You must be some kind of genius, think you can talk to us like that. Our Harvard poet. A genius, boy, a genius. Tell you what.

Me: I never said I was a fucking genius! Do you think a genius would come back to the middle of nowhere and sit around with his thumb up his ass day and night?

Them: Well, you said it. Not us.

I learned soon enough that it was useless. They didn't care what had really happened. All they wanted was my brown face with

Harvard attached to it. They wanted me to jog the eleven miles down to the highway wearing a Harvard T-shirt and a pair of shorts with Harvard tattooed across the ass, so all the white folks would see what a real Indian was made of as they came barreling by the reservation. No one wanted me to tell them anything about what Harvard had meant, what I had seen there, why I had come back. No one asked how on earth I could have gotten to a place in my life where I believed this home was the only one I had.

BACK TO MONDAY. I finished reading my article. It described a wildly popular television show about six twentysomething New Yorkers. I took my time refolding the newspaper when I was done. I had never seen this show. I had not been reading the article in the first place. But there was a principle in the matter. I knew I was being watched.

Look, there was no political divide at the academy between Indian and non-Indian teachers. It was much more subtle than that. Most of the teachers were Indian, but there were a few who weren't, and that was no big deal. We hired whoever could do the best job. That was always our policy. But there was also a way in which many of the Native teachers saw me as a gateway to Elliot. If they were having an issue, they came to me first. We discussed it over dinner on the reservation, and the next morning they went to Elliot. Elliot wanted it this way. He knew there were all sorts of things that wouldn't get done if he didn't have someone interpreting the culture for him, and vice versa. Most of the time I was very happy to do it.

Still, it was hard to miss. We could all look around and notice that the preeminent institution educating our brown children was entirely in the hands of a white man. Though Elliot Barrow was, by popular consent, considered to be just, kind, fair, there was no doubt in anyone's mind that he was also white. And he *thought* white. Maw-Maw would have had lots of opinions on this pretender in our midst.

Elliot's office sat at the end of a long hallway in one of the "temporary" buildings that had been standing for nearly ten years. There were four of these buildings in a line, facing west toward the basketball court and, beyond that, the mountains. To the south was the Bugle House, where Amelia and Elliot lived, where math was taught, and where the children ate on winter afternoons. Elliot had built the school like a mini-university, with distinct buildings for distinct centers of thought. This wasn't so unusual for the elementary school, which took up residence in two of the temporary buildings, with some spillover into a couple of classrooms in the third. But the middle- and upper-schoolers were sent all over the place: math up on the hill, science in a squat, fortified structure built almost entirely by Elliot and me that first summer, history sprinkled in classrooms throughout, and English in the gym's outlying rooms. "Ode to a Nightingale" and *The Odyssey* were first experienced by the children of Ponderosa Academy with an underlying percussive beat: basketballs taking the treble line, sneakers squeaking a soprano counterpoint.

This was Elliot's grand vision, the vision with which he'd come west. Sure, the buildings were shabbier than he'd originally envisioned, but he loved the scurrying back and forth these children had to do. He loved the layers that had to be peeled and unpeeled as the children entered and exited the sweltering swamp of winter heating. I thought it was ridiculous. Yes, this was how Harvard was set up, and yes, I had survived it, but the academy was by no means Harvard. I didn't think that was what we were aiming for. It seemed Elliot had different ideas.

After dragging me to his office, he told me about the plan he was hatching with Benson Country Day. The facts of it, at least. He framed it a tad differently than he had with Helen. He painted a rosy picture: what Benson Country Day could do for *us*. For *our* children. World-class arts and music education, an exchange program, a chance to be part of the global community. They had computers. We had computers, but they had computer networks: Internet, intranets, e-mail accounts. Money money money.

At first I was too stunned to say much of anything. Sat there nodding like some kind of idiot. Stared over Elliot's shoulder at Mount Jefferson, tracing its familiar outline against the blue sky. He just kept talking and talking, and I knew him well enough to understand that such an abundance of words was a sign of nervousness. Once I figured this out, I realized how to begin.

I leaned forward in a donated chair. Folded my hands across my knees. "Do you know why," I asked—very calmly, I might add— "not one of my people knows the language our ancestors spoke for millennia? Do you know why we don't even know what the language the Neige Courante spoke sounds like? Do you know why we don't even know what that language was *called*?"

Elliot cleared his voice. I knew he knew why. But I wasn't interested in his know-it-all-ness. Anyway, these were rhetorical questions. I didn't want to hear him telling me to proceed. I proceeded. "Do you know why the language of my people is dead? *Deader than Latin?* Do you know why we have to teach our children a language we made up only a hundred years ago? A language we made up for trading? For trading with the exact people who took away our language?"

I stood up, thrust my hands into my pockets. Elliot didn't try to say anything this time. "They sent my grandparents to boarding school, Elliot. And do you know what they did in those boarding schools? They beat the language out of my grandparents. They beat my six-year-old grandparents whenever they spoke the language of their ancestors. They taught these children English. They taught them about the Christian God. They taught them about this Christian God's particular favorite place to send heathens. And then they sent these children back 'home' to a place we had never been before. They took us, who had rivers in our blood, who were salmon people, and they put us in a place with no river. Then they killed our rivers: they killed the Columbia, they killed the Rogue, and they are still killing our streams and our brooks. They built dams, drowned our waterfalls, and murdered the salmon." I was at the door. I couldn't be near him. "I will fight you so hard on this. You will not believe what has hit you."

"Cal—"

"No," I said, coming back, looming over him. "No. If you are walking away from this school, then just walk away. Don't pussy-foot around it. But if you are leaving, don't you dare sell us up the river in the process. We take care of our own."

Elliot shook his head as though he could not believe my gall. He shuffled the papers on his desk. "You are missing the point."

"Is this why you brought in that Helen lady? So she could start to set your little plan into play? I knew she wasn't just some old lover."

"I don't want to insult you, Cal, but you are missing the point. Helen is here to help us. We are in this together."

That made me laugh, a tight, mocking laugh, from another time in me. I hated that laugh. "And even if I am on your side," I asked, "even if I stop 'missing the point,' how do you expect all the people who've put so much time and energy into this school to believe that you aren't sending their children to a similar fate as that of their grandparents?"

"You'll tell them."

"I'll what?"

"You'll tell them," he said.

Which was when I got out of there.

HELEN
Stolen, Oregon ~ Wednesday, October 9, 1996

Me again. Cal, that is. More to say, I'm afraid. Cutting into Helen's version of events. Hear me out. You'll understand soon enough why I need to be the one to tell you that I was not "available" for a meeting until Wednesday. Read: I did not want to see Helen at all, but she got to the school secretary, who also happens to be my second cousin Eunice, before I could fully impart to Eunice that I would not, under any circumstances, meet with That Woman. When Eunice informed me that she had penciled Helen in for Monday afternoon, I knew right away that the best I could do was postpone. Eunice was easy to read, especially when she liked someone. She and Helen had probably compared shampoo brands, or complained about lines in ladies' rooms, or discussed one of those universal topics that make women feel closer without having talked about anything particularly worthwhile. I knew, the moment Eunice stared me down, that a meeting would be inevitable.

I thought the two-day postponement might prove an effective intimidation tactic; Helen seemed to thrive on it. She was beginning to feel at home. Ferdinand was joyful, roaming the land, hunting, exhausting himself independently, and if Helen doubted for a moment whether she had made the right choice in coming west, her beloved dog was a reminder that there were possibilities in rural Oregon that even New York City couldn't provide. Amelia and she were forging a kind of friendship. Elliot had quickly turned stalwart. He was Protestant as ever, and Helen doubted they would again speak as warmly, as intimately, as they had on that first Sunday. The fact that they'd had the conversation at all was enough for her. He had let her know he needed her. It was good to be needed. She'd felt more needed in the past four days than she had in her last twelve years of life with Duncan. Though she never would have breathed a word to Elliot, Helen was even beginning to like her little house on the prairie, the quiet of it, the smallness of it, the way it wrapped around her like a shawl. Duncan was miles, decades, away.

Helen breezed into my office with a smile on her face. I had avoided her on campus, which was hard to do, because she and her dog seemed to be everywhere. Even the Neige Courante women glared at me in the hallways. Gossip spreads fast here, and those lady teachers had surely heard about my desertion of Helen over the weekend. Apparently, gender trumps race where sympathy is concerned.

I opened my mouth to talk, but her words came first. "Look, Cal, I know you aren't particularly thrilled about my being here. I know Elliot spoke to you about his plans with Benson Country Day, and I want to make it perfectly clear that I have no opinion about that at all, that I didn't even know about it until I got out here. So I want to get that on the table. Whatever is going on between you and Elliot is just that, between you and Elliot. I would like not to get involved. I would like for you to think of me, if you can, as independent of all that. I would like for you to think of me as someone here on a project, someone who has been hired to do a job. Someone who wants to do that job right." She pressed her hands in her lap and smiled. She hoped she had gotten her points across eloquently and kindly. She hoped she would not have to get clearer than that.

"Why are you here?" I asked.

"I just told you," she said, her smile faltering. "I'm here to do a job."

"And just what exactly is that job?"

"To direct a production of *The Tempest*. With the children."

"Why?"

"Because Elliot asked me to. Really, I don't see—"

"Surely you can see that if your reason for doing something is 'Elliot asked me to,' it is difficult for me to keep what's between Elliot and me separate from what is between the two of us. I would like to keep it separate, but I don't know if that's possible."

"You don't?" She nodded at me, biting the inside of her lip. I thought she was backing down. I was wrong. "We have a misunderstanding," she said, "and the misunderstanding is this. You think that because I have slept with Elliot, because I have been his wife, that somehow I am on 'his side.' Let me assure you that his side is not one I was on even twenty years ago. Contrary to appearances, I am not the kind to take sides. I am my own woman, Cal. I am here to do a job. Elliot is an old friend, and he is the headmaster of this school. He asked me to help him. But"—she laughed, surprising me—"it is certainly not my intention to turn *The Tempest* into a piece of Elliot-slanted propaganda. I promise you that."

Her laughter threw me off. It somehow made things more serious. I blundered on. "The kids are going to hate this. Trust me. I'm the head of the English department. We read *Twelfth Night* in ninth grade, *Romeo and Juliet* in eleventh, and the seniors tackle *King Lear.* You've never tried to get teenagers to read Shakespeare, have you? This isn't New York, Helen." I dug in to the condescending tone. "Acting isn't 'cool' here. Basketball is cool. These kids . . ." I smiled at her dismissively.

"Amelia has already signed on," she said. "I think that's great. I think she'll bring her friends."

I knew right then that I'd be right. The brutal truth was that with the exception of Lydia (who wouldn't be caught dead in a Shakespeare play), my poor goddaughter, Amelia, was friendless. I would let Helen sink on her own terms. "You want to tackle this, it's your thing, okay? I don't want to hear about it. And we don't have a budget for any kind of production—"

"Look, it's great by me if you want to be this hands-off." She was already standing. Why did she make me feel as if I was losing?

"I plan to check in on you." It was feeble, and I knew it.

Helen turned and smiled, and her look made me feel small. "You do that," she said ever so sweetly. "I really hope to see you at a rehearsal or two." Then she was gone. In the moments after she left, before I grudgingly set to grading papers, I sat at my desk and tried to take comfort in the vision of a lone Amelia Barrow showing up for Helen's first session. Meanwhile, out in the hallway, Helen leaned against my door. She tried to calm herself. Her eyes were stinging with self-righteousness. She dropped her smile. She unclenched her fists. She didn't know why winning was so important. She didn't know why proving herself to me mattered so much.

Chapter Three

CAL

Stolen, Oregon ~ Friday, October 11, 1996

*M*y meetings with Helen and Elliot had not gone well. I suppose I could have just called up Benson Country Day and screamed like a maniac at the headmaster's administrative assistant, threatening medicine circles and rain dances, but that would have put them off only for a while. I figured the best way to proceed was to gather evidence, subtly, carefully, cheerfully, and do my best to sublimate my hostility. So I cornered Amelia after class that Friday afternoon. At its best, it was a halfhearted gesture. I had no idea our short conversation would be half as fruitful as it was.

She was already in the hallway by the time I extracted myself from behind the desk. Yes, I sat behind my desk sometimes, and no, I know that isn't "progressive," but sometimes a teacher is tired. Sometimes we don't feel like perching on the edge of our desks, texts splayed open in our palms, tweed jackets slung over our shoulders. When I got to her, Amelia was standing in front of her open locker, removing two bulky plastic bags, her jacket, her back-pack, her lunch bag.

"You have a minute?"

She glanced at her watch and tilted her head apologetically to the side. "You feel like walking with me?"

"Sure, sure," I said, doing my own calculations. Elliot would be safely ensconced in his office by now, nowhere near the main house. "Let me grab my bag."

We met outside. It was a gorgeous fall day. We'd had a fine rain the night before—unusually blustery, presaging winter—and it had made the earth soft and spongy. It brought the smell of the high desert up from ground level and into our chests: pine, sagebrush, the sweet tangle of juniper where it hits you at the back of the throat. I relieved Amelia of one of her bags.

"So what's up?" She led the way, cutting a path away from the building.

"We haven't had a chance to catch up, have we? Since you've been back."

"No, I guess we haven't," Amelia said, looking at me funny. "If this is about that Pearl Poet paper, look, I'm okay with the B-plus. I'm not interested in rewriting it."

I laughed. "No, it's not about the paper."

"Oh. You just kept reiterating that in class today, and I think your idea of rewriting is theoretically a good one. But I only think it'd be worth all that work if I'd gotten less than a B."

"Good thinking," I said rather absently. I realized we weren't walking in the direction of the house. We were walking away from campus, into the wilderness. But I had her bag and I wanted to keep her talking, so I didn't mention it. "Any wild plans for Columbus Day weekend?" (Look, I know it's not politically correct, but the truth of it is, we at Ponderosa Academy like having days off. Even if it's because of a genocidal maniac and the race that followed him into these United States. We take every holiday off we can, thanks to my early suggestions. Columbus Day. Martin Luther King, Jr., Day. If Flag Day fell during the school year, we'd take it off too. Hell, we'd take off Simchat Torah if it were up to me.) Amelia's answer was an eye roll, so I changed the subject. "How was Benson Country Day?"

She shrugged. "Fine. Good. Just wasn't for me, I guess."

"How so?"

"For one, you have to wear a uniform. Which is about the dumbest thing ever. I mean, I guess I know why they do it, so that there's this equality and everything. But there's never equality, because somebody has really expensive shoes, or someone else has diamond earrings. Anyway, everyone knows who's on scholarship and who isn't."

"You weren't the only one boarding there, right?"

"It's a day school with some boarders. I think they want to expand that, though." She gave me a sidelong glance. "Awfully interested in my education, aren't you? You just now deciding to take your duties as a godfather seriously?"

I lied. "I read an article about Benson. I'm just interested to see if they're living up to their promise."

"It's nothing like this, if that's what you're asking." She gestured around us. "They have landscapers. They have actual staff members, not just volunteers. They have *money*. But. You know. I think the kids also miss out a little."

"Oh? Like how?"

Amelia sized me up, smiled, looked at me warmly. And then she opened up. "Like there was this one teacher? Really popular with the kids. Really nice, accessible. *Too* accessible, turns out." Amelia shot me a knowing look. I got the significance.

"You're kidding," I said.

"No," Amelia said. She shrugged. "There were no consequences. The school sided with him. Protected him. Just sent him to another school." She shook her head, laughed. "I mean, you and my dad would have *killed* the guy." She stopped in her tracks, concern flooding her face. "Oh, shit. Cal. You've got to promise me you won't tell Elliot any of this, okay? He doesn't know—and I don't—oh shit . . ." She pleaded with her eyes. "Can you keep that a secret? Please?"

Should have been a moment of crisis. Should have presented me with a conflict between my loyalties as standard-bearing teacher vs. godfather. Not to mention that this just might be the thing to nip

Benson in the bud. Most important to me was the little thrill I felt at having been Amelia's confidant in a secret she was withholding from her father. She trusted me; she *entrusted* me with a secret. She didn't want to talk about it anymore, and she wanted me to agree not to notice.

"Anyway, we're here," she said.

We were cresting a hill and looking down at the old shed Elliot had been working on with some of the kids. It dawned on me who was staying there, and by then it was too late. The door opened and Ferdinand bounded up to us as Helen waved from the doorway. "Hey!" Amelia's hands were too full for me to shove the bag back in them. And if I had gone that direction, my next step would have been to turn tail and run. I wanted Helen to think I had more dignity than that.

"Hey!" called Amelia, her voice full of light. She tore down the hill and left me alone to fend off the stupid dog. By the time I got to the shack or shed or whatever it was, Amelia was inside and Helen was leaning against the door frame. I didn't like her watching me.

"How kind of you," she said, her voice twinkling. She called her dog to her, but he just kept slobbering on my hand. I tried hard not to feel mocked.

"Yeah," I said lamely.

She reached out her hands and took the bag, peering inside. "Oooh, clean towels. Amelia, you shouldn't have!"

"I thought you could replenish your stash at the gym." Amelia was huddled over Helen's bunk, stripping the bed. My eyes adjusted to the darkness inside. The dog wouldn't leave me alone, so I crossed my arms as I sized up Helen's new home. The space was small, but there were already pictures on the walls, an oilcloth on the desk that doubled as a table, flowers in a mason jar. The place looked positively pastoral.

"Amelia's been taking good care of me." Helen turned to me conspiratorially, the way adults do when they are speaking fondly of children or the elderly. "She keeps all my affairs in order. I don't know what I would do without her."

"You know, it's going to get cold in here." I couldn't help it. All I wanted to say were mean things.

Helen didn't blink an eye. "That's been a concern of mine too. But Elliot insists we'll figure it out. I have more comforters than I know what to do with. And the woodstove."

I grunted.

"I've made us tea." Helen moved into the kitchen area, which was about three steps from where we stood.

"You know," said Amelia, "people lived like this not too long ago, Cal. Like, half a century. And they didn't have woodstoves to keep them warm, or water purifiers, or hot showers to go to."

I grunted again.

"Here we are," said Helen in a chipper voice. She handed me a cup of foul-smelling boiling water.

"And they didn't have gas stoves to heat their water!" continued Amelia.

"So." Helen sat on the newly smoothed bunk and handed Amelia her cup of tea. They sat side by side, and I was forced into the chair. Ferdinand lay down on my feet, trapping me in the most uncomfortable seat I have ever occupied.

"Do you want some?" asked Amelia. "I feel bad. We took both your mugs."

"I've been drinking tea all day," said Helen, picking a piece of lint off Amelia's jeans.

"Hey, do we have to read all of *Midsummer Night's Dream* for Wednesday, or will we only be discussing Act One?"

"I'd like it if you could read the whole thing." Helen looked warily in my direction as she answered Amelia.

Amelia was the one I addressed. "You're adding Shakespeare to your busy schedule?"

Amelia shrugged. "Why wouldn't I take a Shakespeare class with one of the preeminent Shakespeare experts of our time?"

I tried to drink the tea. Everyone was being so *nice*. I added, midsip, midgag, "I didn't know there was going to be a class. In addition to the play."

"It's not *poison*," Helen said. "The Bard will not *kill* people when measured out in large doses." I could tell I'd gotten to her. Amelia was lost. But then Helen regained herself and was stronger than ever: "Look." The whole building seemed to stand at attention around us—the furniture, the windows, the ceiling. Her voice implied a frankness I thought I'd welcome. "I know you're upset about the whole Benson thing."

"What whole Benson thing?" Amelia eyed me suspiciously.

Helen didn't answer. She kept talking to me. "I would like for us to be friends, Cal. We got off on the wrong foot. But you've got to see things from my perspective, don't you? Just dropped here, with no idea what to expect. I feel I've walked into a lion's den. But I have a job to do."

"*What* whole Benson thing?" Amelia repeated.

I coughed and looked into my tea as though it were the most interesting thing in the world. Helen answered for me. "An exchange program your dad wants to set up."

"Oh my God." Amelia set her mug on the floor, then stood, nearly bumping her head on the slanted ceiling. "Oh my *God*." She looked very fierce. I could see her mind putting together our conversation. "You were trying to get information out of me?" She shot me a look of pure alarm, utter disappointment. "I can't believe I trusted you. Cal, you promised. You better keep what I told you to yourself." She looked righteous. Just like Elliot. "Promise me, Cal. On everything you hold dear."

"I promise," I said, trying not to smile at her solemnity.

I doubt she heard me. She careened out of the house, and because there was nothing reasonable to slam—the ancient wood slab set on rusty hinges would have broken the house down around us—and because there was wilderness around us, a few moments later, it seemed she had never been there in the first place.

"Hmm." I looked down into my mug again and swirled the sodden leaves back and forth. "That didn't go very well, did it?"

"No," Helen said. The amusement in her voice made me look up. She was smiling.

"What?"

"I'm glad to see I'm not the only one locked in a little war with you. Makes me feel better about myself. Makes me recognize my actual odds of mending things between us."

I'll tell you the truth right here. It made me smile to hear her say that. It was as if I were King Tut and she cut through all my mummy bandages and found my tiny, ossified carcass inside. It was as if she understood that carcass, as if she weren't disgusted by it at all, by its smell or look or its ugliness. It was familiar to her. There was something funny there, something strange and good about her trust in me, about her willingness to be amused by my arrogance and anger, and it made me laugh. I sat in her tiny shack and laughed my ass off until my stomach hurt so bad I swore I'd never laugh again.

AMELIA
Stolen, Oregon ~ Friday, October 11, 1996

Elliot's office door was flung open with such speed and force that he didn't have a moment to protest before his daughter was looming over him, fierce and angry. "When were you planning on mentioning your plans with Benson Country Day?" She could be so tall when she wanted to be.

"Now, Amelia—"

"Don't 'Amelia' me, *Elliot*." Her voice was full of mocking. "You can't keep things from me. This place is too small. I hear about them. Don't you get it yet? Your ex-wife shows up, I'm going to find out she's your ex-wife. You send me to a boarding school—a boarding school that I wanted to leave, so it should have been easy for you to tell the place was bad—and now you've decided to set up an exchange program with it? Guess what? I'm going. To hear. About it."

"Sweetheart, you never said you hated it there."

"You're not an idiot, Dad. And you're so proud of being the perfect father. Well, that's not possible, because if you knew me at all, if you really knew me, you'd know that I left Benson for a good reason. And hatred was part of it. I mean, if I'm going to be your live-in educational experiment, at least you should pay attention to how the experiment's going. You should *learn* from it."

"You're not being fair. I've never, ever viewed you as an experiment."

"C'mon, Dad. You're an educator! You mean to say you never once tried something out on me—the violin, for instance—to see whether it would work?" Amelia paused, but her anger filled the pause so fully that Elliot did not speak. "That's not even the important part. Benson Country Day. Don't you care why I left that place?"

Elliot's voice became infused with concern. Graveness. "Amelia, is there something you're not telling me? Did something happen to you there?"

Amelia held her angry silence, a burning coal in her chest.

Elliot went on, suddenly gentle. "Honey, I don't want you to keep things from me. Let's face it. If we're going to move forward together, beyond this, we have to tell each other things. We have to trust each other to understand the truth."

Amelia could feel the nastiness glinting in her voice. "Like you trusted me with the truth about Helen, right? That would be the kind of honesty we need?"

"Sweetheart, all I can do is apologize. I just need you to tell me the truth."

"Truth? You want the truth?" Amelia felt a power rising inside her. "Well, how's this? I wanted to go to Benson to get away from"—she waved her hands in the air—"*this!*" A pure rage sculpted each syllable. "Don't get me wrong, Elliot. I mean *you*. I mean this school." She laughed bitterly. "I'm getting the picture. I bet I was accepted at Benson because of your little scheme, wasn't I? I bet you wanted this exchange and used me to sweeten the deal." She shook her head. "So here's the truth. I wanted to go not just because of a chance to play the violin; I wanted to go because I can't breathe here. In your experiment, day in, day out. I'm suffocating. We're all suffocating." She felt her father's vulnerability and dug in. "Have you ever considered the fact that if your grand vision for Ponderosa Academy accomplishes what it's supposed to accomplish, everyone will leave this place? We'll all go away to college, Dad, and we won't come back. The Neige Courante kids will move off the reservation and see a different life out there, and they won't come back here to do anything. They won't want the lives their parents have. I'll let you in on a secret: *I* don't want it. I know that already. I don't want this stupid school and your narcissism and your myths about how brilliant you are and how many lives you save on a daily basis."

That was when Elliot's temper broke. That was when he did exactly the wrong thing. He stood still, fists clenched at his sides; he raised his voice, boomed forth: "I am your father! I will not allow this rudeness. Don't you ever, *ever* speak to me this way again."

Amelia let her visible anger dissipate before she spoke. When she did, her voice was calm and even. Low. Calculating. "Something pretty fucked up happened at that school. But you're right, Dad. It's better for me to keep my thoughts to myself. You're my father. You know what's best." Amelia turned and left his office. She was mighty. She was victorious.

Chapter Four

Willa wanted to drive. She needed distraction. She needed to live in a trance. When she reemerged forty-five minutes after leaving Nat alone at the car, she held out her hand. "Can I have the keys?" He wasn't about to deny her a thing.

The land flattened. As they plowed through Missouri and into Kansas, she could see farther and farther into the distance. She fixed her eyes on the highway unspooling into the horizon. The sky was blue and enormous. Dirty snow lurked in the fields on either side of the road.

To Nat's credit, he didn't try to fix anything with words. He didn't speak much at all. Which was the right thing. Willa was angry and confused. But she also felt an odd sense of relief, as if her whole life up until this moment had been lived underwater. Finally, she got to know the way the earth scratched under everyone else's feet. She didn't want her father's words to distract her from feeling this, whatever it was named: this sickness at the bottom of her stomach, this chill up her spine, this humming in the cavern of her head. All she wanted was to look at the world and drive into it.

When they got to Salina, Kansas, Willa didn't want to leave the car, even though the night was long dark and she was exhausted.

They had stopped twice since the Mississippi, and both times were only because they needed fuel. The first time Nat brought her a sandwich and a Coke. The second time he made her get out and go to the bathroom. She loved the car more and more with each passing mile. She loved knowing its established perimeters: that the snacks were in the canvas bag wedged behind the passenger seat, that Ariel's favorite spot when she awoke was the sunny armrest between the two front seats, that the old Volvo whined when Willa tried to push it above seventy. The dimensions of the car were Willa's armor. Outside, the world slipped silently by.

HELEN

Stolen, Oregon ~ Wednesday, October 16, 1996

In the girls' locker room, Helen conveyed her shoulders into the stream of hot—nearly scalding—water. She was trying to warm up. Bed was plenty toasty, what with the dog and the comforters and the hot-water bottle and the wool cap Amelia had knit, but by morning the woodstove was ice-cold, so getting out of bed was torture. Even Ferdinand groaned when his feet hit the floor. It didn't matter how many layers of wool socks Helen had on. Her travel alarm went off and she spent a good fifteen minutes wrestling with the terrible reality of having to get out of bed.

That was the worst of it, though. All the other things about the cabin that she had feared had, in fact, been okay (so far, knock on wood). It was not so terrible to be without a telephone. It was not so terrible to own one plate and one set of utensils and cook yourself easy things that a girl who wanted to please you delivered to your door. Eating an apple, because it was so hard to get, was like devouring manna from heaven. And showering? Showering was ecstasy. The steam, the splatter sound of the water, the heat on her back, not to mention the briskness of the early-morning walk from the cabin to the gym where the showers lay, all made her feel so much more *in* herself than she had been her whole adulthood. And the bathroom part of things, which she had been most worried about, was not all that bad. She timed her visits so that only her before-bed pee took her into the outhouse; all other bathroom time was spent with a real toilet up on campus. She knew it was going to get colder and harder. Something would break. But there was an element of fondness in this challenge.

Light curled against the steam. Helen closed her eyes and pulled back into the water. She was scared. Today was the day she was meeting with the children. Today she was starting them on Shakespeare. She had spent so much energy defending her project to Cal, discussing the importance of her project with Elliot, advertising her project to the children, that she hadn't had any time to think about what her project actually *was*. She hated imagining how she would sound outside her head, talking about Shakespeare as though he could save the world. She felt Elliot moving through her when she believed in something with this much conviction: Elliot too was all big thought and salvation and hero worship, but where Helen's heroes were the old masters of drama and literature, his heroes were political: Martin Luther King, Jr., Gandhi, Dorothy Day. She corrected herself: those *had* been his heroes. She didn't know what he believed in these days.

Shakespeare made her think of Duncan. And that was where her heart sank, because she had done a good job these last couple of weeks pretending that she was not married, that she had not discovered her husband in the act of cheating, that the matter of the house wouldn't have to be dealt with, nor that of the theater. She had not thought about how her life was being divided, parceled out. Her real life was a mess—the life away from this Elliot Barrow fantasy camp. It was so nice not to feel that her life was a mess. She promised herself that she'd make a phone call or two this evening, if Elliot and Amelia didn't mind.

WHERE TO BEGIN? What do you say to a group of twenty-two adolescents—fifteen of them lanky boys, seven of them beautiful, big-eyed girls—who are blinking back at you during their lunch period, when it's obvious they'd much rather be playing basketball or flirting on the sidelines? Do you ask them why on earth they gave up their precious lunch period for *this*? Do you tell them you have never known children, never liked them much, never really worked with them? Helen knew teenagers were like dogs: they could smell fear. So she smiled broadly at them, taking comfort in Amelia and Lydia, and greeted the group.

She had suggested, in the apparently successful pitches she'd made to each English class the previous week, that anyone interested in joining her group of actors should read *A Midsummer Night's Dream. The Norton Shakespeare* was a required book for anyone entering the ninth grade at the academy—one of my lovely jobs was cold-calling New York publishing houses and strongly proposing that they donate boxes of books to us brown people out west—so she knew these kids would have the play in their possession, along with all the sonnets, and every one of the tragedies, comedies, and histories. What Helen hadn't expected was this many people. She hadn't expected the few who did come to have read the play. So she was surprised when one of the tall boys who looked like he'd been made for running like lightning across a gym floor raised his hand and asked, "Mrs. Barrow, is it okay if we were only able to read Act One?"

"Oh," she said quickly, "I'm not Mrs. Barrow."

"But aren't you married to Mr.—"

"I used to be"—she smiled tolerantly—"but that was a long time ago. Call me Helen, please." She glanced at Amelia, who, in turn, glared at Lydia. Lydia shrugged. Helen tried to remember that she was the one in control. "Let's start by saying what brings us here. I'm pleased to see so many of you. Feel free to eat." Some of the kids unwrapped sandwiches. Addressing the tall boy who had spoken, Helen said, "Why don't we start with you?"

"Oh." He looked down at his long white sneakers and managed to mumble, "Victor said I should come."

"What's your name?"

"Caleb." He looked terrified.

"Okay." She smiled. "Well, I'm glad Victor encouraged you to join us." She nodded at the boy sitting next to Caleb in the semicircle. "And you?"

"Victor," he said.

"Your name's Victor too?"

"No, man." He laughed. "I'm Jesse. Victor said I should come." He already had the laugh of a middle-aged man, jolly, belly-deep. He had cracked himself up. "I mean, I like old dead English guys as much as the next person, but . . ." He wheezed himself into another fit of laughter.

Helen adjusted herself in her seat. She scanned the faces before her. Victor was sitting in the middle of the semicircle, leaning back in his chair. Laughter seemed the furthest thing from his mind. Helen asked, "How many of you are here because Victor asked you to come?"

All but Victor, Amelia, and Lydia's hands were raised. Fourteen strong boy arms. Five girl wrists, swaddled in bracelets and perfume. Helen nodded. "Well, Victor, thanks for spreading the word." She knew her voice sounded threatened, but she couldn't help it. This was all so . . . odd. The sole explanation seemed to be that she was being mocked. She scrutinized Victor's face, looking for a break in it, for an indication that he was making fun of her silly little project. She couldn't help herself. She asked Victor, "And what brings *you* here today?"

"I'm here because Amelia invited me."

A chorus of "ooooooooh" flared up through the arc of chairs, rippling through the bodies of the boys like a wave, followed by a round of air kissing. Amelia blushed and looked at the floor, but Victor hardly batted an eyelash. His silence had a power all its own; as soon as the boys noted his steadfast stature, they quieted down and recomposed themselves. The girls tossed jealous glances in Amelia's direction.

Lydia's hand shot up. Helen nodded. Lydia's face was painted with genuine surprise as she said, "Well, then, I guess I really *am* the only one who doesn't want to be here. No offense, Helen, but I'm here because Amelia *made* me." Amelia looked like she might die of embarrassment. Her glance had not moved from the wood floor.

"Thanks for your input," Helen said. "And I think that's a good place for us to begin: anyone who doesn't want to be here doesn't have to be. You're free to go. Because I will say this: if you decide to stay, this is not going to be easy." She made eye contact with each person as she spoke. She wanted everyone to know she was taking this extremely seriously. "I will expect you to do homework just as you would in any other class. For now we will meet twice a week, on Mondays and Wednesdays, during lunch. I will expect you to attend our sessions regularly. Skipping will not be tolerated. Neither will lateness.

"That said, I know this will be a lot of fun. We're going to start small, doing scenework, reading plays, discussing them, playing some drama games, learning about projecting and being onstage, and then we're going to begin work on *The Tempest*, the last play Shakespeare ever wrote. We'll build the sets, make the costumes, learn the lines. As we go along, the time commitment will increase, maybe extending to five afternoons a week, and beyond lunch period, to after school. We will perform *The Tempest* this spring, in front of your teachers, classmates, and families." She noticed more than a few nervous glances passing down the chain of listeners, but she didn't want to spare them. This was going to be a lot of work. They needed to know what they were in for.

"Shakespeare—" She sighed. She wanted to hook them. She wanted them to get it. She leaned forward in her chair, breaking her teacherly stance for the first time. "Shakespeare saved my life. Jesse, is it? You called him an old dead English guy, and he certainly is that. But he's not just difficult language, and he's not just elaborate plots that could never really happen. He doesn't live in my brain. He's not a man of ideas. He's a man of feelings. I *love* him be-

cause when I am sad or lonely, or feeling brave or scared, I can always find a character or a play that will talk to me about what I'm
feeling, that will help me do a better job with my place in the
world. That may sound silly to you, but I bet if you stick with this
project, really make a commitment to be a part of it, you'll begin
to see things from my point of view."

Lydia raised her hand again. It hung eagerly in the air until
Helen nodded in her direction. "Have you worked with people
our age before?"

"Well, I've worked with young actors, if that's what you mean."

"Yeah, but those kids were professionals in New York, right?
And most of your experience is with adults."

"I'm not sure what you're getting at."

"I mean, why do you think we'll be good at this? Shakespeare
is like really, *really* hard. I have no idea what he's talking about most
of the time." Some of the boys nodded. "I'm just saying, I think this
project is kind of ambitious. And when in the spring? 'The spring'
is so general, and if we have to build the sets and make the costumes . . . And what if none of us are *good*? Even if we wake up
one morning and magically understand everything Shakespeare
ever wrote, that won't make us good actors. Most of us have never
even seen a play before."

Helen let Lydia wind herself down. The kids were slumping in
their seats. Amelia was staring fixedly at the floor. Victor was looking straight into Helen, and she felt as though she were speaking
for his benefit when she said, "You can do anything you set your
mind to unless someone tells you you can't."

"But—"

"I don't have the answers, Lydia," Helen said sharply, back in
control. She felt herself shifting into second gear, a clutch of ambition propelling authority into her voice. "I don't have any answers.
If you're afraid of doing this, and you think that fear will keep you
from trying, then by all means, please leave. Those of us who are
here want to be here. We want to try."

And so Lydia was silenced. Books were opened. Act One was tackled. Amelia regained her color, and it seemed, in the twenty minutes before afternoon classes began, as if everyone might actually be having a good time.

CAL
Stolen, Oregon ~ Saturday, October 26, 1996

The second skirmish in the Fleecing-Barrow standoff took place at the first board meeting of the year. We're talking the end of October. It always took us awhile to get our acts together and schedule something. The board was composed of twelve people, including Elliot and me, and Elliot was the one white face in the bunch. Besides the two of us, there were five men and five women. They ran the tribe: they were consulted by the Forest Service on land matters, they held places of honor at powwows and tribal ceremonies. They were all over the age of fifty. They were all related. They were all related to me.

I knew going in that my opinion would be unpopular, if only because my way wasn't as showy as my antagonist's. Elliot had placed twelve crisp collated and stapled packets on the "conference table." We met in the gym, so the conference table consisted of two of those awful institutional tables that are supposed to be portable but end up propped in hallways for years on end because they're too heavy to drag in and out of the damn storage closet. I was late. Eunice was the only nonboard person in the room—she kept the minutes—and outside of this room, she agreed with me only occasionally. One glance at her as I tiptoed into the already-in-progress meeting, and I knew she was not going to take my side.

I let Elliot do his talking. He laid it all out before them, and even I felt myself a little seduced by how he pitched it: "The Benson Country Day Conservatory for the Arts is a world-class institution. What they are offering is nothing short of a miracle. As we've discussed ad nauseam in previous meetings, the private money we be-

lieved would be in place by now to keep Ponderosa Academy
afloat has simply not materialized. It has been my great pleasure to
use my inheritance to get this institution off the ground, and you
all know that a considerable part of my duties as headmaster are
taken up with fund-raising. We are technically a private school that
does not charge its students any tuition. So even with considerable
private funding, we are in the constant, precarious position of losing money.

"Benson Country Day wants to help us. They know we are a
vital institution in this area, providing an essential resource to
Neige Courante children, and they do not want to change that. Let
me make this abundantly clear: their offer would in no way hurt
the education of Ponderosa Academy's Neige Courante. On the
contrary, Benson's proposal would accomplish for our children
something Ponderosa isn't able to attain on its own: an expansion
of space, an improvement of philosophy, an enlargement of resources for all Neige Courante students. It goes without saying that
the contribution our children would make to Benson's community
is inestimable. I'm talking about what Benson would give our children in return. Our children would spend time at Benson, living in
Portland and utilizing Benson's world-class facilities: science labs,
the World Wide Web, exposure to a larger world. In exchange,
Benson students would come here, expanding our cultural understanding—they have a very diverse student body—"

"How many Indians go to Benson?" I guess I'd decided it was
my turn to talk.

"Well, um, I don't have that information in front of me, Cal. But
I do know there are Vietnamese, Japanese, Chinese, Korean, not to
mention African-American—"

"They haven't exactly shown much interest in Indians until
now, right?" I was getting a whole room's worth of dirty looks.

Elliot glanced back down at the packet balanced in his hands. "If
everyone doesn't mind, I think I'd like to get back to the proposal
before opening up the room to questions."

"Actually, I do mind," I said, which was met with groans.

Sandra Courrament tried to shut me up. "Let him finish, son."

I hate that. I hate being called "son." I leaned back in my chair and waved my hand to let him talk. I'd get my turn. He droned on about financial matters and dichotomies of self and tribal empowerment and and and. Then they all applauded, which I should have expected. It made me angry to see them lined up like ducks in a row, beaming up at him adoringly.

I raised my hand. I mentioned the boarding schools our ancestors had been sent to. I drew brilliant comparisons between that "good" idea and this one, both introduced by white men, both in the interest of brown people who weren't wise enough to stand up for themselves or to look ahead to the future. Nearly everyone was tsking and booing, but I kept talking because I was angry and because they refused to listen. And when I was done, there was silence. We sat in silence. Then, slowly, as if he were tapping energy from the rest of the elders, the oldest Neige Courante in the room, and quite possibly the world, straightened in his chair as everyone swooned in his direction. His name was Robert Terrebonne. I have no idea how old he really was. All I know is that his skin was leathery and his eyes rheumy, and that he was already a man when my father was born. His role in meetings such as this was usually limited to nodding occasionally. But today his reedy violin of a voice had a lot to say.

"We're not idiots, son. Some of us lived through that very bad time. You did not. You forget that. Those schools were bad. We were beaten there. Our language? Taken from us. Our land? Taken from us. Elliot's plan and that plan are different. We're living in the twentieth century. Our children need to be"—he paused, savoring the next word—"globalized. They need to see something out in the world besides the Neige Courante Way."

"At the expense of losing the Neige Courante Way?"

"What makes you think we would lose it?" Sandra was glaring at me, and her fingers were white where they gripped the tabletop.

"You don't have much faith in this school, in our leadership, if you think a trip to Portland will take our children away from the Neige Courante way of life."

"Trust me," I said. "The kids at Benson are undoubtedly spoiled rich brats. We can check that out with Amelia Barrow if we need confirmation. It's not hard to guess that they're children of privilege. Their parents have sent them to a so-called world-class institution—something I know about—one of those places full of all those amenities about which Elliot just spoke so glowingly. And you'd better believe that one of the primary reasons Benson is so hungry to get their hands on our kids is that brown-skinned children bring dollars to private institutions. The place will be eligible for lots of grants and will be awarded all sorts of money, all sorts of recognition, for being so devoted to our 'charity cases.' I'm sure it doesn't hurt that we've got some prime land here—well, *Elliot's* got some prime land here—ripe for development. It's no secret that the land east of the mountains has risen in value in the last ten years. And let me remind you folks, Elliot owns this land. Not us. Not the Neige Courante. Will Benson buy it? If they do, I'll bet you anything—"

"Don't embarrass yourself, son." Robert Terrebonne again.

"I'm not your son."

"You're certainly acting like a child." Sandra's finger chided me.

"I'm trying to help you all! I'm trying to help you see before it's too late! Before those assholes come in—"

"You got to go to Harvard." Robert's voice was laced with judgment.

"I worked damn hard to get in, and I worked damn hard once I was there."

"We know all that. You think they would have looked at you? If I hadn't gone to one of those boarding schools? If I didn't have my language beaten out of me? If your father didn't pay good money? He pulled strings to get you into that Phillips Exeter."

"Oh, come on—"

"Shame on you. Shame on you. Thinking you know. You don't know. Your father saved you. He got you out of the reservation school. He took you across the mountains. He sent you to a place where they could educate you right. The rest of us were here. We know what it was like. Before Elliot came. Before Elliot came, only we cared about educating our children right. We did a good job teaching them the Neige Courante Way. But we could not teach them the ways of the world. Don't tell me an uneducated Indian is better than an educated one. My grandchildren? They will never think they are less important than anyone else. Just because they're brown like me. Elliot has helped us on this path. He helps us make things right for our children. Now he thinks this other school will help us more. When he thinks that, I am behind him. He has my blessing."

The rest of the table mumbled agreement. I shook my head. They would never understand. They would never see that I had lived it, this so-called globalization dream they all held for our children, the one filled with college-educated Neige Courante who set out believing they could change the world. These elderly dreamers were so blind that they couldn't see me, or that I was the ultimate specimen of that dream's failure.

Then Robert said one more thing that would burn in my ears for months and sting me into silence. "Figure out what you're afraid of, Calbert. Your fear keeps your heart from living with the Neige Courante. It even keeps you from living in the rest of the world. You don't have a home. You don't know where you live. Stop blaming your poor father for that. Jasper Francoeur may not have been the best father to you. Because he was a father to us all. You're more like him than you think. Time you stopped worrying about that. Started being proud of it. Started living like the rest of us."

The Fish Story

Once upon a time, the boy was still a boy. But each time the sun came up, the boy looked more and more like a man. This was a fact not lost on the father. The father had been watching the boy and saw the way time was going.

Let it be explained here that the father was not often in the house where the boy now lived. This helped the father notice the change in the boy. The father was often away on official business. He left the cooking and cleaning and raising to his capable wife, who was kind enough to the boy, given the circumstances. The boy was nearly the same age as the second of the wife's three children, all girls. The middle daughter had such a beautiful face that there was nothing she could do to keep men's eyes off of her. When she got old enough to own her own body, this girl closely shaved her head, pierced every surface imaginable, and got tattoos on her arms and back. It didn't matter. Every man who saw her still wanted to make her his own. But that is not what is relevant about the girl, although the boy would often look at her across the dinner table when she was still a girl and wonder at the burden of such luminosity. What is relevant about the girl is that it was undeniable—given the two months that separated the boy's age from the girl's—that the father had cheated on his wife and that the boy was the product of this adultery.

The wife clothed the boy and fed him and made sure he got to school on time. Sometimes she forgot to pick him up, but he supposed he couldn't blame her. If he were her, he would have forgotten him too. For a time, the boy attended the most prestigious school in the whole city, which was where the wife's daughters also went to school. When people asked questions, the boy was to tell them that he was a cousin. So he did. He did all the things that he was told.

Why did the boy do all the things that he was told? At first he did it for the memory of his grandmother. She had pulled strings for him beyond the grave. He owed it to her to make the most of the life she'd haggled for him. But as time went on, he started to forget her voice and face, and started to love the things around him. He started to obey because he loved these things and did not want to risk losing them. The father's home was a beautiful house made out of glass up in the hills above the city. It was where the rich people lived. In the father's home, they ate food the boy had never heard of. The father owned thousands of books—he had whole rooms devoted to them—and let the boy borrow these books whenever he wanted. The father told the boy, in between his official business, that he knew they could be the best of friends. He told the boy he had waited many years to have a son. And the boy knew, because of what his mother had whispered in his infant ear, that there was a threat curled up somewhere in the language and the life, but he wasn't interested in discovering what that threat could do, so he chose to ignore it.

One morning the father told the son they would be taking a trip together. A fishing trip. It was a school day, and the boy had looked forward to school. But he dutifully got into the father's car and listened to the father's music as they drove out into the country. They drove fast. The car found a road that knifed beside the river that the boy's and the father's people had been fishing for millennia. It was a wide blue river. It was fed by streams, by tributaries, by waterfalls. But the father did not stop to look at the beautiful country. He did not stop until they got to the dam that had been built across the river and had ended their people's fishing for good.

"Celilo," the father said, and pointed.

It was just water where the father pointed. But the boy knew what the father was talking about. There had been a waterfall there, before the dam was built. At that waterfall, people had fished for thousands of years. One day, when the dam was built, the waterfall was drowned under the river. To make cheap energy. Forget about the people who had been fishing there for thousands of years.

"Yeah," said the boy. "It's too bad."

The father grunted. "Do you know what I do? Every day?"

The boy didn't know how to answer that. "You mean your job?"

"Yes. I mean my job."

"You're a lawyer."

The father laughed, but the laugh wasn't supposed to make the boy feel happy. "My job is to make sure this never happens again."

"You want them to stop building dams?"

"My job is to get the salmon back for our people."

"Okay," said the boy. He didn't know how the father was going to accomplish this. On the walls of the father's office, there were dozens of framed photographs of him shaking hands with luminaries; the boy liked this word. He liked looking at the pictures.

"There are three types of salmon on the endangered-species list. This river is swimming in chemicals now, so even if we catch a salmon, it isn't safe to eat it. By the time you're my age, all my work may have been for nothing. But we have to try, don't we?"

The boy nodded. He wanted to return to school. The boy said, "I thought we were going fishing."

"You thought wrong."

"But you said—"

"Don't believe everything you hear."

"Are we going home now?"

"First I'm going to show you where I met your mother."

They drove into the town that was perched beside the river. The father stopped the car next to a place where women danced nude. The building thrummed with the thump of heavy bass. There were neon outlines of women's bodies on the front of the building. The boy felt himself blush.

"Your mother was a dancer here," the father said.

The boy was trying to imagine what kind of woman his mother must have been. He knew he was supposed to feel ashamed, but he couldn't think about her any different than he ever had. She had always felt like a ghost to him. Seeing where she'd done her dancing didn't change that.

The father had a smile worming at the edges of his mouth. "She was something," he said. "It's time for you to choose. You can be nothing, like your mother. I don't blame her for doing what she did—she did the best she could. But the best she could be was a slut and a liar, because that's all she was offered. I'm offering you something more. I'm offering you the chance to be something. Do you have an interest in making something of yourself?"

No one had ever asked the boy a question like this. But he said what he was supposed to say. "Yes."

"Then you must let go of the past. Forget about that picture you have of your mother. Forget your grandmother's books. Forget the stinking reservation. That was never our home. That's not where we were meant to live. I'm telling you that your mother was nothing because that's what the world will tell you. The world wants you to think you are worth nothing, the same way she thought she was nothing. The world wants you to stay on the reservation and drink and fuck. The world wants you to turn your mind stupid, to forget that you're smart." The father wagged his finger. "But not me. I want you to be like me. I want you to be a leader. I want our people to look up to you, to listen when you speak. I want you to be full of what made me."

"And what is that?" the boy asked.

The father didn't answer. Instead, he said, "I'm sending you east. To boarding school."

The boy opened his mouth, but the father silenced him with one look. "It's the best thing. To learn how the rest of the world is before you come back. You'll be prepared. You'll show everyone who doubts you exactly what we're made of. I only wish someone had handed me the same opportunity. You're a lucky boy. Someday you'll understand."

Chapter Five

Be not afeard. The isle is full of noises,
Sounds, and sweet airs, that give delight and hurt not.
Sometimes a thousand twangling instruments
Will hum about mine ears; and sometime voices,
That if I then had wak'd after long sleep,
Will make me sleep again, and then in dreaming,
The clouds methought would open, and show riches
Ready to drop upon me, that when I wak'd
I cried to dream again.

So speaks Caliban, Prospero's slave, in Act Three of *The Tempest*. Helen had never thought much about what this speech meant. She was a professional, so she *thought* she had. She'd considered the zigzagging tense of it: present to future to conditional to past. She'd mused on the rain metaphor woven into the end of the speech, especially in contrast to the title of Shakespeare's play; in Caliban's version of a storm, the clouds bring riches and hope, not rain. Helen had explored the open vowels of the words distributed throughout the monologue's first half: "noises," "sounds," "sweet airs," "a thousand twangling instruments," "hum," "voices." All these sound words indicated that the island onstage should be peopled with aural stimulation, should be tropical and wet, full of birdcalls, full of mystery. She had directed *The Tempest* three times in her career—once as an undergraduate, once at summer stock, once at the First Stage—and those productions had reflected the times: at Columbia in the late 1960s, Prospero's island had been peopled with flower children; at summer stock in the early 1980s, the setting had been a metaphor for the post-industrial complex, set inside a corporation called the Island; and four years ago, she had reversed the gender roles, as per Duncan's suggestion, casting in the role of Prospero a two-hundred-pound black actress and in the role of Caliban a hunched, elderly white woman.

Each time Helen directed *The Tempest*, this speech in the middle of Act Three provided a sweet nugget of beautiful rest, set amid the comic subplot of Caliban, Stephano, and Trinculo's drunken tromp around the isle. Each time Helen got to this speech, she would make her actors stop and devour it, explore the clues it gave them about the island. They would discuss Caliban's humanity. They would argue that anyone who had put such language in the mouth of "the savage" was doing something subversive. They would say that Shakespeare obviously believed Caliban was just as human as Prospero was, to put such fine words, such complex thought, such elegantly rendered concepts, in his mouth and mind.

But she had never truly gotten it until now. She had never gotten it until the phone call she'd made to check in at the front desk at the First Stage, until she heard that life was going on fine without her, that things were A-OK. She had supposed these last three weeks, that this was what she wanted, but now, hearing that things were fine, she was not as satisfied as she'd thought she'd be. It became apparent that Duncan was there, that he was asking poor young Nick at the front desk to hand over the phone, and then before Helen knew it, she was speaking to her husband, and he was furious and loving at the same time, if that made any sense, and he was asking her when she was coming home, and why she hadn't called him, and how this could happen between them, and promising her mending and hope and future. His voice pulled so hard at her heart that she made herself hang up. She was glad to have Amelia and Elliot's apartment to herself so that she could gather herself, the self that had seemed so gathered since she'd gotten here but which she now saw was frayed and frazzled, and then she called Michael Reid and told him what had happened, and he asked her if anything had *happened* with Elliot and she told him no, it didn't seem that was even on the table, and she didn't even think she wanted it there. She hadn't realized this until she said it. Speaking to Michael Reid took Helen's feelings from a vague, dark place and made them true. She was greatly relieved when she heard herself explaining that something had shifted between her and Elliot, something that made her believe she still loved him but not the way she thought she had all these years, and perhaps that wasn't as disappointing as she had assumed it would be. Michael Reid said to her, "Why are you still out there, then?" For that she had no answers.

Then she was back at the cabin, standing in her doorway—the one place that had ever been only hers—looking out at the high desert, at the mountains in the distance, at the azure expanse of sky above her, and at that moment, Caliban's words floated to the surface of her mind, and suddenly, she understood. She had never loved a place the way she loved this place. She had never felt so at home. She had never believed that a place could save her. She had only believed that about activism, about words. She had never felt that way about love.

Caliban understood this, how a place could give you freedom. In the middle of his enslavement, his desperation, his beatings, he had hope because he could look at the sky and dream. She felt she had never seen the sky before she got out here. She was glad it was getting dark. She leaned her head against the door frame. She watched and waited. The stars came out at last.

AMELIA
Stolen, Oregon ~ Friday, October 25, 1996

Two weeks had passed since Amelia and Elliot's tangle in his office. They'd reached an uneasy kind of truce, but things were far from warm. He'd apologized to Amelia and said he wanted to talk to her more about Benson as things developed further. She'd said she didn't care anymore—Ponderosa was his school, after all, and yes, she did believe he was a wonderful headmaster—and all that was mostly true. The explosion in Elliot's office had somehow taken the edge off her panic. She had no idea what would result if her two worlds did collide.

She felt as though she and Elliot were two separate celestial bodies orbiting opposite each other around the same star, each obscured from the other by the glowing thing between them. It was a lonely feeling. She didn't yet know it was the feeling that comes with growing up.

Which is not to say that she had been sitting home mourning the downfall of her relationship with her father. On the contrary, over the last few weeks, Amelia's social life had blossomed. The other kids at school now spoke to her. They treated her like a friend, and she knew the reason for that inclusion was Victor Littlefoot's respect for her. She didn't know where his loyalty had come from, but it felt amazing. Lydia was loyal, but she didn't have any power. Everyone liked her, sure, but she was a known entity, and hence held no sway. But when Amelia mentioned to Victor that it mattered to her to have a lot of people show up at Helen's first day of Shakespeare, he got the job done. When they were walking down the hallway in opposite directions, he stopped her for a conversation. He waved to her from the basketball court during break. He sat at her lunch table on more than one occasion.

The trail of the lost baby had fallen cold, but Amelia didn't think about that much. What mattered to her about the lost-baby mission was riding in Victor's pickup and hearing stories about

Chicago and getting to look at Victor up close when he laughed. If anything, she liked believing that this baby project would take years of research. She liked that Victor had said he hoped they could keep this project a secret between the two of them. She didn't ask why. She just thought: "Hours alone with Victor Little-foot? Yeah, I think I can handle that."

That first day they asked around at the Rudolph Ranch. The oldest rancher they could find was monosyllabically unhelpful. His longest sentence consisted of gesturing out at the great expanse of field and saying, "Not exactly a place for babies."

"Do you remember if anyone abandoned a baby here? It would have been nine years ago." Amelia loved watching how politely Victor spoke.

The old man glanced at Amelia and shook his head as if they were crazy people. The skin around his eyes was deeply lined, as though he had been squinting for centuries. "We bought this ranch seven years ago," he said. "Hell if I know."

So that was the first dead end. When they got back in the car, Victor laughed, then said grimly, "Lucky you were with me. Did you notice he only looked at you?" They sat in the car for a few minutes as the rancher's dogs eyed them from their spots in the sun. "Do you remember what the baby looked like?"

Amelia shrugged. "I don't know. It was just a baby, you know?"

"Indian or white?"

"I don't remember. I guess I didn't really notice that kind of stuff then."

Victor turned on the motor and made a U-turn on the rancher's gravel drive before saying, "Yeah. Neither did I."

THEY SHOT A Friday afternoon in late October checking the Bend library for records, but they didn't know what they were looking for. They checked birth records, but all they ended up with was a list of names of local children born in 1987. Victor and Amelia realized they couldn't just walk up to people's houses and ask if they'd ever abandoned a child when it was baby. But they figured that as long as they had the official birth registration records of all the babies born in or around Stolen, Oregon, in 1987, they had a start.

"But really," Amelia said as Victor was driving her home, "do you think someone abandoning their baby would actually register it with the local authorities?"

Victor shrugged. "Maybe the baby wasn't abandoned."

"That doesn't make sense either. Babies don't crawl, don't drag a blanket by themselves, and then hang out on it smack dab in the middle of the wilderness." She glanced out at the late-afternoon light beaming through cracks in the thick cloud cover. This was her favorite kind of day, when she imagined herself as the kind of person who could look at light shafting from the heavens and fervently believe in God. She felt emboldened. "We don't even know what we're looking for."

All the energy spent looking for the baby had awakened something ancient and familiar inside of Amelia: the feeling of enchantment she'd shared with Victor when they'd been little and had played those make-believe games combined with a grown-up sense of purpose. As children, they'd pretended to be fairies, but they'd also been ranchers and elk hunters and schoolteachers and traders. She remembered the long days when they seemed to slip out of the Ponderosa world into a sweeter place that looked like their regular world but glowed with unspoken possibilities.

She found herself saying, "It's weird, but you know, back then, I sort of felt like we'd had some kind of spell cast on us. Like we were playing in some magic kingdom." She was staring straight ahead, a smile on her lips, but suddenly, she felt afraid that Victor would make some crack about Disneyland, about how woo-woo she was being, so she took a quick look at him. He glanced at her, silent, a smile on his lips too. She went on. "You know what freaked me out about the baby is that a little bit of me believed that *we* made it up, that *we* made it happen." She rushed ahead. "Oh, not that we lied, but that we made that baby appear out of thin air, you know? And then it got swallowed back up." She stopped, embarrassment now silencing her.

"Wow," said Victor. He smiled appraisingly. "You sound just like my grandma." He laughed out loud. "She's got some interesting theories about the whole baby thing."

"You've talked to her about it?" Amelia felt a pang of jealousy.

"Yeah." Victor shrugged noncommittally.

"Does she know anything?"

"Nah," he said.

"But that's perfect! She must know everyone in the area. Have you interviewed her? Like, formally?" Victor was focusing on driving. Amelia pressed him. "We should talk to your grandma," she said. "We could borrow my dad's tape recorder and interview her—"

"No," Victor said sharply, and in one move his fingers went to the radio dial and began fiddling. He turned the country station up so loud that Amelia could barely hear herself think, and he dropped her off without making any plans for the following Saturday.

THE PHONE WAS ringing as Amelia raced up the stairs two by two. Elliot still wouldn't buy an answering machine ("Anyone who needs to reach me that badly can leave a message in my office"), and Amelia hated the gnawing curiosity that came when she missed a call. Apparently, Elliot was across campus at his office, so she burst through the apartment door, flung her backpack onto the couch, and dove for the telephone: "Hello?"

"Hey. Is this Amelia?"

"Yeah." She was winded. "Yes, it is."

"Hey, it's Sadie!"

Amelia was genuinely surprised. "Sadie. Wow. I didn't think you'd call." Then she was embarrassed and covered with this: "Well, I know you said you would, and I'm glad you did. I mean, it's great to hear from you!"

Sadie laughed. "Oh, 'Melia, you sound just like yourself! I miss you. How *are* you?"

"Good, fine, I mean things are crazy."

"Please tell me life sucks without me. How's your dad? Have you told him how he ruined my life?"

Amelia laughed. "I don't think he remembered what a pain I can be sometimes."

As the two girls chatted back and forth, Amelia grew comfortable. She asked, as nonchalantly as she could, "How's Wes?"

"Oh my God. Wes." Sadie paused. "He's been . . . down. But he's applying to Juilliard. Apparently, Jackson Rice called in an audition. Friends in high places."

"Great," said Amelia. She wondered if Sadie knew yet about the exact nature of Wes and Jackson's "friendship." But then Sadie didn't falter over Jackson's name, so that was a sign that Wes's secret was still safe.

"Don't you want to know why I'm really calling? I mean, beyond just catching up?"

For a moment Amelia's breath caught in her throat. The twinge of shame sharpened and flashed and flooded, and she was afraid that somehow Wes wasn't as neatly contained a topic as she'd hoped. She remembered Wes's angry glare, the hard way he'd pressed the money into her hand. She said, "Sure. What's up?"

"Be sure not to sound too excited."

"Tell me, tell me, tell me!" Amelia feigned eagerness. Sadie loved it when she talked like a little kid.

"It's nothing much unless you count the fact that yesterday old Sylvester, our crazy headmaster—oh yeah, you know him, I forgot—called an assembly and announced that a bunch of us are going to come to Ponderosa Academy in the spring! They're setting up an exchange program between our schools! Did you know?"

Amelia hesitated, and that was all the answer Sadie needed.

"Why didn't you call me? I can't believe you were holding out.

I mean, I knew your dad was the headmaster of Ponderosa, but I didn't know he was such a big fucking deal. Isn't it cool? I'm already filling out my Ambassador application. You have to talk to your dad if I don't get in. I absolutely have to come see you. Wes might come too, if I can convince him you're actually interested in seeing him. He's got some weird thing about you. I think he's, like, in love or something. What. Ever. But seriously, Amelia, we have to see each other before the spring. You have to come over the holidays. If I'm not in Aspen. But I don't think we're going until New Year's . . ."

As Sadie droned on, Amelia conjured up the dorm room where Sadie was sitting, the smell of the stale air, the cool rainy windowpanes, the mismatched linoleum tiles on the floor. She could intuit Sadie's exact sprawl on the bed, and she imagined Wes letting himself in and finding a spot in the corner from which to flip his lighter on and off, a freshly rolled cigarette tucked in the divot of his mouth. She imagined the brother and sister until the picture was complete. Only then, in knowing exactly how they looked and smelled, and the grayness of the light, and the sad sound of a muffled cello rumbling up through the floorboards, did Amelia feel ready to see that it didn't matter whether they came, or what happened when they arrived. Sadie and Wes belonged to her past, and that past was over, set in Portland. Sure, she had to straighten things up a bit before they came. But she could do that. She had time to do that. Sadie and Wes would be coming to Ponderosa Academy in the spring, and the spring was a very long time away.

Chapter Six

CAL
Stolen, Oregon ~ Saturday, October 26, 1996

I wasn't in the best of moods when I left that board meeting. I'm sure I don't need to tell you that. Rarely was my father mentioned to my face. Usually, people bit their tongues when his name was brought up in my company. I never knew if it was out of respect or fear, but I was pretty positive that whichever it was, it was out of respect or fear of *him*, not me, even when he was just a memory. It was close to never that I was called to task about my anger at him, because most people knew that was risky territory. But most people weren't Robert Terrebonne, Most Highly Respected Neige Courante Elder of All Time. Even I was cowed when he issued forth.

My car was alone when I got to it. Everyone else had gone. I got in and turned on tribal radio. There was Joe again: "Good evening, indigenous dudes and dudettes!" I turned the radio off. I listened. There was nothing to listen to. Not even wind. So I cranked on the engine and sat for a few minutes, idling. I could see lights on in Elliot's apartment. Frankly, I was too exhausted for the fight anymore. I'm admitting this to you in confidence, but I began to think, sitting in the car, that Robert Terrebonne was kind of right. I wasn't sure what I was so upset about anymore. Maybe I didn't care about the Neige Courante kids as much as I thought I did. Maybe I *had* made it all about me.

There is a road that winds up around the school and then points due east, toward a great expanse of unnamed, unowned wilderness. It is not entirely unusual that I found myself driving on this road. It's a track I've driven since my teenage summers. I knew of it long before Elliot Barrow came to town, because it heads toward nothingness and gives a person room to breathe. I suppose the fact that it also comes within a hundred yards of Helen's house is, in retrospect, another reason I might have headed that way. The sound of an engine that far out is unusual, so some part of me must have known she'd come to the door and peer out, then smile, wave, and beckon me in.

Rudy's, on the road down to Bend, is the kind of place you think will be full of racist, dirty men. I discovered it when I was sixteen and carrying a fake ID and a will to smart-aleck myself into and out of as many sticky situations as possible. Rudy's looks, from the outside, like a great place to be beaten senseless. But Rudy is just about the nicest guy you've ever met, and the bikers who frequent his establishment on a nightly basis are good men who savor the vegetarian wood-oven pizza he slaves over every night. The parking lot is thick with bikes and dudes smoking weed who, when we pulled into the lot, waved at us like suburban moms waiting for the end of their children's soccer game. It was only nine, and Rudy's was already thumping with the delta blues.

I'm a big fan of Muddy Waters. I'll take early Dylan any day. Give me Desmond Dekker, give me Springsteen's *Nebraska*, give me Ray Charles. I'll sing along with all of them until my voice rasps, until my knees are weak, until my ears bleed. And then I'll sing some more.

It's possible not to advertise this trait, because in these parts, one spends a lot of time alone in one's car. I've got a secret stash of these guys under my driver's seat. I've always felt something shameful about my love of music, as though it risks weakening me in the eyes of those who believe they know me well; even as a boy, when I discovered that records could uncork you, I kept them locked away, to protect me from the magic they could effect. They made me want more than I had. They made me courageous. Let me tell you, there have been some lonely moments in my life when the lyrics to Dylan's *In the Summertime* or Jimmy Cliff's *Sitting Here in Limbo* have been the only things that have gotten me through.

So it was to my own great surprise that I took Helen to Rudy's. I guess I knew the second I pulled up the road winding past her shack that Rudy's was where we'd end up. I guess I hoped by the end of the night, we'd be drunk and happy, grooving to the deep dirty bass line of Billy Lick's four-piece band, that Billy's gravel voice would wash over us and set our conversation down in a dancing place. We ended up with our arms around each other, moving slow and leaning in. I had never seen Helen look the way she did that night. It was the first time I truly understood what Elliot had seen in her. She was flushed and bright, cackling at jokes, swaying up against the chords Billy let loose. She looked twenty years younger.

I told her we didn't have to stay long, but we stayed all night. We stayed long enough to get drunk and sober and drunk again, and then just sober enough to drive home. As we neared our destination, the question began to press at both of us. As I turned in to the school, and as she glanced nervously at Elliot's dark apartment when we passed it, and as she leaned her head against the passenger seat and gave me an apologetic smile, I knew what the answer was. I didn't need her to say what she said, which began with the word "listen" and ended with the word "uncomfortable." I fought my desire to tell her I hadn't had any ideas about where this was going, that all I had wanted was to give her a taste of this world outside of Elliot's vision of it. But I wasn't sober enough to say those things, so I watched her get out of my car and head down toward her cold shack in the light of the moon. And then, for the second time in my life, I sped away from her, fast and angry and afraid.

AMELIA
Neige Courante Reservation ~ Saturday, October 26, 1996

If you've researched the last one hundred years of aboriginal life in central Oregon, chances are you've thought about the Confederated Tribes of Warm Springs and the beautiful Warm Springs Reservation. Their story combines tremendous strength of character with a canny sense of negotiation. For what seemed like forever, the Wasco bands from the East had met yearly with the more nomadic Warm Springs bands at the fishing camp at Celilo Falls on the Columbia River. There, dip-net fishermen built scaffolding and harvested salmon and recognized themselves and one another as people with a common goal. Different languages—Kiksht, Ichishkiin—different customs, sure, but a common goal. To get to live the way they always had. By 1855 these two tribes had had the fight beaten from them. They decided that the best way to continue was together. Under what one can politely call "pressure," they were forced to relinquish ten million acres of land throughout Oregon in exchange for exclusive rights to the Warm Springs Reservation. In 1879 a group of thirty-eight former roaming high-plains Paiutes from eastern Oregon joined the other tribes at Warm Springs.

These days, most people try to find some way to speak tactfully about the dimensions of this staggeringly unjust loss—this spiritual heist—by pointing to the impressive fortitude and good-hearted cooperation of many current reservation residents. This is just another way to avoid talking about the larger problems of poverty and racism and lousy educational funding in much of America.

The Neige Courante dipped their nets in the Columbia too, but as a people, they flowed like water away from any negotiations. Years later, at threat of death, inevitably forced off their mountain land, they discovered that the parcel still "available" for reservation life was dry and tufted, cracked and gorged, earth that fell off from the mountains and looked out across desert.

What I'm trying to say is that the Neige Courante learned to live on their little reservation by watching how the cannier Warm Springs people coped. When the Neige Courante listen to the radio, they tune in to KWSO, the Warm Springs station; when they want to play golf, they drive over to Kah-Nee-Tah. They gaze up at Mount Jefferson and dip their toes in the icy Metolius and visit the Museum at Warm Springs and read about the way things were.

Even though Amelia knew something about Indians and the differences between the Neige Courante and Warm Springs bands and the Wascoes and the Paiutes, she didn't know much. What she knew best was this: ever since she'd been a little girl, going to Lydia Cinqchevaux's house had felt like going to heaven. The house was a standard Neige Courante Monopoly ranch with some pleasant additions. Lydia's dad was the kind of man who built garages with his bare hands. Lydia's mom was the kind of woman who liked stuff in her yard: gazebos, flamingos, wishing wells, smiling gnomes. Something was always being hammered, sawed, or spray-painted in the driveway, and an endless round of meat loaf, mashed potatoes, or fry bread or macaroni casserole was ready to be dished out to innumerable batches of noisy relatives bursting through the front door at unexpected moments. Brothers farted. Aunties arranged bowling tournaments. There was always a group of two or three women beading at a corner of the kitchen table; little boys practiced the Duck and Dive for the coming powwow even though the uncles claimed the dance was traditionally Nez Perce. What Lydia always wanted was some peace and quiet, so she preferred sleeping over at Amelia's, and because Lydia was bossier, she usually prevailed. On most Saturday nights, both girls curled up on Amelia's couch, shared a bowl of popcorn, and watched videos while Elliot typed away in the other room.

Lydia's house provided a home when Amelia needed some coddling, so it wasn't unusual for both girls to head there when Elliot's typing got annoying or Amelia craved distraction. On this particular evening, Lydia's older brothers were dribbling the basketball in the driveway when the girls arrived. Lydia had to lean on the horn to get them out of the way, and then Gordie and Howie mooned the car. This was pretty standard behavior at the Cinqchevaux house.

"Do you want to make our guest sick? You are fucking disgusting. Seriously, I just threw up in my mouth and then I swallowed it again." Lydia was half laughing as she emerged from the car and tried to kick one older brother while the other began pounding on her back. "Ow! Ow!"

Gordie repeated every word Lydia had said in a singsongy mocking voice that only made her angrier and only made them torment her more: "Ow! Ow!" "Ow! Ow!" "Bastards!" "Bastards!" Lydia begged for Amelia's help. Amelia grabbed her backpack and slid past the three siblings into the house as Lydia's whoops and screams floated up and over the yard.

"Stay away from those boys. Being nasty. Lydia too." Suzanne, Lydia's mom, was big and breasty. When Amelia was younger and shorter, she'd been oddly thrilled by the idea that Suzanne might smother her in a hug, drown her in too much eager love. But now Amelia stood a head taller than this woman who loved all children unspecifically and unconditionally. Suzanne pinched Amelia's hip and frowned. "Your father is starving you as usual, I see. We'll fix you up. Help me peel apples. Making a tart tonight."

Suzanne's home was crammed with wonderful stuff. Every single surface, each shelf, each corner, held a treasure. A collection of cowboy-and-Indian salt-and-pepper shakers perched on every available ledge in the kitchen; snow globes from twenty-seven states graced the mantelpiece; defunct exercise equipment hovered behind the easy chairs; and stacks of catalogs cascaded from the end tables. Amelia loved nothing more than snuggling up on Lydia's couch with a glass of ice-cold Pepsi and ten catalogs while the rest of the family watched a sporting event. She loved being invisible and at the heart of things at the very same time.

Amelia followed Suzanne into the brightly lit kitchen, sat and chatted as Suzanne spun out a feast from commodity foods, called "commods": open cans and boxes, cartons and bushel baskets. Bread steamed, corn boiled, pot roast burbled in its thick gravy, potatoes sizzled in deep hot oil. Amelia marveled at the bounty, the generosity, of Lydia's family. Suzanne's meals overflowed with welcome.

The older woman made sure that Amelia wielded the sharp knife. She took the dull one herself and got to work. "Lydia tells me about you and Victor Littlefoot."

Amelia kept peeling her apples. She didn't know what to say.

"You like him. There, in that smile you're trying to hide. Nice kid."

"We're just hanging out," Amelia said. She could tell Suzanne was heading somewhere specific.

"You call on his grandmother yet? Old Adele Littlefoot? You take her some salmon? Tobacco?" Suzanne paused and peered at Amelia, a smile playing in her eyes. She knew the answer, but she asked one more question. "You doing things right for that old lady?"

Amelia felt herself blushing even before she had a chance to open her mouth, before she had a chance to lift her eyes from her task. She was glad to glimpse Lydia entering the kitchen.

"Ma, lighten up. We'll take care of it. If that'll shut you up."

"You've got the supplies?"

Lydia grinned. "Not exactly."

"I knew it."

"So you're a mind reader. Happy?"

Suzanne scolded them both: "Shame on you." She opened a high cabinet and pulled a long plastic bag of dried salmon from behind the cereal, shoving it into Lydia's hands. "People are going to think I didn't raise you right." She went into the living room and returned with a Ziploc of tobacco, then left again. They heard her in the bedroom, rustling through drawers. She came back with two folds of blue cotton cloth. "Lydia, I tell you every time. Always keep these things in special places." She wagged her finger in Amelia's direction. "Even you know better by now." She perched her hand on one hip and looked at the girls. "Well? What do you say?"

"Thank you," said Amelia, barely audible. She felt so clumsy in Lydia's world sometimes.

Suzanne leaned down and pecked both Amelia's cheeks. She smelled like cinnamon and talcum powder. "What would you do without me?"

Amelia had hoped they would run into Victor on this trip to the reservation. But she hadn't said anything to Lydia. And she couldn't believe that Suzanne could see right through her. What Amelia hadn't gotten around to telling Lydia was that Victor Littlefoot had made it clear his grandmother was off limits. More than once Amelia had suggested they hang out at his place; she wanted to meet his family. His answer? "There's just my grandma." When she said, "Well, I'd like to meet her," he responded, "No, you wouldn't." She got the distinct impression that it was more like *he* didn't want Amelia to meet her. Case closed. But now Suzanne had made such a big deal about visiting and gifts and how those presents were coming from the Cinqchevauxs' own pockets, that there was no way to go back and explain.

Suzanne had summoned Louie Cinqchevaux, Lydia's father, from his spot on the couch and informed him that tonight he'd tell Amelia about Adele Littlefoot's husband, Gavin Littlefoot, the fastest wild-horse rider ever to appear from the shadow of the Cascades.

"They say there's only been three men ever rode that good, and Gavin Littlefoot was the best. He also died the youngest. Out at a rodeo in the Wallowas. He was *the* rider. You know what I mean by that, girl?" Louie Cinqchevaux sank into the easy chair in the corner of the kitchen, watching as his women cooked and ladled, set the table, counted out forks.

"Sure she does, Daddy. You calling my friend ignorant?" When Lydia spoke to her father like this, no one considered it sassing because Lydia spoke to everyone the same way.

Amelia felt at home enough to chime in, "Shut up, Lydia. Can't you see he's telling a story?" Everyone laughed at that.

"Well, you know the three jobs: mugger takes the neck, anchor controls the lead-line, rider throws on the saddle, then throws on his own self. He gets bucked. Meantime, nine other teams are

doing the same dang fool thing. Most say you can't win this event."
Louie sighed. He knew about horses; he made his money helping
Chester Marron break his wild stock in order to breed with the Indian ponies. He went on, "What you girls got to remember is a
good horse becomes a man. He's never quite broke in spirit. But
he's full of respect. When you ask him to do a thing for you, if you
ask nice, he'll consider the request." He chuckled.

"Get on with the story, then," Suzanne urged.

"So this Gavin Littlefoot was real young. Couldn't have been
more than twenty. He's the best. His wife's real young, maybe seventeen, they have their little girl, Victor's mother's mother"—
Amelia realized the grandmother they'd been talking about was
technically a great-grandmother, although no one else seemed to
note this distinction—"and she's mad. Mad at the horses who flow
like flash floods over the desert. Mad at them for taking her husband from her. She yells at him. He promises he'll go out one last
time. He'll win the biggest purse ever." He shakes his head. "Wanna
guess what happens?"

Suzanne clucked. "What always happens when a good woman
tries to keep her husband from his own foolishness."

"Now, Suzy, who's telling this story?"

"You asked."

Louie waved his wife off. "Sure, he goes and wins. But just as
he's winning, he's bucked off. Hoof right in the skull. Head
crushed in. Gavin still wins the purse, though. His friends take the
money to Adele. But not the horse. They don't dare take the horse
back." Louie paused. Reflected.

"This is way too sad," Lydia said, fishing in a cabinet for a serving dish. "I hate stories that end like that. What's the point?"

"The point is to tell you about how come Adele Littlefoot is the
way she is. Ever since that wild horse crushed Gavin's skull, that
woman became an expert in all the old Neige Courante ways. Believed Gavin died because he didn't take the proper precautions. She
became fierce in those matters. An expert. Thing is, lots of people

thought she made them up. Pulled them right out of thin air. Even so, people from all over take her their problems. Believe her solutions. Burn some of this. Sprinkle some of that. Do it naked before daylight, you'll be safe. Put on buckskin, you'll change your luck. Lots of crazy stuff no one ever heard before. Until now. Now she's so old, everyone thinks she must know the old ways."

"Ignore this old man." Suzanne's voice cut through the kitchen. "Adele Littlefoot takes care of a lot of people on this reservation. She's a good soul." She glared at Louie. "What he's not telling you is women run the show. Women like Adele Littlefoot. They have for generations. It's our job to carry the traditions. Besides, that father of yours can't imagine what grief might do to a person."

"True enough." Louie chuckled. "She can be one tough old woman, though. Be sure to take some good tobacco."

"Oh, they will," Suzanne said, satisfaction creeping into her voice. "Haven't you noticed? They're taking yours."

ALL THE WAY on the winding gravel road the following morning, Amelia couldn't tell whether she was more afraid of seeing Victor or his grandmother. She couldn't tell whether she was more afraid of telling Lydia that Victor would definitely *not* be glad to see them, or of waiting to let Lydia see for herself how Victor felt. Instead of saying anything, Amelia pressed her cheek against the car window as they passed trailers and ranch houses, rusted-out tractors, scrawny dogs. Yellow traffic signs designated wild-horse crossings, and the girls both laughed at that; how were the horses expected to read where they should cross? Who would ticket them if they crossed at the wrong place? What neither of the girls wanted to say as they drove through the poorest land on the reservation was that Lydia lived an entire tribal life about which Amelia knew relatively little. As they were sheltered in the warmth of the Cinqchevaux house, that difference seemed insignificant, but out here with the old washing machines, abandoned cars, and unmarked roads, Amelia felt lost.

Out in the middle of nowhere, Lydia turned left and the car

crawled up a dirt path, dust spewing behind them. They approached a neat little trailer surrounded by a few wooden outbuildings, a couple of lean-tos made out of corrugated tin. Victor's truck wasn't there, and Amelia felt a sense of relief overwhelm her. "He's not here. We can go."

"Are you crazy?" asked Lydia. "My ass is definitely on the line here. We've gotta say hi or I might as well never go home again."

Both girls climbed out of the car, and Lydia said, "Don't slam the door," just as Amelia slammed the door. A tiny, ancient woman with two neat braids and a flowered housecoat stepped down from the trailer into the light. She squinted at the girls and said something Amelia couldn't understand. Lydia answered in a strange language—not Sahaptin, Amelia knew what Sahaptin sounded like—and gathered the salmon, cloth, and tobacco leaves from Amelia's hands, offering them to the grandmother. Lydia placed the gifts on a ledge by the trailer steps as Amelia held back shyly. She watched as Lydia pointed at her and the old woman gestured and answered. Finally, Lydia called her over with a commanding "Don't be rude, Amelia. Come say hello to Mrs. Littlefoot."

Much to Amelia's surprise, Mrs. Littlefoot said, "She's not so much rude as scared of me. Look at her. Like a little rabbit, and I'm the hawk." When Amelia came near, the old woman took the girl's hands in her own and stared her in the eyes. Amelia blushed. Victor's grandmother's irises were bright and clear, nearly the deep purple hue of blackberries. Amelia would have expected the eyes of someone so ancient to have broken blood vessels, cloudy film. But it was as if the old woman could see into all the places Amelia didn't want her to see.

For a minute it felt as if everything was going to be fine; this was a proper thing, the kind of thing teenagers ought to do more often. Take treats to the elderly, keep them company, smile and chat. Had Lydia gone alone, the visit would have become just that.

But Mrs. Littlefoot held tight to Amelia's hands and said, "I know about you. You're Victor's white girl. Victor's little white girl with the fairy games. You took my Victor into the wild. You pretended you were kings and queens. During all that play, the world shattered. You're the careless girl who cracked the world open. You made a baby leap out. It fooled with you. That's why Victor had to go to Chicago. To get the trouble in his mind out. But even in Chicago the world cracked. Because of what you did to him. The drugs were what you did to him. You put those drugs in his hands." The old lady said this almost without expression, but fast, as if she had been waiting to give this speech for a long, long time. Amelia tried to pull away, but the old woman continued. She was surprisingly strong. "Your life is bad now. I know that. Now that Victor's clean, I told him, 'If you can't stay away from her, just bring that broken white girl to me. I'll try to fix you both, the Neige Courante Way, the Old Way.' But he said you'd never come."

A grin just like Victor's spread across the old woman's face, like a wildfire across the prairie. Amelia didn't try to pull away anymore. She stood transfixed as the smooth breezes washed over her, carrying the brisk sage scent and the calls of birds whose names she didn't know. The old woman released one of Amelia's hands and pointed to a circle of embers. "I've been calling you for many nights now. And see? Now here you are. I made you come."

The old woman leaned in close and gestured the girl down to her, so Amelia could feel her hot radish breath against her cheek. "It's because of your mother. You think it's your fault. But it's because of her. The only Way you knew was to crack open the world. That was the only Way your mother knew. That was the Way your mother left you. What you saw was another baby. But don't worry. I can help you with that." The old woman made a cooing sound that brushed Amelia's cheek. "Poor girl. You couldn't know any better. She left before she could fix her mistake. All this time you've been so lonely. But there are ways to fix that."

Lydia had grabbed Amelia's free hand, but Amelia hardly noticed. Lydia pulled, but Amelia couldn't move. She felt things she had never felt before, things she had no words for, although, if pressed, she could have said that part of what she felt was fear and part was excitement and part was shame. She also felt something else; she felt *seen*. She felt *known*. She felt *identified*. Just as she registered that feeling of being known, and began to relish what it might mean to her, it was over. Victor appeared. Amelia heard no engine, but here he was, slamming the door of his truck, a cloud of dust surrounding them. He was yelling. "What are you doing here? Get off our land. Leave my grandmother alone."

That broke the spell. The next thing Amelia knew, she and Lydia were in the car together, barreling fast down the dirt drive, but instead of being friends the way they should have been—the way they always *had* been—Lydia and she sat far apart, as if old Mrs. Littlefoot's assertions had created revelations that occupied the space between the girls. Lydia loosed her anger into the air. She put it into words, questions: "What the hell was that about a baby? And about giving Victor drugs?"

Amelia shook her head numbly.

"We weren't even invited, were we? You lied to me. Apparently, you've been lying to me about other things too."

"Like what?"

"Like drugs. Like a baby."

"I didn't lie. She just—"

"And what was that she said about your mom? What was she saying?"

"I don't know."

"I'm taking you home." When Amelia didn't answer, Lydia fumed, "I'm your best friend, Amelia. And I didn't even know what she was talking about." When Amelia kept silent, Lydia asked, "Did you?"

Amelia did and Amelia didn't. She didn't know how to explain. It was as if she'd been told a story about herself, one that was mostly true but with parts she didn't recognize or know how to understand.

"You can't just do that, go up to a woman like that uninvited, and have her say something like that to you." Lydia shook her head. "We messed with something really powerful back there." Amelia stayed numb and unresponsive. "Well? Don't you have anything to say?"

"Not really." Amelia finally spoke, but her voice sounded distant and distracting even to her. Her head was spinning. She was trying to get her mind around what the old woman had said. About cracking the world open when they found that baby. About how it was all her mother's fault. And how vicious Victor had looked when he said those words: "Get off our land."

"Amelia—"

"Can you give me a minute?"

Lydia looked at Amelia agape as she turned onto the highway. "No. No, I can't. I don't even recognize you. You're acting crazy."

"You mean like you?"

"No. I mean like you. Like the way you've been ever since you came back from Portland. So fucking cool. Wes and Sadie and Viiiiiiic-tor."

"I can't talk about that right now."

"*You?*" Lydia mocked shock. "You don't want to talk about something? What a surprise! What a goddamn surprise! Amelia Barrow avoiding the subject of herself."

"Just let me out, please."

"You're kidding, right?"

"I'm *not* kidding." Amelia gripped the door handle. She didn't know why she was so angry, but she couldn't see through it. She needed air. "Slow down and let me out."

Without another word, Lydia pulled onto the shoulder and put on the brakes. Gravel spilled down over the side of the road as the car careened to a halt. Amelia opened the car door and slammed it behind her. She started walking. She didn't care how long it would take her to get home.

Chapter Seven

WILLA
Day Four
Salina, Kansas, to Boulder, Colorado ~
Saturday, May 10, 1997

*W*hen you enter Colorado on Interstate 70, heading west, it is impossible to believe the Rockies are right there, lying just out of sight a few miles ahead of you. You've been driving for hours through one of the flattest, broadest plains on the face of the earth. As far as you can tell, this flat land will go on forever. Nothing but bunch grass and scrub and a few far-off sheeplike clouds that race quickly across the sky. These cotton-candy clouds sometimes cast the car in shadow, but that is the most exciting thing to happen for miles. The simplicity of this life becomes comforting. In Willa's case, it was just what she needed. Nothing in sight challenged her steady grip on the steering wheel.

Then comes a moment when you realize that all those dark thunderheads that haven't budged in miles—those grayish splotches hovering stationary above the horizon—are really mountain peaks bathed in snow and shadow and light. It dawns on you, as it dawned on Willa, that the first white settlers who thought the scariest thing they were going to encounter was Indians hadn't yet caught sight of these ruthless, monstrous mountains lying in wait, ready to swallow horses, splinter wagon wheels, and dash spirits without a second's hesitation.

Willa glanced at her father. He smiled at her. He'd been smiling at her for two days. She hadn't been giving him the silent treatment, but she'd been keeping talk to a minimum. This morning, lying in bed in Salina, listening to him showering, she allowed herself the realization that it must have been difficult for Nat to tell her these secrets he'd been carrying. She was still upset that he'd kept them from her all this time. But she knew there had to be a reason that he'd kept them to himself, even if she didn't want to admit it. This was how it always was. He was too good to her to stay mad at for long.

"You can drive," she offered.

"But you're doing such a good job," he said. "Unless you're tired. I'm happy to take over if you want a break."

"Nah."

"You've never seen the Rockies before."

She shook her head.

"They're something, aren't they?" They were. They reared up out of nowhere. He paused, then added, "Take the turnoff for Boulder."

"But we have to keep going," said Willa, keeping to herself the words "even though you won't tell me why going matters."

"I want to show you something," Nat replied. So Willa followed the signs that fed them onto highways careening around Denver and up to Boulder. All the while, the mountains soared redder and more jagged against the sky.

The town of Boulder was exquisite—a sturdy downtown with all sorts of gift shops, cafés, restaurants; wooden cottages with wide yards and dogs lazing in the sunlight; tall trees everywhere. Willa felt as if she were on a movie set. Boys on skateboards whizzed past as Nat directed her through town. "Did you guys stop here? When you drove across the country?" she asked.

"We did," he said. "Your mother loved this place."

The conversation was safe like that, skirting the edge of the issue, as they made their way out of Boulder and toward a mountain road that wound its way up through a national park. Willa leaned forward to get a better purchase on things. She could see what was ahead. She'd never driven at such an incline, with such a drop-off just at the edge of the car and no guardrail. In the past, Nat already would have offered to drive. Willa was scared to steer up what seemed like a sheer cliff.

"I don't think the car's gonna make it, Dad," she said hopefully.

"It'll be fine."

She shook her head and looked at him again. "Could you . . . ?"

"You can do it," he said.

"I don't *want* to do it, I think." And she laughed a little at herself. "Please?"

"You sure?"

She nodded and relinquished the driver's seat at the next tiny shoulder. She was glad as he directed the groaning car carefully around the curves of the alpine road. She locked her door and tried not to look down. She found she was happy to have something real to fear, something tangible. The car could go off the cliff and they could die.

She relaxed her tense hold on the car door as Nat angled in to a turn-off and parked. They had been climbing for twenty minutes, but it was as if they were already in another world. "You're going to want your camera," Nat said, reaching his long arm into the backseat and gathering up her equipment. The car shuddered in a gust of wind.

Willa gasped as she stepped onto the lookout and gazed down at the world below them. She had never been in an airplane, but she thought this was what it must be like. The fields of Colorado were far below, like squares of an old, never-ending quilt sewn in tones of beige and brown, with tufts of white snow as batting. Denver was a distant flash of glass and steel. Willa glanced back at the cold mountain behind them, a solid white column that rose into the sky. "Don't let Ariel out of the car!" she called. One mis-step and any of them would be gone.

"You came up here with Mom?" she asked when they'd brushed the snow off a boulder and huddled there together. Willa was shooting, but lazily. She wanted to stay where she was, see what pictures she could make from one vantage point. In her viewfinder, she caught a family of four sharing a sunny picnic on the other side of the lookout. She snapped the long hair of the little girl, blond like spun gold, tossing about in the wind. She clicked the shutter as dozens of chipmunks skirted the edge of the human activity, greedy but ready to run at any sudden movements.

"This is where we watched the fireworks."

"There were fireworks?"

"It was the Fourth of July. We timed it so we could spend two nights in town and I'd still get back east in time for my apprentice-ship. We told this woman at a diner that we were newlyweds, even though we weren't. She told us the most romantic place she could think of to watch the fireworks was up here. So we came up here expecting, you know, the usual kind of thing—you lie on your back, the fireworks are above you. What we didn't know was how high we were. When they started, we realized we were not only above the fireworks but above dozens of displays going off across the plains." Nat's hand swept the scene in front of them. Willa snapped the world below. "Denver's fireworks, sure, but also ones from the small towns, and ones that teenagers were setting off in backyards. We tried to count them but couldn't keep track. I'm telling you, Wills, there were lights all over the place. Your mom got the giggles. We stayed up here even after the fireworks were over, looking up at how huge the stars were. And then I asked your mom to marry me. I didn't have a ring or anything, and we'd already talked about it, so it wasn't a total surprise. But I wanted to ask her for real. This seemed like the right place to get down on one knee. She said yes. She said she didn't need a ring. All she needed was my promise." He felt Willa nestle against him. "I've wanted to take you here for a long time. It got so cold after I asked her that we had to drive right back down to town and take hot showers. We got back on the road the next day."

Willa's sigh was heavy against Nat's arm. She let her camera come to rest in her lap. She said without a trace of indictment, "You don't have to pretend anymore, Dad."

"Pretend what?"

"Pretend that everything was so great. That you guys . . . I mean, I guess you always let me believe that my mom was this really great person. You know? But she was horrible. You don't have to make her sound so fantastic anymore."

"I'm not pretending."

"I can't believe she did those things, Dad. Those things you said. Bombs. What happened to that man. If she, you know . . . murdered him. Like you said."

"I know," he said. "I know. I'm sorry."

"You don't have to be sorry, Daddy." Willa turned to look at him, and he saw that her face was glossy with grief. "It's *her* fault. *She's* the one to blame. Right? She just fucking left us. I hope I'm nothing like her. I wish I didn't look like her at all."

"Your mom loved you. She loved you so much. You can't forget that."

"I hate her," Willa said. "I hate what she did to us. I hate that you kept it all a secret. I wish I had known what a terrible person she was so I didn't have to—" Willa's expression splintered as she began to weep.

Nat gathered his daughter to him as he had a million times before. She was always like ice at first, but he melted her rigid stance. This was how she had cried as an infant: inconsolable, angry and alone. Grief presenting like a tidal wave. Minutes passed. He felt her begin to drift to the blessed calm after the storm, felt her grip loosen against him. She started to speak into his chest, and he tried to hold her tight. He didn't want her to be met with another wave of reality. But she was strong now. She pulled herself away from him and asked, "Why would you do this? Why would you give her what she wanted? After what she did to you?"

"What do you mean?" Nat had gotten so good at playing the innocent that he forgot he didn't have to anymore. He offered her his shirtsleeve for wiping her nose, but she shook her head. The family at the other end of the lookout was packing up their car and shooting indiscreet looks in Willa's direction.

"That guy. That Elliot Barrow guy."

"You mean why are we going to see Elliot Barrow?"

"Yeah. Why would you try to find him? Who is he?"

Willa looked exactly like she had at four. At seven. At nine and a half. Determined. Her eyes were big and blinking. Her breathing was shallow. She bit her lip once, the only gesture to belie her apprehension. She wanted to know who Elliot Barrow was.

Nat took a deep breath. "Elliot Barrow was your mom's lover. She had an affair with him. And then she chose him. Instead of me."

Willa imagined, for a fraction of a second, pushing her father over the cliff. There would be no more terrible things to know. No more truth.

HELEN

Stolen, Oregon ~ Saturday, October 26, 1996

Helen was drunk enough after our evening out that she ignored her newly stocked woodstove and the glow of the kerosene lamp. Perhaps I do not mean "ignored," perhaps what I mean was that things had become so surreal in the last few hours that this oddness seemed in place with everything else. Had she really almost invited me in for a night of sex, and was it solely her lame attempt at reason that had kept me from coming in? Had she really pressed herself against me on the dance floor like a schoolgirl? Her body was angry at her mind for turning me down. She hoped she'd said the right thing. That she hadn't been insulting, only clear. Ferdinand nuzzled her as she dizzily sat down on the bed and giggled against the comforter. And then the comforter sat up.

Helen screamed so loudly that night crawlers of every variety scurried away from her as fast as their little legs could carry them. In the seconds after her screaming, the land around her cabin was as bug-free as it had been in centuries. She was about to race off into the night herself when the comforter disentangled itself from the tear-soaked face of one Amelia Barrow, equally terrified and terribly apologetic.

"Oh my God, Helen, I'm so sorry, I must have fallen asleep and—"

Helen was gripping her chest, looking as though she might never recover.

"Here," said Amelia, getting up from the bed, bringing the cabin's only chair to Helen, and helping her sit down.

Helen didn't say a word.

"I should go," Amelia said lamely, and began to sniffle again. The sound of her tears brought Helen back to herself, because they were the ragged tears of someone who had been crying for hours and could not stop. Amelia was bending over the bed, gathering things into her backpack, when Helen found her words again.

"No, no, stay."

"It's okay."

"No, it's not. Stay." Helen stood. "Just give me a few minutes to catch my breath." She went about making a pot of tea, and as she did so, she began to laugh at the absurdity of the whole affair. She hoped she could pass herself off as sober. She didn't want to embarrass herself, though it seemed like she'd already done a pretty good job.

"I'm sorry," Amelia said again as Helen placed a hot mug in between her cold hands.

"Next time leave a note on the door or something. Or lie on top of the bed. How's that?"

Amelia nodded, and her face dissolved again.

"Oh, it's not that big a deal. It's funny, really. I promise. We'll be laughing about this for years to come. I couldn't have choreographed a more ridiculous scene myself. Oh, now, Amelia, don't cry . . ."

Amelia was unreachable. Finally, Helen got her to speak but couldn't understand a word she was saying. Amelia hiccupped the words: "It's just. That I ruin. Everything." And started to cry all over again, this time uncontrollably.

Helen held the girl in her arms until her sobs abated some. And then Amelia told her about the argument with Elliot, and mentioned a boy named Wes, and told her about the trip to Victor's grandmother's, and Lydia hating her, and how no one would ever speak to her again. She began to babble about what a terrible person she was. Ferdinand licked Amelia's tears. Helen held her and asked, "Does your father know where you are?"

Amelia nodded into her.

"Good." Helen had never held a child like this before, so close, so needed. Even though Amelia no longer had the body of a child, she was holing into Helen like a three-year-old into her mother. Helen could smell the girl's scalp. She realized that neither of them had ever had this, the burrowing in that most women had with children of their own. She was reticent to move at all, because it was a nice, foreign sensation, to be necessary, to soothe, to comfort.

Then Amelia sat up straight. It jolted Helen's body back into itself—her back was aching, her foot was asleep—and she expected Amelia to say something further about why everyone hated her, to dissolve all over again. But her voice was steady when she said, "You knew my mom."

"Yes," said Helen, "I knew her." So it was time for this.

"I need to know. I know what you're going to say, that it's my dad's job, but he never tells me anything. He won't talk about her. All I know is that her name was Astrid and that she died in an accident when I was a newborn. That's it. I'm sixteen, and that's the only thing I know about my mom." Tears welled up in Amelia's eyes, but they didn't spill over. She'd gained control. "Please. Please help me."

Helen withdrew her arm from around Amelia and folded her hands in her lap.

Amelia was gaining courage now. "My dad gets so sad whenever I mention that she existed. I've tried to ask him, but he doesn't even have any pictures of her. He left them behind when he moved us west. So then I think he moved us west because he wanted to get away from the sad memories he had in the East. Then I think they're *my* memories, and he didn't have the right to take them from me. He didn't have the right to leave those pictures behind." Helen could feel Amelia's eyes searching her face, begging. "I've never met anyone else who knew her. *Please*, Helen. I'll never mention it again. I promise."

A part of Helen had known, on the first day she decided to come west, that this very conversation with Amelia was inevitable. She knew what kind of father Elliot was (the kind of man who "protects" his child from difficult things), and she knew what kind of woman she was (someone who believes that truth is an unrivaled salve). Until this moment, she hadn't given this implicit agreement any thought. It had been wordless, the pact, and it was only now, in hearing Amelia's "please," that the necessity of telling truths was revealed. As though "please" were a magical word used to unlock a vault of terrible memories. Helen hadn't known, until this moment, that she had made a pact in the first place. But now she saw it. There it was. She was doing something necessary on behalf of the Astrid she had known and hated and envied and been broken by. For the Astrid who had borne a beautiful baby Helen could not bear. It did not matter anymore whether Helen had wanted a child in the first place. It did not matter that for so many years, Helen had blamed Astrid as the person who had taken her one chance for a child. What mattered, for the first time, was the child. This child. The one Astrid had borne, the one Helen sat beside right now. The child deserved some answers.

Helen already knew she would spare the girl the hardest truth of all. She would be kind, then leave the rest to Elliot. She knew this was perhaps not the best way. Perhaps not the way she would have handled it in the past. But she could not bear to see what it would do to tell the girl what her mother was. She needed to nudge the girl along, so Amelia could find out for herself what had truly happened.

Amelia was giving up. Helen could feel it in her, the despair building, for every second Helen kept quiet. But Helen thought long and hard about what she was going to say before she said it.

"Your mother and I were not friends. I wish I could say that we were, because that might make things easier for you. We were in love with the same man. Practically everyone I knew was in love with your dad. I know it's impossible for you to imagine anyone ever feeling that way about him, but your father and I were in love in our day. We met at Columbia. We stood up against the war. Your father, well, you know this, but imagine the charisma he has now, doubled, tripled, quadrupled. He motivated people. He got people to *do* things. He got me to fall in love with him.

"After college, we moved into a communal apartment on 102nd Street and Broadway. That's on the Upper West Side, the same neighborhood you were born in. In those days, people got married very young—listen to me, I'm talking like an old woman. But I suppose that's the truth. Elliot married me because it meant he got his inheritance—and no, now, I know more about this than you do. I know that it wasn't *only* because of that. At the time, I didn't know it was about that at all. I thought love was enough. But I got older and wiser, and I saw that I was the kind of girl your grandfather wanted your father to marry. I may not have had the kind of breeding Elliot's mother had envisioned for her son's bride, but your grandfather noticed immediately how loyal I was. A good girl. Your grandmother died before I met your dad. But your grandfather was wonderful to me. I wish he hadn't died before you were born. He always made me feel welcome in the Barrow family, even though I was the daughter of a single, Jewish, working-class woman from New York, and they were these very upper-crust Boston Wasps. We loved the Mets. They loved the Metropolitan Opera.

"In any case, when I married your father, I guess I didn't think about what it meant. I don't think either of us did, truly. What I thought about was being wanted. I hope you don't mind me speaking to you like an adult, but I think you need to hear this, because someday someone will want you like that, and you will have to know if you are strong enough to bear it. I thought I was. I thought I could be who Elliot wanted me to be—someone who would help him in his vision for changing things. But I was already interested in theater by then, and I began to see that I was not a leader in the causes Elliot fought for. *He* was the one who wanted to stand outside prisons and hold candlelight vigils. *He* was the one who wanted to picket outside nonunion supermarkets. But I wanted to grow up. I wanted a career.

"Anyway." This was the hard part. "Astrid. She moved into the commune about six months before I left Elliot. She was a nice girl, very sweet. Very beautiful. Long hair like a curtain. Tall, like you. Striking blue eyes, like yours. I wish I could tell you more about where she came from or what she was really like. But in those later days, I felt so far from what the commune believed in that I didn't spend much time with those people at all. I really only used the commune as a place to sleep, which was dangerous, because they were the kind of people who could turn against you quickly if you were not living the 'right way.' The irony is, Elliot fought hard to keep me from getting kicked out. Even though he was the one who wanted me to leave.

"I came home one afternoon and found Elliot and Astrid making love in my bed. They were happy. Seeing them there together made me realize I hadn't been happy for a long time. They'd obviously fallen in love. So I left your father. I left the commune. And that was the last time I saw your mother.

"I can tell you this. Your father and your mother moved out of that commune the instant they knew they were having you. They set up a home together because they loved each other and they loved the thought of you. They couldn't wait for you to come into their lives. Trust me. I know how badly your father wanted a child. Even though I didn't know Astrid well, I saw how happy she was with Elliot. He made her happy. Your mother loved you, Amelia, I know she did."

Helen could see Amelia sorting through all this new information. "Why are you so nice to me, then? Why would you come help my dad if he was so terrible to you?"

Such a simple set of questions. Helen wouldn't have been able to answer them even a month before. Now she knew. "I'm older. I can see it as a story that happened to someone long ago. And I feel lucky. In those days, I believed I would never love again. I believed I would never survive. I believed I would never have anything to give another person. But I kept living, and pretty soon I realized that life gets good sometimes and it gets bad sometimes. I realized it wasn't the only story I was going to get to tell."

"And my mother? What happened to her? I mean, I know she died in an accident, but I want to know everything."

This was to be managed very carefully. "That's something you need to ask your father."

"But he won't tell me. He'll never tell me. I know he won't."

"Ask him."

"I can't."

Helen took the girl's hand and clasped it tightly. "You take all the time you need. Ask him about her when you know you're ready. And when you're ready, I promise you. I promise you he'll tell you everything."

We each make promises we cannot keep.

The Yarn

Once upon a time, the skinny woman was no longer a skinny woman. Yes, she was still slender, but her bones no longer made her sad. She did not look at herself in the mirror and think: "A bag of bones." She had come to accept her body, though only a short time had passed since she'd found the husband rolling in bed with the different woman who was like a bird. Already the discovery seemed decades old. At first leaving the husband had been like trying to breathe in a place without air. Soon enough, the no-longer-just-skinny-woman realized the terrible truth: not breathing was the same as dying. Dying seemed like an opportunity for a while. But when she saw how much the dog needed her, she began to see dying as an inconvenience. As she fed and walked and threw sticks for the dog, she saw that, at least in the dog's eyes, her death would be a tragedy. So the woman decided to keep her breathing up. The air was sticky and sweet and thick. It was a city's summer air, which is lumpy and full of the smells of others. She hesitated to let it in her lungs. But she watched the dog and tried to be like him. She taught herself to inhale and process and exhale the sticky maple syrup that had replaced the air in what was now her life.

Let us begin to call her the satin woman. Once she started breathing in the maple syrup, and life opened with a sweet daily measure of hope and opportunity, the skinny woman began to notice that her skin was softer than it had ever been before. From head to toe, she began to have an extraordinary luster. She exuded confidence, and even she began to notice the way people—men, especially—looked at her. They looked at her the way she had noticed people looking at the husband in days gone by. Every day she became the satin woman more and more. Every day the world slipped off her like rain off the eaves of a well-designed roof.

She was not going to stay a satin woman. Up until this point and, in fact, for the rest of her life, she had been and always would be in a state of fluctuation between the skinny woman and the satin woman. These states of being were two extremes of the pendulum's swing. Sometimes the pendulum swung over a matter of days. Sometimes it took decades. But if it went one way, it would always go back. The satin woman knew nothing about this. She thought, now being made out of satin, that she would never have to be skinny again. She did not see that she was given both options so that one day, when she was older and wiser, she could choose to hover in the sweet spot between them both. She did not see that both states of being were equally good, that though the skinny woman was scared and unhappy, she was also clearheaded and brave, and that though the satin woman was witty and elegant, she was also vain and shortsighted. But we are getting ahead of ourselves. Let us not be distracted from the story at hand.

The satin woman had started meeting with a group of actors every week, reading plays by dead men who wrote about the human condition. The satin woman loved the moments when ancient words would soar from her. She loved feeling that these words made her bigger than her own small self. She loved inhabiting the hearts and minds of others. And she loved being part of a group of people who were working toward making something, not taking something down. She remembered how the clan she had belonged to with the husband had only pretended it was a clan. Instead of making a good feeling that was bigger than itself, all the clan seemed to make was a set of angry whirlpools through which each person daily descended. It was as if the clan started the day braided together like a thick, useful rope and ended it a frayed set of weak strings. To be part of the clan, you had to believe that the world was in a state of deadly hopelessness. You had to believe that the clan (and only the clan) had the power to change this world. You had to believe change came through anger. That meant the satin woman, when she was still the skinny woman and living with the clan, had felt terrible and alone at the end of every day. While remember-

ing how this felt, the satin woman looked around at the group of actors she was now a part of, and she smiled. She started every day as a single strand. She ended every day braided into something thicker. She ended woven into a tapestry. What can I say? It was the early 1980s. She listened to a lot of Carole King.

One evening the satin woman left her acting group and strolled down the bustling avenue where she lived. She heard trains rumbling below her and watched old women pushing carts of food. She looked forward to taking her dog out for a long walk when morning came. Then she saw him. And she remembered. Not just what it had been to love him but what she had wanted from him all those years and what she saw in his arms. A baby. He had a baby.

The husband and the woman who was like a bird had made a baby together. Now that the satin woman examined it, she understood why the few people who were in the clan and with whom she still sometimes spoke had been so strange around her the past few months. They had known the baby was on its way, but they hadn't known what to tell her. So they had told her nothing at all.

She decided to pretend she had already known. She sidled up beside the husband who was now someone else's husband and said, "Congratulations." The husband looked up at her, and tears seemed to leap to his eyes the second he saw her. Even without the tears, he looked tired and worried. The satin woman hoped a little that he was sad on her account. But she also saw the beautiful baby—really just a lump of pinkness, so new and bright—curled against him. She let out a sudden laugh that clapped against the people milling beside them. "She's beautiful!" the satin woman exclaimed.

"Thank you," said the no-longer-husband. He was solemn. She wanted to punch him in the shoulder and say, "It's okay. Bygones and all that." But she could see that he was about to say something big, and she didn't want that. All she wanted to think about was how she would be taking her dog on a walk in the park the next day. So before he could say another word, she took a step back.

"I've got to get some milk," she said, and walked away.

She did not buy milk. The next thing she knew, she was in the yarn store buying soft pink baby yarn. Apparently, she was going to make a sweater for the husband's baby. She thought this very odd indeed but didn't know how to stop the transaction. She wondered at herself. Why would she buy yarn for the different woman's baby? Perhaps because she felt sorry for the baby itself, being held by a man who looked so sad. Perhaps the satin woman sensed something so true and invisible, that the woman who was like a bird and was now a mother was in far over her head, and this pink sweater was a method to try to stop what was already on its way to happening. Or perhaps the satin woman was simply planning to let the different woman know she had won after all, and leave it at that.

By the time the satin woman got the phone call five days later from the husband himself, she had knitted only one sleeve of the baby sweater. She was not a very good knitter, after all. As she heard the panic in his voice, the sorrow, the need, she fingered the soft little sleeve. She set it down and got her coat. The different woman had disappeared. The husband was in a panic. The baby was with him, yes, but that was not the point. He was going mad. He thought something that wasn't true. She told him it wasn't true. But he needed her, and she heard it. She left the beginnings of the sweater where it lay and never worked on it again.

Act Four

[OR]

Let Me Live Here Ever;
So Rare a Wonder'd
Father and a Wise
Makes This Place Paradise

Chapter One

When I was a boy, and Maw-Maw sat at the center of my life, love and anger were two strong feelings I could easily tell apart. As I grew older and felt the forces exerted by desire and betrayal, things grew more complicated. I could desire something I knew I might grow to love, but when life betrayed me—by denying me the object of my desire—I felt anger and pain. That was when fear entered the mix. Soon the terms got jumbled around, and over time—long time—a pattern emerged. Say, for instance, I desired someone I felt I could love. Afraid of the inevitable betrayal and the subsequent pain, I'd grow enraged at *her* for making me want her in the first place. In a grand gesture of preemptive punishment, I'd be the one to initiate betrayal. Because she was the one to blame for being so damn *wantable.* Which is a long way of saying that, in matters of love, I had become a self-justifying, lonely asshole.

Many problems arose from this strategy—many losses were tallied—but the greatest loss was the one I couldn't even register. Because love and pain, desire and fear and anger, all appeared at the same time, I lost my ability to tell them apart. Sure, they still gave rise to loud, sharp roars in my body and soul, or a slow, raw keening in my heart, but let's face it, all I could tell is that I

was being jerked around by something huge. Pretty sophisticated, huh?

ALL THAT IS a prologue to my dealings with Duncan. Yes. Helen's
Duncan.

It was during the second week in January that I began to get the
phone calls. Hard not to see now, with the benefit of hindsight, that
Duncan must have made a New Year's resolution. I was sitting in
my office, grading papers, when Eunice buzzed my line. "There's a
guy on the phone. Wants to speak to the man in charge. Elliot's in
class." She knew I'd bite.

"Yup?" I said into the receiver.

"Hello?" came the man's voice.

"Hey. How can I help you?"

"Hello. Who's this?"

"Who's *this*?" I wanted a name.

"This *is* Ponderosa Academy, isn't it? I've been trying to reach
someone there since last week."

"Yes, this is Ponderosa. We've been on break."

"Thank God *someone* finally answered the phone. I need to
speak with Helen Bernstein." His voice dripped with irritation.

"May I ask the nature of your business?"

Silence. Then, a little huffily, "Is she there or not?"

Now I was the silent one.

"May I ask to whom I'm speaking?" A reasonable question, if
you think about it.

It was my response—the promptness of it—that surprised me.
"Elliot Barrow," I said without thinking.

"Elliot Barrow!" The man paused. "I thought you were in class.
Your secretary said—"

"I'm not in class. I'm here, with you. Now may I ask who's calling?"

"Duncan Reilly. Helen's husband. Her *current* husband. Let me
speak to her, Elliot."

That's when my fear and anger merged into a rather manipulative, albeit stupid, wiliness. "But you see, my good friend, she's unavailable. She's in a class right this very minute. And the truth is, the first thing out of her mouth the second she stepped on campus was that she would rather be drawn and quartered than ever have to speak to you again. I assured her I would do everything in my power to make sure she got her wish. Now I find myself in a rather tricky situation." I felt like Elliot—sure I did—only braver, more honest, slightly more British. I went on. "Between us, Duncan, if anyone can empathize with your position, it's me."

His voice softened. "Is she okay?"

"She's thriving," Elliot replied.

"Well, there's a lot we have to talk about." He wavered. "I really want to talk to her. *Need* to talk to her."

"Naturally." As if impersonating Elliot weren't bad enough, I did something worse. "I've got an idea," I said. "Since Helen doesn't want to hear about you, but you want to hear how she's doing, why don't I just pass along my private office number and you call me from time to time?" As soon as I spoke, I knew my ruse might work. I never answered the phone by giving my name—I hated the stuffiness of that—and instead uttered a trademark *"Yup?"* Fortunately, Duncan didn't know of either my existence or my trademark. "That way I can keep you posted on how Helen's doing. Serve as sort of a go-between. Let you know when she's ready to initiate contact again." I let him mull it over. "What do you say?" I sounded like Elliot at his most patronizingly friendly.

"You're sure she won't talk to me now? Will you at least tell her I called? That I want her to call me back? Whenever she can?"

"Trust me," I said.

He trusted me. Then we hung up.

There you have it. In the space of a few minutes, I had managed to commit three relatively brutal acts: I'd lied to Duncan, impersonated Elliot, and infantilized Helen. Four brutal acts, if you count me as another one of my victims: I'd set myself up for a colossal downfall. At least some part of my pea brain must have known that I'd pay for this. Big-time. Once it was undertaken, it was something I couldn't undo.

So why do we think I did something that was so bad for so many? Let's forget all that crap about love and desire, betrayal and anger. They are relevant but not necessarily helpful. Sure I desired Helen, knew she was loveworthy. Sure I felt betrayed by her continuing rectitude, and that made me mad. I think I hated Elliot for lots of reasons. But that wasn't why I did this.

I did it because I wanted something clean and basic, something that I'd never allowed myself to have. I wanted to talk about Helen in the way you get to talk about someone you care for. I wanted to brag about her a little. Smile as I reminisced. I wanted to share this talk, these feelings, with someone who could get how simple they were, how justified. I wanted Helen's name to live in my mouth, her stories on my tongue. It seems that I, Calbert Fleecing, couldn't let myself be a man who got to have such rudimentary, good things without stealing them from another man.

I heard from Duncan again a week or so later. This probably had something to do with the fact that I never told Helen that Duncan had called. I know. I know.

I lied to him. I told him I'd passed along the message and she'd asked to be left alone. But let it be noted that there were limits to my arrogance: that was the last time I ever spoke on her behalf. I never said, "She does not forgive you." I never said, "Never call here." So he kept calling. Sometimes we'd shoot the shit. Sometimes he would reveal deeply personal fears to me, like his terror that, having cheated on his wife and been left by his mistress—who was not his mistress in the first place but, rather, some pretty young thing who'd wanted to bed Power and figured out soon thereafter that she had simply bedded Pathetic—he was going to die alone. Or his fears about his career, about the people in New York who had turned against him now that he did not have Helen on his arm.

He became something of a friend. I pretended to be Elliot only in name; the rest of it was me: listening, offering advice. He liked me. He was a troubled man, but he was also good. Funny. Smart. He wanted to be better than he was. He was asking me to help him decipher where that missing piece of him had gone. He once said to me, "I never thought we'd be friends, Elliot. And the truth is, I don't have many friends. I don't think I know how to make people trust me. That's why losing Helen is so terrible. Maybe it's not even losing her. Maybe it's losing who she thought I was."

I became kind toward him, and not just because I pitied him. I didn't side with him, certainly not, but I began to see their story as an orb, something with smoothness to it, where one thing would lead to another and fault was not involved. I began to understand Helen from another point of view, like seeing the moon from the other side of space. Every time he called, and every time we talked, I knew I was one step closer to being found out. But I began to like him. Some days I even hoped he'd call.

Given all the world's loneliness, I don't know if there was anything wrong in that.

HELEN
Stolen, Oregon ~ Wednesday, January 15, 1997

Helen stopped me in the hallway a week past winter break. By this point we were being nice to each other, but we certainly weren't at an easy-breezy "stop in the hallway and say hello" phase. What had happened the night we went to Rudy's was still making things awkward between us. Lord knows why. I'd done a lot more with women for a lot less drama. But Helen was careful. I had begun to realize this about her, and it would be a good while before I would like her even more because of it. She wasn't the kind of person who accidentally almost slept with people. This truth was something she repeated, alone to herself, as she lay in her icy bed and thought, into the darkness, about me. I didn't know this. All I knew was that I wanted to blame the awkwardness on her. Which was unfair, to say the least; it takes two to tango.

I was surprised she stopped me. She was surprised she stopped me. We were both mightily surprised.

"Cal," she said, two steps beyond me, before her brain had a chance to still her tongue. We were walking in opposite directions.

I was turned by her. I remember cocking my head to the side, as if I were listening up and listening down. "Yup."

"Can we talk?"

There was a thunder pounding in my breast when she said those words. We sidled off the beaten path as children raced out of the building into the free afternoon. We leaned like schoolgirls against a pair of lockers.

"I'm wondering if you'd mind sitting in on my auditions."

Why didn't these people know how to ask a question? Helen and Elliot had a way of framing things so you were damned if you did and damned if you didn't. I stood there in the stuffy hallway and tried to figure out who was wondering what and what there was to mind and what sitting in on auditions meant.

She thought I was going to say no. She had the sudden fear that she would burst into tears. For though she had surprised herself in speaking to me, she had been hoping for some time now that I could help her. She had imagined many different ways of asking. She knew I would say I did not want to help her. But she also suspected that I actually would. Would want to and would help. She had devised all sorts of suave ways to ask and tried to memorize them, so she would not bumble them up. And then she had gone and done exactly that. She nearly ran away.

"Do you need my help?" I asked. I guess I wanted to know.

She glanced at her hands. They seemed too far away, folded against her jeans. "Yes," she said after a moment. She was hoping that wasn't too forward.

"Why?"

"I don't think I can manage on my own, actually," she said. "Just the auditions." She laughed. The laugh was like a gust of wind that filled my sails. "At least for now."

It was enough for me.

CAL
Stolen, Oregon ~ Monday, January 27, 1997

The children of Ponderosa Academy are a good lot. They are most often kind. They give back to their community, and not just because they have to. They honor their elders almost every day. They are not, however, actors. Or at least most of them were not actors of promise on that Friday in late January when Helen and I sat on folding chairs in the gym and listened to sixty-two of them perform scenes: "I might call him / A thing divine, for nothing natural / I ever saw so noble"; "A howling monster; a drunken monster!"; "You have often / Begun to tell me what I am, but stopp'd." We watched as they hollered out monologues: "Ye elves of hills, brooks, standing lakes, and groves"; "Be not afeard. The isle is full of noises"; "If by your art, my dearest father, you have / Put the wild waters in this roar, allay them." Helen, judicious, even-handed Helen, considered it fair to give anyone interested in auditioning the chance to do so, including those kids who had not been meeting with her on a regular basis. Ten minutes after nine, I saw the error of her ways.

Eunice kept order in the hallway. We could hear them buzzing out there, and in retrospect, I have to admit that was a good thing. I didn't say this out loud, but I'd never witnessed at Ponderosa anything like this bubbling desire to participate.

Elliot was in Portland for a week, engaged in serious negotiations with the folks at Benson Country Day. The rumor mill—well, Eunice—had passed on the news that somehow Elliot had found out about certain irregularities concerning the dismissal of a teacher who'd indulged in some inappropriate behavior, and Elliot was making sure the two schools saw eye to eye on such issues before any possible merger. My anger over the entire merger question had

ebbed into something less tangible. I took refuge in the knowledge
that I was under no obligation to Elliot Barrow, Ponderosa Academy, or the Neige Courante. I could walk any time I wanted to.
Maybe taking that walk would be cowardly, but letting myself think
about it provided me with a nice warm blanket of self-justification
in which to wrap myself at the end of exhausting, frustrating days.

So there I was, helping out. Helen's play. I was not blind to the fact
that the promised production of *The Tempest* might well have become
the proverbial cherry on top of the diversity cake that made Ponderosa Academy look so damn delectable to Benson Country Day.

Even if I had wanted to mull this over, even if I wanted to relish some irony, the children were too loud, too excited, too insis-
tent for me to think about anything other than *them*. Man, they
commanded attention. Ever the practiced professional, Helen insisted on conducting the auditions as if the gym at Ponderosa were
Broadway. Each "actor"—her preferred term—filled out a detailed
résumé: name, age, grade, hair color, eye color. Naturally, over 98
percent of our applicants wrote some combination of "black" or
"brown" in those last two categories. There was a space to record
previous experience—one child had done some modeling one
summer after being approached on a Portland sidewalk by a talent
agent. Amelia's violin recitals were the sum total of our "previous
experience." Another space, left blank by everyone, was labeled
"future aspirations." Helen explained that meant "dreams and
hopes." But most kids still left it blank. The final, vague category—
"interest in Shakespeare"—made a few of Helen's loyal followers
write things like "You said to come." Otherwise, all we saw were
the occasional smiley face and obscene word.

By lunchtime, I had a pounding headache. I was supposed to go
back to my office to see if there were any school disasters that
needed my magic touch, but Helen asked me to stay and talk with
her. It was the damn way that woman asked for things. She made
me help her even when it was the last thing on my mind.

"So what did you think? Have we seen a Prospero yet?"

"You're really asking me?"

"Be honest."

I decided to try both honesty and tact, avoiding the subject of the kids' lack of talent, focusing on the glory of the old wizard Prospero. "Honestly, no. And I don't think you're going to. Prospero is . . . larger than life. Powerful. It takes balls to be that big. And we don't have anyone who's going to fill those shoes. I just don't see it happening."

"And a Caliban?"

I smiled and settled back in my chair. "Same thing," I said. "I hate to disappoint you, but if Prospero's got big balls, then Caliban's the only one with gigantic ones. The play is a battle of wits—"

"I don't know if I'd call it that."

"I don't want to debate you." I laughed. "You'll win. But you asked for my opinion, and now you have it."

My candor got me out of one job: Helen didn't ask me to help her with casting. For the rest of the day, I warmed my seat as the children filed in and out and slaughtered the Bard. At the end of the day, I went home and lay in bed and smiled to myself. I didn't know if I was smiling because she was going to fail or because I'd spent the day in her company.

ON MONDAY SHE posted a cast list that was so crazy, so bold, I sought her out the first chance I got. Which happened to be a lunch meeting in Elliot's office.

"You cast Amelia as Caliban?"

She was sitting, prim as can be, her knees up against the front of Elliot's desk, one of Amelia's lunches spread before her. I would recognize that fifteen-year-old Tupperware and the signature combination of hard-boiled egg and peanut-butter sandwich anywhere, even if it hadn't been sitting right next to an identical meal spread before Elliot Barrow.

"And what's wrong with that?" she asked innocently.

"Nepotism? For one?" I gestured to the meals on the desk and in Elliot's general direction. "And she's a girl? And no offense,

Elliot, but the truth is, she isn't very good. Which brings me back to nepotism."

"Oh, nonsense," Helen said. She had an odd way of looking like Maria von Trapp when she wanted to. The Julie Andrews version, not the real one, with the wrinkled face and Nordic brow. Helen pinned me with her eyes and asked with a smile, "Is it because she's white?"

"No," I said vehemently. "Honestly, no."

"And what do you think of my Prospero?"

"Victor Littlefoot?"

"Yes. Do you think he has enough portent?"

"He's certainly something of a deity around these parts. If that's what you were going for." Two can play at the fancy word game. "To tell you the truth, I'm surprised he even showed up. That kid lives for basketball."

"And Lydia?"

"As Miranda? Well, she sure won't play the role as it was written. Lydia's not what we call a wallflower."

"I was going for putting the best people in the parts I had available."

"Well, you know my opinions on that."

"We certainly do," said Elliot, with an annoying trace of amusement in his voice. It was then that I wished I'd kept my opinions to myself. "Care to sit?" he asked.

"I should get back."

"Just sit down," said Helen, and before I knew it, I was sitting. "Sandwich?" she said, beginning to slide a lunch baggy in my direction, but that was where I drew the line.

Elliot and Helen had been talking about his trip up to Benson Country Day. I had interrupted an apparent flurry of excitement about the day of what we were now calling the Ponderosa Festival, which would take place on May 6 and feature a daytime powwow, a musical performance by the elementary students, and, in the evening, *The Tempest*. There was much to be done, but as I listened, I was surprised at how much had already been scheduled. Teachers and parents had already signed up to volunteer, and as they went down the list of names, it seemed mine was the only one not included. In fact, my name was noticeably absent. As Helen and Elliot discussed their vision, and the vision of every other adult member of the school community save me, things took a turn for the uncomfortable. I couldn't very well excuse myself, if only because that would have drawn even more attention to me.

Let it be noted: I did not want to help. I did not want anything to do with the hoopla required to ingratiate ourselves with Benson Country Day folks. But it was inevitable.

"And Cal?" Elliot looked in my direction, one eyebrow raised.

"Cal is helping me." So Helen was also going to pretend I wasn't sitting there.

"Really? How?"

"Working with the actors. Scene work. Stage work. Building sets."

"Good. Wow, Cal." I hated it when Elliot took this tone. "That's great. I must admit, I'm surprised."

After we stepped outside and before we parted ways, Helen said, "You owe me one."

"Are you kidding me?"

"I just saved your ass in there," she said, rippling into laughter.

"I'm not working with the kids," I said.

"Oh, yes, you are."

"I don't know anything about acting. Or the theater. Or Shakespeare."

"Hah! That's a good one! You went to Harvard, got your degree in English and American literature and language, didn't you? Harry Levin's famed lectures? Any of that ring bells?" She laughed again. "Don't look at me that way! I know you know Shakespeare better than anyone else around!"

"Except you."

"Well, yes. You would be right about that."

"Since when did you get to be the boss of me?"

"Since I saved your ass."

Which was how I became her slave.

Chapter Two

AMELIA

Stolen, Oregon ~ Friday, February 21, 1997

*F*orgiveness. Forgiveness is what must come after rage. Amelia had been raised to assume that an apology functions a little like a reset button on the hair dryer. The dryer blasts heat, then refuses to turn on the next time you plug it in, you push the reset button, and voilà—more hot air! Things are back to normal. Except for the part where you no longer count 100 percent on the dryer working in the dead of winter. So you don't wake up at dawn to wash your hair before school; you begin to plan ahead. Your life changes a tiny bit, reorganizes itself, and you don't notice. You think it's the way it's always been, and it sort of is. But not completely.

When Amelia decided to forgive her father about Benson, it was a matter of offering an apology. She'd decided to forgive him because, honestly, she was sick of the flouncing drama of everyday life. That, and the fact that after her collisions with Lydia and Victor, she couldn't even imagine what might happen if Sadie and Wes popped up in her Ponderosa world. Her imagination failed her, she knew, not because the confrontation would be huge but because Sadie and Wes hardly mattered to her now. She'd deal with those two when she saw them, *if* she saw them. It helped that, even before the full apology had left her lips, Elliot was eagerly apologetic in return—"Sweetheart, how selfish of me not to have consulted you!"—but Amelia chalked that up to Helen's influence. She knew that things would never really get back to *normal* normal.

That had to do with Lydia. Never before had Amelia realized what Lydia meant to her. Lydia was still in her daily life, sure, but she wasn't really there. Things had changed. Naturally, there had been apologies and explanations. Naturally, Suzanne and Louie Cinqchevaux had gathered Amelia up, had sided with her plight, had accused old Mrs. Littlefoot not of lying but of craziness, which meant they needed no explanations from Amelia. Old women were crazy sometimes, what were you going to do about it?

But Lydia was different. Lydia required stories, explanations. When Amelia told her the story of the baby at Wiggler's Creek, of Elliot's anger at the time, of Victor's desire to search for a real baby, and when Amelia swore that she knew nothing about Victor and drugs, nothing about Chicago, it was clear that Lydia believed her. It was clear that Lydia would keep these secrets. Lydia's anger, her hurt, weren't about who should know what. They were about too little, too late. They were about what she and Amelia had said to each other after they'd been terrified by an old grandmother who'd unearthed blatant secrets that both girls felt too young, too scared, to explore.

It was also about the other thing, the unspeakable thing; Amelia had crossed an invisible line. She had grown up mourning her plight at Ponderosa Academy, trapped, lonely, in her father's realm. Lydia had listened, all these years, as Amelia complained, all the while probably thinking the white girl had no idea how good she had it. Amelia knew Lydia didn't call her "the white girl." But she also knew that Lydia wouldn't look her straight in the eye for a long time after they'd gone to visit Mrs. Littlefoot. Because something serious had happened, something Neige Courante, something deep and strange and baffling. It wasn't about craziness, not really. And it wasn't about poverty, although both girls had been trained—oh, man, had they been trained—to be politically correct about poverty. It was about a possibility that was true and wild. Neige Courante. Indian. That was what they couldn't say.

For the same reason, Amelia didn't know what to do or say to Victor. Normally, she would have sought advice from Lydia, but not this time. This time Amelia knew she was on her own. She wished she could get up the guts to do something, to say something right. She should apologize for going to visit Mrs. Littlefoot, but not because she'd defied Victor's will; that was the wrong reason. Maybe she should have gone sooner; maybe she should go again. What could she say? Everything felt unfinished, raw. These were the circles of thought Amelia's mind orbited in the three months between the time Victor stopped talking to her and the day that he was cast as Prospero and she, his slave.

IT WAS ABOUT three weeks later when they got onstage together for the first time ("stage" being a loose term; it was a rectangular area marked in electrical tape on the floor of the gym. Helen had high hopes that someone—read: me—would help by building a low stage that could be assembled in pieces for rehearsals and the performance. I assured her we risked no such progress). Victor and Amelia had read their scenes together a couple of times, but that was always with a big group of people, during what Helen insisted on calling "a table read," and they were always seated far apart and thus not required to make chitchat. This time it was just Amelia and Victor. And Lydia. Who had been cast as Prospero's daughter, Miranda. Which made things weirder.

"I have some ideas for blocking, but I want to see what you do naturally, okay? So just read the scene and try not to get too caught up in the language, but remember to *move* where you want to move." Helen gestured to stage right (which, I've "learned"—I already knew this, but everyone, including her, was excited to be the first to explain it to me—is named from the point of view of the actors. Leave it to the audience to be blamed for getting everything backward). "Prospero's cave will be over here. But you do have the whole stage to work with. So let's just see what happens."

Amelia stepped "onto" the stage and stole a glance at Victor. He was engrossed in his script. They'd been issued the same bulky folders with three-hole-punched, one-sided, photocopied, and enlarged pages from an unannotated version of the play. Helen had shown all the actors how they could open a script to any page and write down blocking or notes on the blank page facing it. I know everything about those scripts. Guess who was roped into making them?

Back to the tale at hand. They read the scene once, standing there. Amelia knew they should be moving, but Victor wasn't moving and Lydia wasn't moving, and she herself didn't know how Caliban stood or how his voice sounded (or why she'd been cast as him, for that matter), so she delivered her lines as best she could. It was the angry piece of Act One, Scene Two, when Prospero and Miranda gang up on Caliban. He tells them:

> *This island's mine by Sycorax my mother,*
> *Which thou tak'st from me. When thou cam'st first,*
> *Thou strok'st me and made much of me, wouldst give me*
> *Water with berries in't, and teach me how*
> *To name the bigger light, and how the less,*
> *That burn by day and night; and then I lov'd thee*
> *And show'd thee all the qualities o' th' isle,*
> *The fresh springs, brine-pits, barren place and fertile.*
> *Curs'd be I that did so! All the charms*
> *Of Sycorax, toads, beetles, bats, light on you!*
> *For I am all the subjects that you have,*
> *Which first was mine own king; and here you sty me*
> *In this hard rock, whiles you do keep from me*
> *The rest o' th' island.*

Prospero recounts, as Miranda looks on, how Caliban once tried to rape Miranda. Cheery. And oddly reminiscent. But I am not a revisionist. I do not believe Shakespeare was some kind of prophet presaging the abuse of Native Americans at the hand of the white man. What I believe is much simpler: that what happened to us brown people was so fucking predictable that Mr. Stock Scene himself wrote it down when our version of it was only beginning in the world. That Shakespeare gave Prospero these words: "I pitied thee, / Took pains to make thee speak, taught thee each hour / One thing or other. When thou didst not, savage, / Know thine own meaning, but wouldst gabble like / A thing most brutish, I endow'd thy purposes / With words that made them known" was not because Shakespeare was a genius (perhaps he was a genius, but not in this, and really, who's sick of the genius debate? Let's call them all geniuses and be done with it) but because he was a story-teller. Centuries of genocide and rape and false promises do a great story make. It doesn't take a genius to think that up.

They were not good actors. Amelia knew this. Not just because Helen looked befuddled when they lowered their scripts but because Amelia could sense mediocrity hovering above her like a swarm of gnats. But all Helen said was "Again, please. And Victor, this time, remember, Caliban is your slave. He's disobeyed you. You must put him back in line."

Amelia had to start the scene by entering. She had to curse at them, but the curse was long and hard and tangled: "As wicked dew as e'er my mother brush'd / With raven's feather from un-wholesome fen / Drop on you both!" She stumbled over the words and tried to imagine how Caliban would stand, but all she could muster was a halfhearted hunch. So she was surprised when Victor's lines emerged from him bold, and loud, and angry.

"For this, be sure, to-night thou shalt have cramps," he began, and she blushed because he was looking right at her, and the face he had on was the same face he'd worn that day when he found his grandmother holding Amelia's hand. She wanted to shrink from him. But since her next line was bold, she tried to be bold too. Because it began with "I must eat my dinner," she thought, "Well, maybe that means Caliban's going somewhere," so she walked in front of Victor and, out of the corner of her eye, caught Helen nodding and smiling, so she knew she'd done something right.

She tried to be as dominant as Victor. His next line began "Thou most lying slave," and he was in her face, and she felt afraid but thrilled at the same time. She had felt this before when she was with him at the bonfire and on the brink of something she had never expected. Being near him had felt good and terrible at the same time. Now they were face-to-face, and she felt a challenge well up inside her.

"You taught me language," she said, "and my profit on't / Is, I know how to curse. The red plague rid you / For learning me your language!"

He had another line, and as he was saying it, she looked at her next line, at what she was supposed to say, and she realized he was going to win. Prospero threatens Caliban with magic, and Caliban pleads for mercy. We see this is not the first time Prospero has punished him. We feel pity for the slave. But Amelia did not know how to back down to such a place. She felt her heart thudding against its four walls, and she wanted to go on. She did not want to leave the stage. She did not want to lose yet. But she delivered her lines and exited.

"So much better, you guys!" enthused Helen. "Why don't you take a three-minute break and we can block it out?"

Victor left the stage. Lydia left her post on the stage and, as she passed by, whispered to Amelia, "He's *good*. And by the way, Miranda is a fucking twit. I can't believe I have to sit here with a straight face."

Amelia watched Victor as he got a sandwich out of his bag. He was not going to speak to her. Even after this, even after the way she felt and the way it felt to act together, trading lines, *pretending*, there was going to be nothing. Which was going to get stranger as the show progressed. It was up to her. She was going to have to figure out exactly what to say.

CAL
Stolen, Oregon ~ Wednesday, March 19, 1997

Amelia never came to my classroom unless she wanted something. I learned this about her when she was five, because I kept lollipops in my desk drawer and she had an uncanny ability to show up at the most opportune moments, licking her rosebud lips in anticipation. But Amelia's the kind of person who isn't always aware of what she wants. Part of the trick is teasing her desire out of her. When she slumped in under the weight of her backpack after my last class of the day, I knew with one look at her that she had no idea what had brought her to me.

We shot the shit. We were masters at avoiding big topics. I asked her about the play. I knew we'd get to whatever was on her mind eventually, but I didn't know it'd happen so soon.

"I can't do it," she said.

"Let me guess: for moral reasons. You don't believe women should be on the stage."

"Very funny. No, Cal, I mean, I can't do it. It's too hard. All these lines to memorize—"

"You have a great memory. You've memorized all those violin pieces for years! You're going to be fine."

"No." She was shaking her head. "Why did she cast me in the hardest part in the play? I'm the only girl who has to play a boy. And he's not even a boy. He's a monster! You know? And then I have to be funny. And I'm not a funny person. You know I'm not. I am absolutely not funny."

"So you're scared of being funny?"

"Never mind," she said, gathering her things.

I got her to sit back down. "What's so hard about it? And I don't mean that the way it sounds. I mean, explain to me why it feels so hard."

She sighed. She was quiet for a good period of time, during which she looked out the window. I watched as her mind zigged and zagged. Then she said, "Forget it."

"No, tell me."

"I can't figure out a way to say it."

"Yes, you can."

"It sounds conceited. It sounds terrible."

"So we'll close the door." I got up and pulled the plywood door closed, which in turn rattled the Sheetrock walls. Closing the door for privacy's sake was more of a gesture.

Amelia gripped her backpack with a stricken look. The first time she said it, it was impossible to hear her. I made her repeat herself. She said: "I don't know how he feels."

"Who?"

She swallowed. "Caliban."

Which was an interesting point. And an interesting challenge. Because I know exactly how Caliban feels. I wake up every day and make a choice: to sink under the weight of what he feels or to rise above it. I know I'm not alone, I know all across this country there are brown and black and even white people who wake up every day with that same feeling. But sitting in front of me was one of the lucky few who had only ever known love.

"Ah," I said.

She nodded. I went to that window where she was looking and put my hands in my pockets and gazed up at the whitened mountains. The sky was blue. There were no clouds, and a light dusting of snow lay on the grounds of the school. This was the moment: was I going to do my duty as English-teacher Cal, or do something bold, serious, and—some would venture—inappropriate? "Honey," I said. "I'm talking here as your godfather. Not as your father's second in command. Not as your English teacher. I want you to understand that before I go on."

She nodded slowly, her face full of curiosity. "When I was at Harvard," I began, "there was a girl. She was a poet, and she was married to a mathematician. Really, we were all friends, but I knew from the second I saw her that I loved her. Even though she was married, it didn't matter. Well, it did matter, but I *thought* it didn't. I was sure it didn't. All I thought was: 'How do I make her love me?'

"So I tried everything. I pulled out my most romantic Indian tricks: Coyote tales, stories about my grandmother—women love stories about your grandmother. She wanted to know me, but she didn't seem to want to love me. She seemed to want to love her husband.

"And then one day she touched me right here, on my leg, and I knew she loved me. And it was like . . . it was as if the world spun backward and time didn't exist anymore and I was suddenly in *love* with someone. Which was what I had wanted my whole entire waking life, to have someone just for me, and me just for them.

"Well, now, things were complicated by the fact that she was married. But I wasn't going to let that stop me. I was so determined to keep her, because I had wanted her for so long. I had possessed the idea of her even before I knew her. Naturally, I was sure that meant she was my true love. I believed we had been destined for this for eternity. I wanted only her.

"She and I began to meet. Not in hotels or anything like that, but in Boston Common. We'd spend hours watching the swan boats. Or we'd walk down Newbury Street and pretend we were rich people getting ready for a trip to Europe. We did not kiss. And we did not have sex. We convinced ourselves that by not doing those things, even if we were more than friends, at least we were honorable. At least we were not cheating on her husband. The agony of wanting her and not having her was a thrill in itself, because I fancied myself something of the romantic poet, pining, needing, unsated. Some days, when we were daring, we held hands, lightly. Even that was risky because we knew someday that someone who knew her husband would see us and we would be found out. She never mentioned leaving her husband. I never asked her to. Things seemed so perfect, and I thought, 'Why ruin it?' I enjoyed that she glimmered like a fish I could not hold in my hands.

"So one day we're sitting together on a bench in Boston Common, and I see a woman all the way down the path. She's homeless. She's pushing a grocery cart. She looks crazy. But she also looks exactly like my mother. Now, my mother left here, the reservation, when I was, oh, seven months old, and I hadn't seen her since. So you're right to be suspicious. But I just knew: 'That's my mother and she's walking toward me. I wonder why on earth she's in Boston and what on earth I'll say to her,' but more than that, I think, 'This is amazing. This is beautiful. Two women I love, together in the same place.' My mother gets closer. I stand up. She's dirty and old and her hair is matted but I'm sure it's her. I'm smiling. And then the woman I love, sitting beside me, grabs my arm. I look back at her. And she gives me this look. Like, 'What the hell are you doing?' My mother is getting closer and closer and I step forward and greet her, my arms are open, I say, 'Ma, do you know me?,' and the woman I love looks at me with horror, absolute horror. She holds her handbag closer. She lets go of my hand. And then I see: my mother isn't my mother. She's just an old Indian. I also see: I do not love the woman I am sitting next to. In that single gesture of repulsion, she becomes a bad person. She is a person I have trusted. But in that second, I see the truth: this old homeless woman, who smells of piss and shit and vomit and blood. I would rather sleep with her at night, and kiss her, and love her, and even put my thing inside her, than love the woman sitting next to me. Because the woman sitting next to me thinks I am nothing. Or rather, she thinks I am something only because I have overcome the nothing that I really am."

Even in my role of godfather, I couldn't believe I'd told Amelia all that. But I knew there was a reason she'd come to me: I was the only person in her life who was willing to tell her how the world really was. The light had fallen a little in the time I'd been watching the mountains, and when I looked back at her, her face was cast in orange. Golden sun glinted off the fuzz of her hair, making a halo about her head.

"That's what it feels like," I said.

Chapter Three

*S*o that's why, isn't it?" Willa's father was driving again, and she'd been letting her mind drift in the passenger seat. Ariel was tucked against her as the Volvo groaned up the mountain passes and sun streamed into the car. Willa didn't realize she'd said anything until Nat responded.

"Why what?"

"The reason we moved all the time. Because of what Caroline did. Isn't it, Dad?"

They had spent the afternoon and night in Boulder. Nat had declared it an official break from all grim talk. So they'd grabbed burgers at a corner pub, sipped tea in a really cool Russian pavilion, seen the kind of dumb-girl movie Nat usually complained about, and eaten roasted chicken at the nicest restaurant in town. Willa pretended they were on the kind of vacation they had never taken when she was a child. The kind of vacation she'd dreamed about. The problem was that even though she didn't want to think or talk about the new facts that had come to define her life, they were unavoidable. Her father paid cash for everything. That got her to wondering: if Caroline really had died so soon after seeing Nat, why was he still hiding? What had he done to help Caroline that was all that bad? He wasn't telling Willa something crucial.

It was a relief to be back in the car. To be finally climbing the Rockies. The air in those mountains was crisp and clean. Piles of snow, peaked by soot and dirt, had been pushed back off the highway. The car sped past mountains and evergreens and kept climbing. Willa's camera was on her lap. She wondered why she was calling her mother Caroline instead of Mom.

"*Isn't* it?" Willa looked over at her father and willed him to answer.

"Your mother was a fugitive."

"But she died, Dad. Which means she wasn't a fugitive anymore. Which means we didn't have to—"

"We *did* have to, Willa." Nat's voice was honed to a point. It was like an arrow meant to end the conversation. But Willa pressed on.

"Why? She was dead. It's not like you—"

"I helped your mom. I loved her. I helped her out when she asked me."

"How?"

Nat was keeping his eyes on the road. "Not yet," he was thinking. "Not yet."

"*How*, Dad?"

"She asked me to hide something for her."

"I don't understand."

"To keep something safe. Until it was time to deliver it."

"What kind of thing?"

"Something that kept us moving. We had to move so no one would discover it."

"Something dangerous?"

Nat tilted his head to the side, considering. "Depends on who you ask, I guess."

"Don't joke, Dad. I'm serious. What did you have to deliver? And who gets it?"

"I promised her I would take it to Elliot Barrow."

"You mean whatever it is is in the car right now? Something dangerous is in the car with us?"

Nat put his shifting hand out to pat Willa's leg, but she recoiled. Fear tightened between them for one of the first times. "I promise you," he said as they headed into a tunnel, "it's not going to hurt either of us."

"So it's some kind of information, right? Some kind of message? Or is it money? But why would the police, after all this time . . . why would they care? It's not like it's some issue of national security. Anymore, at least. That was seventeen years ago." Bars of light scuttled across Willa's face as they made their way through the darkness. She closed her eyes and tried to gather the facts. She decided to take a different tack. "Dad. You have to tell me. You have to tell me what it is. So I can help you. What if something, you know, happens? It's better if we both know."

Nat shook his head, but it was so dark on his side of the car that Willa couldn't see. The white iris of day at the other end of the tunnel made an appearance. Willa snapped a picture of this lighted keyhole. "I've kept it safe all this time," Nat said finally.

"But why didn't you deliver it sooner? If that was why we had to move? If the police were really following us because of it?" Nat could hear doubt in her voice. Good. There was a part of her that still thought he was a little off. Paranoid. "Good girl," he thought. She went on. "Because if you'd just gotten rid of it, then we wouldn't have had to move all those times, Dad. If the police were really following us. They would have stopped, right? They could have gotten that thing, whatever it was. And it would be over. We could have settled down so much sooner. Things would have been so different."

"You're right, Wills. They surely would have." He spoke deliberately. "But I didn't just make a promise to your mom about Elliot Barrow. I promised her that I'd guard you with my life. And if the police caught me, well . . ." He paused. "I knew if I went to jail, I'd lose you. Then I couldn't guard you the way I promised."

"I don't understand," she said, and her voice was sinking. In the darkness, he could imagine the daughter sitting beside him was only six years old. It was that daughter he had to speak to, the one who could trust him to make everything okay. "I understand why you'd take care of me. But I don't understand the stuff about Elliot Barrow."

"I made a promise to your mother," he said, and he was going to go on, but Willa understood that he was telling her something different, and that was where he got his out.

"You promised her you wouldn't tell a soul, right? That this was a secret you would keep until you handed it over to Elliot Barrow?"

Nat let his silence speak. He was glad for the darkness. The daytime was so close now. He was beginning to make out the edges of the other side.

"I understand," said Willa. "Not all of it. But I understand. You made a promise. But I don't get why you didn't break it. She was dead, Dad. And she was a bad person. I can see that now. She used people. She used you to get something dangerous to her . . ." Willa swallowed. "To Elliot Barrow. I don't understand why you helped her. After she used you like that. Why would you help someone who was so awful?"

"Because I loved her," Nat replied. Day was upon them.

AMELIA
Stolen, Oregon ~ Monday, March 31, 1997

Amelia was Caliban and Victor was Prospero, and they couldn't even speak to each other. They couldn't speak because except for those moments when they were working side by side, elbow to elbow, Victor was doing everything in his power to pretend Amelia did not exist. Amelia didn't like this one bit. The scene at the Littlefoot trailer may have taken place months earlier, but she still felt its dreamlike potency tugging at her conscious mind.

More than that, she realized that earlier in the fall, when she had been Victor's friend, and everyone had known it, kids at Ponderosa Academy who had never noticed her had begun to nod and wave when they passed her in the halls. She hadn't necessarily loved the attention, but she could have grown to like it. By November, all that formerly unwanted attention had stopped. And by Thanksgiving break, Victor had told as many people as possible that Amelia had never been his girlfriend—what made them think something crazy like that?—so there was nothing further to mention. No, Victor and Amelia hadn't broken up, because breaking up means being together, and they had never technically been together. That didn't mean his rejection, his denial, didn't hurt.

Interest in the state of affairs between Victor Littlefoot and Amelia Barrow had dwindled by the first week of December. But it had been refueled once that cast list had gone up. As it became increasingly obvious that Victor was not going to speak or look at Amelia unless he was forced to by what was written in a four-hundred-year-old script, she knew it was best to bite the bullet and get the job done.

They'd been working on that angry scene again from Act One. Lydia had to run off to her brother's birthday dinner, and Helen was going right into a costume meeting. So Amelia knew it was the right day. She went up to Victor as he was putting his script into his backpack. "Hey."

He looked at her as if she were a stranger. "Hey."

"Can we talk?"

Victor carefully zipped up his backpack and put on his polar fleece before saying evenly, "You can walk me to my truck."

They burst out of the gym doors together as if they were friends, except neither of them was smiling. The air was cold and it was dark and Amelia pulled her scarf tighter. Her heart was pounding. From his pace, she knew he wasn't going to give her any more time than he'd agreed to. She was going to have to make it snappy. She started right in with what still mattered most.

"Look," she began. "About going to your grandmother's that day? I know I shouldn't have gone without telling you. I'm sorry."

Victor shrugged. "Whatever."

"No," said Amelia. "Not whatever. I'm sorry."

"Okay."

"She said some things to me that day. You heard her. Don't act like I didn't too. I want to know what they mean." This last came out in a passionate rush, and Amelia held back the tears burning her eyes.

Victor was silent as he stalled in his tracks. They were already at his truck. She knew he might just drive away when he said gruffly into the air, "Leave my grandmother out of this."

"But, Victor, she's already *in* it, don't you see? She's in it and through it and all over it! What do you think I've been thinking about all these months? What the hell do you *think*?" Now she was crying, a little fierce, a little proud, a little stupid, but she didn't care if he saw.

"My grandmother isn't crazy. If anyone says she's crazy"—Victor's voice clenched, and he looked around like a cornered animal seeking escape, then relaxed as he saw his way out—"I'll just quit this damn play. I'll walk out. I don't need this shit, Amelia."

For a moment Amelia was speechless. Then she was mad, and at that moment *The Tempest* was the furthest thing from her mind. "Victor Littlefoot, you're an ass. Crazy? I don't think your grandmother's crazy! I think she's one of the most sensible people I've heard in my whole life!" She stopped. "Maybe you're the one who thinks she's crazy." Her anger lifted as she watched Victor let his body go slack against the side of his truck.

Silence.

Then Victor's words came out quietly, with a white puff of breath against the cold night. "You don't think she's crazy?"

Amelia found herself answering, "All that stuff about the baby and how the baby changed everything? Victor, that's what I'm try-ing to tell you. I don't know what I believe about much of anything, but I think your grandmother's at least a little bit right. That day *did* change everything. Maybe not in the way she says it did, but it did. You know it. That's why you wanted to find out who the baby was, right? Because it changed everything. We weren't allowed to play together anymore. You and your mom moved to Chicago. My dad and I . . ." More silence. Then she spoke again. "You know, when your grandmother started talking, I felt like I'd been waiting my whole life for her to say those things, and I don't even know what they mean."

Victor smiled. "Well, she can definitely have that effect." He opened the truck door, tossed in his backpack. "You want to get warm?"

Amelia nodded, went to the far door, opened it, climbed inside. The truck smelled right in the cool air. It smelled liked Victor—sweat and metal and something unnamed that made her knees weak. The cracked vinyl seat received her weight.

Victor got in too, sat behind the wheel, turned the ignition. "You have no idea the grief she gives me. But you know, she's the reason I'm getting my education. She's the reason I'm bringing home good grades. She's the reason I'm not using anymore."

Amelia nodded solemnly.

Victor went on. "I don't know what the baby means, Amelia. That stupid baby. What my grandma calls 'our broke lives.' When I first moved back, I thought if I found out once and for all, she'd shut up about how that was the reason for my troubles. I never should have told her about that baby, but I was only eight then, so I guess I didn't know that you shouldn't tell certain people like your grandma every single thing that happens to you. When my mom sent me back here, my grandma told me I should ask for your help. She said if we found out about that baby, maybe things could be right again. But I don't care anymore. I don't even think the baby matters. What matters is my grandma believes this Neige Courante stuff, and when she says it to people, it sounds true." He shrugged. "I don't know if she's right, but all it takes is someone else acting like she's crazy or wrong and— Well, she's my great-grandmother."

Amelia relaxed into his warmth. "I get it," she said, and the atmosphere cooled.

"No, I don't think you do get it, Amelia."

"Yes, I do."

"No, man," Victor said, shaking his head. "You don't know what it feels like to be poor or Indian or living in a city where the drugs on the street corner have your name on them. To live in a place where no one can tell where you're from." He turned and faced Amelia. His voice was earnest. "If someone asked you, 'Do you know who you are?,' what would you say?" He didn't wait for her to answer. "You're Amelia Barrow. Daughter of Elliot Barrow, head of the Ponderosa Academy. You get to live one life, and maybe it feels lonely, maybe you screw up and lose friends, but you always know who you are."

Amelia let him continue.

"Things are different for me, for *us*. We don't get that one life. Hell, there is no such thing as one kind of Indian when you're an Indian, but when you're out there in America, you can't tell anyone about who you really are. All they see is brown skin and black hair and they think they know. And being Neige Courante is even stranger. My great-grandmother, the expert on these things, doesn't even think the Neige Courante are a tribe! Can you believe that? She thinks the first ones were a band of renegade Wascos and Paiutes and others who hid in the mountains and then got rounded up by whites, so that last reservation could be established and the mountains taken for the government. She thinks the Neige Courante were made up by some white guy so there could be a story that sounded good and pure and true. And the white folks gave the old Indians horses and cigarettes and all that jazz, so the Indians said, 'Sure, we'll be your Neige Courante tribe.' My grandma says whites took everything else from the Indians, so why not take over their beliefs too? When she gets going, she'll tell you

Neige Courante is just a white dream." He laughed and said almost to himself, "If that doesn't make her sound crazy, I don't know what does."

Amelia was astounded. "But what does that mean?"

"Nothing much, because according to her, time makes everything real. That and the stories people tell about things. It doesn't matter, Amelia. I'm Victor Littlefoot. I'm Neige Courante, and I'm just as real as you."

They were silent for a few minutes. Then Victor said, "You must be getting pretty excited about the Benson thing. Lydia told me some of your friends are coming. That guy Wes, right? Who was what? Your boyfriend? And his sister?"

Suddenly, Amelia was mad. Up until this moment, Victor had seemed like Victor, the old Victor, even better, in fact. In control, maybe, but open, vulnerable. He had welcomed her into his truck, and she couldn't help that she'd imagined they would be friends again. But just as that was happening, just as warm air was beginning to blast out of the heater, he'd drawn the line, and he'd drawn it by bringing up the Benson people as if they were hers. "Wes is not my boyfriend."

"Okay."

"I don't know why you have to put it like that."

Victor rolled his eyes. "What's the big deal?"

"What did Lydia *say*?"

"She just said . . ." Victor shifted uncomfortably. He knew it was best not to tread into girl territory. "She just said you made some really good friends there. I don't know why you're so pissed. I don't care if you have a boyfriend, you know. It's not a big deal. I'm not into you."

Amelia was embarrassed, and that embarrassment spun quickly into more anger. She knew it wasn't fair to be angry at Lydia. Lydia could have mentioned Wes's name offhand, and Victor could have taken that the wrong way. As words began to fly out of Amelia's mouth, she knew it wasn't fair to be mad at Victor either. But he was there to be mad at. "You don't know anything about me." She shoved open the door and let the cold air blast in. "Or Wes. Or the terrible thing he did to me. How he made me feel like nothing. Like less than nothing. It isn't any of your business, Victor, and I wouldn't have dared to inconvenience you or Lydia with why I really came back from Benson." She jumped down to the ground. She could barely make out Victor's features in the darkness. "But I'll tell you this much: I would have told you." The night was cold. "All you needed to do was ask."

Chapter Four

HELEN

Newport, Oregon ~ Saturday, April 5, 1997

She pulled up in front of my house at eight A.M. on Saturday and honked twice. First I thought it was Elliot, because she came in his car. "Oh, shit," I thought. "Here we go." I didn't even have my pants on, and I let the kitchen curtain fall before I thought he'd be able to see me. What I didn't consider was his car was the only car she could borrow. Eunice said from the couch, "She's here."

"Who's here?"

"Your ride. Your day."

I had no idea what she was talking about. All she said was "Oh, just get your pants on. Get outside already. I finally have the TV to myself."

Outside was Helen, leaning against Elliot's car with a big smile on her face.

"How did you find me?"

"I have an in." She knew she'd gotten me. "Get in."

"I don't make it my habit—"

She got in the car. I stood for a minute in the morning light and looked over my shoulder. The wind was coming up behind me, moving like a comb over the grasses. It was chilly. So I got in.

We drove off the reservation and back out onto the highway.

The whole time Helen was making that kind of small talk women excel at: weather, books, movies. Nothing controversial or risqué. I was utterly at her mercy.

"Where's the dog?" I asked.

"It's just you and me today."

We passed the school and kept driving.

"Elliot doesn't lend out his car to just anyone, you know."

"He owed me one," she said. "Actually, he owes me more than one. So I cashed in."

"Where are we going?"

To which I got the smile.

We headed south down 97 toward Bend. I thought: "Restaurant." But it was too early for lunch, and she had to assume I'd already eaten breakfast.

"How long have you been planning this?"

To which I got another smile.

We turned west after Terrebonne onto a road that starts out flat in the desert air and then begins to climb and climb. If we'd turned the other direction, we would have come face-to-face with Smith Rock, the climbers' mecca, all dry air and brown walls, a hot yellow place where lizards and rattlers nestle in baking crevices. But that was east. We were heading west. The mountains' sentinels, the foothills, produced our first real challenge, and what we had next was a groaning, wheezing car on our hands (given that we were in Elliot's Camry from the mid-1980s; my truck does just fine in the mountains, thank you very much). We began carving our way through the ponderosas and western larches and Engelmann spruces and Douglas firs, the blue-green branches spreading over us like a vast umbrella, creating darkness in a morning where it was only bright. Herds of elk glimpsed at us through the tree trunks. The bucks stopped still in the hibernating underbrush and watched us blast by. The air our car set in motion pestered their pelts. I watched them turn tail and head back into the green.

As we crested the pass, we noticed a dusting of snow over everything—icing the conifers, slicking up the road. We were among the first to see this snow; there were only two sets of tire tracks with which to play catch-up.

I told her, "The Neige Courante loved these mountains. You've met us living on the steppes, but we've been living down there only since the government made us move. We're originally people of the volcano. That's why we lived on these high alpine slopes whenever we could. We knew it was our job to cool down the hot lava running just below the surface. It was our job to cool down the mountains in the fervor of the earth to escape its own plight."

"Is this something you memorized?" She was amused, impressed.

I shook my head and kept talking. "The lava we could detect bubbling under the surface of every dried cone, the steam we felt on its escape from tiny vents in ancient moraines, all of it attested to the intolerable situation of the earth's displacement. This huge rock that we lived on—Earth—had once made its home in the skies. Now it was trying to get back up there, but we needed it down here, because here was where we lived. It was the Neige Courante who kept the earth cool. It was the Neige Courante who kept the earth from aspiring to the unattainable condition of the stars. That's really how we got our name. To answer the question you asked me when I first picked you up at the airport. Yes. We gave ourselves this name."

I could tell I'd made Helen happy. I was glad to see her shine. I leaned back in my seat and turned up the heat. It was cozy, looking out at a kind of winter this woman had never seen. Somewhere in there, I stopped worrying about where she was taking me and said, "The snow's because of the rain shadow effect," and explained how the Cascade Mountains are like a wall; the moist air comes in off the Pacific and drops its wet all over the western side of the wall, so that by the time it makes it all the way over, the air isn't moist anymore. And that's why Ponderosa Academy and the Neige Courante reservation rarely see rain, because the air is bone-dry by the time it gets to us.

She saw I was right as we came down the other side of the mountains; the moisture had been dropped not as snow but as rain in the lower elevations. It clung to the upper boughs, refracting light. It was beautiful. All along, the land burst green. She read names and I repeated them back: Black Butte, Camp Sherman, Santiam Pass, Three-Fingered Jack, Tombstone Pass, Menagerie Wilderness, Sweet Home. She wanted to know everything she could, about land formation, about the dormant volcanoes and their residual lava rocks, about the buttes left over from the time when the mountains were being made. She wanted to know about winds, and weather, and birds, and flowers, and trees. I told her what I know. I surprised myself in knowing so much, as I never thought I'd be the kind of man who would want to know this place like the back of my hand. In talking, even I was impressed by the strangeness of this wild, natural world that was mine.

Waterloo, Sodaville, Tangent, Philomath, Eddyville. These are the towns you pass through before Newport, and Newport is where the world opens. Newport is where the land meets the ocean. Helen gasped when she saw it. It was truly erotic, that gasp. Made me chuckle. Made her blush.

Then we were standing on a dun-colored beach blasting with ocean wind. The air was icy. She had her arms around herself, as if she were her own armor. She said, "I wanted to be with you the first time I saw this." She said, "I've never seen the ocean so cold or so wild." She said, "My husbands were not good to me," and that was when I put my hand upon her waist and pulled her to me. That was the first time I kissed her.

You'll notice by now that I've lost my slip on her. I've lost my ability to imagine things from her direction. This is her section, after all. But I can't see it, no matter how hard I try, from her point of view. Maybe there's fear there. Maybe I don't want to imagine all the other things she was likely thinking in that moment when I was closer to her than I had ever been before. Maybe all I want to believe is that she saw things just the way I did, that all she wanted in the world was to have her lips on mine, because that was all I wanted.

All I know is this: knowing Helen at first was like a friend explaining a delicious dish to you, an unusual assortment of ingredients that a well-known chef has crafted into something new. You are unimpressed at the description, sure you won't enjoy it. But your friend insists you give it a try. You're sure you'll hate it. You can live your life without it. But your friend's enthusiam has made you curious. You start to wonder if you're missing out. And then. One day. You score reservations. You order your meal.

Reader, Helen was the best thing I'd ever tasted.

CAL
Stolen, Oregon ~ Wednesday, April 30, 1997

I knew Duncan would call again. His phone calls had dropped off in recent weeks, and most of me hadn't much noticed. I'd won. Helen was mine. I knew the dimples that appeared below her scapulae when she shifted her weight onto her elbows, the drowsy swell around her eyes in the morning, her embarrassed thrill when I told her she was beautiful. Hence, it was convenient to forget the way I had been betraying her. Subtly, yes, and in her best interest, but still and all, I had been reporting to her husband, and lying to her, and impersonating a friend, and those were not honorable activities. I was going to get caught.

In those few moments when I did think about hearing Duncan's voice again, I felt sure I'd come clean. "Here's who I really am, here's how to get ahold of Helen, she's been willing to talk to you all along," etc. etc. The reality was much different.

"It's me," he said.

"Good to hear from you! How are you, old man?" I often found myself slipping into Elliot's mock Briticisms, which were truly just snob.

"Actually," and his tone was a different color than it had been in the other phone calls, murkier, more purple, "I need you to pass along a message to Helen. I know she doesn't want to speak with me, God, she's made that abundantly clear, but her good friend Michael Reid is very ill. He's . . . It looks like he hasn't got long to live. He's just deteriorated . . ." His voice trailed off. "I know she'll want to see him. Please tell her I'll do anything to help her make that happen."

I had heard her speak of Michael. She'd described his house in Vermont and how she was going to take me there, how he was going to love my furrowed brow. I sat in my office and thought about how she'd told me, after one of the six times we'd made love, that she believed Michael Reid was the real love of her life, that that's who wonderful friends were, your love affairs. I had held her in my arms and listened to her voice pattering the air as I fell asleep. It was time to tell her the truth.

It was the middle of the day. I had a class to teach. But I poked my head in the classroom and told my ninth-graders to please read aloud from *The Odyssey* until I got back. I headed over to the gym, but she wasn't there yet. So I made my way down the path, each step heavier than the last.

She opened her door with a broad smile. "You're supposed to be teaching an English class," she said, taking my hand, pulling me in.

"Helen," I began, and the look on my face was enough to stop her.

"What is it?" Her voice was newly grave. We had not done this yet, the taking in of each other's sorrow. It broke my heart to hear her worry.

"There's no easy way to say this."

"I knew it." She stepped backward. "I knew it. You're married, right? Or—"

"Nothing like that. No, it's just . . . I spoke to Duncan just now. He left you a message. Your friend? Michael Reid? He's very sick. So sick that Duncan's concerned he isn't going to hold on much longer."

"Oh God." I've never seen tears spring to someone's eyes that quickly. "Oh God," and soon she was doubled over, bent in sorrow, and I was holding her up, but it was that odd tangle of not knowing how to touch someone when she is in the throes of sadness. She had a stunned look to her, but after the initial blow, I saw her mind beginning to work. She was putting on her jacket. "I have to call him," she said. I didn't know if she meant Duncan or Michael, but it didn't much matter at that point, because all I wanted was for her not to cry anymore. "How did Duncan get your number?" she asked, one shoe nearly tied.

I shrugged. "He called me."

"How strange." It was strange. But I didn't know how to begin it. Then she was winding a scarf around her neck and kissing my cheek and saying, "I can use your phone, right?" and I was handing her my office keys and she was racing out the door and she was gone.

SHE CAME BACK two hours later, her eyes rimmed in greasy red. "Please leave me alone," she said, and I knew that Duncan and she and Elliot had figured things out. She had figured things out with her husbands.

"I'd like to tell you—" I began, but she pointed to the door.

"Please."

So I left.

Chapter Five

*T*hey spent the night just short of Salt Lake City. In the midmorning light, they turned abruptly north, shooting past the Great Salt Lake, where the light fell crisply from the open sky. Willa traced the curves and bends of the roadbed in the atlas and glanced at her father. His eyes were trained on the road.

"Dad?" she asked.

"Hmm."

"Did you . . . Did you *do* something?"

"What do you mean?"

"To help her. Is that why you think there are people after us? Did you hurt someone?"

She meant it seriously, but Nat smiled at her from his eyes so she knew he wasn't lying when he said, "You know me, Wills. I couldn't hurt a fly."

She took a picture of a slice of the Great Salt Lake out the driver's window, between her father's arms. She wished she could crunch the crusty white salt underneath her sneakers, but she didn't suggest they stop. She knew that Boulder had been the vacation. Now her father was all business. He was hunched in a different way over the steering wheel. Reluctant to give up the driver's seat. Unwilling to tell her anything beyond what he must. She had tried begging for information. Now she had to try patience.

AMELIA
Stolen, Oregon ~ Tuesday, May 6, 1997

Amelia was agitated. Shaken up, nervous, unable to relax. On a daily basis. She felt this way when she ate dinner alone with her father. When she walked to class with Lydia by her side. When she imagined Wes and Sadie coming to Ponderosa Academy. When she passed Victor in the hallway. When she endured my lectures on *A Tale of Two Cities.* She had felt this way every day since the morning Victor's great-grandmother told her things were the way they were because she'd cracked the world open with a fairy game.

The one time Amelia didn't feel agitated, the one time she could relax, could fully look Victor in the eye and not feel embarrassed, could put her arm around Lydia and believe entirely in their friendship, was when she was onstage. *The Tempest,* and acting in it, had become Amelia's refuge.

Acting felt the way playing duets had felt. Good. Flowing. There were rhythms and pauses, courteous interruptions, moments when you raced ahead. She liked playing music with Wes, so she had let herself believe she liked Wes, maybe even loved him. Acting made her understand this. It made her understand that she'd been wrong to think she had a crush. She hadn't liked Wes *like that,* but it had been easier to believe that than this other, more complicated truth: she loved merging, through art, through music, with someone else.

Amelia's friendship with Lydia limped along, a little bedraggled, a little torn. What made Amelia feel good about Lydia was simple: she trusted that when this was all over—and by "this," she meant the play, the school year, the Benson visit—she'd be able to sit down and explain everything to Lydia, and Lydia would do what she'd always been able to do. Lydia would love her, if only because Amelia had taken exactly one hundred dollars of Wes's eleven-hundred-dollar bribe and bought Lydia a Walkman and a music-store gift certificate. Amelia was planning to give it to her friend when the summer began.

Wes surprised Amelia by writing a letter. It was earnest and handwritten, and it profusely apologized for accusing her of tattling. He'd found out through the grapevine that it was a third boy who'd gone to the principal and confessed that Jackson Rice had touched him inappropriately, then added he'd heard Jackson was "hooking up" with some other boys too. *So I guess I've got to learn a lot about men and the lies they tell,* Wes wrote. He had started seeing a therapist, and he noted enthusiastically that he was making "real progress." It was this therapist who had urged Wes to send the letter. Wes wanted to hear from Amelia whether or not his presence was welcome at Ponderosa during the exchange. He understood if she never wanted to see him again, but he would be honored, truly honored, if she would let him come. He wanted to see her again, to tell her about Juilliard, how good New York City would be for him. Could he come? Amelia wrote back a simple yes. She decided that his visit would give her the chance she wanted to press Wes's money back into his palm. To tell him he had no right to treat another person the way he'd treated her.

THE TEMPEST SETTLED the agitation in the pit of Amelia's stomach. That didn't mean it was easy. The play was hard. Memorizing lines was hard. Creating a character, no matter how many times she met alone with Helen for "character work," was hard. Doing homework on top of all that was hard. Amelia didn't even try to practice the violin. No matter how difficult things felt, no matter how exhausted she was, every day was laden with excitement. It was as though *The Tempest* were single-handedly giving everyone at Ponderosa the chance to see a future. Even Victor had renewed hope about college, as soon as he found out there were scholarships for actors. Lydia was already sending away for brochures from conservatories as far away as Boston University.

Then there was the matter of the cast parties. There were going to be two of them. One after the show, in the gym, when the lights went up and the set was shoved back against the wall and all the parents and teachers mingled and congratulated the students and everyone ate cookies and drank juice. Then, despite the lectures they'd gotten as a student body, as a cast, as a set of individuals, the kids were organizing a party of their own. Elliot worked hard on those kids at assembly: "We are inviting children from a very different student body into our homes. In doing so, we are making a promise, to their parents, their teachers, and to them. That promise? We, as their hosts, will look out for their best interests. I know I don't need to remind you that holding a party where there will be drinking, or reckless behavior of any kind, is not only illegal, it is irresponsible. And I'll thank you to remember that holding such a party under the noses of this institution will result in serious consequences." I missed the rest of that lecture. I had to step outside and roll my eyes.

Naturally, the question of the party set Amelia on edge. Not only would she be disobeying her father's personal and professional wishes by attending, but there was the matter of Sadie and Wes. They would be there too. As would Lydia and Victor.

ON THE DAY of the performance, the cast spent the morning in a dress rehearsal and most of the afternoon correcting lighting errors and fixing the prop business they'd fouled up in the dress. Amelia did not see Sadie or Wes at all, but she didn't think about them. She and the cast had entered that fabulous phase when the play is going to happen. No matter what. There is nothing more that can be fixed. There are no more lines to memorize. There is only the play as a whole to discover, as it becomes something new: a living thing with its own rhythms, its own humor, its own heartbeat.

Elliot came backstage while Amelia was applying smudges of brown to her face.

"It's supposed to be dirt," she said.

"Very convincing."

She went back to her makeup, expecting him to step away from her in order to make some kind of general announcement to the cast. Everyone else seemed to anticipate this too; a hush had fallen over the makeshift dressing room. But he squatted next to her and lowered his voice. She looked at him, surprised, as he began to speak.

"I just want to tell you to break a leg. I know you'll be fantastic. Helen's been telling me how talented you are. I know how hard you've worked—"

"Thanks, Dad," she said. It wasn't that she was dismissing him. It was more that she was nervous. She wanted to believe no one was going to be out there in the darkness, watching her.

He stayed beside her. He was fiddling with the top button of his dress shirt.

"Leave it undone," she said.

"Is that the style?"

"Yeah. You only button it if you're wearing a tie."

"Oh."

She set down the pancake makeup as she said, "Dad. Can I help you with something?"

"I just wanted to say—" He cleared his throat. "I just wanted you to know why I chose this play."

She rolled her eyes. "I know. I already know. Because of the colonialism, and the native stuff, and the slavery, and you wanted to do a Shakespeare play to show Benson how 'world-class' we are, Dad, I've already heard this lecture."

"I chose this play because it was your mother's favorite. Her absolute favorite play in the world." His voice faltered, and he lowered his eyes. But he went on. "I took her to a production of it in Central Park in the dead middle of winter, when she was pregnant with you. I knew how disappointed she'd be later, when she read about it in the *Times* and couldn't go. She was so enormous that she couldn't even fit into my clothes. So I went down to the Salvation Army and found her a muumuu and a man's coat just so she could go see that play. It was the middle of winter! Who does a play in the middle of a snowfield? Totally impractical. But it was sunny, and really, the light on the snow made the whole world feel like a fairyland.

"The actors performed while moving through the park. Your mother loved it. I knew she was going to love it. We tromped through the snow with the actors, as though we too were part of the production. And even though Astrid was huge, and even though it was freezing, she smiled the whole time. Even though she couldn't sit for two hours, and she had to keep moving. It was one of the happiest days of my life. And I didn't even know it. I guess you never do."

This was the most Amelia had ever heard her father say about her mother in one sitting. Her father seemed so soft and kind. She put her hand on his cheek. "Thank you," she said.

Helen came into the dressing room. "Fifteen minutes!" She glowered humorously at Elliot. "All nonactors are strongly encouraged to take their seats!"

Elliot pecked Amelia on the cheek. "Break a leg," he whispered. As he walked to the door, he began to clap. "Break a leg," he said to each of the other children. He smiled and waved and popped out the door.

That was not the last time Amelia saw her father whole. She saw him after the play was over, when she was drenched in adrenaline and thrilled at what they had all just made. But when he gave her a hug, and told her how proud he was of her, it was not real talking. It was not just the two of them. Everyone was watching and excited, and the audience was boisterous and the actors were giddy, and all Amelia was thinking about was getting out to the cast party. All she was thinking about was the next big thing that would make her feel as happy as being inside the play had made her. So although Elliot's words to Amelia about her mother were not the last words he ever spoke to her, they were in the ways that matter. She can still see him sometimes, waving to her from the doorway. She can still taste the possibilities of truth his words offer as they swirl inside her. And then he is gone.

The Sea Story

Once upon a time, a group of children put on a play. This play was about a storm on the ocean, and a shipwreck, and a tired but powerful wizard, and his innocent daughter, and their slave, and their sprite, and the men who were shipwrecked, who feared they were dead but weren't. In order to put on the play, the children had to work very hard. They had to memorize and build and paint and ponder and sew and worry and hammer and wait.

They were waiting for the night when the play was ready.

They were waiting for their audience.

None of the children had ever put on a play before. So they didn't know quite how things went. They didn't know, until the night they performed their play, whether it was any good or not.

It was good.

It was so good that the babies in the audience did not cry. It was so good that the old men in the audience did not fall asleep. It was so good that the dogs in the audience did not bark. It was so good.

There was a girl who was bright like a song in her everyday life, but she disguised her songness and played the slave, who was a beast, and everyone forgot she was not really a he. There was a boy who was sleek and new like a pine sapling in his everyday life, but he was so good that he disguised his pineness and played the wizard, who was all bluster and power, and everyone forgot he was not ancient and magic. There was a girl who was rowdy like a hurricane in her everyday life, but she disguised her rowdiness and played the daughter, who was still and curious, and everyone forgot that when she laughed, the world shook around her. There were many other *children who accomplished similar tasks. They left themselves. They became the play.*

The words the children spoke when they became the play were words the audience had never heard. When the children spoke those words, they made the room electric and hushed and rapturous. The hairs on the arms of the children and the audience stood at attention. The breath in the lungs of the children and the audience filled with something that was not only air.

The room became an island. A storm blew in, and the people inside and outside the play were afraid. A wild ocean lapped at the edges of the room. The island was full of the sounds of magic, magic that misled the bad and tempted love for the good and conjured feasts and secured justice and set a good man free.

It was this man who came to the edge of the island at the end of the play and reminded the audience that there had to be an end. The end would be brought by clapping. This man, who was the wizard, who was really the boy like a pine, begged to be released.

Though the audience did not want to leave the island, they knew it was time. All the words were gone. All the children were exhausted.

And so the people clapped.

Chapter Six

AMELIA
Where-We-Have-the-Parties ~ *Tuesday, May 6, 1997*

The children gathered out in the darkness after their play. They whooped in their cars as they drove, speeding up the gravel road. Amelia's body was buzzing, as though in disbelief of what it had just accomplished. All those words! They'd come out of her in the right order! Her mind smoothed over the memory of how inevitable it felt: once the shipwreck began, the play was a long line of dominoes. First this, then this, then this. No other way to go. No way to end what they'd begun. No way she could have forgotten her lines even if she'd tried. No way she could have stopped midstage, looked out at the audience, made a time-out sign with her hands, and said, "I'm Amelia," even if she'd wanted to. That was what made her feel buzzy and exhausted and exhilarated all at once as she hurtled through the night with Lydia by her side. That was what made her shiver and feel a little afraid. She *wasn't* Amelia when she was Caliban. She was only Caliban. It was a scary and powerful and perfect feeling. She wanted to feel it again.

But for now she could relax. Now she could have a good time. Sadie was already at the party—she'd made friends with a few Ponderosa girls. As Amelia waved to them and garnered their congratulations, she hit on a crisp truth: these girls were more like Sadie than Amelia could ever dream of being. These girls *want*ed to giggle at the idiot boys taking turns hurtling themselves over the fire pit. These girls *want*ed to suck on cigarettes and complain about how fat they were. Because they were all genuinely impressed with how hard Amelia and the rest of the cast had worked, it didn't feel so sad to Amelia to recognize how different she was. She didn't feel sad that these girls had never been truly kind to her, and that she had never been truly kind back. Instead, she put her arms around them and accepted the beer they placed in her hands.

Lydia was wild with joy. She didn't threaten anyone's life or yell obscenities. In fact, she'd developed something of a crush on Caleb, the boy who'd played Ferdinand to her Miranda, a shy kid with a hangdog attitude who had somehow been transformed into a dashing, loyal lover the second he'd stepped on the stage. Amelia watched Lydia toss her hair and laugh at Caleb's jokes as Bobby Marron, Lydia's sometime boyfriend, sulked in the shadows. Caleb looked simultaneously panicked and thrilled, trying to take Lydia all in as she gestured exuberantly.

Victor was at the party too. Amelia and he nodded at each other as they gathered beside the bonfire. Amelia didn't know what was going on. She and Victor had achieved a strange kind of closeness, just being onstage together. She'd had the same feeling with Wes during their duets. Amelia felt as though she *knew* Victor deeply because of the work they'd done together, but without any of the facts of his actual life involved. As though the talk in his truck had been an agreement between them not to let real life get in the way of the acting work they had to do. Victor was an astonishingly good Prospero. Amelia knew his acting talent, and his passionate devotion to the character, were a significant part of her attraction to him. She also felt a strange stirring inside every time she looked at him, remembering how she'd been plunged into embarrassment when he said he wasn't "into" her. So that was that. He wasn't. And yet there was this knowing, this gnawing. She dropped his gaze and decided not to talk to him until she'd had a few more beers.

Wes interrupted Amelia's thoughts. "You were just great." He grabbed her into a long hug, and over his shoulder, Amelia caught Sadie explaining to another girl her impression of the nature of her brother's feelings. Amelia could read Sadie's whispering lips: "He really likes her," and Amelia closed her eyes and hugged Wes back.

"You look great," he said as they pulled away. "Congratulations. Really. I mean it. That's the least boring Shakespeare play I've ever seen."

Amelia remembered her first impression of Wes, how hot he'd seemed, how distant and artsy and brooding. Now she laughed and ruffled his scruffy hair. "So you're letting it grow?"

He shrugged. "Jackson liked it short. So I thought, 'Screw Jackson.'"

"Speaking of Jackson, I want to talk to you," Amelia said, nudging him in the ribs. "We've got some unfinished business." But Lydia was calling everyone to attention for a toast, and afterward, there were more congratulations and Benson people to meet, more beer to drink, more boisterous stories to tell about nearly missed entrances and lines. Then Amelia was standing face-to-face with Victor.

"Good job," he said simply. She was the one who made the move to hug him, and he obliged.

"You too," she said.

"You were really funny," he said.

"Thanks. And I loved that epilogue. I think you made a lot of people cry."

Victor looked pleased and shy. Light from the fire rippled across his face, and Amelia tried not to feel a pang of regret. She'd missed her chance. He'd told her, to her face, that he didn't like her, at least not like *that*, but maybe she could have done something different at the beginning that would have changed his mind. She tried to memorize him. This was probably the last time she would be this close, get to see his shallow breath as it moved up and through him, the rapid way he blinked. She wanted to say something perfect. But nothing came.

Victor cleared his throat. "Um, listen," he said.

Amelia smiled. "Yes?"

Wes appeared beside her. "*There* you are! I've been looking everywhere. You ready?"

"Sure," said Amelia, bringing her voice to a public tone. She was about to introduce Wes to Victor and Victor to Wes, but Victor was already bumming a smoke off another girl. He was as unreachable as if they'd never been talking.

"Sorry about that," said Wes as they walked away. "I thought you two were talking to that group behind you. I hope I didn't ruin a moment."

"No worries," Amelia said, pushing aside her disappointment.

"He's hot. Is he your boyfriend?"

"I don't have a boyfriend! *You're* the closest thing I've ever had to a boyfriend. And we know how well that turned out."

They found a log away from the others to sit on. "Look," Amelia began, "I don't want this to be a big deal. I just wanted to kind of, I don't know, tell you something. About that day when you gave me that money?" She sighed. "I know you meant well. But I don't want that money. I never did. And it has nothing to do with whether I'm poor or rich. It has to do with the way you made me feel. You made me feel like I was nothing to you. Like all you cared about was your secret. And it hurt me that you couldn't trust me, that you thought—"

"I'm sorry," Wes said. "I was really messed up. Jackson had told me that if anyone found out—"

"I know," said Amelia. "But here's where you promise me you'll never, ever do that to someone again. Okay? We're friends. I'll keep your secrets. You don't have to bribe me."

"Okay," Wes agreed.

Amelia fished the thousand dollars out of her back pocket. "I was pissed off, so I spent a hundred of it on my friend Lydia. But I want to give you back the rest."

"Keep it," Wes said. "I owe you."

"That's the point: you don't owe me. Friends keep secrets. I'm not going to tell anyone. I don't want this money."

"Well, I don't want it back," Wes said, but Amelia took his hand and pressed the stack of bills into it.

"I don't want your blood money—"

"Hey!" Victor's voice rang out in the darkness. Amelia turned toward the fire, and he was standing there, his arms crossed. "What is that?"

Amelia could see that Victor was angry, even though he was in shadow. Wes answered before she could. "It's no big deal."

"Yeah?" Victor was closer now, towering over them. "Why don't we let Amelia answer?"

"Victor, it's no big deal." She held up the money and waved it. "Wes lent me some money. I'm paying him back."

"Looks like a lot of money to lend someone."

"Don't worry about it, man."

"It's really no big deal," Amelia said.

"You're that Wes guy, right? Amelia told me about you."

Amelia saw a flicker of fear pass across Wes's face. "What'd she say?"

"That you got her into something bad."

"It's no big deal," Amelia said again, but she wasn't being heard.

"You know what I think?" Victor went on. "I think some rich kid from the city shouldn't come out here and sell drugs."

"Drugs?" Amelia couldn't help the shocked laugh that accompanied the word. "That's insane. There are no drugs."

"I told you, man, this is none of your business." Wes was standing now, and Amelia found herself rising to make herself a barrier between the two young men.

"This *is* my business. This is my home. This is my reservation. You can't just come in here—"

"This is just a big misunderstanding. Wes just lent me some money, Victor."

"And that's why you called it blood money? Maybe it isn't drugs, but this kid did something to you, and I don't trust him."

Amelia wedged herself between the boys and tried to push Victor off. She realized she was much drunker than she thought she was. She could barely budge him. "Look," she said, "Wes is my friend, okay?"

Victor sized Wes up and snorted. "Yeah. He seems like a great guy."

"You don't know anything about me," Wes said, and Amelia had to move against him as he lunged.

"It's okay," she said, "just let it go."

"You don't know anything about me, man." Wes ducked around Amelia and swung at Victor.

"This is insane," Amelia said. "We're all drunk. Let's forget this." But the boys were not going to forget it. Amelia looked toward the fire. A few people had noticed that a fight was brewing. She hoped they were coming to help stop things.

It didn't matter how many people came to try to pull the boys from each other. The boys were both angry, both afraid, both sure of what they knew. Both ready to fight.

Victor knew what he had carried with him from Chicago: people sold drugs. People lied. Amelia was innocent to the ways of people like that. He liked her that way, wide-eyed, optimistic. He wanted her to stay sheltered. Who was this Wes fellow, anyway? Lydia had told him that Wes was Amelia's boyfriend, and then Amelia had said he wasn't. But here he was, arrogantly cornering Amelia when Victor was trying to tell her something important, something personal, something about the way he felt. And Victor was tired, from the play, from caring for his great-grandmother. He was scared because in the last six months, he had discovered a terrible secret about himself. He loved acting. He knew he was good at it. But maybe he wasn't good enough. There were people like Wes in the world, and they were white, and rich, and arrogant, and they were the people who got to do what they loved. They were the people Amelia was going to want. Not someone like Victor, a poor brown kid who lived in a trailer and wanted to be . . . what? An *actor*?

Victor swung back.

Wes knew what he had carried with him from Portland: he was really, truly gay, and no matter how he tried to cast it, that meant Sadie would never look up to him anymore, that meant his father would be ashamed, that meant his mother would lock herself in her bathroom and cry. It didn't even matter that Wes had fallen in love, because Jackson Rice was a bastard who'd been fucking three boys in total, telling each one he was the special one. Yes, Wes was going to therapy, and yes, most days, with enough effort, he didn't hate all of himself, but here was a boy accusing him of being a bad person, here was a boy saying he had heard something from Amelia about who Wes really was. Suddenly, Wes was forced to wonder if Amelia had kept his secret as she'd promised, or whether everyone here knew about him and the sweetness he felt when he kissed a man, and then he became all tangled in fear and anger and rage. He wanted to be beaten. It seemed just.

Wes punched Victor across the jaw.

The fight was so visceral, so raw, that not many noticed Amelia going off into the night. Lydia certainly didn't. But when a few boys had finally pulled Victor and Wes from each other, Victor asked where Amelia was, and a girl standing beside him said she'd noticed Amelia heading off in the direction of the abandoned barn. Victor called her name and took off into the night.

Amelia was nearly to the barn when Victor caught up with her. She was crying. Scalding tears sheeted down her face. She was humiliated and angry, and she yelled at him when he caught her by the elbow. "How could you hurt someone like that?" she asked. He apologized. He told her he couldn't stand by and let someone hit him. "He's my *friend*," Amelia cried. "You don't know anything about him." She told him to leave her alone. She stomped into the barn, and he followed.

Back by the bonfire, Wes was angry and breathless. Sadie and Lydia tended to him, but he told them he wanted Amelia. They couldn't find her. Someone mentioned that Amelia and Victor had headed out toward the barn, and Wes grabbed a burning stick from the fire and said he was going to find her himself. Sadie begged. "This is stupid. You're just going to fight again."

"I want to make sure she's okay," Wes slurred, and a gaggle of children followed him as he made his way into the night, a torch in his hand. That was when Lydia decided to get help.

HELEN
Stolen, Oregon ~ Tuesday, May 6, 1997

Helen made her exhausted way back to her house. The play was over and she was proud. No big flub-ups; just three late entrances. Only a few lines dropped, and the audience hadn't batted an eye. She'd watched from the back of the gym and known immediately that this was the best kind of crowd, one that laughs at the comedy, gasps at the denouement, and holds its breath for the lovers. All around her, in the darkness, there were people who had never seen or heard this story before, and as she walked home in the quiet night, she smiled at how rapt they'd been. It would be the first thing she'd describe to Michael when she landed in Burlington.

Elliot had nodded gravely when, a week before, she had told him she was leaving. She didn't say she was leaving for good, but it was assumed. She would stay the week, to see her project through. Elliot didn't need to ask her to do that; she was loyal to the children and the play. But after the performance, her task was over. "My friend is dying," she said. "He needs me." She knew Michael would disagree with this phrasing. The truth was, he needed her more than anyone else in the world did, and that counted for something. It would have to be enough. It was time to get back to her life.

She lit the kerosene lamp and the stove, and rubbed her hands together as she waited for the little room to warm up, then filled Ferdinand's water bowl. She had become so fond of her cabin. Even though a chill lurked in its corners, she could tell spring was firmly on its way. She had smelled it each morning since deciding to leave, and there was a part of her that longed to stay and unfurl with the season. She opened one of her suitcases onto the bed.

There was a knock and the dog startled. Helen's heart fluttered. She hoped it would not be Amelia, because she had not yet told the girl she was leaving. She hoped, for that matter, it would not be any of her students, because she was prepared to tell them in the morning, with a clear head, of her evening flight back east. She hoped it would, and she hoped it would not, be me. For reasons too complicated to name. Still, as she swung the door open, there was a part of her that glittered at the thought of me standing there.

It was Elliot. He was beaming broadly and enfolded her in a tight hug. "It was glorious! I wish you'd been able to come out for dinner with the Benson faculty. They were thrilled, absolutely. Helen, you have no idea. Come to breakfast with us tomorrow and they'll gush. I have no idea how to thank you."

"Come in, come in."

"Oh, I know you're busy packing. I don't want to disturb you."

"Elliot." She took him by the arm and pulled him inside. "I need the company. And I've got a bottle of rum. Hot toddy?"

Elliot, who did not often drink, said yes.

It took him some time to bring up the real reason he had come to see her. By then they were loose and reminiscent. He was sitting in her chair. Ferdinand was curled around his feet. She did not see the sober expression cross Elliot's face—she was consumed with fitting her socks into the nooks and crannies of her shoes and books—and his seriousness was odd to her, jarring.

"Cal is going to be sad to see you go."

"Oh," she said. "Well."

"It's hard to forgive someone when he betrays you."

She nodded.

"But—this is none of my business—perhaps he deserves another chance? He's a very good man, even if he sometimes acts—"

"Like a child?"

"I was going to say 'as if he doesn't know how to love someone.' Perhaps your version is more . . . honest."

Helen went back to packing her socks. "I've made up my mind," she said. "I appreciate your point of view—"

"I understand," he said. "I have to admit I liked watching you both grow to care about each other. I flattered myself that I'd found a second career as a matchmaker. But I understand."

They sat in silence for a few minutes, the pause between them growing from hesitant to anxious to awkward.

"I'll let you get back to your packing," Elliot finally said but made no move to leave.

"I guess I'll see you tomorrow, then."

"I suppose." Still he stayed where he was. Helen busied herself with the suitcase until she heard him say. "I've been wanting to talk to you."

"Uh-oh. You've put on the serious voice."

"No, no, it's nothing bad. Just . . . illuminating. I hope."

"Okay."

"Remember the first day you were here? When I first told you my plans with Benson? And then I thanked you. For that night, seventeen years ago, when you helped me. After Astrid disappeared."

"Yes, of course."

"Well, I didn't tell you everything."

"Okay."

"Why don't you sit down?"

She sat beside the suitcase.

"Remember what I told you? About how I was starting to understand hope again?"

"Yes."

"It's real. My hope was real."

"I have no idea what you're talking about."

"I thought for many years that I'd gone crazy that night. Yes, I was out of my mind. Astrid had just left me alone with our infant with no warning! None at all. I found out three days later that I was right to have lost my mind a little, when I found out what my wife had been up to. That the bombs she'd been helping make were what killed her. That she'd kidnapped and helped assassinate that poor Simpson boy. That she and her comrades, as hideous as their own crimes were, had to die in such a horrific fashion. That my daughter would grow up without a mother. I blamed myself for making Astrid marry me. For trying to keep her safe from herself. I saw then that I'd been a fool to try to cage that kind of bird."

"It was a terrible time," Helen said.

"Yes, it was. A tragic time. I've been thinking about it a lot." He nodded to himself twice, as if encouraging himself to continue. Then he met Helen's eyes. His own were shining. "I was right," he said with conviction, as if she knew what he was talking about.

"Right about what?"

"Do you remember what I said that night?"

"You said a lot of things."

"Yes, but do you remember what I kept saying? What I kept telling you?"

Helen looked down at her hands, folded in her lap. Of course she remembered. But she was not about to repeat the ravings of a madman to the man, transformed, before her. "It was a long time ago," she said finally.

"I've found her," he said. "And that's why. That's why I've been in talks with Benson Country Day. That's why I want so badly for you and Cal to work out whatever is between you. Because I can't be here anymore."

"I don't understand."

"She's real, Helen." He was beaming. "It's time to go and get her back. To let her know I tried everything. To try to make it up to her. To tell her that no one would listen when I told them the truth." He rose and came to her, grasping her hands in his, kneeling before her. "Listen to me, Helen. You will change the future of this school. You and Cal, together, are exactly what this school needs. I will place it in your capable hands. You will usher—"

"What are you talking about?" Helen was looking at Elliot in hor-ror. She hadn't gotten past his first sentence. "Who have you found?"

"Her." The word was a whisper.

Helen took a deep breath. "Astrid is dead, Elliot."

"I know."

"She's never going to come back."

"I know she's not. But that's not who—"

There was another knock on the door. The dog, instantly alert, bounded to the door as Lydia opened it. She blushed when she saw Helen and Elliot so close, and touching. "I'm sorry," she said, "but I need help."

"What is it?" Elliot was standing already.

"I'm sorry, Mr. Barrow, but there's a party. And everyone's pretty messed up, and I'm worried that something bad's going to happen. I don't know how to explain, but we need someone to come." She looked at Helen with pleading eyes. "And maybe someone to call the police. I'm sorry."

Elliot shot out the door, and Lydia followed on his heels. The car was still running, and they took off into the darkness. It was amazing how quickly they were gone. Helen ran flank to flank with Ferdinand. The nearest phone lay waiting at the school.

CAL
Stolen, Oregon ~ Tuesday, May 6, 1997

Here is what great art does to me: it opens me. It opens me dan-gerously. That woman I loved in Boston? Her poetry was the most exquisite thing I had ever heard. It made me see the world in a way I had never seen it, and once her words inhabited me, it was as though there was no other way to see the world. Even now, when I run across one of her poems in the occasional literary magazine, I feel as though my breath has been taken from me in the most de-licious, necessary way.

Helen's play did that for me. All that crap about Benson Country

Day and Elliot? It flew out the window as I stood backstage and sent our children out into the footlights. I was opened dangerously by that play, by what it did to the people in that room. It made me ache. It made me ache for that moreness that great art makes me ache for.

When the play was over and the children had dispersed, and the chairs were folded and the gym swept, and Eunice had convinced Helen to get home and pack—Helen, whom I had not yet spoken to, Helen, who had not even told me in person she was leaving— I was left alone in the dark, vast room, so recently full of hundreds of pumping hearts, quick tongues, clapping hands. My own heart beat as if it might burst out of my chest.

I locked the gym door behind me. I found myself sprinting across the field that separated the school from Helen's home. I was fast and blinded and breathless. I would knock on Helen's door and hold her and love her and tell her I was sorry and that she was the brilliant thing in my life, the fire in my heart, the sun in my sky, that I was a fool to have hurt her, that she could not leave me or the school, that I would not let her. I would make love to her until she glowed.

At the house, I thought, "Better look inside first." Funny how those little thoughts pop up and you listen. For the rest of your life, you wonder what if.

I did not see that room from the inside, where things were positively fraternal. I did not know that Elliot was pleading my case. No, what I saw was what Lydia saw: a man and a woman, once married, holding hands like lovers. I stopped short and I knew: "Well, that's it." I could not compete with Elliot. I would not win. I hiked back to the parking lot, trying to close the open part of me. I thought I heard a car engine behind me, but I didn't turn to look. It was as if I was outside the world.

I WAS SHOCKED when Pete held up the phone over the din of the jukebox and hollered, "Your girlfriend's on the phone."

"What girlfriend?" I was already into my second whiskey.

"That teacher," he said. "The one from New York."

"How'd you find me?" I asked into the mouthpiece.

"Eunice," she said in one breath, and in the next, she began to speak so fast I could hardly understand her. The noise from the bar wasn't helping. What I got clearly was "Come quickly." She needed me. I headed back out to the school, speeding the whole way.

DRIVING OUT TO Where-We-Have-the-Parties, I assured Helen things were going to be fine. "Elliot's there," I joked. "He's an expert at ending teen fun." She was amazed that the police and I both knew exactly where the party was. "I grew up here," I said. "It's not that hard to guess where the kids go." Aside from that, there wasn't much to say. Yet I was glad to be near her. I was still thinking of myself.

We knew, as soon as we started up that last little hill, that things were going to be terrible. We felt it, the horror growling in the root of our stomachs, when we saw the flames. They were the tallest flames I've ever seen, and when we crested the hill, the world was lit up. The whole place where the old barn had once been was now fire. And around that fire was a circle of silhouettes, watching like statues.

We were out of the car and running into the smoke, but the police were already there, and they held us back. "Is everything okay?" Helen kept asking, over and over. The children's faces were different in the orange light of the blaze. I searched them for the people I knew, and even though the next day, many of them told me they tried to talk to me, they said it was as if I never saw them at all. I was looking and looking, but I could not see.

The fire department arrived about five minutes later. It seemed to take forever, but I'm told it was five minutes. Those men are skilled at quarantining forest fires in an area where a lit match can ignite a whole mountain. They ran toward the fire, and that was when I noticed Amelia and Lydia. They were wrapped around each other, intercepting the firemen, begging them to help. "He's inside!" I heard Amelia cry. Then I squinted into the heat of the blaze and saw a tall boy, his face wrapped in a shirt, being pulled away from the fire. Victor.

"It's all right," I said, coming up to the girls. "Look, he's fine."

"Where?" asked Amelia, frantically searching.

"There," I said, pointing at Victor.

"No," she said. "I don't mean Victor. I mean my father." She stepped back from me. "My father went in there looking for me."

I looked back at the blaze as it groaned, the great structure bowing and bending. It made the sound of a thousand coyotes howling at the moon. It made the sound of a thousand pine trees blown down by a mighty wind. The heat from the fire blistered my face and singed my hair, and the smell of it was to be on me for days. The water truck pulled up in front of us, blocking our view, and I began to move us around, but Amelia buried herself in me. "I don't want to see," she said. "I don't want to watch this." Which was wise. Because the barn collapsed, but before it did, they found Elliot. One of the firemen carried Elliot out on his shoulder, but it looked like that man was carrying a deer or a dog. I could not see clearly, but I could see that Elliot no longer had a face. I held down my bile as they put him on a stretcher and the ambulance screamed away.

The Flight of Fancy

Once upon a time, there was a boy who became a man but was still a boy, except for on the outside. This boy did as the father said. This boy went east to boarding school. He did the father proud. He got the highest marks in every class. He learned the rules of all the games that the other boys knew—lacrosse, tennis, crew—and all the invisible games as well—girls, money, drugs. By the time he finished boarding school, he had been admitted to the most prestigious university in the land. The father was very proud. He sent the boy a generous monthly check in off white, watermarked linen envelopes, with the father's name and address hand-pressed on the back. The boy earned the nickname "the Indian Prince."

As the father had advised, the boy forgot his grandmother. He forgot his mother. Until the day he thought he saw his mother again, looking like a hobo, begging men for food. That was when he knew he had forgotten how to love.

This matter of what love was, and whether or not the boy could do it, had already come to haunt his life. He thought he'd fallen in love with a girl, the girl who was with him on the day he thought he saw his mother. But the girl turned out to be terrible. When the boy discovered she was terrible, he thought that would mean he didn't love her anymore. But what it really meant was that he started to love her in earnest. This real love was selfish, and cold, and unkind. So perhaps he had not fully forgotten how to love. Perhaps he had only forgotten how to love well.

Let it be noted that as the boy pleased the father and did exactly what the father said, the boy also thought he fell in love with Poetry and Prose. He found salvation in words, with the lingering sigh of sentences, with deft, *squat punctuation, with prosody, with scansion, with rhymes across the caesura. He fell in love with the idea of telling people "I am a writer." He fell in love with the idea of receiving an advanced degree in the esoteric. The boy told the father about this. "I will never be a lawyer. I will never be a doctor, or an astronaut, or a senator, or a scientist." The father stopped sending checks.*

Anger had been building a house around the boy for some time now. Everywhere the boy walked, he was slapped with either the sweet figlike memory of the girl, or with the stark white silence of his own inevitable anger, and the combination of these two loveless things made a tight, hard knot inside of him. He began to think of the knot as the Dread. The Dread glinted at him in café windows. It reflected back at him every time he passed a mirror. It clanged down on his head each time the bell tower struck the hour. The Dread was what reminded the boy that he had no home. That he had no friends. That he had no way to love no one.

He found himself at the airport. The blond woman behind the counter examined him with scientific fascination. "It'll cost you three thousand dollars to get on the next flight."

The boy slapped a thick stack of bills on the gray-flecked ticket counter, and the Dread flicked her a slick smile.

It was night when the boy got to the house of the father. The house was dark, and the boy believed that no one was home. But the father was waiting in a chair, in the dark, when the boy came in the door. It was as if he had a sixth sense for estranged, deranged, enraged offspring. "You're no writer," the father said.

Words like that fed the Dread. It coursed and cursed through the boy's veins. He said, "And what would you know about it?"

"Writers sit at home and write."

The boy wanted the chance to get physical. But the father was sitting still, perched in an armchair, with a sincere smile on his face. The boy held his luggage tight in each hand. "I don't care what you think."

"Of course you do. That's why you're here, isn't it?"

The boy would not be confused. "You're an asshole," he said.

"*Maybe.*"

"*I need to know something.*"

The father nodded as if the boy were asking him permission.

"*Why did my grandmother make you come get me? I know she didn't like you. But she did something to make sure you'd take me in after she died. I need to know what it was.*"

A smile slunk across the father's face. "*She made me promise.*"

"*I know,*" said the boy. The Dread was whirling out the top of the boy's head, like a tornado tightening the room. It was a mighty Dread. "*I need to know about that promise.*"

"*She made me promise I would stay away from you.*"

The boy's grandmother came back in a flood of sound and smell: her to-bacco breath, her froglike crackle, her cough rattling him awake. All this time he had done it because of her. Even if he'd forgotten why, at the root of him, she had been the reason he'd obeyed this father, done exactly what was expected. It all came together: the father was the reason the boy had become the Dread. The father was the reason the boy could not love.

"*You lied to me,*" the boy said, and spat upon the freshly polished floor.

"*Of course I did. You are my son.*"

"*Stay away from me.*"

"*You're not a writer,*" the father called to the boy's departing back. "*You care too much. You're meant to tell our stories, but not to a blank page. To our people. You're just like me. That's why you came back to me. Your grandmother kept us apart. But I knew I could teach you to be a great man. To lead our people.*"

"*You should have left me,*" the boy said over his shoulder. "*I didn't want this. You lied to a dying woman.*" It was the last time the boy saw the father alive.

The father died that very morning. The boy was out on the highway by then. When he got to his grandmother's home, where his people lived, the news met him there. "*He's been sick for months,*" the people told him. "*Didn't you know?*"

That the father had died only made him more of a hero. The boy didn't wish to speak of the words he'd cast against the father. He did not wish to *tell that story. It was no one's business. But that story was the story every person wanted to know. Yes, the father had been ailing. Perhaps he had not told the son that he was ailing, but wasn't it a miracle that the son had somehow known? Everyone wanted to know: what loving words had been said to bring the people's hero to the land of peace?*

It was not until much later that the boy saw his curse: he could never tell the story of what had happened that night. Not a soul could know. But it was the only story the boy had. And the father had been right: the boy had been born to tell stories. People wanted him to tell them. They wanted him to begin with the story of that night.

It was then that the boy saw how right the father was. If the boy told the people anything—of the Dread, of the girl, of the grandmother, of the love he could not feel—they would listen to him. They would follow him. That would make him just like the father.

So the boy shut his mouth with drink. He brawled and yawned and shat. He wasn't good for much else. He had to spend all his energy focused on keeping the stories inside. Sometimes they were too much for him to bear. But he was not going to let them out. He was not going to become what the father had stolen him to make.

That first night, before the boy knew the father was dead, he left the father's house and the city the father had made his own. The boy walked down to the highway and stuck out his thumb. The highway led to his grandmother's house. He stood for hours in the brittle darkness, waiting for his ride. Dawn came as a bloody line across the sky, as if a knife had been drawn across the bruised throat of night. Day began to startle. Across the city, the father drew his last breath. The boy shivered. "I will not lead them," he thought. "But I will go home."

Act Five

[OR]

O Brave New World,

That Has Such People In't

Chapter One

*A*melia went into the wilderness. She did this twice: once, on the night that her father was burned on over 85 percent of his body, and again, nearly a week later. The first time she was gone for only a few minutes. The second time she was gone for twenty-four hours.

She stepped away from the party, and then the barn, to get away from Victor and Wes. It took the police a long time to reconstruct what had happened at the party, and as is always the case, not every story matched up, so we'll never know for sure. But this is approximately what occurred: Amelia, distraught by the fight between Victor and Wes, ran toward the ancient barn at the edge of Where-We-Have-the-Parties. Victor caught up with her, but she was inconsolable and ran into the barn alone. Victor followed her in, but when he called her name, she did not answer, and it was too dark and full of cobwebs and debris for him to go on. He was cautious and sorry. Amelia, on the other hand, fueled by her frustration, was oblivious to the spiders, to the rusty nails, to even Victor's voice pleading for her, so she decided to slip through a hole in the far side of the barn. "Let them fight," she thought. "I'll be gone."

Victor was still searching for her when he heard Wes calling for Amelia outside. Wes had a torch in his hand, and Victor was to say

later that it looked like the end of *Frankenstein*, when the towns-
people have come for the monster. It was hard for him to see the
faces of his friends in the shadows, and everyone was talking over
one another, so it was confusing. Wes was there to help Victor look
for Amelia, but Victor said he didn't need any help, and soon another fight had begun, this one with words. Wes lunged for Victor,
Victor dodged, and Wes and his torch launched into the side of the
barn, all brittle wood and dry beam. Soon the fire had begun.

"Amelia!" Victor called, but by this time she was a hill beyond
them, heading east. She sat down and looked up at the stars. She
needed some peace and quiet. Her back was toward Where-We-
Have-the-Parties, or she would have seen the orange glow from
the blaze much earlier.

Immediately, Victor and Wes and the other children lost track
of which side they'd been on. They sobered up and took turns
running into the doorway of the barn and calling Amelia's name.
Soon the whole structure was engulfed in flames. It was awe-
inspiring, the speed and heat with which the fire licked the old
barn. The children stepped back. They mentioned forest fires. Victor was the only one running close to the building now, and some
of the other boys tried to hold him back, but he fought them off.

Then Elliot arrived. It was good to see an adult who knew how
to solve problems. Elliot gathered, from the jumble of words flying
toward him, that Amelia was trapped inside, in the fire. They had
tried to save her, especially Victor, but the barn was not a barn anymore, it was a fire, and there was no way to step inside it.

All the children tell it like this: Elliot didn't stop to think. He
didn't say a word. He just ran into the flames. Faster than they
knew how to stop him.

Out in the wilderness, Amelia began to hear something strange.
Pops and groans from behind her. She stood and turned and saw a
glow so bright she thought it was the headlights of cars driving up
the hill after her. But then she smelled the smoke, and then she was
running back up the hill, and then she was standing in sight of the

blaze. She ran around it, beginning to make out people in the shimmer of the heat. A girl saw her and called her name, and one by one, the others fell back at the sight of her. One of them told her that her father was in there, trying to find her, trying to save her, and Amelia didn't understand. It took six or seven others saying the same thing for her to believe it. Lydia found her in the middle of the crowd and wrapped her in her arms, and then the police arrived, and soon after, Helen and I were upon her, and then came the firemen, and the water, and sometime in there, her father was found, but she was not watching because she could not bear to see.

THE REST OF the night and into the morning, there were the hospital and the police and the statements to be made. We were all exhausted. We were all sad. But Amelia was particularly functional, offering to make us peanut-butter sandwiches and cups of tea. She stayed responsible and together for days. I knew we were in trouble.

Each day Helen drove her back from the hospital in the early afternoon, while I kept a vigil at Elliot's bedside. When they got back to the Bugle House, Amelia would always take a nap. "Feel free to lie down with me," she added. But Helen had phone calls to make and food to prepare. Seven days later, Amelia convinced her to lie down beside her. Helen watched as the girl drifted into a long, still sleep. Only then did Helen close her eyes too, with the girl safe beside her.

Amelia waited until Helen's breathing slowed. Then she opened her eyes. She was good at the pretending-to-sleep trick. Her father called it "playing possum." He was the only one who knew when she was faking. She moved slowly off the bed, grabbing her backpack as she went. In the kitchen, she took the can opener and the canned corn and chili that had been in the top cupboard for years. She took a bag of bread and the newly opened peanut butter out of the fridge. She wished they were the kind of family who had beef jerky. She found two water bottles and filled them. Before she tip-toed out the door, she grabbed the afghan off the back of the couch.

It wasn't that she wanted to scare anyone. And it wasn't that she thought it was all her fault. Both things had crossed her mind. She knew that had she not gone into the barn one way and out an-other, her father would be fine. But she was a rational girl, even in the deepest pit of grief she'd ever known.

Mostly, she went into the wilderness because she wanted to be alone. She wanted to think it all through before everyone told her what to believe. It had already begun. She had heard it in our voices, Helen's, mine, the policemen's: "Your father is a hero." But she knew it wasn't over; she knew the world had to be healed. All she wanted was to be alone.

WILLA
Day Seven
Boise, Idaho, to Bend, Oregon ~ Tuesday, May 13, 1997

The seventh day bloomed sunny.

He was going to tell her.

He had believed he would tell her at the Mississippi River. But she had looked at him in such a way in that instant when he told her what her mother was. She had looked at him, and he had been cowed. Too much truth would have spelled disaster.

While packing up the car a week before, he had thought, "Surely I'll have told her by the time we get to Kansas." But the two days after their conversation above the Mississippi had been bound by silence. Willa seemed on the edge of breaking. Telling her would have been cruel.

Then there was the chance of Boulder. A perfect place. But she had started crying before he could begin to steer the conversation to where truth could begin.

After that, the Rockies. In the Rockies, he'd realized: it wasn't because of *her* that he couldn't tell her. It was because of him. All these years he'd believed that she was far too delicate for his honesty. Now he could see, in the confident way she sat beside him, offering up snacks, taking her photographs, singing to keep them both alert, that she wasn't delicate at all. She was her mother in her mother's best ways. She was strong. She was going to be fine.

He was the one who was the coward.

"So we're going to walk into the hospital? Just like that?" she asked.

"I will."

"Is he . . ." Willa put her feet on the dashboard. "Are you sure he's still alive?"

"I called the hospital in Bend this morning. He's still in the coma. He'll surely die. But he's still alive."

"Wow." Willa fiddled with her shoelaces. Nat knew her nervous habits because he was her father. "Dad?"

"Hmm."

"I'm coming in with you, okay?"

"We'll see," he said.

"That's what parents say when they don't want to say no. It's basically lying. Just let me go into the hospital with you."

"We'll see," Nat said. Really, Willa was right. He was lying. He wasn't going to see. He already knew that he would make her stay in the car. But in the scale of things, he thought grimly, this tiny lie didn't matter. There had been so much lying all these years. He reminded himself: he had told the lies to keep her safe. Then he thought: "Safe from what?" And then he thought: "Enough. I am going to tell her."

He was the driver of a car, and his daughter was the passenger. They were vaulting across the eastern Oregon desert as a May afternoon began. Malheur County, the Stinking Water Mountains, Rattlesnake Creek, the town of Burns, Sage Hen Valley, Silver Creek, Glass Butte, Harney County, Lake County, Pine Mountain, the Badlands, were each, one by one, left in their wake. The wake that Nat and Willa made together.

Neither noticed the names of the desert. Neither noticed the greasewood or spiny hopsage spreading out for miles in either direction. Neither heard the steps of the western whiptail or the leopard lizard, nor those of the white-tailed antelope squirrel, nor of the marmots as they made their way about the warming day. Instead, Nat's mind and Willa's mind worked deftly: his, on the problem at hand, hers, like a comb, running over her father's words, trying to find the catch in them. There was something more. She was smart enough to know that.

"I am a coward," Nat thought.

In the same instant: "I am going to tell her."

And then he comforted himself: "Not yet."

Chapter Two

AMELIA
Stolen, Oregon ~ Tuesday, May 13, 1997

She still swears to it that she had no particular destination in mind. I've asked her over and over again, because the chances of her accidentally ending up where she did unplanned are one in a million. But if she's lying, she's the best liar I've ever seen.

She walked out of the house in broad daylight, and no one saw her leave. Helen didn't awaken for four hours, until the evening, and it took her another three to track me down, since she assumed I'd picked Amelia up while Helen slumbered. Amelia had a seven-hour lead. In most parts of the country, we would have been able to drive after her, because a seven-hour lead on foot doesn't mean much compared to sixteen cylinders and four wheels. In our part of the world, however, there are no roads after a certain point. Yes, there was the chance she'd hitchhiked out of here, but I had a feeling she wouldn't leave her father's wounded body that far behind. Other people were worried about her physical well-being: she could be raped, she could fall into a ravine, she could get dehydrated. I wasn't worried about Amelia's body surviving. I was worried about her mind and her heart. I know where you can go when you let those broken pieces of yourself lead you. I wanted to save her from that. So we searched. For one night and one day, we roamed the wild country and called her name. She says she didn't think about that. That's the part she's most embarrassed about.

She won't talk about what she did out there. I respect that. I don't think she'll ever tell another soul, and I've told her I believe that's the best way for things to be, because it's Her Way, and that's the only way that matters when you're healing.

What she *will* talk about is how strange it was to find herself behind a trailer and to see Victor Littlefoot emerging. When she saw him coming out, she realized she'd seen the trailer from the other side. But she didn't know how she got to be there right when Victor happened to be making breakfast for his grandmother, just in time for him to glimpse Amelia out the window.

"You don't want me here," she remembers saying.

"Yes I do," he said. His grandmother was behind him, in the doorway. "It's Amelia," he said. "You remember Amelia."

"I called her here," she said, peering closer. "She's the one with the broken heart, the broken life. And the one with grass for hair."

Victor lifted Amelia in his arms. "Let's get you safe." It was the first time Amelia felt like crying.

Victor's grandmother cooed over her. "You don't have to cry, girl. Your wholeness is coming for you. You don't have to cry."

"Of course she does," Victor said, bringing Amelia into the house. "Of course she does." He placed her on the couch. He laid himself down beside her. His body was warm against her whole length, and she buried her face in his chest, which rose and fell like that of a sleeping creature. Victor didn't say another word. He let her cry until she had no tears. He let her cry until she slept. After that, he carried her to his truck. He brought her home.

HELEN

Stolen, Oregon ~ Tuesday, May 13, 1997

The day after the fire, Helen called Michael at the hospital in Vermont. She was cautious and did so while Amelia was sleeping.

After Amelia ran away, Helen feared she had not been cautious enough. She feared Amelia had overheard her and misinterpreted what she'd said. She feared the girl thought she too was going to abandon her. She was supposed to be getting on an airplane in two hours.

Michael was asleep. She left a message with the nurse. "Tell him I hope to be there soon," she said. "There's been an accident. Tell him . . . tell him I won't be there tomorrow morning. But I'll be there soon."

Seven days later, when Amelia was gone, Helen answered the phone and heard Michael on the other end of the line. His voice was strained and thin, as if his vocal cords were pressed against something sharp.

She did most of the talking. Michael was horrified to hear about Elliot and squeezed out every medical detail Helen could remember. "I fancy myself something of a diagnostician these days," he said.

"It's just awful, Michael. He's just—there's nothing left of him. As if he's been obliterated. Like in one of those cartoons where someone's a pile of ashes. One second he was right there, talking to me, and then he was gone. He's not even really alive anymore. And then I think that's a terrible thing to say."

"It's true," he said. "It's true."

"I'm sorry." She realized how breezily she'd brought death into the conversation. "That was very insensitive—"

"Oh, shut up," he said. "I may be skin and bones, but at least I *have* skin and bones." He laughed grimly. "See, now I'm the one who has to apologize. I just reined myself in from making barbecue jokes."

Helen laughed grimly. "That's awful."

"You spend more than a day in the hospital, and you get a free pass to make jokes like that. Especially if you're dying."

"I'm coming to see you," she said. "But something very strange happened before Elliot's accident. He asked me to stay. And even though he didn't know that anything was going to happen . . ." She shivered. "It's spooky. He told me he was leaving the school. He told me he needed me to help run it in his absence." She lowered her voice. "It's like he *knew*."

"I've decided I don't want you to come at all," Michael announced.

"What?"

"I said, I don't want you—"

"I heard you. But I'm coming soon. I promise."

"I don't want you here. I'm musty and wizened, and I make the most terrible smells."

"Please don't be angry with me."

"Au contraire, my dear. Au contraire. I'm the furthest thing from angry. Here's how I see it: you've got one dying guy in a bed in Oregon and one dying guy in a bed in Vermont. So that pretty much evens the scales. Here's the thing: you've got something more out there than you'll ever have here. You have a life."

"That's silly."

"Don't you dare call it silly. I would give anything to have a life. You know I would. Don't you dare denigrate that gift. You have Amelia. You have Cal. They need you."

"I have a life back there, with you."

"No, you don't," he said. "We have a friendship. But we don't make a home for each other. I've heard it in your voice, ever since you got out there. You've finally found your home, haven't you?"

She shook her head as though he could see her. "I'm coming to visit." She heard a car pull up, and as Ferdinand began to bark, she guiltily asked Michael to hang on a minute. She shouldn't be jamming up the phone line. What if something had happened to Elliot or Amelia? She ran to Amelia's room, and, peering down at the driveway, she saw Victor's truck. She ran back to the phone, breathless. "I'm sorry," she said, "but I've got to go. Someone's here."

To which Michael Reid responded, "Good girl. Back to life."

Chapter Three

*I*t was when they were parked across the street from the hospital that Nat said, "I'm sorry about the art show, kiddo. We're three days and three thousand miles away."

Willa shrugged. "I've shot, like, fifteen rolls of film. And if even one picture is better than the *Scars* crap, it was worth it."

"I know," he said. "I just wish we hadn't had to choose. I promised you four normal high school years. And then—"

"It's okay, Dad," Willa said solemnly. "I had a good time with you. And you let me decide this time. I liked that."

Nat nodded and looked out his window at the hospital. He didn't want Willa to see him like this. But he'd invited her along.

"Well?" she said after a minute or two.

"Well, what?"

"Aren't we going to go in?"

"Yup," he said. "Except for the part where *I'm* the one going in. You're keeping Ariel company."

"Dad."

"No buts."

"Haven't I been responsible?"

"More than I could have imagined."

"Then it totally isn't fair. I can't believe you'd bring me all this way and make me sit here, waiting for you. You haven't even told me *why* you have to see him. All I know is that Caroline wanted you to pass something along. But he's in a fucking coma! So whatever you tell him, he's not even going to hear you. And here I am, your poor daughter who's driven three thousand miles with you, and you won't even tell me *why*."

"I *can't* tell you why."

"Fine. Whatever. The point is—"

"It's not fine. I *should* have told you why. But I couldn't."

Willa was baffled. She'd been drawing a perfectly fine argumental line, and now he was interrupting her with a grammar lesson. "The point is," she said, "that I need to go into that hospital with you. It's gonna kill me to sit out here with the dumb cat."

"I know," Nat said. "But you're going to do it. Not because I'm telling you to. Because I'm asking you to. I'm asking you to do me a favor. It would mean the world to me if I could have a little time . . . just to think. Just to be alone with him."

Willa scrunched herself down against her legs and looked at her father from below. "Did you know him? I didn't think you knew him until now. You seem . . . sad."

"Yeah," Nat said, "I feel sad."

"But we made it! All the way across the country!"

Nat took his wallet from the dashboard, removed five hundred-dollar bills, and placed them in Willa's hand. "I want you to hold on to this," he said.

"What is this?"

"Just in case."

"In case of what?" A knot rose in Willa's throat. She sat up. This was happening too quickly. She had thought they were done with all this. She thought they had arrived.

"In case . . ." Nat smiled, and Willa realized he was smiling to keep himself from crying.

"In case what?" she asked.

"I'm supposed to tell you something now."

"Okay."

"Something big."

"Okay, Dad. Okay. You can tell me. You can tell me anything."

"Not this." He shook his head, once, twice, and then he brought it down to rest against the steering wheel.

Willa waited. At any moment, Nat was going to sit upright and he would be her capable, strong father and he would tell her he had changed his mind and that they were going to go inside together. Then they would go find Elliot Barrow, and she would sit in the waiting room and let Nat have his privacy, and she would give Nat back his five hundred dollars and then he would explain that there had never been anything terrible to tell her. Because that was what she feared. His face told her everything. Whatever the secret he was going to spill, it contained terrible things.

"Dad." She touched his leg. He barely moved. "Dad," she said again, more powerfully. "Listen. You don't have to explain anything. Okay?" As she spoke, she realized she didn't want this secret, whatever it was, to be loosed upon her. Not yet. It was the first time in her life that Willa didn't want to know a secret. She didn't want to have to know another awful thing.

She spoke with confidence. "You can do this. It's easy. You're going to go in there and do whatever you have to do with Elliot Barrow, and then, afterward, if you still want to tell me this . . . thing . . . you can, okay? But not now. Let's make a deal. Not now."

Nat shook his head. "I have to."

"I don't want to hear it," she said with finality. "I don't think I can stand to hear something else."

"I've been terrible," Nat said.

"No," Willa said. "No. You've been wonderful." She didn't know what they were talking about anymore. But she knew that he was wonderful and that she didn't want to hear otherwise.

She tapped him on the leg. "You better change your shirt," she said. "That's the one you've been wearing since Utah. Anyway," she added, "I've got to help Ariel stretch her legs."

"Stay in the car," Nat said, alert in an instant.

Willa leaned back against the window. "Okay," she said. "Okay."

After that, Nat was all business. He changed his shirt and ran his fingers through his hair. He took a mint from the glove compartment and looked straight at Willa. "Stay in the car," he said.

"I'm *going* to."

"You remember when I told you—that we've been hiding? Well, they may well be looking for me here. I'm a fugitive."

Willa started giggling when she heard that word. Her laughter was incredibly inappropriate, but she couldn't stop.

Nat went on. "There's a distinct possibility that the FBI is waiting for me in that building."

"Then clearly you can't go in," Willa said, her anxiety still laughing through her.

"I don't have a choice."

"Yes you do. We can wait out here, see if we notice anything. And then tomorrow—"

"He'll be dead tomorrow."

"Why? What do you mean?"

"They don't have a burn unit at this hospital. What does that say to you?"

"I don't know. I don't know anything about burn units, Dad."

"It says they're not trying to fix him. It says they're just trying to keep him comfortable."

"Oh." The money was damp in her hand. She didn't like the smell of it.

"It can't be helped, Willa. It's too late," Nat said, but he seemed suddenly cheerful. Optimistic. As if announcing the word "fugitive" into the conversation had been the best decision he'd ever made.

"Don't go in there. You don't *have* to."

"Oh, but I do."

Later, Willa would replay this scene, wondering what she could have said to stop her father from going, but every time she replayed it, her father was too fast for her, all words and purpose. In the memory, Nat didn't feel like a person to Willa, he felt like water. Flowing-away water.

Before he left the car, he turned in his seat and looked Willa squarely in the eye. He was completely lucid, in control. "This won't happen. But if. If they take me . . . if I'm identified, arrested, I will send someone to come and get you. To take you somewhere safe."

"This is insane." Willa's whole body was vibrating, the way it did when she'd had too much caffeine. She felt as if she were outside herself, and that a part of her was laughing at how strange this was. But only she could hear the laugh.

"It sounds insane, yes, it does. But promise me. Promise me that if someone I've sent comes to get you, you'll go with them."

"Who?"

"I don't know. But I'll figure something out."

"How will I know who they are? How will I know you sent them?"

Nat nodded at her sensibility. "You'll know. It will be someone you can trust. They'll tell you they're taking you somewhere safe. Just to be sure, when they come to get you, don't say a word. Wait to speak until you see where they take you. If they don't handcuff you, then you can trust them."

"They're going to use handcuffs?"

"No, of course they aren't. Only the police would. But if the police get me, I'm not saying a word about you. I promise. They won't know you're here."

"But who—"

"Just promise me."

Willa bit her lip. "I promise." There was a secret world of people waiting to rescue people like her from the police, the FBI, whoever they were. She wanted to ask, "If you are a fugitive, does that make me a fugitive, too? Will going with someone you send make me a fugitive if I'm not one right now?"

"I love you, Willa," Nat said. "I want you to remember, no matter what happens, how much I love you." He grabbed her in a hug, squeezing all her air out. She wanted to hold on to him, but he slipped through her fingers. "I'll be back," he said. And then he was gone.

As she watched Nat disappear into the hospital, Willa tried to calm her heart. No undercover agents in trench coats followed him in. No police cars careened into the parking lot, lights and sirens blaring. Nothing unusual happened at all, and Willa told herself that everything was going to be fine. He was going to reemerge from that hospital in twenty minutes, and they were going to drive to a hotel with a swimming pool. There, the terrible secret would not be so terrible. He would tell her whatever it was, and she would wave her hand and say, "No biggie." Things would be back to normal. They had driven across and through and over all this country—all this vast strange country packed with a zillion Denny's and Wal-Marts, cheap motels and bad coffee—and if they'd made it this far, there was no way they could lose each other now.

Willa believed this wholeheartedly until the Indian man knocked on her window.

"Your dad wants you to come with me," he said. "He wants you safe." The Indian put his hand on the door handle. "Come on. Come with me. You don't have to say a word."

CAL
Bend, Oregon ~ Tuesday, May 13, 1997

When I wasn't out looking for Amelia, I was sitting at the hospital, waiting for Elliot to wake up. I'm no fool. I knew the chances were slim. But at first his waking up seemed possible. Miraculously, he'd avoided breathing in too much hot air, so his lungs weren't fried; his heart was strong. I took those for good signs. Everything had happened too fast, and it seemed that all I could do was sit down to try to gather the bits of truth I knew and to catch up to reality.

The hospital was a good place to do this. Otherwise, it looked like I wasn't doing anything. Otherwise, everyone kept asking me if I was all right. When I say "everyone," I mean people like those from Benson Country Day, who seemed to be mighty relieved when I told them no charges would be pressed against Wesley Hazzard. People like the Neige Courante elders and their children, who kept showing up on campus even though I had canceled classes for the time being. People like Helen, although, to her credit, she asked only twice, and the second time she saw I could not stand the question, and after that I knew she would not ask again. I restrained myself from talking harshly to Helen, because I didn't want her to consider me, in this moment of crisis, as impossible as I actually am. I did not want Helen—who was cooking, and fielding calls, and beating herself up about not keeping a closer eye on Amelia, who'd run off—to hate me or to leave. Helen had postponed her trip to see Michael Reid. That was encouraging.

Even after I knew Elliot was never waking up again, I went to the hospital to sit in the dark room where Elliot lay barely breathing, and I tried to account for what had happened and why Elliot was holding on. I looked at the heap of bandages before me, at the machines blinking and beeping and whirring, and wished I had Elliot back so he could tell me the story himself. Why wouldn't he let go?

I valiantly assumed I'd figured out everything on my own. I figured out that Elliot couldn't die because his daughter wasn't there for him to lay eyes on. I figured out that was the reason Amelia had decided to run off in the first place. She knew her father was way too polite, way too cultured, to leave without bidding us all adieu. He wanted, and deserved, a proper deathbed scene. I know that sounds trivial now—maybe even snide—but both Helen and I knew Elliot and his daughter well enough to recognize that even if this wasn't completely true, Amelia might believe it was true. So I was feeling a little irked at Amelia, a little annoyed, for leaving her father in the lurch like this. For not having the nerve to say good-bye.

I was thinking these thoughts as I headed back downstairs and one of the nurses took me aside. She wanted to ask me something, but I shook my head. "Not now," I said. "Later." And strode on. What caught my eye then was the remarkable contrast between competence and utter grief. There stood nurses, all clipboards and rainbow-hued scrubs, gleaming and confident, while the others— *us*—the real people, felled by the suffering of those we loved but could not save, mumbled and churned in unkempt clothes, or put on bright false countenances and read glossy magazines and sipped from giant thermoses. We waited in vain.

None of this was new. But today, in the center of the visitors' lounge, stood a tall thin white man, and he was weeping, un-abashed. Tears flowing. His face a mask of agony. No consolation possible. Looking at him was at once unbearable and irresistible. His grief was so pure that it should have shamed us all. He was los-ing someone before our eyes, and there was no help for it.

What happened to me then was remarkable. I had—let's put the right name on it—a revelation. I saw that I was mad at Amelia, irked at her, as I believed, not because she was holding up her fa-ther's demise but because I, Calbert Fleecing, her godfather, was worried sick about her. What if I lost her too? Not just Elliot but Amelia? I felt a stab of pain that I recognized as love and fear— both at once, as usual. Then I was out of there, racing out the front entrance of the hospital, on my way to find the person who, I now knew, was becoming my daughter.

To say that I found her immediately makes it sound as if I'm lying. But that was what happened. No sooner had I opened my eyes in the glare of the daylight than there, in the front seat of a car, I saw what we'd all been looking for.

I'd like to say that love filled my heart with kindness, but no. I felt good and mad. I also felt a rush of relief and a dawning realization that Amelia was wounded, wounded like an animal, and more than anything, I had to lure her home. I couldn't afford to scare her. Maybe she'd been hitchhiking. I wouldn't make her tell me anything. I'd just take her, safely, home.

Amelia stiffened when she saw me. Her eyes panicked, even though the rest of her stayed still, and I dreaded knowing what had happened to her in the world to make her look at me that way. I tapped on the window. I said, "Open the window, please."

She unrolled it a sliver, so that my words had to fly through a tiny space to reach her. "Your dad wants you to come with me," I said. "He wants you safe."

She shook her head.

"Come on," I said. "Come with me. You don't have to say a word."

When she opened the car door, it was clear she'd gathered things on her lap: a jean jacket, a backpack. I didn't recognize these things, but I don't pay much attention to stuff like that. She reached down to the floor and picked up a cat, old and stunned, and—I was proud of myself—I didn't say a word. Hell, we could handle a cat. Even Ferdinand could. I was surprised that she leaned on me, given how she'd looked at me through that window. But she leaned on me hard as I walked her to my truck. It felt as if she was crying, though she didn't make a sound.

We drove north, and she was silent the whole time. I'd decided to wait to speak until she did. She didn't say anything. She leaned her head against the window and angled her face away from me. I was glad I'd found her when I did.

We pulled into the school and in front of the house, but she made no move to get out of the car. Finally, I said, "I'd leave you here alone, but I'm concerned you'll run away. So you're going to have to come inside."

She nodded once.

"Do you think you can manage?"

She held her things to her chest as I walked around to her side. She held on to my arm as she stepped down from the truck. Then she shrugged and handed me the cat. Her eyes searched the house, and that was the first time I had a moment of pause. It looked as if she had never seen the house before. I thought, "She's traumatized." So I led her to the doorway and up the stairs.

"Helen!" I called. "Look who I found!"

Helen appeared at the top of the stairs and went white at the sight of Amelia. "She ran away again?" She scrutinized Amelia. Stern. Then asked, "How did you get out of your room?"

"I just found her down by the hospital—"

"But Victor brought her back about an hour ago. I've been trying to call you."

"Victor?"

"He found her this morning up by his house. He brought her back himself."

By then Amelia and I were at the top of the stairs. Helen enfolded her in a hug and shook her head. "You can't keep running away like this. I know it's hard. But honey, I'm too old for this; you're going to give me a heart attack."

Amelia stood there, her things still in her arms.

"What's all this?" Helen asked, but couldn't pry them away.

There was a noise behind us. We turned one by one to see a second Amelia, standing in the doorway of her bedroom. "I'm trying to sleep," she said. "Could you keep it down?"

Helen screamed. It was a note that hung in the air long after it started. I dropped the cat and stepped back, speechless. Helen stumbled as if her legs were giving out, and propped herself against the door frame.

There were two Amelias. They stared at each other, and their expressions were like those of people who have never heard of the existence of snow, and then open their eyes one morning and find that the world is a miracle of white. Or people who have never known the sea, and the road turns left and there's the Pacific, all wild and wide. It was as if the girls were seeing the whole world for the first time. Hell, it was as if *all* of us were seeing the whole world for the first time. Looking at them was seeing the world coming together. No one said a word, and then Helen murmured, "You weren't crazy, you were never crazy."

The girls moved toward each other. I looked at Helen and her eyes were wet, and she was gasping, but I'm ashamed that I can't explain in words the euphoria spangling through her. She told me later that I looked the same.

"Where's my father?" the first Amelia asked me.

"Elliot?" I said.

She shook her head. "His name's Nat."

"I have no idea," I said. The wheels of my mind were stuck in the mud.

"I'm Willa," the first Amelia said. "I want to make sure my father's okay."

"Yes," I said, but I didn't move. I watched the girls take each other in.

"I'm Amelia," Amelia said. They took each other's hands.

The Song and Dance

Once upon a time, there was a girl who was like a song. She was like a song because she preferred to hold still, and when she held her very stillest, that was when song, pure and clear, emanated from her deepest self. She was shy about this song. It was her great gift.

Once upon a time, there was a girl who was like a dance. She was like a dance because she could not hold still. She ricocheted off of everything. Her dance was frenetic and funny, and often she would whiz by and people would wonder, "What was that?" She was not shy about this dance. It was her great gift.

The girl who was like a song did not know about the girl who was like a dance. Likewise, the girl who was like a dance did not know about the girl who was like a song.

But the strange thing was, they looked exactly alike.

Before they figured out how it was they looked exactly alike, before they figured out that they had the same parents, before they figured out that these parents had kept them apart for their song-and-dance lifetimes, there was a moment. This moment was before the girls were sad or angry. This moment was full of wonder. This moment was when the song realized she had always missed the dance, and the dance realized she had always missed the song.

The song said, "You look . . ."

The dance said, "You look . . ."

And together they said, "Like me."

The dance reached out a finger to touch the song's cheek. "Maybe I'm asleep," the dance thought.

The song stood still and started to cry.

The dance said, "Why are you crying?"

The song said, "I'm scared."

The dance said, "I'm fucking freaking out."

There were adults in the room. The adults were supposed to have the answers. The adults were even more bewildered than the song or the dance, because the adults were seeing double. They had known the song since she was a baby. They had sung to her and changed her and held her in their arms as she cried. But they had never imagined there could be two of her.

Well, that is not entirely true. One of the adults was the man-who-had-once-been-the-boy. He knew about fathers and their lies. The other adult was the satin woman. And as soon as she saw the song and the dance, face-to-face, she began to weep. She tried to speak. She tried to say, "He told me about this. When you were just a baby." The satin woman pointed between the song and the dance, trying to tell the song she was speaking to her. "He told me there were two of you." But she couldn't get the words to sound clear.

The song and dance said, "What?"

The satin woman finally got it out.

The song and dance said, "Who?"

"Your father."

The song and the dance looked at each other, bewildered. They were each thinking of her father, but they were thinking of different fathers.

The song and dance said, "When?"

"Seventeen years ago. On the night your mother left."

The song and dance said, "Where?"

"New York City."

The song and dance said, "Why?"

That would turn out to be the biggest mystery of all.

Epilogue

Spoken by
CAL

*W*e've arrived at the end in the play. And though it may be almost time to quit our seats, the damn story—the one we've been caught up in—will never be over. This is hard on all of us. The players, caught up in the spell of otherness, must plunge down to earth, taking on their skinnier daily identities. The audience's job is even harder. The audience, whose attention cast this spell in the first place, must shrug the charm from their collective eyes and concede that the other life—the one outside the theater—is the life they're stuck with. It awaits them. But if the play has worked its magic, then that waiting life, that coming death, can look a lot like peace, a lot like rest. A place to give way to sleep without giving up hope. The time has come to scramble into coats, dry our eyes, roll up the playbill. Exeunt.

So. Elliot. There are only a few more things to tell. And then you can choose. To go or to stay. To be or not to be.

Should I start with your daughters? The way they sit on either side of you, whispering their secrets into your ears? That's one story I can't tell. It's not mine. Anyway, I know you have already heard the heart of it. You hear them the way a father hears, love them the way a father loves.

So what is left?

First in line stands Nat Llewelyn. Willa is asking you to forgive Nat, her father. Dammit, we *all* are.

Ah, the mysterious sins of the fathers. Apparently and reasonably, kidnapping is considered a crime only if the person you've kidnapped officially exists. Unless you've met that simple condition, no charges can be filed, even if you turn yourself in to the police and seek out a hard-nosed judge who's willing to listen to you until you run out of talk and tears.

No one, except perhaps you, Elliot, can blame Nat Llewelyn for basing his entire life of caring for Willa on the mistaken belief that he was wanted by the feds. No one can blame him for assuming that Willa was your only child with Caroline aka Astrid, and that you were devoting all your resources, all your might, to locating that precious daughter, to retrieving her, to punishing whoever had stolen her. Since Nat loved her the way he did, with such a pure singing heart, he could imagine what Willa meant to you. He did not know that Willa's birth had never been registered, even though Amelia's had; he didn't know that once your wife—Astrid to you, Caroline to him—had been killed in that blast, along with her comrades, you were the sole living person, other than Nat himself, who knew that Willa was rightfully, biologically, *yours.*

Why didn't he keep his promise to Caroline, bundle that baby up, and deliver her to your arms? What made him wait until now? Think about it, Elliot. There was a good chance that you were as wrongheaded and strong-willed as Caroline had proved to be. As far as Nat was concerned, you had fallen in love with that terrorist knowing full well that she was a terrorist; as Caroline had confided to him in a horrible rush of candor, you'd taught her everything worth knowing about life. Caroline was referring to your idealism, your inexhaustible search for justice, but how was Nat, listening through a fog of heart-wrenched jealousy, not to think of violence? How was he supposed to know you weren't the one who'd taught her bombs?

As the years passed, and no agents knocked at his door, and no private eyes flashed mug shots of Caroline at his boss or neighbors, hoping to make an ID, Nat began to wonder whether you'd given up the search. If you'd done that, what kind of father did that make you? He'd look at your scrambling, gorgeous girl—now *his* scrambling, gorgeous girl—and know that you didn't deserve her. Nat had promised Caroline that if anything happened to her, he'd guard Willa with his life, and he'd return her to you, Willa's father. He figured that he'd kept the best part of that promise, even after he read of a man named Elliot Barrow who'd started a school out in Oregon for Indian kids. Willa was seven when Nat read that article. He thought: "Maybe this isn't the same Elliot Barrow." He decided, just in case: "We do not go west of the Mississippi." He vowed: "I will forget I ever read this." He burned the article up. There was a hectic dailiness to attend to: school lunches to pack, swings to push, bedtime stories to tell. Nat didn't let himself stop and think about the enormity of what he'd done. Just kept moving. Once he and Willa had settled down in Connecticut, once he'd put a roof over their heads, a life of secrecy was no longer a daily improvisation; it became a habit.

That is, until he turned on his radio that morning a few weeks ago and everything changed. As Bob Edwards's voice broke the story, Nat could feel his life breaking apart. First came the name: Elliot Barrow. Then the urgency of the accident: the man was as good as dead. For an instant Nat was tempted to think this might be a different man, a different Elliot from the one who'd fathered Caroline's child, the stranger he'd read about in that education magazine. Then Bob Edwards clinched it. This Elliot Barrow had once been linked to radical activism in the 1970s and early '80s. Seems his wife had been a terrorist. Killed by a bomb. What an incredible man, a true hero, an inspirational story, Elliot Barrow was. He had gone on to found Ponderosa Academy in hopes of showing people that radical change was possible through daily, peaceful endeavor. That, finally, was what brought Nat to his knees.

There in his kitchen, watching the goldfinches mobbing the thistle, Nat saw the collapse of his world. When he had first lifted Willa out of Caroline's arms and made his promise, he hadn't been thinking about Willa or Elliot. He'd been thinking about Caroline. He'd always wanted to woo her, to please her, to earn her trust. Nothing had changed. A few days later, Nat saw Caroline's picture in the paper and read her other name: Astrid Lux Barrow. That was when, for the first time, he thought about Elliot. Right then, right there, with the newspaper spread open in front of him, he decided to break half that promise and be damned. As far as he was concerned, you'd died alongside the woman who'd married you and not him.

Only then did he think, *really think*, about Willa, who'd grown accustomed to greedily gulping formula from the bottle he held, peeing her way through those mounds of disposable diapers he'd grown adept at changing. First she would cry and he wouldn't know what to do, but once he picked her up or slipped her into the Snugli, she'd smooth down into a lump on his chest, and he'd gather her into his rhythm and place his hand on her back. Already he loved, without measure, without reason, the astonishing mewing girl in his arms. He loved her as if she were his own.

For over seventeen years, Nat was able to believe that you, Elliot Barrow, were a monster. For over seventeen years, Nat was able to believe that even though the FBI might want him for kidnapping, he'd done the right thing. Hell, he'd done better than keeping Caroline's promise; he'd kept her daughter. And he'd kept her daughter safe by giving her a life of love.

That thought sustained him. Then the radio told him that Elliot Barrow was still alive, that Elliot Barrow was not a monster; Elliot Barrow was a great man among men. Suddenly, forcefully, Nat realized he still had time to fulfill the rest of the promise. He couldn't make Willa come with him to the dying man's bedside, but he could make her feel that she should, so he packed the car.

No one can blame Nat for being racked by a hideous, irreparable grief and guilt over what he'd done once he realized the enormity of his transgression. Stealing another man's child is not just a crime against the man; it is a crime against the child. In this case, a crime against *two* children. How great a crime it was became obvious the moment Nat laid eyes on Amelia, and Ponderosa Academy, and his own Willa standing in the middle of a life that could have been hers, except for him.

The minute the police dropped Nat off at our door—he was to pick up his Volvo later, in Bend, where he'd spent the night in custody—Willa forgave him absolutely, with her entire heart and body. She clung to him and wept, murmuring, "Daddy, Daddy, Daddy."

Amelia, knowing that you would never hug her again, stood to the side, looking on in wonder, and then Nat opened his arms even wider and welcomed Amelia into his lanky embrace. "Look at you," he kept saying. "Just look at you." And then; "I am so sorry. Please forgive me, I am so sorry."

Which brings me to you, Elliot. As all of us—led by your daughters—ask you to forgive Nat, we also ask you to forgive yourself. We know now that you were looking for Willa, and look! Elliot, something even better has happened: she has found *you*.

After Willa walked into our midst, after Helen screamed and sobbed and yelled, she began to murmur, "You weren't crazy after all, you were never crazy." She was talking to *you*, because seventeen years ago, you laid your head in her lap and cried, and she thought you were crazy. Ravaged by grief, exhausted by the countless number of police interviews needed to establish your complete and utter lack of awareness of Astrid's devastating illegal activities, you were undone. The moment you'd heard about Astrid's death, you'd begun ranting about Willa, your other baby. And guess what—I don't have to tell you this—everyone, lawyers, police detectives, family, friends, assured you *there is no second baby*. There was only one birth certificate. Only you and Astrid and her midwife at the birth, and the midwife was nowhere to be found. By the time you called Helen to you, you'd begun to believe you were truly insane. Helen was your test; Helen would advise you what to do. So you confided in her too.

You told her about the existence of the two girls, and that one of them had disappeared with Astrid when she'd fled. Later, after the explosion, your lawyer was not so indulgent as he'd been at first. He'd attempted to expand the scope of the investigation, but the remains at the explosion site were all adults. Six people, including Astrid and the midwife, identified by their dental records. Then there was the fact that no one had ever seen the second baby. The lawyer had neatly explained this part of the argument by the time Helen showed up. You wanted Helen to know that this meant simply that no one had ever seen the two babies together at once, which, as far as you were concerned, meant nothing at all.

What Helen did that night was to hold you in her arms, to gather up your baby girl Amelia, and to tell you that Amelia was reason enough to pull yourself together. Didn't you realize you could lose *her*, Amelia, if you let grief drive you mad? By morning, true to form, you rose from Helen's lap, washed your face, and declared, "Enough of this craziness!"

Seventeen years later, Helen knew that you'd managed to keep Amelia, but it was only at the end of your life that Willa had come back to you. Worse still, you'd tried to tell Helen about this loss more than once. In fact, she understood that you'd been talking about Willa moments before you'd tried to rescue your other daughter from the fire. You'd sounded optimistic, and this optimism was what sent her, on the morning after Willa's appearance, straight to your office. In your desk, she easily found the file folder labeled WILLA. Inside, she read the letter from the detective and a printout of two hundred names and addresses. Red checks by all the names from A through K. Willa Llewellyn was on that list. A circle around her name. Her phone number underlined. You were right. You had found her.

You were on your way to your Willa. That was the reason you

wanted us here, at the school, to go about your business in your stead. That was the reason you were so tempted by the possibility of collaborating with Benson Country Day. You were leaving. You were going to get your lost baby yourself. Summer was approaching. You had a plan. You were on your way. But you couldn't abandon us utterly. You knew that in Helen's and my hands, with the helpful expertise of Benson, the Neige Courante children you had come to love would continue to thrive at Ponderosa Academy. Sure, it was an arrogant plan. Then again, that was your style; you excelled at I-know-what's-right-for-you. I used to hate this about you. But now I wonder: what if you were right? The headmaster of Benson Country Day called me the morning after the fire to express his condolences, to offer his support. I was cynical. But he has called every day since. He has been down to visit you three times. He tells me he sees our schools as two separate entities bound together by tragedy but also by possibility. He hopes we can carry on your vision of collaboration, and he is encouraging about financial possibilities for your Ponderosa Academy. I hate to admit it, but his ideas don't sound so bad. I bet that doesn't surprise you.

What comes next? Helen. I bring you Helen. Not as your ex-wife, not as your next in command, not as the woman who is marshaling and cajoling your girls through this hard, hard time. No. I bring you Helen as the woman I love, the woman I'd want to tell you about if we'd ever shared these things.

Helen stayed. I knew at first that she was staying for Amelia and Amelia alone. After Elliot's accident, Helen was the one who got the grieving Amelia up each day, fed her, helped her shower, did her laundry. I don't know what I would have done if Helen hadn't been here to get us all through that first awful week. When Willa showed up, I saw that the second girl and what she brought with her—that pain and glowing need—was another reason for Helen to stay.

I knew that Calbert Fleecing was not the reason Helen woke in the morning. To be fair, Helen wasn't my reason for getting through each day either; like her, I had an eye on those girls. I was caught up in worrying about you and holding your proverbial hand and getting the school through to the end of the year.

So Helen and I didn't have much of a chance to talk about the weather, let alone what had or had not passed between us. I'd like to tell you that I didn't think about her romantically at all that first week or so. I'd like to tell you I was so selfless that when she pressed past me on the stairs, I didn't remember how salty her skin was, or that her loosened hair smelled of fig and cassis. But now that I'm a responsible adult, I'm trying to keep my lies to a minimum.

The first moment we had alone was the night when Suzanne Cinqchevaux scooped up Amelia, Willa, and Nat and took them up to her house for a good hot meal. You were suspended between life and death, and that seemed to have become the pervading metaphor for all of us: we were holding our breath. For what, we didn't know. I was finishing up washing a sink full of dirty dishes. I found Helen downstairs, on the porch. The night breeze carried the promise of summertime.

"I didn't know you smoked," I said.

She jumped at the sound of my voice. "Seemed like a good time to start again." She offered me one. I took it and hoped she'd lean in to me and touch the glowing orange of her cigarette to mine. She offered me a box of matches instead. "Beautiful night," she said, looking back out again. She leaned against a porch beam, and I saw how badly she needed something to hold her up. It figured. We had all been leaning on her.

"When do you think you'll head east?" I asked.

She took another drag, then looked me in the eye. "You're really asking me that? After all I've done?"

"I didn't mean it in a bad way. I meant, I know you have another life. One you want to get back to . . . right? The ticket you had to Vermont?"

"I guess," she said.

I picked my own porch beam to lean against and looked where

she was looking. Nothing much to see. Just the headlights out on the highway, pointing north and pointing south.

"How is Michael?" I asked carefully.

"Dying."

There's not much to answer to that. I tried another tack. "I didn't mean to bother you." I turned to go. She called my bluff and let me walk away. She wasn't going to stop me. Had I not turned back, I would have ended up inside. "Actually—"

"Yes?"

"Can you tell me why you're so angry with me? Because you know I'm sorry. I told you I'm sorry about the phone calls with Duncan, and—"

"You really think this is about Duncan?"

I came back beside her. "Isn't it?"

She took another drag and watched me. "You know"—she exhaled—"you always want to talk about *me*. About *my* life. You want to hear about what I've done and who I've loved and where I've lived. At first I was flattered. I mean, it really goes well with your whole sensitive-new-age guy routine. But I get it now: you just don't want to have to talk about yourself."

"Maybe," I said, and I couldn't believe it, but gladness tugged at the corners of my mouth.

"Maybe," she said, shaking her head.

"What do you want to know?"

"Maybe I'm not interested anymore."

"Maybe not," I said, "but here's your chance to decide."

She raised her eyebrows and looked me up and down. The light from the porch lamp made her whole self yellow. "Your father," she said.

"What about my father?"

"Why do you hate him so much?"

That was when I smiled for real. Because that was how well she already knew me. She knew exactly the question no one had ever been brave enough to ask. "He's dead," I said.

"I used the present tense because he's obviously quite present in your . . . well, in *you*. You walk around acting like he just beat you up."

That was when I told her everything I could about Jasper Francoeur.

When I was done talking, it was much, much later. Suzanne had called to inform us everyone was bedded down at her house. Helen and I had moved inside. We sat side by side on the couch. I lit another cigarette, even though I knew you'd be horrified to find me smoking in your house.

"So," Helen said. "He changed your life. I guess you'll never forgive him for that." I had to look at her to see whether she was mocking me or not. She was dead serious.

"No," I said.

"No, you will? Or no, you won't?"

"I don't know," I said. I stubbed the cigarette out in the dry glass in my hand and held it in the tips of my fingers.

"Okay," she said, "confession time. Amelia told me about that pep talk you gave her. Your Caliban advice. She was so matter-of-fact. She made me promise not to tell anyone else. But what you told her about the affair you had in Boston? With the married woman? That helped her, Cal. It helped her think about her role, sure. But it also helped her think about life." She was moving toward me. "I know I shouldn't be breaking her confidence. But I wanted you to know that story helped me too. I needed to hear it. I wanted to understand if it was just your stubbornness that drove me crazy, or if you were the kind of man I could fall in love with." She reached out her arm and put it on the small of my back. She pulled me in. She said, nearly whispering, into my ear, "You must understand this about me: I will never be like that woman. I will never believe that you come from nothing. I will never believe that you are nothing." And then she held me. She let me close my eyes and press them against the heartbeat thrumming in her neck. She let me lean.

★   ★   ★

You can see that there is plenty of guilt and grief and joy and forgiveness to go around in the old Bugle House on Antler Hill; there is a particular way for each of us to feel bad and to feel fabulous, like the wretched and essentially good people we are. Seeing that, getting that in our brains, has been the first stage in our recovery. The second stage has been finding a way out. That began when Suzanne Cinqchevaux drove up with old Mrs. Littlefoot and two other old women and three men, and the ceremonies of eating and sleeping, praying and dancing, began. The vigil began. You lived on, refusing to go, as Mrs. Littlefoot put it, until we did things right.

Her requirements were simple. The first thing we needed to do was find out about that baby. Yes, *that* baby. The one the kids, Victor and Amelia, had found at Wiggler's Creek all those years ago. To be honest, I was ready to tell the old woman to give it a rest, but it was Lydia who hushed me for good.

She'd found the baby. Of course she had. That's Lydia for you. She'd begun nosing around right after Amelia slammed her way out of her car, and had come up with a nine-year-old girl, Lucy Randall, baby sister of Lucas Randall, who was now married to Doris, one of Lydia's cousins.

The story was simple, kind of romantic. Two kids in love. One Indian girl, one white boy. The boy's a big brother who's told to care for his baby sister for the day. He thinks that means he can woo his girlfriend, he can take her out on the land and lie down with her. The trouble is, she's shy, doesn't want to lie down in front of the baby. So the boy makes it right, takes the baby off a little span, flags the site, assures his girlfriend the baby is fine.

That's when those kids show up. One of them's that white girl, daughter of the schoolteacher. When the little boy runs off and the little girl hides herself away to pee, the big brother, wily and silent, slips right in and scoops up his baby sister before the adults come back and whip him for good. Doris and Luke fall even more in love after this, and the story is one they begin to tell on themselves in front of family about six years into their marriage. Up until the moment Lydia asks to hear it, everyone else has believed it to be one of those lies people tell about the time they fell in love.

When Lydia finishes her rendition, Mrs. Littlefoot is nodding like crazy, rocking back and forth in her chair, even though it's an ordinary kitchen chair and not a rocker.

Amelia, who sits with Willa on one side, Victor on the other, pipes right up, "I don't get it. I mean, I don't think I believe in all the magic stuff"—she blushed—"but I thought I was the one who made the baby appear. You said I had." She looked straight at Mrs. Littlefoot.

The old woman looked right back. "You *did* make that baby appear. You needed to see that baby. Now the real baby you missed has come: your sister. Now you let that other baby, the one you found that day, have her own realness."

Then she looked at me. "Time's come," she said, "for you to pick up the work your daddy made for you." She chuckled when she saw my face. "You don't like me saying that. 'Course I don't mean the lawyering. I mean the work where you do what you was put here to do. I'm looking around me, Calbert. If someone doesn't begin to tell this family's story, doesn't close this story down, there'll be no end to it.

"You know what I'm talking about. Your old maw Daisy Lesmures knew as good as me. Unless you tell a person his story, how's he gonna know it's over? How's he gonna know it's all right for him to go now?" She shrugged. "That's the job your daddy saved you for. Can't flee it."

WE ARE GATHERED here around your bedside: Helen, Amelia, Willa, Nat, and I. We sit around you, a circle of the family you have made. I know you feel us here. There is one more story to tell.

This time I don't have any of the facts. You are silent and Astrid, or Caroline, is dead. But it is the story that we need. It is the story the girls need to hear in order to put some meaning into what kept them apart for seventeen years. It is the story Nat needs in order to understand why the woman he loved left him for you. It is the story Helen needs in order to understand the man she married. It is the story I need because I need it.

All the falling in love around me makes me wonder: were you and Astrid in love? In the beginning? When Helen found you together in her marriage bed, was what she saw really love? I wonder this because I've done my research, and I know now that nine months and twenty-two days after you made those girls, your wife walked out of her apartment with one of them tied to her chest, hidden under her coat. It was Wednesday, March 5, 1980. Astrid Lux Barrow—the name she'd made up, because her name was really Caroline—walked twenty-eight blocks downtown and struck up a conversation with a young, handsome man. She asked him for directions. When he offered to help her, they walked together until they passed an alley. In the alley waited her friends, her comrades, who put a pillowcase over the head of this young, handsome man named Jason Simpson, who also happened to be the son of the president of one of wealthiest banks in the world. Astrid got in that van with the newborn Willa tied to her chest and left her life behind her.

I don't know what made her do it. I don't know why she brought her baby along with her. I do know that what she and her comrades did to that young man was an act of terrorism denounced in newspapers all over this country. I know that a few days later, Caroline appeared at Nat's door to drop Willa off with a man she knew she could trust. I know that this same woman's life ended at a split-level in New Jersey a week later, when the safe house where she was staying exploded. She had gone to that safe house after leaving Willa in Nat's care.

All these stories depend on one great, strange truth that none of us fully understands. Why did you and Astrid keep the twins a secret? That is the question that gnaws at us. It keeps us restless in the night. It infuses the girls' sleep with nightmares. It keeps you from having your peace.

I wish I could speak the truth for you. I wish I could tell this family of yours why you did such a strange thing. But I can't. I wasn't there. What I can do, what I *do*, is tell stories. So I can guess. And that's why we're gathered here today. So that I can tell you all the story of how Willa and Amelia first came into the world. Together.

It was a cold February night, and Astrid was not due for another week. But her water broke early in the evening, and her contractions came on fierce and rapid. Elliot called the midwife, and she, of the patchouli-scented everything, arrived at the door in a swirl of wool and linen and declaration. "Your son will be an Aquarius!" she announced, as if Elliot didn't know that already. For you see, the midwife was sure the baby was a boy, and even she believed there would be only one baby.

That could still happen in those days. Before ultrasounds. It was just a doctor in a clinic with five minutes and a stethoscope, who could mistake one back, one head, and one set of legs as all belonging to one baby. Who, in his rush, listened for only one heartbeat and, hence, heard only one.

Elliot would have liked to get Astrid better prenatal care. He had the money, for God's sake. But pregnancy had made Astrid more political and angry than she'd ever been. She was fiercely independent. She insisted on riding the subway alone, even though her belly swelled to epic proportions. She told him that if women in Harlem were doing fine with the prenatal care up there, so could she. She had been sullen on their wedding day, but he'd chalked it up to cold feet, to the strange circumstance of an unplanned pregnancy. Instead of lifting, the sullenness had spread, turned bitter. She asked him, six months in, "Why did you make me marry you?" This was when he knew his marriage had crumbled. This was when he began to wonder who it was he'd married. Because in pregnancy, Astrid was no longer the giggling girl who'd taken him to bed. She was fierce and determined. Not at all like other preg-

nant women he'd seen. He insisted they move to their own apartment and out of the commune. It would be better this way, he assured her. But more often than not, when he came home from
work, she was not there. He would call the commune, and someone would vouch for her safety, then hang up the phone. The
commune was angry at him for insisting on keeping his family unit
separate.

As Astrid got closer and closer to her due date, and it became
harder and harder for her to get around, she and Elliot began to
argue. He had agreed to a home birth with the midwife of her
choice. He thought this was more than a little reasonable. She
wasn't satisfied. She told him she felt like now that she was full of
a baby, she could no longer be full of dreams. She wept, but she
would not let him hold her.

He would have been willing to do anything to see her smile.

On the night when Willa and Amelia were born, the midwife
and Elliot held Astrid's arms and spoke in soft tones. Astrid had decided she wanted to have the baby swim into the world; they were
lucky to have a bathtub in their small apartment. The midwife advised her that it would be difficult to climb in and out, but Astrid
was stubborn like an ox. She could make decisions even when her
body was not hers. She asked for more ice chips and assured them
that she was having this baby in the bathtub.

Amelia Barrow was born at 4:03 A.M. She swam out into the
world, all fists and sputter and wild eyes. In planning for the birth,
Elliot and Astrid had talked about this moment as though there
were still a partnership between them: Astrid would pick the baby
up out of the water, pull her onto her breasts, and nurse her straight-
away. But in the minute after Amelia was born, Astrid could only
moan and cry. Contractions were still coming hard, and the midwife's uncertainty was nearly more than Elliot could bear. So he
reached down into the lukewarm water himself and pulled out the
baby girl, clutching her in a towel. She looked up at him with wise
eyes, and he was washed in happiness. He waited to cut her cord.

"The placenta's coming," the midwife said by way of explanation. Four minutes later, it was not a placenta that emerged from Astrid's womb, but another baby girl. A baby girl none of them had known would come. This girl was smaller and more serious. Already so serious that in the seconds after her birth, she looked up through the water and caught her mother's eyes, and her mother felt for the first time in her life that she was known.

After that, one thing led to another. It was daytime when the midwife left, and before she did, she and Astrid spent a long time alone in the bedroom, talking. Elliot didn't want to disturb them, but when he let the midwife out, she winked at him. "Our little secret," she said.

He asked Astrid what the midwife meant. Astrid was exhausted by the birth and the sheer hard work of the girls' constant demands for her breasts. She kept saying it was too much. "Look," she said, "fuck the government. They want us to fill out a slip of paper saying how many future taxpayers we're providing them with. Well, fuck that. Let's tell them we just had Amelia and leave it at that."

"You've named her?"

"Amelia. After my grandmother."

"And her?" He held the tiny hand of his second daughter.

"Her name's Willa. I was going to name our boy William, if we'd had a boy. But Willa's a good name too."

Elliot looked at his wife, just a girl, really, and decided the sadness rushing through him could be chocked up to sheer surprise and exhaustion. They were all going to feel euphoric tomorrow. He would talk sense into her then.

"We have to fill out birth certificates," he said the next day as he spooned soup into Astrid's mouth. He'd told her to invite her friends over, that he'd make a vegetarian stew. But she said she wanted to be alone with the babies. She didn't mention him.

"Technically, we only have to fill out one birth certificate," she said.

"What about the pediatrician? School? Having a life?"

"You love rules," she accused, pushing away the spoon. "I need to sleep, Elliot."

Twenty-one days passed. Elliot noticed how strangely divided his family had become. Every time he tried to talk to Astrid about the reality of both girls, she got angry. She started to rage at him. "They came out of *me*," she said. She looked wild when she said this. He saw something of a threat in her eyes, and he was afraid. He'd keep the second girl a secret one more day. He'd wait to talk to Astrid again when she was more reasonable. Just one more day. In the meantime, he took Astrid's lead; when she picked up a crying baby, it was always Willa she picked up first. "She's so tiny," she would say. Elliot found that he was the one who picked up Amelia more often.

When Astrid started to venture outside, she took Willa with her. When Elliot went out to the grocery store, he carried with him his firstborn. People from the neighborhood congratulated them on their daughter's birth. Note the singular. When Astrid disappeared, Elliot called the police, and the first thing he said was "She's got my baby with her." Because by then there *was* only one birth certificate, and he was holding a baby in his arms, and no remains of a baby were found at the scene of the explosion a week later, his claims were dismissed. He was experiencing a break of sorts. These things happened. His pleas for baby Willa were ignored.

Months later, when he knew all that Astrid had done, when he wondered if his second daughter still lived and breathed and looked up at the stars at night, Elliot Barrow blamed himself. He worried night and day about his other girl. But he could not find her. If the FBI denied her existence, how could he begin to look?

Until he figured out how, he would do what he could. Since he could not help his own, he would help as many other children as he could. He would take his inheritance and make a difference. Oregon sounded like a beautiful place. And that was when he brought his Amelia west.

★   ★   ★

WE ASK STILL why. Of course we do. The "why" is at the center of our tale—why did Astrid want to hold only one of her girls? Why did she take this same girl with her when she kidnapped a man? Why did she leave one daughter behind? Why did she bring her other daughter to Nat's arms, and not home, to Elliot's?

We would love to know the answers to these questions. We believe that if we have the truth, we will be able to forgive. Ourselves. Each other. Her.

But no one can tell us why. I suspect that even Astrid—were she still alive and now a middle-aged woman, serving time—could not tell us. I know, I know: having answers to these questions would be so easy. It would be so good. But it is not how this story, this life, will go. No matter how many times we ask, there will never be answers, since those who might have known them cannot speak, and perhaps they were answers that even then could not be named.

Meanwhile, those of us left behind are hungry for our lives. I see why you've been holding on, Elliot. Why we all have. We have put our lives on hold, because we hope there will be answers. We hope to be rescued from the terrible moment when Astrid picked up one baby girl and left the other one behind; we believe rescue will come in knowing why. But the truth is simple. We will never know why. She is not here to tell us. We will never know what was in her heart: if she was scared, or angry, or crazed, or cruel, or if she was so delusional that she believed she was doing good. The "why" of that moment will never be answered. That truth is brutal. But it is still the truth.

You see that now, don't you, Elliot? You see why we are here.

We are here to set you free. To forgive you for that fleeting second in which you made a decision: to say yes to Astrid's insistence that you acknowledge only one daughter, a decision that changed all our fates. We are here to forgive the woman who bore you these beautiful girls, the woman who took your wholeness from you, who separated your daughters from each other. More than that, we are here to help you. Because the girls are back together

now. We are here to promise you that in the face of this great gift
of their togetherness, we are letting go of why. We are letting go
so we can get back to living. We are here to promise you that
when we are heartbroken, and when we are angry, and when we
are afraid, we will not return to the never-answered why, because
we know that it leads nowhere. Instead, when we remember you
and Astrid together, we will choose to remember the time before
your world began to unravel. We will imagine the extraordinary
moment when you first became a father, when you first saw your
daughters, pink baby salmon, swimming in the waters. We know
that in the instant when you and Astrid first saw these girls slip
from their mother's womb, you both meant good. You meant no
harm. You were hopeful in the act of creation.

What more can we expect? How else could we ever offer you
our mercy?

You are my brother, Elliot, and here, with our mercy, is your
story. I give it to you. We give it to you. With our great love, it
winds above us. It sneaks out through the open sash of the window. It streams skyward. It calls to you. Follow it out of this room.
Be not afraid.

Author's Note

I am no Shakespeare. But that doesn't stop me from entertaining a fully Shakespearean ambition: to devise a world in my mind and then to present my "insubstantial pageant" so broadly, and with such respect, that you too will be caught up in it.

In order to create this book, I—like so many fiction writers—dreamed and invented various characters, read voraciously, and researched deeply. Finally, after much deliberation, I dreamed and invented the Neige Courante. I am not of Native heritage and thus cannot write from the advantage of belonging.

I offer my invention with deep gratitude and respect; I could not live long enough to adequately represent the elaborate heritage and worldview of any of the extremely culturally rich Northwest peoples. All faults are mine.

Of particular help in my research was the Museum at Warm Springs in Warm Springs, Oregon; the National Museum of the American Indian in Washington, D.C.; and Frank B. Linderman's book *Pretty-shield: Medicine Woman of the Crows*, which Cal encounters under its original title, *Red Mother*.

I drew inspiration and understanding from Janet Catherine Berlo's *Spirit Beings and Sun Dancers: Black Hawk's Vision of the Lakota World*; Ella E. Clark's *Indian Legends of the Pacific Northwest*; Luther S. Cressman's *The Sandal and the Cave: The Indians of Oregon*; *Northwest Lands, Northwest Peoples: Readings in Environmental History*, edited by Dale D. Goble and Paul W. Hirt; Eugene S. Hunn's *Nch'i-Wána "The Big River": Mid-Columbia Indians and Their Land*; *Myths and Legends of the Pacific Northwest*, selected by Katharine Berry Judson; *Coyote Was Going There: Indian Literature of the Oregon Country,* compiled and edited by Jarold Ramsey; *Teaching American Indian Students,* edited by Jon Reyhner; *First Fish, First People: Salmon Tales of the North Pacific Rim,* edited by Judith Roche and Meg McHutchison; Robert H. Ruby and John A. Brown's *A Guide to the Indian Tribes of the Pacific Northwest;* Cynthia D. Stowell's *Faces of a Reservation: A Portrait of the Warm Springs Indian Reservation;* and Charles Wilkinson's *Messages from Frank's Landing: A Story of Salmon, Treaties, and the Indian Way.*

The *National Audubon Society Field Guide to the Pacific Northwest,* by Peter Alden and Dennis Paulson et al; and David D. Alt and Donald W. Hyndman's *Roadside Geology of Oregon* gave me the right terms, trees, and animals. Judith Clavir Albert and Stewart Edward Albert's *The Sixties Papers: Documents of a Rebellious Decade; Weatherman,* edited by Harold Jacobs; and the Weather Underground's publication *Prairie Fire: The Politics of Revolutionary Anti-Imperialism* all gave me deeper understanding of Astrid Lux Barrow's beliefs.

Acknowledgments

Thanks to my team of readers, Daniel J. Blau, Annalisa Brown, Jennifer Cayer, Caitlin Eicher, Amber Hall, Emily Raboteau, and Wendy Salinger, for being so cogent and so kind; to Mona Kuhn, Maia Davis, Jock Sturges, and Marine Sturges, for the gifts of space and art; to Se-ah-dom Edmo, for her encouragement and diligence; to Althea Pratt-Broome and Willowbrook, for casting me as Feste when I was ten years old; to Sid Eaton and Steve Saslow, for inviting me on a life-changing voyage to Montana; to the people of the Crow Reservation and Pretty Eagle School, for their exuberant welcome; to Amy March, for recounting her adventures; to two extraordinary friends of my mind and heart: my father, Dr. Robert Dunster Whittemore II, and my sister, Kai Beverly-Whittemore; to my husband, David M. Lobenstine for his friendship, sagacity and resolute faith—I am besotted; and to my mother, Elizabeth Beverly, for planting the seed, watering the sapling, and pruning the branches.

Thanks to my agent, Anne Hawkins, for her vision and friendship; to Rick Horgan, for his early advocacy; to Emily Griffin, for all she does; to Beth Thomas and Penina Sacks, for their keen eyes; and to my editors, Amy Einhorn and Frances Jalet-Miller, for their wise insight and generous guidance.